# THE DEVIL WEARS HIGH HEELS

*A Premiered Erotic Collection to Release Stress After a Busy Day's Work*

Margareth Moore

© Copyright by Margareth Moore.

In no way is it legal to reproduce, duplicate, or transmit any part of this document in either electronic means or in printed format. Recording of this publication is strictly prohibited and any storage of this document is not allowed unless with written permission from the publisher. All rights reserved.

The information provided herein is stated to be truthful and consistent, in that any liability, in terms of inattention or otherwise, by any usage or abuse of any policies, processes, or directions contained within is the solitary and utter responsibility of the recipient reader. Under no circumstances will any legal responsibility or blame be held against the publisher for any reparation, damages, or monetary loss due to the information herein, either directly or indirectly.

Respective authors own all copyrights not held by the publisher. The information herein is offered for informational purposes solely, and is universal as so. The presentation of the information is without contract or any type of guarantee assurance.

The trademarks that are used are without any consent, and the publication of the trademark is without permission or backing by the trademark owner. All trademarks and brands within this book are for clarifying purposes only and are the owned by the owners themselves, not affiliated with this document.

## TABLE OF CONTENTS

FORCED TO WATCH ................................................................. 4

YOU DON'T GET TO CUM YET, BUT I DO ........................... 8

THE FOLLOWERS .................................................................. 12

CALL ME SIR ........................................................................... 17

MASTURBATION AND A SHOW ........................................... 22

MOVIE TIME .......................................................................... 26

TASTES LIKE MORE ............................................................. 30

A WOMAN'S WORLD ............................................................. 34

THE FIX .................................................................................. 39

HER FANTASY ....................................................................... 46

WIFE GETS WILD ON CRUISE ............................................. 52

OUTDOOR TREAT ................................................................. 57

HIS FANTASY ........................................................................ 61

GIRLFRIEND CUMS .............................................................. 67

DESIRE FILLED ..................................................................... 71

AWAITING AN ANSWER ....................................................... 75

SINFUL ENJOYS DISPLAYING ............................................. 78

## FORCED TO WATCH

"Fuck you." The smile on her face when she spat those words in my face took most of the impact off, and I stuck my tongue out at her.

Her wrists, so nicely tied together in my favourite red rope, also prevented her from moving, as they were strapped to the bedstead. She was not used to lying on the floor and she liked to pretend to fight with me for it. She had half-heartedly wrestled with me when I had tied her to the bed. We both knew I was going to win, and we both enjoyed the road we had travelled until then. I knew that with every curse that came out of her mouth, she got wetter, and I knew that too.

"Hmm, what kind of language is that?" I asked playfully, clicked my tongue at her and slid my hand over her panties. I pulled her down and could see how her excitement glittered on her pussy lips. I wanted to put my fingers between them and push them hard inside her so I could hear her moaning, but she didn't deserve that yet.

Her eyes turned to mine and she said, "Fuck you. Just untie me so I can go fuck myself if you want to tease me like this forever. It's not fair."

I pulled her wet panties together and stuffed them down her open mouth before she could protest. Her eyes fluttered in equal parts surprise and excitement.

"Oh", I mocked her in a mocking tone, feigning her innocence. "Do you want to be touched? Do you want to get out? Don't you want to be tied up just so I can take you off piece by piece?" Slowly I drew a finger in her neck and pulled my fingernail across her chest, a red line blossomed behind it.

"You don't enjoy just being tied up and naked so I can look at you and touch you and do whatever I want with you? Not only does it excite you more and more when you are exposed and vulnerable, when you are forced to watch and cannot do more than what I allow you to do? My fingers found her nipple and pinched hard, causing a sharp gasp from her lips.

I crawled onto the bed, kneeled beside her head and she had a clear view while I pushed my black lace panties to the side and stroked my fingers against my own growing wetness. She moaned longingly and bit her lip as I pushed my fingers inside with ease. As much as she enjoyed it that I teased her, I enjoyed it even more.

She pulled on the rope that was holding her back from me, whimpering that she could not touch me. I picked up the pace, fucked with my fingers and circled my clitoris with my thumb.

She spat out her panties and said loudly: "No! No, there is no way you can get away without letting me cum and without letting me touch you. No! You're not so mean either."

I put one hand on the bedstead next to her bound hands to support me when I felt my body start to cramp. Somehow she managed to twist herself so that her fingers could touch mine, then she bit my inner thigh, because that was all she could reach.

The pain of the excitement I felt from the teasing and how hot it made me feel pushed me over the edge and I screamed. My thigh began to tremble and I could barely stop falling on it when my orgasm overtook me. At some point she had stopped biting me and was just watching attentively.

I pulled my soaking wet fingers out of my pussy and pushed them into her mouth where she eagerly licked them clean. Her eyes glowed and I could smell her excitement. I moved to spread her thighs and took both hands down to walk across her neck, chest, stomach and hips. I leaned forward to kiss her hard, our bodies pressed tightly together and I could feel her body grinding against mine.

"Please," she whispered and broke our kiss.

She leaned back so I could see her face, her eyes were big and hopeful, empty of the bratty attitude of the past.

"Please," she said again softly, "please let me cum. Please let me jerk off. I want to come for you."

With a smile I reached between her legs and watched her gasp for air as I stuck two fingers inside her. "All right," I said as I snuggled up against her neck, "You're on."

## YOU DON'T GET TO CUM YET, BUT I DO

With my lips wrapped around the base of your cock and your head at the back of my throat, I look up to make eye contact with you and you moan loudly. "OH FUCK", you scream, your hands clenched in the air where they are tied above your head. You growl, whimper and sigh, and I can see your arms pulling on the shackles. The rope that bites your wrists looks delicious and you whimper. I can only imagine the tingling in your fingertips, and the thought is enough to make my nipples hurt.

I bounce my head up and down faster, suck hard and swirl my tongue around you. The whimpering turns into a loud moaning and you jerk your hips into my mouth and try to twist them away from me.

You know you're not allowed to cum until I tell you.

I suck long and hard and let your cock slowly slide out of my mouth while I pull my tongue along the underside of your shaft. My lips are wrapped around you wet and I kiss the tip while letting your cock out of my mouth. You take one deep breath while I refrain from touching you, then I flick my tongue along the edge of the head of your penis, causing you to lose your breath in another groan.

I lean back so that you can see my body better, and move my hand down my neck, down my chest and to a stiff, eager nipple. Slowly I circle it with my fingertips and let out a scream of my own as I pinch it hard. Her eyes are closed on my hand while her tongue rushes out to lick your lips.

My hand falls from the nipple over the belly to the inside of the thighs, while a grin spreads across my face. I pull my nails up and leave bright red lines on the sensitive skin. I have to let my other hand rest on your thigh to calm me down while I let two fingers slide easily into my finished and waiting pussy.

You are begging now; begging me to finish you, to let you help me come, because I don't even know what. I can't hear the sound of your voice anymore when I close my eyes and concentrate on how good it feels to fuck myself.

Suddenly I pull my hand away and push my fingers, dripping wet from my juice, into your whining mouth. "Just shut up and clean this one up, will you?" I say with an eye roll. You nod as your tongue wraps around my fingers, greedily licking and sucking.

"Fine," I say when I feel the job is well and truly done. When I take my fingers out of your voracious mouth, I pat your cheek crisply and remind you why we are here. "Now," I say, "I'm gonna suck your cock again, but don't you dare come. You haven't earned that yet."

I kiss the length of your cock down to your balls, lick slowly over them and wrap my hand around your shaft before kissing your thigh. "No reply?" I say between kisses. Pinching your tender flesh with my sharp teeth, I continue: "If you want me to stop now because you can't control yourself, just say the word.

I'll squeeze your cock and slide my thumb over your leaky head. Your mouth hangs open for a second and then you whisper, "Please don't stop. I won't stop. I will not come. Not until you say I can."

"Glad to hear we're on the same page," I say cheerfully. I use your precursor to lubricate my palm and start stroking you slowly. At the same time I bite your thigh and bite harder and harder while I work your cock faster and faster. Your breath now comes in tattered blasts and a quick glance shows me how ambivalent you are.

You are so close, and getting you there has made me so wet. I feel the moisture on my inner thighs and wonder if I could hose down without touching myself. Just thinking about how much I want it, I need it more and more, and I'm tired of holding back. If you could look into my face now, you would see the sparkle in my eyes, but you are so lost in lust and try not to give in that your eyes are squeezed tight.

But not for long. Surprisingly, I stop every touch and pull myself away. As I stand up, your eyes fly open and slowly focus on my naked body. Your gaze wanders down between my thighs and you move to get up from the bed, forgetting again the rope that holds you. It holds you in place and you practically growl.

I look at you while I lean my head to the side and let a hand slide up and down my thigh. "Hmmmm," I pretend to be brooding. "No, no, I don't think you're allowed to cum yet. But I can." I bend over so my ass is in the air, while reaching under the bed for my toy box, I pull out my Hitachi and my favorite rainbow dildo. I throw the Hitachi over one shoulder and lick the dildo, then I wink and stroll out of the bedroom into the living room.

I make sure I hose down extra loud so you can hear it from where you are.

## THE FOLLOWERS

I lick my lips while you look down at me, kneeling between your thighs after you have just swallowed one sperm spot after another. After over an hour of teasing, while you were theoretically "working" from your home office, I finally let you climax and the orgasm hit you hard. Just the way I like it. Your breathing slows down and you stroke my hair with one hand. I kiss the head of your cock and enjoy how your whole body twitches during the action. I put my hands on the arms of your office chair and slide your body up.

You lightly stroke my hips, caress my ass and grab it, pulling me firmly into your lap. You spread your legs and how wet I am becomes immediately obvious when I get used to you. I kiss your chest up, over your collarbone and into your neck and bite exactly where it meets your shoulder. Slowly I increase the pressure of the bite and sway my hips, rubbing my clitoris against you. The harder the bite gets, the more you press my bottom and I scream. Suddenly I stop, licking over the spot I just bit on as it turns red, and kiss it gently before continuing on your neck. When I reach your ear, I briefly suck your earlobe into my mouth and then let my lips stroke your ear while I whisper, "Don't you have work to do?"

Leaned back, I take your hands out of my ass and put them back on your keyboard. "I cannot allow all these followers to be deprived of their contents," I say before giving you a playful kiss on the lips. As you withdraw, you look at me with something between lust and glare, and I can't help but smile. "I, on the other hand, have no work to do and have to hose down quite desperately. So I'm gonna take care of this right now. But don't let me distract you from your work." You're definitely tight now, but you're absent-mindedly licking your lips, and I know you've got that game coming.

I take my hands off the armrests of the chair and let them run up my sides and up my breasts. I squeeze them together, your eyes twitch down and your breath becomes faster. "Nu uh", I say, move one hand to your chin and direct your head back to your computer screen. When I hold your head there with one hand, I squeeze my nipple firmly with the fingers still on my chest and scream. "You have a lot of work to do."

I hold your chin down, let go of my nipple and let my hand fall between my legs. Normally I'm all for build-up and teasing, but letting you go was enough. My fingers circle my clitoris and press firmly on my clitoris while I crunch my hips against my hand and your pelvis. "Oh yes", I whisper and close my eyes while I feel an orgasm already building up. My hand falls from your chin to your shoulder and holds on tight while I ride with my hand and pull my body against your body.

I haven't noticed the absence of typing sounds, but I know that you stop working when I feel one arm around me and the other on my chest. When I open my eyes, I am about to say something snappish to you when you lower your head and bite firmly on my nipple. "Oh FUCK", I scream and squeeze my fingers even harder against my clitoris. "Oh FUCK, I'm coming, I'm coming..." The orgasm breaks out over me when you suck on my nipple. I keep riding against you and slowly letting myself sink to the ground. When you're sure I'm done, your hand gets knotted in my hair and you pull my face towards yours and kiss me hard. I wrap my arms around you and press my body firmly against yours.

Suddenly you pull my head back and up. Your other hand on my hip pushes me back and away from you, towards your desk. I am now standing half standing, half sitting, my bottom on the edge of your desk and my legs spread wide apart. I lean back, my hands on your desk, and you push your chair away, kneeling between my thighs. When you start kissing my leg up from your knee, I roll my eyes and reach forward. "Foreplay is great," I say as I push your face into my pussy, "but I want you to make me cum again, and I want you to do it now.

Not one who is disappointed, you suck my clit in your mouth and I lean back on both hands with a shiver. "Fuck, yeah," I whimper, "just like that." You flick your tongue against my clitoris and make my thighs tremble, you lean back and slowly pull your tongue along my whole slit, making me gasp. I look down on you while you are working and our eyes close while you circle with the tip of your tongue around my clitoris. Moaning, I slam my hand back on your desk, and my eyes close. If you clasp my clitoris with your tongue, you do your work: "Oh shit, yeah... Gods, I'm so close," I say. "Please," I moan, "please let me cum again."

Your fingers slam into my soaking wet pussy and you fuck me hard with your fingers without letting my clitoris out of your mouth. I scream now and hum again, harder and deeper than before. I feel your keyboard pressing under my back and your monitor pressing into my shoulders and I just don't care. My hand is running through your hair, you keep going until my whole body is shaking against you and I have to pull you away. You slide your fingers out and sit on your heels again, you smile at me and you are proud of yourself. I come with you to the ground, suck my juices from your fingers, then wrap myself around you and kiss you deeply. We are locked in this embrace, kissing and touching each other with none of the urgency of an hour before, but still fully enjoying each other's bodies as your text alarm goes off.

You reach for your mobile phone and look at the message and your forehead wrinkles. After poking around in your phone for a few moments, you burst into laughter and show me the screen. Your professional Twitter account is open, and I see a tweet with a jumbled text from 6 meters ago. "I guess your ass had its first tweet and reached

100,000 followers," you say as I blush before I laugh along too.

## CALL ME SIR

"I want you," I whisper in your ear. Lying on my bed, making out like a high school boy, things have stayed pretty PG so far. Your arm tightens around me, and I press my body into yours. I lick around your ear and kiss your neck, soft kisses, trying to tease you gently. My hands run along the sides of your body and pull along the top of your jeans. Your body is stiff and tense as if you are holding back. I look into your beautiful, hazel eyes as I come closer to kiss you. Your lips are soft against mine, only slightly parted. Your hand slides from my back under my arm, over my chest and up to my breasts. I moan slightly and try to slide my hand down the top of your pants, and suddenly your hand is around my neck, pushing me back onto the bed. You're not hurting me, but I'm surprised.

You bend over me and also pull an arm over my head and pin it. "Say it again," you tell me. I bite my lip unsteadily, and you press a little harder on my throat, your eyes are full of lust. "I told you to say it again," you say softly.

"I want you," I whisper and feel my nipples harden as the words leave my mouth. You push my legs apart with your knee and put your body between them, pressing the bulge in your jeans against me. My skirt is pulled up around my hips and exposes me as I am not wearing panties. One hand is still wrapped around my throat, you let go of my hand and lead the other down my body, stopping to pinch my nipple hard before you let your hand rest at the waist of my skirt.

"Are you wet for me?" you ask and breathe a little harder.

"Mmm," I groan and rub against you. You pull your body back, and I let out a little whimper.

"Use your words," you say with a grin. "And look at me when you tell me how wet your cunt is for me."

I moaned again and opened my eyes. I look up at you and say, "I'm soaking wet for you right now.

"Sir," you say, sliding your hand down my thigh, "call me sir."

"Yes, sir," I say, panting, as you pull your fingernails up the inside of my soft thigh. "If you touch me, my pussy gets all wet for you, sir." Your fingers finally reach my shaved lips and slide gently between them.

"Gee," you say hoarsely, "somebody's really wet for you, sir." You slip a finger up my dripping cunt and into my rear bulges. I bite my lip hard and my eyes close as my head rolls to one side. You pull your finger out and bring my head back in the middle. "Look at me," you command. I open my eyes and swallow hard, using all my self-control not to ask you to enter me again. You bring your finger, enveloped in my juice, to my lips. "Lick it off and tell me what you taste like." I greedily take your finger in my mouth and stroke it with my tongue. I want you to know how good I can be with my mouth. You moan softly and then pull your hand away. "That's enough," you tell me. "Well, how do you taste?"

"Good," I murmur. You raise one eyebrow and I catch myself. "Fine, sir," I humbly say.

"Better," you say affirmatively. "If you are good, I will fuck you." I feel my thighs start to shake when you say "fuck". "But you will have to convince me that you really want to. Tell me how much you want me." You take your hand off my neck, and I gasp for the sudden freedom, then as you reach under my shirt and pinch my nipple hard, you pull up and twist a little. "I can't hear you."

"I want you to fuck me, sir. My pussy feels so empty and I want your huge cock to fill it. I want you to push hard and fast inside me, I want you to fuck me raw. I want you to scream for you, sir." I was so caught up in my own fantasies that I didn't realize your hands had left my body. With your pants down around your thighs, you kneel there naked, slowly stroking your hard cock. At this sight I almost came off.

You lay down on me, your hard cock wedged between our bodies, grabbing my hair and holding my head. "Beg me", you say, as you push my legs roughly further apart

"I need you, sir." I whimper, I covet, and I must color my voice with despair. "I need you to fulfill me. I need you to fuck me to oblivion, sir." You adjust yourself so that your dick head is at the entrance to my smooth pussy. I try to push my hips forward to get you inside me, but you pull back

"Say please", you whisper in my ear and push forward just a fraction of an inch so that I can feel the top of your head inside me.

"Oh shit", I moan, "Please, please, please, please, dear God! Please, sir, please! Please, fuck me! Please, please, please..." I choke in my words when you finally ram your giant cock into me and try to stuff it. When you ram your dick so hard in me that your balls are beating my ass, your pubic bone is dragging on my clitoris. All I needed was a few slaps.

"Oh, God... Sir... I'll be right there..." I say right before my body tense up. I grab the sheets and clench them in my fists while my toes curl. My back is arching and I feel my cunt arching around your cock. You don't let up at all as you fuck me through my orgasm and I come down slowly, panting and moaning.

"That was fucking hot, baby," you say breathlessly. "Now you're gonna lick your own cum off my dick, then let me finish your pretty little face." You stab me hard one last time and then you slip out again. My body screams for you again, but before I feel too empty, you're kneeling on the bed You pull my head towards your cock and you slap it deep into my mouth. I feel your dick head sliding down the back of my throat and taste my own sweet cum on your hardness. You moan as I greedily suck you and make my head slide back and forth while my tongue swirls around your cock. I reach up to play with your balls and you inhale sharply and put a hand on my shoulder to keep your balance.

I look up at you, your cock fills my mouth and I feel your balls tighten. You reach down and pull your cock out, then you hold my neck just below the jaw and give your cock a few quick punches. I make eye contact with you while your hot cum shoots out and covers my face. You're shaking and I gently lick your head up to get the last drops.

You look at the mess you made of my make-up and face and smile. "Yeah, you're gonna be a lot of fun."

## MASTURBATION AND A SHOW

The sweat runs down the side of the face, tinted blue by the stage lights. Her eyes are intense under the thick, black eyeliner that makes her stand out all the more. When you strike your bass, the heavy notes pulsating through me to my innermost being as I dance near the front of the crowd, I think of the fingers running over my body instead of over the instrument. The thought: "What a sexy smurf" comes to my mind, and I can't help but laugh. Then you bite your lip as you dive into the song and I stop laughing.

A soft moaning gets stuck in my throat as I feel a hot flash running up my chest and neck. The pressure of the bodies, strangers forming the crowd around me, holds me tight and I feel exposed and invisible at the same time. Fortunately, the music covers all the sounds I could make, and my too short plaid skirt is just the right length to slide my hand under it with ease.

And that's exactly where my hand is, which almost unnoticed has made its way between my thighs. My fingertips caress the wet fabric of my black thong and run lightly over it as I jump to the music. I think of finding you backstage, of sneaking into a dark corner where I can get down on my knees and mess up my carefully applied make-up between your thighs, your hands wrapped tightly in my pink hair while I lick and kiss and suck you and feel myself getting wetter and wetter as I build you up to orgasm.

The song ends and a slow, crunchy number begins. My hips sway back and forth and my fingers push the thin fabric aside. I hardly need to apply pressure to split my smooth pussy lips and my eyes close as I gently slide over my clitoris. I imagine your breathing getting harder and harder the closer you get to orgasm, I close my eyes with you while I continue using my mouth until you tremble and scream my name, I can't help but push my fingers deep into my pussy. I moan while the heel of my hand crunches against my clitoris, my fingers damn deep and hard, I feel my knees getting weak. Do my fellow concertgoers know what I'm doing? Do they know that I would fall to the floor now if they didn't support me, if the mass of the rabble didn't hold me up? I don't know, but I do know that I want to see you when I come.

I pull myself away from the fantasy and look back at the stage. You're standing right in front of me now, and I take a deep breath when I realize you're looking at me dead. There's no way you can see what I'm doing, is there? When so many people are crowded together, you can't see down to the hand in my cunt and the wetness spreading over the top of my thighs, can you? We have eye contact, and I'm sure you know everything; everything I imagined, everything I did to myself, everything I would do to you now on stage in front of everyone if you said you wanted me to...

And then you go away, you walk back across the stage, stretching your eyes out for every other admiring fan. I whimpered and took a breath I didn't know I was taking. When I see you strolling back and forth, my tongue flicks across my lips and I know that I am on the verge of orgasm. When I look around me, it seems as if the rest of the audience is caught by the show on stage instead of the one I'm performing. My cheeks burn when I think of the embarrassment of being trapped. It turns me on even more. I want you to see what I do, I want you to pull me up in front of all the people and finger me to the climax in front of this whole venue while you stand above me and keep on playing. I want you to bend me over the speaker and press me firmly against it so I can feel the vibrations rolling through my body. I want you to make me beg for release. I want you to let me...

Every inch of me shakes when the orgasm begins to wash over me. I struggle to keep my eyes open, watching you and thinking about how much I want you to know what I'm doing right now. I would try to stay calm, but everyone else is screaming and singing along, and I've gone too far to care anyway.

Screaming I come hard, feel the pulse of the music around my body and the pulse of orgasm around my fingers. I ride on the feeling that my senses are suddenly heightened because the music is almost a bit too loud, the people around me almost a bit too close, the feeling of my climax almost a bit too much. I want to laugh and have a nap and lick my fingers clean, then I fuck you till dawn. Instead I smile, wipe my dirty hand up my skirt and go back to dancing.

## MOVIE TIME

Your fingers stroke against the outside of my naked thigh while you pull the hem of my skirt up a little further. When I sat next to me on the couch during the movie night, wrapping a blanket over us, in which we were all crowded together, I paid more attention to your presence than to anything else on the screen.

As your fingertips begin to caress more forcefully, to go over to the top of my leg and promise to keep going if I let you, my breath stops and you look at me. Without taking my eyes off the screen, I nod my head slightly and say with my mouth: "Yes, please".

Your hand slides gently to my inner thigh and you let your sharp nails touch my tender flesh while you pull your hand up my leg. I feel the warmth between my legs, and I'm sure you feel it too when your fingers reach my wet panties. I suppress a moan when you slip under the flimsy fabric and immediately get soaked how wet I am. Your finger runs over my clitoris and my eyes close. It takes everything inside me to keep still and not start rubbing your hand.

And then it's gone. I open my eyes to see you licking your fingers. I blush, glad the lights are dim and no one can see. "I think I need some water," you say and give me a sharp look as you get up.

"Yes," I say, while fumbling to get up from the ceiling and off the couch, "Me too." As I follow into the kitchen, I'm pretty sure I hear a giggle, but I don't really pay attention. All I can think about is how you're gonna get me back in your hands.

I turn the corner and you're on top of me. Your hands grab my hip and pull me close, my arms go around your shoulders almost by themselves. Our mouths are hot and passionate, tongues scamper together and lips caress each other. I groan into you and push you back against the fridge.

"Hey", you say, as you slide one hand down the front of your skirt and panties, your fingers circling straight around my clitoris, "Imagine seeing you here". I gasp and kick my feet a little further to give you better access. It took longer than I'd like to admit, and when your first touch sent electricity through me, your fingers that bring me to orgasm are like a constant charge.

"Oh God yes", I whimper in your ear as I kiss along its edge, and enjoy the feeling of each of my piercings touching my lips. I breathe heavily as you start pumping a finger in and out, in and out, before you add another. I bite your shoulder and scream out when you start to bend your fingers.

With your free hand you pull my head back by my hair and take my body away from yours. I whimper when you pull your itty-bitty fingers out of me and you push them into my mouth when you push me back against the kitchen island. I lick and suck my own juice from you as you push me firmly into the granite countertop, then you replace your fingers with your mouth and we kiss violently. Your hands move down to my nipples and I feel my knees weaken as you roll them between your nails.

When you break the kiss, you fall to your knees and bury your face between my legs. You hold my hips firmly in place with one hand, bring the other back up and start fucking me with your fingers. I've been so close since you walked through the door at the party and now, with your tongue flicking back and forth on my clitoris and your fingers pumping in and out of me, I can't hold back any longer. I reach for the counter as I groan in rhythm with every stab, your fingers bury themselves deep inside me and rock hard into me while my pussy grabs them too tight to keep pushing. You suck hard on my clitoris, your tongue caresses it while my whole body trembles against you. I'm not sure what I'm saying now - I'm screaming loudly right now, but I'm pretty sure it's not safe for work. As the ecstasy begins to subside and you slow down, I gently push you back and sink to the ground with you.

By wrapping my body around you and kissing your mouth, which tastes like my orgasm, I notice that the house is very quiet. Suddenly laughter breaks out of the projection room downstairs, and then thunderous applause. We laugh, and then I put my hand between your legs. There must be another encore.

## TASTES LIKE MORE

When I wake up, I feel the soft fullness of the pillow that I had stuffed between my legs during the night. I reach down and adjust it and give my hot inner thighs the joy of the new coolness. As I do so, my hand gazes over my smooth, damp hill. I feel very excited and wonder what time it is. I long for more of you and especially for her.

I open my eyes and look at the other side of the bed. You are just out of my reach, lying on your stomach and breathing deeply. The sheet is wrapped around your legs and your beautiful, muscular butt is completely exposed. As I slide closer to you, you turn on your side and offer me a glimpse of your smooth cheeks. I feel the presence of another person in the bedroom and lift my head from the pillow.

I see her sitting on the other side of the room in the candlelight. She is draped over the living room chair, smoking and looking directly at me. She smiles as she exhales and asks me if I had enjoyed myself earlier. Her voice is deep and rough, thick with desire. Quietly I slide my hand down my stomach while looking at her, shaking my palm around my wetness. The simple sound of her voice alone has made my clitoris stiff. She slowly, almost imperceptibly, begins to nod, nodding her head, while I let my other hand slide along the sheets towards your ass.

Gracefully she rises from her chair, flicks her cigarette and slides along the length of the floor, her body is slim and strong. Her breasts move as slowly and sluggishly as they do under water, swinging in a kind of floating suspension. Her long legs quickly exploit the space between us, and in no time at all she is sitting on the edge of the bed next to you.

To reach her, I have to move over you. Again she smiles knowingly and puts her hand over mine, which now rests on your hip. My view of her body is now broken and through the tangle of our arms and your hips only small parts of her are visible. I get more and more wet as I stare at her and realize that every piece of her that is cut into pieces is absolutely desirable.

You stir slowly and adapt to the new weight that is on you. Still dozing, you must feel our presence and I continue to watch her face to see if it shows me that your cock is beginning to harden. She continues to hold my gaze and with her hand she guides my hand along the front of your hip. I move closer to your back and begin to gently push my crotch into you. Our hands do the fall together and land on your stand. Together we wrap our fingers around it and start to caress you until you are completely full. I think you must be awake now, although I cannot see your face. I wonder if your eyes are open and if you are receiving the vision of her loveliness within you.

She bends over to your face, her eyes still on mine, and offers you her breasts. I hear you moan and cling greedily to a nipple. She twitches as you suck, pull and bite. Again I move closer to you and lift my face to her. I want to taste my juices on her lips again. While she leans towards me, I can smell my scent on her. Your cock is rock hard as we stroke you. I put my tongue in her open mouth and fill my cunt with the fingers of my other hand. I am slippery and dripping wet while rubbing hard against my clitoris.

She gently begins to roll you onto your back with me. She carefully pulls her breasts out of your mouth, fills her mouth with my spit and slowly slides down your upper body, taking you full length down her throat. I try to move my hand away, but she holds on to my clasp and we press harder on your cock. Your breath is fast as you watch her swallow you. You arch your back and lift your groin to meet her mouth and start to stick your cock deeper into her throat. She raises her gaze to meet ours and I move quickly towards her and start sucking your cock with her. She pulls it up, then lets go and I swallow you. I suck it, then I let go and she goes down. My hand grabs your balls while her hand caresses you. Each of us with the other hand goes up your stomach and takes a nipple between our fingers. I turn left and she turns right. We look at you both and hear you moan while you rest your head on the floor to watch us.

Your appetite for you is fierce! She sucks your dick fast and furious, she breathes hard and loud. I go away to watch her She now sucks your dick very deep and strokes your shaft with both hands now.

She slowly begins to move her body, swinging her slender leg across your chest and grabbing you while sucking. Just as she spreads her cream-coloured pussy over your face, I move in the opposite direction and crawl on my stomach between your legs. I lift both legs up and bend them in my knees. You feel my hot breath on your asshole, spread your legs wider and offer them to me. I stick my hard tongue up your ass, the fingers of both my hands rub your balls and cheeks. Her head pats on your dick right above me, and I look up and meet her eyes again.

As our eyes close, you arch your back and start shooting your load into her throat. Then she pulls loose and we watch as your coming splashes on both our faces and lips. I take my tongue out of your ass, lick your load out of my face and stand up to hit her creamy lips. Her juice is hot and salty between our mouths as we fuck each other with our tongue down each other's throats.

"Mmmm, baby," I whisper to her. "This definitely tastes like more!"

## A WOMAN'S WORLD

In a fast-forward to 2027, 20 years after George Bush choked on a peanut allegedly planted by Jimmy Carter, Laura Bush was appointed President of the United States by unanimous decree.

After two terms as President, her daughter Barbara ended two terms as President, and her twin sister Jenna just began her first term as President. Instead of roses, the rose garden is filled with bushes.

Although gas prices are $30.00 a gallon, hair salons, childcare, Pilates classes, curves, breast implants, Victoria Secrets underwear, shoes, slim-fast weight loss supplements, dildos and vibrators, and condoms and Viagra are subsidized by the federal government through high taxes on beer, sports betting, live sporting events, and televised football, baseball, hockey, and basketball games.

Paula Abdul is governor of California, and America's most popular television show is American Midol, in which women win cash prizes for humiliating their husbands on network television.

"And today's American Midol winner of a two-week vacation in Jamaica is Debbie Knowles from Dayton, Ohio, for proving that her husband John has the smallest penis in America. Happy birthday, Debbie. And John, thank you for being a good sport. What's the consolation prize for John, Murray?"

"We got a brown paper bag he can wear over his head so he doesn't have to show his face in Dayton."

Miss America Pageants are a thing of the past. They're being replaced by Mister America Pageants where men have to strut their stuff across a long runway while wearing a codpiece thong. And their erect penises are measured backstage by Burt Lars (yes, he's back) and announced over the loudspeaker while women guide them down the aisle.

"Here he is, Mister America. Chad Morris is a senior at Cal Tech with a 7-inch penis. Tyrone Jones is a junior at Florida State with, oh, my God, a 10-inch dick"

The term Dead Beat Dad is no longer a figurative term, but should be taken literally, as fathers who do not pay their court-ordered alimony are beaten to death by their ex-wives. Needless to say, there are no more Dead Beat Dads, and child support now extends not only to financial support but also to physical, emotional and spiritual support, not only until the child is 18 years old, but until the child is married and makes his own living.

Since pregnant women are not allowed to smoke and/or drink, men are not allowed to smoke and/or drink while their wives are pregnant. Vasectomies are considered mandatory whenever the wife deems it necessary.

Marriage vows are rewritten and force men to recite "And I will love, honor and obey...".

The three major car manufacturers, once General Motors, Ford and Chrysler, are now Toyota, Honda and MacDonalds. MacDonalds made the world's first edible car, the Ronald, where you drive the car for a week and eat the edible portions for breakfast, lunch and dinner while driving to and from work, and then the following week you buy another car for $99.00. The gasoline for running the car is pressed from French fries. And every automaker in the United States has to have a place for a handbag.

Bill Gates is the world's first billionaire after announcing his plans to produce and mass-market the first all glass car called, what else, Windows. Oprah Winfrey finally comes out of the closet and declares her love for Tyra Banks, and Donald Trump and Martha Stewart, now penniless, are arrested for fraud after their reality TV shows were exposed by the winning candidates who had not been given real jobs in their companies. There is no truth to the rumor that Rosie O'Donnell and Donald Trump were secretly married, but there is a rumor that the rumor still exists. Barbara Walters, still alive and on TV at 98, refuses to retire and will never die.

The newest and bestselling product that came on the market is an inflatable latex doll designed after Brad Pitt and Johnny Depp and named DepPit. The doll has a remote-controlled steel vibrating rod that is inserted into his rubber-like penis to give pleasure to lonely and/or horny women. Pitt and Depp receive generous royalties for their permission to allow the manufacturers to design the dolls according to their ideas. Now everywhere they go, they are grabbed by women who tug at their clothes and want to know if their tails are like those of the DepPit dolls. Of course the celebrities tell them that it's just longer, thicker and harder. Apparently they don't mind the attention, as they laugh all the way to the bank. There is no truth in the rumor that the company makes a doll after the grandmother, Barbara Bush, who is still alive at 99, called Bush, for the older men in nursing homes who still want a little but can't stand up fully.

It is an offence for a man to give a woman a bad connection, a false name and a first date without calling her 24 hours later. Rape does not exist because the punishment for rape is the surgical removal of the perpetrator's two brains, the penis and the cerebral cortex. Women can now finally roam the streets safely in the dark. Unfortunately and inexplicably, there is a sudden and enormous increase in violent crime by women against men. In reality, women persecute, assault and rape men

Since the colours of the American flag have changed from red, white and blue to pink, yellow and evergreen, there have been no more wars.

Do you think the world is a better place when it's run by women? What do you think? What suggestions do you have for improvement?

## THE FIX

Cynthia sat restlessly in one of the plush chairs in the waiting area, directly in front of the hotel lobby. She fingered the envelope in her hand - the envelope that had been left for her at the desk. She smiled to herself as she examined her name, which was neatly printed in Chad's handwriting. Today would go well - he knew the routine. He knew her daily routine and his limits. He did not necessarily understand her preferences, but he had learned that it was worth his while to follow her instructions. She frowned a little as she felt the electronic ID through the envelope. There was something erotic and powerful about it, like a key slipping into a lock. The mechanical noise it made. The flicker of worry as you turned it - "Will it work?" "Do I have the right room?" The ID took some of it away. Oh, yes, another thing that has been "improved" by progress.

She looked at her watch and noticed it was 2:22. She wouldn't go to the elevator until at least 2:27 - Chad was probably getting ready. As she fidgeted, the glow spread throughout her body. With one of her "regulars" she was never nervous - only anxious. It was always nice to be confident that everything would go smoothly. With a new "appointment" came excitement, but also - additional worries. As usual, the butterflies were dancing like crazy in her tummy. Her pussy got wetter by the second. She pushed her "librarian glasses" onto the bridge of her nose, stood up gracefully and smoothed her trousers. She remembered that she had to change hotels again soon. Although she was 15 miles "out of town", she was married and needed no one to notice her. Of course, she knew that she not only had her husband's "permission" but also - his encouragement. But this did not mean that the rest of the community would understand.

At 2:28 a.m. she entered the elevator. Her hair was piled up into a bun. She was wearing a dark chocolate pantsuit with a cream-coloured blouse underneath. She was wearing high heels - not slutty, but not conservative either. She was wearing a leather attaché who looked like a lawyer or real estate agent on business in the city. At exactly 2:30 a.m., the elevator stopped at 5. At 2:31 a.m., she pushed her badge into the lock on the door of room 548. As she entered the room, she found a switch and put down her briefcase, pausing for a moment to allow her eyes to get used to the darkness. The room was dark, but not pitch black. The air conditioning in the room seemed to be on "maximum" - it was 68 degrees, or cooler. The curtains were drawn. Several candles were flickering in their assigned places in the room. The smell in the air - the candles contained essence of patchouli. This pungent smell, which came from the currents generated by the alternating current channels, made them almost dizzy.

She could see the outlines of Chad on the bed. As she preferred, the bed was bare, except for the single sheet that covered Chad. The same Chad whose face she had never seen. His tail - only slightly larger than average - protruded through a hole that had been cut in the sheet. He was not yet fully erected. She took a short breath, as usual, the moment she saw it. It was a raw, sexual contrast to the simple white linen sheet. It was pure sex. It was there for her - not for him, not for any other purpose. She bent over and lightly kissed the end of it. Then she scratched her nails to length. Almost immediately it was hard. Quickly she took off her trousers, folded them and put them on the chair. She took a sip from the glass with Coke and ice that had been prepared for her. Next, there was a bra and panties. Strangely enough, they were made of plain white cotton. Nothing exotic, nothing perverse. With an ice cube in her mouth and no comment, she swallowed his cock. He grunted at the surprise. She muttered her approval as her chin met the fresh linen of the sheets. His cock jumped out of her mouth and she took it roughly in her hands. She was anything but tender as she glided the length of the tail up and down with her hand. Chad groaned, but according to the agreement he did not speak a word. He was literally the "object of her desire" - he grotesquely protruded from the sheets, there was nothing else to distract her; nothing else to concentrate on.

God, how she loved that - actually longed for it. She stroked it. She scratched her polished nails over its shaft, head and balls of Chad. He writhed with each new touch, but never made a sound. She took it in her mouth - first just the end, then the whole thing. She licked him like a lollipop. She smeared the silky drops of the concoction over her palm and rubbed it over her nipples. Whenever she had a free hand, she put her fingers on herself. They nipped feverishly at her throbbing clitoris. They sank, three or four at a time, into her soaking wet pussy. She even shoved her smooth index finger up her ass. Her hips spun with every touch while she worked his cock. She needed it like an addict needs his fix. Her cunt longed to be filled. Yet denial was part of the thrill. It was not yet time. She was in the moment. Here she was - soccer mom, devoted wife, sincere member of the community... behaving like a crazy bitch in a darkened hotel room. She loved having an alter ego. She loved having that secret side that only her husband and her lovers knew about. She loved to have the freedom to live her sexuality the way she wanted to live it. She loved cock, she loved fucking - almost to the point of obsession. Sex made up a large part of her personality.

She wanted to drag things out, but knowing that Chad couldn't take the roughness for long, Cynthia slowed down. She took a sip of her lemonade and lay down on the bed next to Chad. Her fingers stroked him gently - enough to keep him excited, but not so much that he spat.

With her free hand she let an ice cube from her glass slide over her body. Side to side of her neck, around her breasts and over her stomach. She pushed the ice cube through her pubic hair and pressed it against her clitoris while her third and fourth fingers tried to spread her lips. All the while she stared longingly at Chad's cock. The ice made her throb even harder. She moved the rapidly shrinking cube back up her body and sucked it into her mouth. Since the hand was now completely free, she started again by fingering herself. She twisted and bucked against her hand. Her desire to be fulfilled was now approaching desperation. Her breath was heavy and her body did not stand still even for a moment. Even Chad moaned softly - his inability to experience this fully - was almost cruel.

Finally she sat down on him - face outwards, of course, so that he would not remain uncovered. With her left hand she held him while she positioned herself up. She lowered herself a little more and used his glittering head to split her lips. Yet nothing but his cock was exposed through the sheets. He barely made a sound. Her clitoris was swollen, and she was circumcised but not clean-shaven. Outside of the hotel rooms, she was a very conservative lady. Suddenly she let go of her weight and impaled herself on him. He grunted - partly in surprise, partly in pain - it was not a graceful movement. It was an indication of her need. She moaned when he was all inside her. She was soaking wet, and she loved how "dirty" she sounded when she started moving her hips back and forth. Like one of those women in the movies. Her movements became more and more hectic, and her breathing became rougher with every beat. "God, he was feeling good. " All that week she could hardly think about anything else. Now she was there - finally getting the relief she needed. She imagined a junkie having to feel like that when he gets a long-awaited fix...

She started to squeeze her breasts, squeeze them. Her pace quickened, her ass "smack-smack-smack-smack" through the sheet onto Chad's body - filling the room. She was now panting like a dog. With one hand she rolled her nipple hard between her fingers. With the other hand she worked her clitoris as best she could while fucking Chad's swollen cock. What she needed now was his sperm. In these sessions she reached her one-minute moment of weakness - the moment when she started begging. She begged Chad to come inside her. With tears of joy, she begged him to fill her. In her fury, she was almost like an animal. She concentrated only on his cock inside her and how it made her feel. She concentrated on the moment when it would swell and finally break out inside her. Her screams and pleas now came quickly to her - she needed his sperm and she told him again and again. She herself was on the verge of orgasm - she felt it swelling up inside her. Finally she heard him start moaning and his cock seemed to double. "Yes, please" - she begged - "Fill me! Fill me with your sperm" And with that his whole body seemed to freeze for a moment, then spasm. Then another spasm. She felt him twitch inside her. She felt the heat spreading inside her. At what felt like his second or third squirt, her own orgasms began to collapse inside her. Like a thousand blinding, icy headaches bouncing around her body like pinball balls. With a whimper she collapsed and lay down over the groundbreaking form below her.

After she had showered and got dressed, Chad finally left the bed. In the envelope on the desk was a crisp $50 bill - another mysterious part of her "scene". Harmless though, and he could always use the cash. After all - he had the room for a whole day - he could watch the game and use the room service.

When Cynthia went down in the elevator, she felt like a new woman. She imagined that her husband would be happy to hear about her escapades later that evening. She checked her attaché for her day planner. On the taxi ride home, she had to think about her plans for the next week. Hmm. Maybe Anthony, at a new hotel - the Biltmore would be nice.

## HER FANTASY

They had a poker party. It was late. I hadn't been in the way in the study all evening. Since I wasn't in charge of entertainment, I was dressed in jeans and T-shirt - no bra, no underwear (and no jewelry).

The other three boys had just left, and you and the cute guy collected chips and counted the winnings of the evening. I came in and started churning around and picking up snacks, etc.

He smiled at me cheekily. I was a bit embarrassed because my nipples were hard from the breeze blowing through the open windows and I was sure he noticed, so I smiled shyly and started picking them up. He started a conversation to involve me about cards. Was I playing? Did I like cards? What about strip poker?

I said we played when you were in college, before we got married. You didn't say much because you noticed the vibes, the tension in the air and wondered where it would lead. He said, "How about a few rounds just the three of us?"

I looked at you and tried to gauge your feelings about the idea. Personally, I was for it; my nipples were still hard (and now not from the breeze) and I felt a twitch in my cunt.

I knew that I could only lose two hands and I would be naked, but you didn't!

You smiled that it's ok, I love you, it'll be ok, smile at me and say: "Sure, is that ok with you, honey?

I said "ok" - determined to throw away any card worth anything to see his reaction to my naked body and also your reaction to his reaction.

We were all 3 relaxed, not nervous, chatting like close friends (I had only seen the guy I always called "the cute one" in my mind a few times).

Of course I lost my first hand and took off my T-shirt. He seemed to be pretty sorry I lost, but he appreciated my tits with the hard nipples.

The game went on and I felt a foot from his side of the table starting to massage my foot under the table. Somehow I didn't lose the next hand, but every time I reached for another card, my arm grazed the side of my tit and I knew he (and you) were watching.

With the third hand I lost, and I said, that's the game, gentlemen, and he protested "why"?!?

I unzipped my jeans, pulled them down and took them off and said "because I have nothing left to lose".

They reached over and pinched a tit with their hand, pinched my nipple and said "But maybe we can compromise.

The winner of the next hand - if it was one of you two - was allowed to fondle my tits for 1 minute while the other kept "time". And we would proceed as follows:

- Then he'd fondle my tits and kiss me - two minutes

- stroking tits, kissing me, sticking fingers in my cunt - 3 minutes.

- Sitting on the winner's lap while he kisses me, caresses my tits and rubs my ass - 4 minutes.

- i stand in front of the winner while he kissed me and sucked my tits - 5 min

- I give the winner 10 minutes.

If I lost that many more hands, the game would be over and we would finish the game.

We all agreed it was okay, and I had a good feeling about the time limits. You know a kind of "controlled" danger situation. Dangerous because I wanted to be kissed, sucked, touched and fucked by him and wouldn't even protest a little "help" from you.

You lost the next hand, your shirt is gone. Here I was, naked, with two naked-breasted sexy men and I was horny.

My nipples seemed permanently erect and my cunt was still twitching. Not only that, but since He had won the hand, He was allowed to stroke my tits while you "timed" 1 minute. It felt good to have hands on my tits - I was so horny and I loved how full they felt when he pressed them into his big warm hands.

With the next hand he lost and took off his belt. They, on the other hand, got 3 minutes to caress my tits, kiss me and put a finger in my cunt. The three minutes went by so fast. I wanted you to just fuck me good, but no, keep going, your 3 minutes are over!

You lost with the next hand, now it's your jockeys turn and he beat my cards too. I rolled on his lap together with my arms around his neck, he kissed me deep and hard, played softly but firmly with my tits - cupped them, pinched my nipples just enough to make my cunt twitch even more, and he squeezed my ass cheeks and kneaded them as if they were dough; my cunt dripped when you shouted "time".

They won the next hand and I was "loser" again -- OH, POOR ME! I LOVED IT! He took off his jeans and didn't wear jockeys!

You left me standing in front of you for 5 minutes while you sucked and kissed my breasts, because only you know how to do that. I was so turned on! He on the other hand timed us and his cock was stiff and erect - just the way I like them. Since he was behind me with a timer and you were caught in the 5 minute tit-thrill, I noticed once or twice a slight stroke of his cock head over my ass cheek. Could have been an accident, but I don't think so! I noticed your cock was rock hard too, but you still had your jockeys on. It made a nice arch

Well, you lost the next hand, and that nice curvature turned into a hard, finished cock - but he won the hand and 10 minutes of free running with me. His dick was no longer or thicker than yours. But it was just as hard. Since he only had 10 minutes, he pushed his hard cock directly into my cunt, because he knew from my billowing chest and obvious pleasure in our little game that I would be soaking wet. Indeed I was, and I came as soon as his cock was buried in me all the way.

He caressed my tits, kissed me deeply and sucked my nipples until I begged him to stop and fuck me again!

You, on the other hand, looked at the clock and shouted "time"!

Then you asked in front of him if you could help relieve some of my sexual tension left over from the rushed 10 minute fuck. I gladly accepted, and we made madly passionate love. When we both reached the climax, you stayed inside me and turned around so I was on top.

He approached us from behind and kneeled behind me and allowed his hard cock to tease my wet cunt that still had your cock in it.

You grabbed my tits and let your cock slip out. His slipped in with little change of position.

But I wanted to change position. I wanted to be on my hands and knees, with my tit in your mouth and his cock in my cunt. It felt so good.

I came, he came, you played with your cock and came on my belly.

I was full of emotion and you were so great! We all fell asleep and fell asleep.

The next day I was raw all over, but it was worth it.

I wonder when the next poker game will be...

## WIFE GETS WILD ON CRUISE

It is the first day of our ten-day cruise. This holiday is a little different from the last one we have taken in the last 3 years. I have told my wife that she can have any man she wants, as many as she wants, and that she can do anything she wants as long as I am there. She doesn't seem to be interested, so I didn't even mention that a third person was coming to us this time.

We're spending time exploring the ship and having a few drinks. I'll tell her I'm on my way to the Mess Hall. We meet a few hours later and have another drink when she tells me that she overheard three guys talking about how they hope to be happy. She pointed them out, good-looking, late 20s, early 30s, clean-looking.

I smile, "Did you invite them upstairs?" I ask her while she smiles "no".

She said their conversation was interesting because they were not only hoping to be lucky, but also that if they were lucky, they could all be together. My eyebrow raised in interest as I listened, and I think I was already leaking.

"That sounds like the perfect scenario babe, three horny dudes and us" when I giggled and stopped, knowing she wasn't going to do anything.

We both go to our stateroom and before we fall asleep, we have our fun. I take the 3 guys up a couple of times, but only after she mentions them and the cum is hard.

We both woke up early, earlier than usual, so it's no wonder it's noon and we find ourselves on the tired side. Drinks and sunshine didn't help much. I'll apologize in the bathroom. A few minutes later I come back and see my wife talking to two of the three boys. I decide to take my time, come back and order more drinks. She sees me at the bar and signals me to come along.

I arrive with the third man of the group. He has a frightened look on his face and is disappointed when I show up. I smile as Tracy, my wife, introduces me to the two she knows. They introduce their third buddy. We all sit together and make small talk, then Tracy opens up to the fact she was talking about when she overheard their conversation and asks if they've had any luck yet. Turns out they haven't.

The third guy, Jim, looks at his buddies Tim and Tony and asks them questions when they explain. I sit there with a scared and interested look as my wife grabs my hand, I look at her and let her know that she can do it if she wants to.

She seems comfortable with Tony as she grabs his hand: "Jake and I were just about to go to our cabin, take a shower and take a nap. If you'd like to join us after the shower, we'll be in cabin 7363".

They look stunned when we get up and I say before we leave: "I hope to see you again soon".

Tracy and I chat on the way to the cabin and in the shower. She has decided to provide condoms, but is confident that they are clean; they are a bit on the nerdy side. I even made a clever remark about them being virgins.

She knows I loved it when my 2 best friends shot their load into her. I loved the taste and the feeling and I want it again so much, but we don't want to invite any friends over because of the strains afterwards.

We sit on the bed, scantily clad, when a knock at the door comes. I open it nervously and anxiously and see all 3 of our new friends. I invite them in and the five of us make ourselves comfortable while we have a drink and talk. I notice that all 3 have bumps and I can't wait to see what they have.

I start kissing my wife and then I look at her and say: "Are you as horny as I am"?

She pulls me towards her, kisses my lips "hornier I think" while I put them back and start to take them off.

When I have freed her breasts so that everyone can see and enjoy them, I look at the guys with the question "Please help yourself. She is on fire and we have the fire hoses".

All 3 are standing and quickly undressed. I see 3 beautiful, cut, hard cocks, all 3 also with shaved balls. Tracy leans on her elbows: "Oh, they look so good. I can do whatever I want with them," she asks as I nod in agreement.

We had no trouble getting them back into anything as I watch them suck on her juicy breasts that alternate in her pussy. I loved watching their hot cocks stretch her and she enjoyed it immensely to have pleasure as she had one orgasm after another.

The time was getting closer and closer as the guys held back on the scrounging as long as possible. First, Tim announced that he was purring when Tracy broke off our kiss while Tony and Jim sucked her tits: "Come inside me, come deep inside me," she begged as Tim plunged deep inside her. I moved to watch his cock pulsating and throbbing inside her and pumping his semen into my wife's hot, hungry pussy.

She comes back and says she can feel his sperm in her. I watch Jim go next and then Tony. Tony, she held on as they both came and she pulled him over for a hot, deep, passionate kiss. I was about to explode!

I looked at her pussy filled with semen and went right down on top of her. I hear her moaning with relish as I taste her and her. To get a good taste, I come up, position my leaky cock at her entrance. I bury my two and a half centimetres slightly inside her and let out a deep, satisfying moan.

She looks me in the eyes and says, "Do I like the way I feel after being fucked and satisfied by 3 guys"?

I bend over and kiss her with more passion than ever before: "Yes, yes, I do! You feel great, look beautiful and taste delicious".

I start beating on her already well fucked pussy while Jim and Tony stand by her side. She takes a half hard cock in her hand and looks at me: "Do you want to help me with that? I smiled, leaned in and also Jim's half hard cock in my mouth and then felt my wife cum almost immediately as I pumped my own sperm into her too.

This is going to be a great vacation and a great cruise. I can't wait to see what the next 9 days will bring for us.

## OUTDOOR TREAT

It is a cool, busy evening and my husband and I are out late with a cup of coffee, enjoying the night air and the sky. We hadn't been outside long when I saw our friend coming towards us. The three of us are talking and I wonder all the time if he has ulterior motives. If not, I wonder if he does have any. My thoughts start playing with scenarios of what might be, what I might wish for. I gently nudge my husband and give him my little, naughty, bad girl smile and beg him for permission to be a bad girl. He smiles back with a nod and tells me that I am free to get what I want and that what I want is right in front of me, both of them!

I put my coffee on the hood of my truck and move my hand towards the zipper of his jeans. Once he understands what is going on, he looks at my husband for approval, gets it, then quickly helps me to get access to what I want, his delicious cock!

I kneel down in front of his crotch; stare for a short moment at this delicious cock in front of me before I fill my mouth with this hot and wonderful cock. He is immediately hard and throbs in my mouth when I start pumping him hard, I want to enjoy him, but I know that I have to let him cum as soon as possible. We are outside in the driveway between our two trucks, so we don't have much time, and I really want to feel him in my mouth and taste his sperm.

He starts his own pumping action on my mouth in perfect harmony with me, while we both enjoy a moment of forbidden pleasure. Oh, I swear I'm getting wet from the thrill of being outside, possibly being caught, his delicious cock inside me and the fact that my husband is going to ravish me tonight after all this. I want them both so bad and so much that I'm willing to fuck them both right here

My mouth has enjoyed being fucked by his delicious cock and by all indications he may be ready to deliver the fruits of my labour. With slower and longer strokes he pumps his delicious sperm into my mouth. I almost choke to death on the huge amount he delivers, but with everything I have; I take every single drop and enjoy the feeling as it runs down my throat and into my stomach.

When I get up, my husband helps me up and I smile at them. Our friend graciously thanks me while he zips himself. My husband now hits his own hard and begs for the same treatment. With a smile on my face I pounce longingly on my dear man. I want it bad, I want to be bad and I will be bad! Our friend watches with interest as I work on my man with my hot, beautiful cock and do everything in my power to extract his delicious seed. They both moan and I won't even touch our friend! I can understand why my husband does it, but our friend?

While my husband's cock is pounding in my mouth, I hear him telling me that our friend is spreading his back, stroking it and it is hard again! This really turns me on now, I love the fact that I can do this to these two and they want me so much. It works out well because I want them too.

I work furiously on my men who have a hot and throbbing cock and now more than ever want his sweet juices. He has poured big samples into me, which tells me that I am close and he is closer! His own pumping movements are faster in pace. He lets me know that it is indeed time as I walk all the way down on him and bury his hot, pulsing flesh deep in my mouth. My reward is here, I can feel his huge load squirting with force down my throat as his cock pumps his semen into me, over and over again. My goodness, what a load he had! As I suck every single drop of him and slowly pull his cock out of my mouth, they moan again!

"I think I might jerk off with another load," I hear our friend say. Did I do that? I look up at my husband, that turns him on, when I see this I turn to our friend and tell him to stop while I take the head of his cock in my mouth and lick it and suck it while I wait for another load of candy, for me it's candy for sure. He meant it when he said he thought he could get another load, within minutes his cock pumps more of his delicious stuff into my waiting mouth and I drink it down, this time with plenty of it on my lips. I get up and kiss my husband while my hand caresses his still hard cock and he reacts eagerly. As soon as our kiss is broken, I kneel down and rub his sugar cream over my lips and rise to our friend and kiss him. His reaction is not as good as my husband's, but then again we are friends, not lovers!

We are three of us, all dressed and with a smile on our faces. My husband then invites him to his home in the morning to continue a more intense and thorough exploration of the other. He looks at me, then at my husband, we both smile approvingly when he tells us that he will come by around ten o'clock. In agreement, he begins to go home while my husband and I finish our coffee, so that we can go to "bed" and live out our fantasies together and rapture each other.

I am lucky to have him and I really love him!

## HIS FANTASY

My wife and I have often talked about our fantasies, and of course mine are always perverse. After such discussions we are both heated and ready. One of my fantasies is that I love watching her and another man and being with her. I love to watch her put it in her mouth. She looks absolutely beautiful and hot with another man's cock in her mouth. I also love watching her get fucked by another man's cock. Her pussy is beautiful as it is, but even more so in this situation.

While the three of us sit and talk, all of us getting hotter by the minute, I finally break the ice and start talking about sex and how hot my beautiful wife is. My wife is very heterosexual, but every now and then she has some abnormal tendencies, and I hope this is such a moment. She responds, and that is in our favour!

While I slowly undress her, our friend Eric watches very curious. I ask him for help and ask him to undress like I am doing at this moment. We begin to caress her breasts, which are so soft and subtle. He can't help himself as he begins to suck and lick her breast. I follow him while my wife pleasurably puts her hands on the back of our heads. Both Eric and I tease and finger her beautiful and bald pussy by working her breasts with our mouths as she starts to let go with her moaning in ecstasy. She starts to talk dirty, which is unusual for her, but for me it is purely sexy and hot.

Eric starts stretching her stomach down to her sweetheart. Once there, he works her pussy with his mouth and tongue while I move with my manhood to her mouth. She lets out a "Ohhhh yes, lick my pussy!" quietly but with relish. This is just about to get me over the edge as she takes my manhood into her mouth. She's never sucked so much passion from me before, it feels so good.

I watch as Eric starts to penetrate her love channel with his cock. I watch as he slides between these beautiful pussy lips and starts to lick hard when my wife says: "Oh God, that feels so good, fuck me, I want to be fucked". Watching Eric pounding my wife's pussy looks so good, so hot that I start to lick more and my hungry wife sucks and licks everything. Eric responds to my wife's reaction and words with "Your pussy feels good and I will fuck you and your pussy well". After a few minutes of his angry slapping on her pussy and an orgasm from her, he is about to release his load of love juice. My wife rips me out of her mouth and screams: "Give it to me, fill my pussy with your cock and juices, I want it, I want it all". So he did it. When I saw how he poured his semen into her, how his cock and balls twitched with every squirt, I was in heaven.

When he pulled himself out of her, mixing his and her juices, and his cock shining out of them, I became very aroused. I go down and start eating her freshly fucked pussy filled with sperm and it tastes so good. She pulls the back of my head inside with her hands and shouts softly "eat my pussy filled with sperm". Surprisingly it tasted good as I eagerly sucked and licked her cream-filled pussy and watched her hungrily sucking his cock. I got up and pushed my cock into her hot, wet, soft pussy. Her sperm-filled fucked pussy felt so wonderful. When I started pumping her pussy angrily, I watched her sucking Eric's cock, then she moved to his balls and skillfully sucked each one while I fucked her pussy. My animal fury overcame me as I watched her and felt her delicious pussy wrap itself around my cock. I couldn't stop myself, so I took Eric's cock in my mouth and started sucking it.

To my surprise, he felt and tasted quite good and fuelled my passions even more. It must have had the same effect on my wife when she told me to suck his cock, suck it well and enjoy it. All three of us moaned in utter ecstasy as I fucked my wife, watched her suck Eric's balls like she was hungry and she was, and I sucked his cock. I felt his cock splatter little hints of what was inside him and eagerly accepted his gift. As his cock in my mouth became harder and harder, my own passions were about to explode when my wife screamed before another orgasm, screaming, "Fuck me, I want to fuck, I want to fuck you both". With this I released my hot load of love juice as she pulled me towards her so that it penetrated deep into her.

When I pulled out of her now very soaked pussy, Eric continued to go down on her and eat her pussy, which was also very full of semen. He also loved the taste of all our juices. When he came up he took my manhood in his mouth and started sucking me. It felt weird but good at the same time. My wife then posed to suck my balls and with that I worked hard on one again. Eric pulled his hungry mouth off my cock and grabbed my wife by the hips, rolled her into the doggy position and penetrated her pussy from behind. She was now more eager than ever to get fucked and she told us. I leaned back and watched them, my own passions went completely out of control as I stroked my cock. She looked so hot and sexy as she was fucked and the two of them together were almost too much. I slid to her mouth as she eagerly took my cock in her mouth and sucked it as best she could.

After many minutes of her mouth and pussy being fucked she had another orgasm and that was all it took to get Eric over the edge as he squirted another load of his semen into her pussy. She begged us for every drop we had as I turned her over, laid her down and spread her beautiful legs. Slowly I pushed my now rock hard cock into her now well fucked pussy, it felt so fucking good, she can't know how much I love the feeling, how hot and sexy she looks and what a turn it is for me to watch her receive and give total pleasure as she screamed "fuck me, please fuck me well, I want to be fucked and be fucked well". I did my best to fulfill her wish, just like Eric did.

I fucked her while Eric positioned himself over her face and she accepted that he put a tool in her mouth and sucked him with anger. After a few minutes she pulled it out of her mouth and offered me a turn which I gladly accepted as she was obviously excited to see it. She had another orgasm while I worked his cock with my mouth. She started sucking and licking his balls and with every ball she sucked he gave me a sample of its contents which I gladly accepted. I pulled out of my wife's pussy, rolled her on her side and penetrated her pussy again. Eric positioned himself to lick her pussy and my balls simultaneously. This was something I had never felt before and it felt great, so great that I couldn't hold back and let go with another load of cream for my wonderful wife and her hungry pussy

When I pulled out, Eric took my manhood in his mouth and cleaned me dry. Then he put my wife on his back and kicked again into her so well fucked pussy and fucked her with a rage. I leaned back and watched this wonderful sight. It was really erotic to watch her fucking with spread legs. She grabbed his head, pulled his lips to hers, then broke the kiss and begged him to fuck her and fuck her well. It was obvious she wanted to fuck and we were her victims. He told her he wanted to fuck her and he would fuck her and he did. I'm sitting there stroking my own cock and watching these two fuck with everything they have, while he's about to unload another package of pleasure in her hungry pussy, I announce that

I'm ready too and she pulled me to her and shouted for us both to give it to her.

If she only knew how aroused and excited I will watch and share in these mutual pleasures. I also learned that Eric feels and tastes pretty good. We all lay there exhausted afterwards, but within minutes Eric found the urge again and I thanked him by spreading my wife's beautiful pussy lips open so he could enter. His cock felt nice to slide between my fingers into my wife's very hot, wet and well fucked pussy, but she was ready for more and we gave it to her willingly.

## GIRLFRIEND CUMS

Mike went through the front door and found a surprise waiting for him. His wife and her best friend were sitting in the living room waiting for him to arrive. He had no idea that Toni was coming to town. He gently kissed his wife Wendy and gave Toni a big hug. "Hi, girls! When did you come to town? "he asked as he was putting his things down and his wife handed him a beer. Toni replied that she had arrived around 10 o'clock the night before. Mike looked at Wendy with a strange look. They all sat down together and talked a little while sipping the drink of their choice. Finally Wendy looked at Toni and Toni started to take off her shirt. Mike was stunned. He sat still for a few seconds and then watched Toni take off her bra. Her breasts were beautiful! They were perfect spheres with dark pink areolas that rippled under Mike's watch. Mike still said nothing. Stacy then took off her shirt and was without a bra. Slowly both Wendy and Toni leaned over to Mike and began to kiss and caress his neck and lips. Mike had a very breathless feeling. He was not sure if this was happening. Then he was carefully undressed by these two women. He wallowed in the moment and was surprised and shocked as he watched Toni bend over and lick his wife's tits. Talking about immediately applying hard

Wendy arched her back and gave Toni free access to her breasts. Toni spent several minutes on each one of them.

Mike became more and more horny and horny second. Then Toni moved out Mike's wife completely. Wendy stood up and Toni started to caress her all over her body. She ran her hands into the curve of Wendy's ass. Then Wendy started to explore her own a little. Shyly she reached out her hand and grabbed the perfect globe of Toni's breast. Then she started teasing the erect nipple with her tongue, watching her husband's face the whole time. Wendy enjoyed the looks on Mike's face and the feelings Toni introduced into her body. Wendy and Toni started an unforgettable journey for Mike. They explored each other's bodies for the good of the man Wendy loves with all her heart.

Wendy told Toni that Mike's deepest wish was to see two women from nipple to nipple and so they rubbed their nipples together in front of Mike's eyes. At this point Mike noticed the new entrance to the living room. Wendy had bought a huge mirror and put it in the living room so all three could watch what was going on. Wendy found out that she herself was enjoying the view in front of her. She looked in the mirror at Mike and was amazed at the angry Hardon he was boasting about! He stroked his member slowly with his hand. Somehow he needed that to relieve the pain he had but at the same time he didn't want to cum...

Mike watched as Toni and Wendy explored each other thoroughly, and when Toni lowered her head to the top of Wendy's thighs, Mike emitted a tremendous groan. Wendy then spread her legs wide so that Mike could watch Toni eat them. Mike could no longer control himself. He began to touch Toni's tits and cupped them into his hands, rolling his nipples between his thumb and forefinger. His other hand began to caress her abdomen and then his hand dipped into Toni's pussy. He enjoyed the fact that he could touch Toni anywhere. Toni was wet and her pussy had a deep rosy color that was so different from his wife's pussy. When he touched Toni, Wendy reached her peak under Toni's management. Wendy then began to touch Toni in the places where Mike was not. Wendy sucked her tits and stroked her thighs as Mike's fingers brought Toni to her climax. Then Wendy reached down and grabbed Mike's cock in her hands.

Toni looked at Wendy as she offered up her husband's cock. Toni smiled and then greedily took Mike's member in her mouth. Mike gasped allowed. And Toni licked Mike's Precum off her head. Wendy then lowered her head to her husband's balls. She licked and sucked her husband's sack and teased his ass with her fingertips. Mike purred before either of them expected it. Mike's load was huge. He splashed his sperm all over the two women.

Wendy and Toni then began to touch and kiss again. Knowing that Mike would quickly regain an erection. They were not disappointed. He immediately became huge again. Mike then threw his wife on his back as he stuck his stiff cock into her cunt. While he did this, Toni moved her lips and tongue to Wendy's clitoris. Wendy had one more highlight, which was absolutely fantastic... Mike had still not had an orgasm and when he hit his wife's pussy, Toni started to lick his balls. His scrotum tensed up and in seconds it exploded into his wife.

They all lay there for a while, and Mike reversed those events in his mind... With one big question... How long was Toni in town?

## DESIRE FILLED

I just can't help it, my loving husband has made it clear that he wants our friend to come to us whenever I want, and that I can have him to myself from time to time without him as long as I tell him with all the details! Well, this morning was one of those horny moments, and I am horny, my husband is just finding out about it, and he seems to like it. I already asked him if I could give our friend a blowjob on occasion, and he gave his approval after I gave him such a blowjob! I have no problem with it, I love his cock, and I find that I like our friends too, I only got it once, but I was nice.

It's early afternoon and I go out to see if our friend might be on his feet, he is! I stroll down his path and find him smoking in his garage as I walk towards him making small talk. As we both make small talk, I can't help but notice that we both have a smile on our faces and seem to be dancing around what's burning in our bellies, hoping that he will pump his liquid into my stomach and extinguish my burning desire.

I decide that if I want it, I have to go for it. "I want to suck your cock," I say to him, waiting for his response.

He gets up and closes the garage door, then turns to me and smiles: "I'd love to do that.

I lead him into his house, through the living room and into the kitchen. I stand in his kitchen, facing each other, and with his help I start to take his pants off, never taking my eyes off his. With his pants and underwear out of the way and one of my hands already on the prize, I start my way down to him, gently kissing and stroking his chest on the way down. Now that I am on my knees and his pulsating, hot and hard cock is looking at me and waiting to be massaged by my lips and tongue, I take him inside me and do just that. It feels so fucking good and tastes so fucking good. I enjoy it in my mouth; my tongue dances over it, my wishes, begging to be fulfilled. I use the tip of my tongue and I move it up and down the underside of his shaft a few times, only to find that he has left me a reward when I am back at the tip of my tongue. I graciously accept it and hunger for more. I work his burning passion well with my mouth and just wait for him to put out my fire with his fire hose.

After a good quarter of an hour or so, both my knees and his legs get tired. I get up, not really wanting to take him out of my mouth, but I have him too, and pull out a chair for him. When he sits, I eagerly take my place again and fill my mouth with his delicious self. By now he is already licking quite a lot and I am more than ready to take it.

My husband asked me if I would swallow and I told him "maybe", but I was not sure. Well, now I am, with my husband's wonderful gift to my hungry sex appetite, and I want more of it. I could get very used to this.

I feel our friend pulsating in my mouth and his juices filling my mouth more and more, his time is near. After this thought is finished, he tells me what I already knew. I grab his ass cheeks with my hands and let him know that I want it, he seems to like it and my husband seemed to like it at the thought that I take over his burden! He grabs the back of my head and gently pushes me into him, and once his throbbing, hot, delicious self is as far as it can go, and that's all the way through, then it happens! Oh yeah, give it to me, baby, give it to me, I think to myself as I feel his hot and coveted load of treats splashing against my mouth and moving towards my hungry stomach.

He slowly begins to pull himself out of my hungry mouth after he has emptied every drop of cum he had in me. I taste and feel his delicious cock as he slides over my tongue on his way out. I lick my lips as I stand to make eye contact and thank him for my treatment.

"No, I thank him. God, that was great, I've never had anyone swallow before. But I have to ask, what about your husband?"

"He knows, he let me, as long as I tell him everything."

With a worried and anxious look I assured him that he had nothing to worry about; my husband will be no different to him than he would like the three of us to meet more often! He seemed to have no problem with that, he even asked about tomorrow afternoon, and I gently let him know that this part of me would not be available for the next few days.

"I wouldn't have a problem with it if you and your husband didn't, I'll even bring the towels!"

He seemed to want it pretty badly, and so did I, to be honest. I told him to meet us at our house around 12:30, and he agreed. So I let myself out and went back to our house, and I am eager to tell my husband. If I am lucky, he will give me another taste of his own sweet self! God, I could get so used to this!

## AWAITING AN ANSWER

Lust. What's that? Is lust a pure form of sexual desire? Or is it something deeper, more intimate? How can you tell?

Desire. Is that what our mind really wants? How is it different from... lust? Are they one and the same?

For example, I wanted to have sex with a dear friend I've lusted for a long time. Guilt takes over. I love my husband, I desire him, and I lust for him. So how can I lust and desire another man?

The temptation prevails. My eyes are looking for my friend's. My body becomes warm and my cheeks burn with thoughts in my head. I look at my husband. My heart is beating wildly. He knows! What to do? He's such a part of me, I don't have to tell him. He understands immediately what I hope for. The instant guilt. It's overwhelming. But he's in an intense battle with... desire.

Time passes, the desire builds. The pace picks up. My friend is still in my head. I am out of breath with the possibilities. I have to stop myself. I will control my desires. I will do it.

His hand brushes across my chest. Accidentally, I suppose. I'll check to see if my husband notices. He acknowledges with a smile. What? I wonder. Any more touching, and hey, my friend seems to look at me like a woman. Could I possibly evoke the same feelings in him?

Should I ask? We see him all the time, and lately there's more undercurrent, or am I just imagining it?

It's just the three of us here. The touches get aggressive. The flame is fanned. I want to find out the answer. I want to be with him, I want them both! I hold my breath. Questions rush through my head. My body is alive, my senses are awake.

Body language is loud. Finally, the answer. Yes, he too is tempted. My husband knows! He actually seems to want me to taste our friend. My body is on fire. I'm excited and scared. I want that so much. Will it change me forever? Am I going to go through with it? I want it!

My boyfriend touches me, my husband kisses me. I tremble. I'll take control, I will, I say to myself. My friend comes closer, I tremble. I will answer my questions. It's now or never. Will he want me? Will my husband stay by my side?

Oh, my God! They touch me, oh please, I beg quietly, I must explore my desires. Lust rages. I want to be with them both! They taste me. I scream inside. I really want that. I need that. I grab it. I taste him. Surprised, it's better than I dreamed. More, I need more. It can't be over yet. Desire is only fed. The crescendo increases. Both continue to explore me. I finally learn what my mind already knew.

I drink from both. I want her, I want him. Can I take him in? My wetness surrounds his vessel. Uh, that feels good. I keep swallowing my husband. My friend feels so good. My hips are moving in rhythm. My breasts need the endless attention. My femininity is swollen with desire.

These two give me the results. I take my man into the deep. It feels good. I need his loving reassurance. My mouth works our friend. So different and yet so similar.

The three of us have explored the idea together... Lust or desire?

## SINFUL ENJOYS DISPLAYING

Someone told me that sperm running down your lover's leg is disgusting. I feel sorry for him. A well-fucked cunt is one of God's greatest gifts to man. If you can look at a well-fucked woman and you are disgusted, then the disgust is in your heart, not in hers (or mine).

Anyway, I am just the vehicle, although I was lucky enough to pass on some of the experiences I write about. These stories are true. The experiences are as accurate as I can remember.

Cindy was full of spirit that night. The smell of a good fuck was obvious. You could look at her and see a content, confident young woman. She and I had never shared such an experience before. Fucking her with John was a new high point.

We got in the car. I pulled her close as I put the key in the ignition and kissed her tenderly. I took her naked pussy in my hand, and it was immediately soaked with our combined sperm. I did not hesitate. I shoved two fingers inside her steaming cunt and fucked her slowly as I drove off the parking lot.

She pressed her body into my hand. She was trying to get more into her pussy. She slid down on the seat and pressed against my hand and tried to eat my fingers. I pushed a third finger in. Her tunnel of love was tight and hot as hell. I could feel her cunt reaching for my three fingers as I pushed her as deep as I could.

She turned around on her seat so her back was to me and slid down to maximize my access. She spread her legs and offered a view to anyone driving next to us while I kept fucking her with my hand. I drove out onto I95 and concentrated on satisfying my wife while I drove.

Just a moment later a truck passed us on the left side and dropped off in front of us again. Cindy moaned now. I knew that another orgasm was only moments away.

I pulled out to the left, overtook the truck until we were even with the cab, and held the car next to it. He had the full glare of my fingers squeezing into her wet pussy. I turned on the courtesy light.

"He's watching you," I said, although I couldn't really see him from where I was. "He sees your hot pussy taking my fingers."

She moaned and her lower body picked up speed. It was like she was a fucking machine from the waist down. Above the waist, she was barely moving. Her full concentration was directed at freeing herself from the fingers that were poking into her body. The truck driver blew the horn. She picked up even more speed and opened her legs further to his sight.

"He's got his dick out now, Cindy." I said, "He wants to stick it in your pussy. He wants to give you his sperm."

She froze. Time only stopped for a few seconds. It felt like an hour. I kept pumping my fingers inside her. Then she orgasmed. She screamed and slammed into my hand. I barely stayed inside her and I felt her orgasm grab my fingers in waves.

She pounced on me. Her pussy relaxed to where I probably could have stuck my whole hand in if I had thought about it. Well, maybe not, but she was still a good fuck.

I picked up speed, drove in front of the truck, and when I realized we almost missed the turn, I jumped the exit ramp. I pulled my hand out of her pussy and offered her a finger. She sucked it deep into her mouth. "Ummmmmmmmmmmmmmmmmmmm," she said. "We're definitely gonna need more of that."

"I think so too," I said. I pulled my hand from her mouth and sucked the other two wet fingers into my mouth. The mixed taste of fresh female sperm and our previous encounter was indescribable. I knew I was an addict.

She sat upright, tidied her skirt with restraint and snuggled up to me, purring like a kitten. Her head was turned against me. I kissed the top of it as we drove the last mile to the apartment.

Days turned into weeks. Cindy was the happy housewife and I was the breadwinner. I really took my time at work and broke down every night without knowing the world. It was a very busy time for me and very satisfying.

Cindy, on the other hand, was going crazy. She wasn't a soap opera person. There was a fire burning under the happy housewife. Hanging it up in the house put a lot of strain on her. We lived two blocks from the beach, so she spent most of her time sunbathing, splashing and other tourist things.

One afternoon she called me at work. "Lee, I have a favor to ask of you, dear," she blurted out in a hurry. "I met these two guys from Vermont on the beach a while back, and... I want to take them home with me. They said they'd be glad if you came to us, honey. Can I Please?"

My first reaction was anger. Who broke into my cave? Like it was supposed to be a shock, her fooling around. I thought for a minute. Then I laughed, "Sure, tiger, go ahead. If you don't wear her out by the end of the day, I'll be there."

"Thanks, baby," she said, "Hurry home."

Sinful was back.

CPSIA information can be obtained
at www.ICGtesting.com
Printed in the USA
BVHW080757050521
606421BV00006B/1920

+CB19 .L35 1983

# Systems Science and World Order
## Selected Studies

```
           Laszlo, Ervin,
CB          1932-
19
L35          Systems science
1983        and world order
```

# SYSTEMS SCIENCE AND WORLD ORDER LIBRARY
*General Editor:* Ervin Laszlo

**Explorations of World Order**

DE ROUGEMONT, D.
The Future is Our Affair

GIARINI, O. & LOUBERGE, H.
The Diminishing Returns of Technology: an Essay on the Crisis in Economic Growth

LASZLO, E.
The Inner Limits of Mankind: Heretical Reflections on Today's Culture and Politics

LASZLO, E. & BIERMAN, J.
Goals in a Global Community
Vol. 1: Studies on the Conceptual Foundations
Vol. 2: The International Values and Goals Studies

MARKLEY, O. & HARMAN, W.
Changing Images of Man

SAUVANT, K.
Changing Priorities on the International Agenda: The New International Economic Order

TÉVOÉDJRÉ, A.
Poverty: Wealth of Mankind

**Innovations in Systems Science**

AULIN, A.
The Cybernetic Laws of Social Progress

COOK, N.
Stability and Flexibility: An Analysis of Natural Systems

CURTIS, R. K.
Evolution or Extinction: The Choice Before Us

GEYER, R. F.
Alienation Theories: A General Systems Approach

GEYER, R. F. & VAN DER ZOUWEN, J.
Dependence & Inequality: A Systems Approach to the Problems of Mexico and Developing Countries

JANTSCH, E.
The Self Organizing Universe: Scientific and Human Implications of the Emerging Paradigm of Evolution

LAVIOLETTE, P. (ed.)
Systems Anthropology: Selected Papers by Ludwig von Bertalanffy

NOTICE TO READERS
If your library is not already a standing order customer to this series, may we recommend that you place a standing or continuation order to receive immediately upon publication all new volumes published in this valuable series. Should you find these volumes no longer serve your needs your order can be cancelled at any time without notice.

**A Pergamon Journal of Related Interest**
TECHNOLOGY IN SOCIETY*
An International Journal
*Editors:* Dr George Bugliarello and Dr A. George Schillinger, Polytechnic Institute of New York, USA
An interdisciplinary journal for the discussion of the political, economic and cultural roles of technology in society, social forces that shape technological decisions and choices open to society in the use of technology.

*Free specimen copies available on request.

# Systems Science and World Order
## Selected Studies

by
ERVIN LASZLO
*UNITAR, New York*

PERGAMON PRESS
OXFORD · NEW YORK · TORONTO · SYDNEY · PARIS · FRANKFURT

| | |
|---|---|
| U.K. | Pergamon Press Ltd., Headington Hill Hall, Oxford OX3 0BW, England |
| U.S.A. | Pergamon Press Inc., Maxwell House, Fairview Park, Elmsford, New York 10523, U.S.A. |
| CANADA | Pergamon Press Canada Ltd., Suite 104, 150 Consumers Road, Willowdale, Ontario M2J 1P9, Canada |
| AUSTRALIA | Pergamon Press (Aust.) Pty. Ltd., P.O. Box 544, Potts Point, N.S.W. 2011, Australia |
| FRANCE | Pergamon Press SARL, 24 rue des Ecoles, 75240 Paris, Cedex 05, France |
| FEDERAL REPUBLIC OF GERMANY | Pergamon Press GmbH, Hammerweg 6, D-6242 Kronberg-Taunus, Federal Republic of Germany |

Copyright © 1983 Ervin Laszlo

*All Rights Reserved. No part of this publication may be reproduced, stored in a retrieval system or transmitted in any form or by any means: electronic, electrostatic, magnetic tape, mechanical, photocopying, recording or otherwise, without permission in writing from the publishers.*

First edition 1983

**Library of Congress Cataloging in Publication Data**

Laszlo, Ervin, 1932-
Systems science and world order: selected studies
(Systems science and world order library.
Explorations of world order)
Includes index.
1. Civilization—Philosophy—Addresses, essays, lectures. 2. International relations—Addresses, essays, lectures. 3. International cooperation—Addresses, essays, lectures. 4. System theory—Addresses, essays, lectures. I. Title. II. Series.
CB19.L35      1983      901      82-22471

**British Library Cataloguing in Publication Data**

Laszlo, Ervin
Systems science and world order: Selected Studies
(Systems science and world order library)
1. Social sciences   2. Systems theory
I. Title
300      H61
ISBN 0-08-028924-X (Hardcover)
ISBN 0-08-028923-1 (Flexicover)

*Printed in Great Britain by A. Wheaton & Co. Ltd., Exeter*

# ACKNOWLEDGEMENTS

The author gratefully acknowledges permission to reprint, with updating and minor revisions, the following studies:

*The Meaning and Significance of General System Theory*, from Behavioral Science, Vol. 20, No. 1, January 1975.

*A General Systems View of Evolution and Invariance*, from General Systems Yearbook, Vol. XIX, 1974.

*Basic Constructs of Systems Philosophy*, from Systematics, 1972, 10(1).

*A Systems Philosophy of Human Values*, from Behavioral Science, Vol. 18, No. 4, July 1973.

*Biperspectivism: A Universal Systems Approach to the Mind-Body Problem*, from Epistemologia, 1982.

*The Rise of General Theories in Contemporary Science*, from the Journal for General Philosophy of Science, Vol. IV, No. 2, 1973.

*The Application of General Systems Models in the Theory of Scientific Development*, from Advances in Cybernetics and Systems Research, 1973.

*Systems and Structure – Toward Bio-Social Anthropology*, from Theory and Decision 2, 1971, D. Reidel Publishing Co.

*The Reduction of Whorfian Relativity Through a General Systems Language*, from Communication and Cognition, Vol. 6, No. 1, 1973.

*Cybernetics of Musical Activity*, from The Journal of Aesthetics and Art Criticism, XXXI/3, Spring 1973.

*General Systems Theory and the Coming Conceptual Synthesis*, from Kybernetes, Vol. 3, 1974.

*The Purpose of Mankind*, from Zygon, Vol. 8, Nos. 3-4, September-December 1973.

*Human Dignity and the Promise of Technology*, from Human Dignity — This Century and the Next, edited by Rubin Gotesky and Ervin Laszlo, Gordon and Breach, New York, 1970.

*Children and the Future of Humanity*, from UNICEF News, 102/1979/4.

*New Conditions and Obsolete Perceptions*, from Disarmament: The Human Factor, edited by Ervin Laszlo and D. F. Keys, Pergamon Press, Oxford, 1981.

*Global Goals and the Crisis of Political Will*, from the Journal of International Affairs, Vol. 31, No. 2, Fall/Winter 1977.

*Educating World Leaders for the Coming Age*, from Lux Mundi, International Association of University Presidents, Seoul.

*Toward an Early Warning System at the United Nations*, from Technological Forecasting and Social Change, Vol. 8 (1975), American Elsevier Publishing Co., New York.

*Regional Community-Building and Inter-regional Agreements: The New Imperatives of Progress and Development in the 1980s*, from Development Forum, 1980.

*The Future of RCDC*, from RCDC: Regional Co-operation Among Developing Countries — Report on the Findings and Recommendations of the Conference on Regionalism and the NIEO, by Ervin Laszlo with Joel Kurtzman and A. K. Bhattacharya, Pergamon Press, New York, 1981.

# CONTENTS

INTRODUCTION ix

## PART ONE – STUDIES IN SYSTEMS SCIENCE AND PHILOSOPHY

| | | |
|---|---|---|
| 1. | The Meaning and Significance of General System Theory | 3 |
| 2. | A Systems View of Evolution and Invariance | 24 |
| 3. | Basic Constructs of Systems Philosophy | 38 |
| 4. | A Systems Philosophy of Human Values | 48 |
| 5. | Biperspectivism: A Universal Systems Approach to the Mind-Body Problem | 62 |
| 6. | The Rise of General Theories in Contemporary Science | 72 |
| 7. | The Application of General System Models in the Theory of Scientific Development | 81 |
| 8. | Systems and Structures – Toward Bio-Social Anthropology | 97 |
| 9. | The Reduction of Whorfian Relativity Through a General System Language | 112 |
| 10. | Cybernetics of Musical Activity | 122 |
| 11. | General System Theory and the Coming Conceptual Synthesis | 139 |

## PART TWO – WORLD ORDER STUDIES – IN A SYSTEMS PERSPECTIVE

| | | |
|---|---|---|
| 12. | The Purpose of Mankind | 149 |
| 13. | Human Dignity and the Promise of Technology | 162 |
| 14. | Children and the Future of Humanity | 187 |

| | | |
|---|---|---|
| 15. | New Conditions and Obsolete Perceptions | 191 |
| 16. | Global Goals and the Crisis of Political Will | 197 |
| 17. | Educating World Leaders for the Coming Age | 213 |
| 18. | Toward an Early Warning System at the United Nations | 219 |
| 19. | Regional Community-Building and Inter-Regional Agreements: The New Imperatives of Progress and Development in the 1980s | 236 |
| 20. | The Future of RCDC (Regional Co-operation Among Developing Countries) | 243 |
| 21. | Toward an Age of Human Ecology | 248 |

INDEX 257

# INTRODUCTION

This volume brings together studies written over the better part of the past decade in order to illustrate the meaning and relevance of the concepts 'systems science' and 'world order' individually as well as in combination. It also serves to focus, under a single cover, the topics and concerns of the volumes which have appeared to date, and will appear in coming years, in the Pergamon Press Systems Science and World Order Library.

Thus the message of this volume, while expressed in terms of the personal insights of the writer, transcends them in significance. To write on the complex and at first sight disjointed subjects of 'systems science' and 'world order' goes beyond the question of *how* one writes about them: it shows that these topics can, and indeed should, be addressed together. The volume before the reader is, therefore, both the record of the evolution of the thinking of one writer over a period of some ten years and, more importantly, the exposition of the relevance of this evolution to contemporary science and world affairs.

Systems science is a newcomer in the sciences and is often misunderstood. It is not another academic specialty but a broad new orientation that permeates many different fields. Its roots lie in the fact that reality, both natural, and human, does not stand still: it evolves, complexifies, sometimes regresses, but always changes. Change can be haphazard or ordered, constructive or regressive. It has been the subject of controversy since time immemorial. Heraclitus thought it the basic characteristic of reality; Parmenides believed that it is but illusion. But modern science must cope with it in earnest. It cannot go as far as Heraclitus, who was said to be able to do no more than point to objects since they were changing all the time ('one cannot step into the same river twice'), but it also cannot assume that constancy is the order of the day. Rather, science attempts to comprehend the logic and the order of change through concepts and formulas that themselves do not change. Individual uranium atoms change and decay; the laws of radioactivity remain constant. Objects fall to the ground; the equations of gravitation maintain their validity.

Systems sciences are especially capable to cope with problems of change and development since in the real world change occurs in interaction between 'systems' and events of all kinds. (There are no longer any purely 'material' objects and entirely 'relational' entities: this distinction of classical science has collapsed. In the last analysis even the most solid material object turns out to be a combination of force fields and elusive, short-lived subatomic particles, integrated in relatively stable atomic and molecular combinations.) General System Theory and other branches of systems sciences can give increasingly rigorous formulas for expressing change in interaction between object ('system') and environment. These formulas and models apply to a wide variety of systems, defining them by their common structural and functional properties.

Systems sciences are also able to explain change because they are supradisciplinary. Reality does not fall into conveniently watertight categories that we can label 'physical', 'biological', 'human' or 'sociological'. Evolution in the organic and social sphere builds up some sets of relationships, destroys others, but tends on the whole to produce more organized and less entropic systems. In the physical realm the trend is toward increasing entropy, although the final word on the fate of the universe has not been spoken yet. It is clear that we need to comprehend the many entities which appear in the course of time under some general concept. It is here that system concepts and theories have unparalleled advantages. 'The system' does not mean that establishment against which youth and revolutionaries rebel, but simply a set of parts or elements in mutual relations. The relations are sufficiently stable to permit one to identify the system as an entity that stands out from the background of change. Rocks and trees, atoms and people, societies and china dolls are all stable objects. Some are created by nature, others by people who in turn have been created in natural evolution. Some are evolutionary and tend to build up, others are entropic and tend to run down.

The world, looked at in terms of systems, is a very different world from that of classical science, and even more different from everyday commonsense. But it is a world which may be more important to know than either of these alternative conceptions. Today, the pace of change is accelerating, and always new entities are called into play. They appear on the scene, they may gain dominance, and then further evolve or disappear. We ourselves accelerate this play of change and evolution by creating vast numbers of artificial systems and interfering with the stable processes of self-maintaining natural systems. We are in rapid evolution and must learn to cope with its problems. Concepts and theories based on the idea of interacting parts and elements in dynamic interplay with their environment have optimal advantages.

For pure meaning and understanding, as well as for practical problem-solving we cannot do better than work with systems concepts and theories. There are, obviously, limitations to the scope and penetration of contemporary systems sciences and we should not press them beyond the range of what they can do. For example, there are many more dimensions and aspects of 'world order' (or 'world problematique') than we know how to handle rigorously through systems sciences. Therefore we should not hesitate to use whatever language and mode of thought is adequate to the task. Systems thinking can nevertheless inform our thinking on a deeper level. It is not necessary to use any specialty language to truly exercise that specialty; the determining factor is the use of the type of thinking engendered by it. One can think systematically without expressing oneself in systems terms. This is true of a large number of world order studies, amply illustrated by both the Systems Science and World Order Library, and Part Two of this volume.

The unmistakable need is to move toward a clearer understanding of the nature of change and evolution, and a better ability to cope with its effects on human beings and societies. Both these attempts can benefit from the use of system concepts and theories. In time, we can even envisage replacing 'systems science *and* world order' with 'theoretical and applied systems sciences'. But we are not there yet, and in the meanwhile we have many urgent problems to consider. Hence the philosophy that underlies this volume of collected studies, as well as the entire Systems Science and World Order Library, is to promote the development of systems science as a peculiarly appropriate mode of understanding the world around us and, at the same time, allowing free rein to the exploration of the multifold problems of world order.

Some further clarification is in order concerning the use of the concept 'world order'. The 'world' meant here is the human world or, even better, the world in which we humans are the major and determining actors. This world, thanks to our ever increasing interactions, is now growing into a global web of relations. It is becoming a 'system' in the sense of a set of strongly interacting parts and elements that stands out against the planetary backdrop. We should learn to look at it in this way, since we cannot solve the problems of global interdependence except by referring to the global set of relationships that generate them. Oil shortages and gluts, inflation and unemployment, deforestation and the depletion of mineral resources, the growth and urbanization of populations; these and myriad other factors are elements in the seamed web of interdependence we created — if unwittingly — on this planet. We have seams where national and multinational private and public interests operate, and where geography and cultural factors introduce differentiation. But the seams are not broken, and as we tug at one end of the fabric the other ends feel the stress, on both sides of the seams.

As in other realms of natural and social evolution and development, the world system of our day is a multilevel edifice made up of human individuals and their immediate surroundings and resources, integrated for better or for worse with their families, communities, states and provinces, nations, and the family of nations. Because we ignore these continuities and interdependencies we create untenable stresses: the rich and few by their wealth and power, the poor and multitudinous by their numbers and collective demands.

There is as great a need for innovations in systems science as there is for explorations of world order. Whereas in the former the system concept is explicit, in the latter it is often only implicit. This does not prevent the growing together of these fields, if they are brought into productive interaction with one another.

These are precisely the considerations that inspired the creation of the Systems Science and World Order Library a few years ago, and which now prompt the appearance of this book. What the two sub-series of the Library do through their individual volumes — and do in great detail and with remarkable insight — the here following studies of this book do within the limitations of this writer's time and insight. But whereas the volumes appear separately, and for the most part treat *either* systems science *or* world order issues, this book, despite its brevity and shortcomings, has its *raison d'être* in bringing together the two fields of inquiry under a single cover and exhibiting their mutual relations.

Our times of change and interaction call for new and innovative modes of thinking, and detailed as well as applicable guidelines for concerted action. Systems science is there to fulfil the former task while world order studies respond to the latter. That in time they should join forces is almost inevitable, but the acceleration of this process could be important. We urgently need the most appropriate forms of understanding to bear on the widest range of issues of practical concerns. This is the rationale for the present book, and for the Systems Science and World Order Library as a whole.

It is my privilege to acknowledge here the farsighted and dynamic leadership of Pergamon's Chairman Robert Maxwell in calling the Library into life and nurturing it through its first delicate years of existence toward growing strength and maturity, and the expert management of Peggy Ducker, and now Kim Richardson, in transforming manuscripts (and often merely ideas for manuscripts) into readable and attractive printed volumes. May their faith in these endeavors be rewarded by the continued cross-fertilization of systems science and world order studies, to combine the benefit of achieving a clearer understanding of the nature of the human condition, with enhancing our ability to cope with its problems.

New York

# PART ONE

# STUDIES IN SYSTEMS SCIENCE AND PHILOSOPHY

# 1

## THE MEANING AND SIGNIFICANCE OF GENERAL SYSTEM THEORY*

System theories excite increasing attention and find increasing application in many parts of the world today. Their novelty attracts extravagant praise as well as severe criticism. Both are often biased and a more balanced assessment is badly needed. We shall contribute to it by examining the prospects and summarizing the principles of the most general of the contemporary system theories: general system theory.

### PROSPECTS OF GENERAL SYSTEM THEORY

One could hardly find a more powerful set of words today than general system theory. System is one of the most popular terms currently in the scientific vocabulary. It has penetrated the language of everyday life, and has created a vague assumption that if something is or acts like a system, it is efficient, up to date, and even good. General connotes size, scope and power. It is a high military rank, a part of the name of large multinational corporations, and a prefix attaching to broad-based studies and sciences. Theory has made great progress since the 1930s when scientists such as von Bertalanffy faced a barrage of criticism for advocating theoretical biology. It is now recognized as a basis not only for the empirical sciences, but also, albeit in tacit form, of much of human behavior. Even the act of observation has turned out to be, in Hanson's words, "theory laden".

Were it merely a matter of conjoining popular terms to attain popularity in a branch of science, general system theory would enjoy the height of intellectual fashion. Yet, as all new and revolutionary developments, it is still going through a phase of exploration, with a generous dose of scepticism, and criticism from informed as well as uninformed opponents. Since the systems movement as a whole is undoubtedly making great strides forward, and to date no other general theoretical

---
*Reprinted from *Behavioral Science*, Vol. 20, No. 1, January 1975.

formulations of systems *per se* have made their appearance, we must take a closer look at the origins and development of general system theory to come to an understanding of what system theories can offer in science and, through science, to society.

In recent decades significant similarities have come to light between the concepts and theories of a number of scientific disciplines. These disciplines constitute what Warren Weaver called the sciences of complexity: biology, ecology, psychology and psychiatry, anthropology, sociology, political science, management and organization theory, the policy sciences, international studies, as well as the related 'sciences of the artificial' (Simon): cybernetics, computer science, network theory and their mathematical correlates. Until recently these similarities have gone unperceived by all but a handful of scientists. In the 1920s only Ludwig von Bertalanffy and Paul A. Weiss in biology, and Alfred North Whitehead in philosophy, became aware of the potentials of developing a general theory of complex phenomena — a general theory of biological systems, or a general philosophy of organism. By the 1940s and 1950s, however, a small group of scientists at the University of Chicago, and later at the Mental Health Research Institute at the University of Michigan, became concerned, both on theoretical and on practical grounds, to evolve a general theory of behavior. Physiologist and psychiatrist James G. Miller, whose perceptions were formed in his youth through his personal contact with Whitehead, together with economist Kenneth Boulding, mathematician Anatol Rapoport, and other natural scientists including physicist Enrico Fermi, formed a working group dedicated to developing a general theory based on the possibilities offered by the emerging parallelisms in the disciplinary sciences. They were concerned to develop a basic vocabulary of terms common to differing specialties and analyze their meaning across the disciplinary boundaries. A society was formed to investigate the potentials of a general system theory in 1954. A few years later, the society began publishing a yearbook jointly edited by Bertalanffy and Rapoport. In the 1960s the visibility of this group increased and today it has chapters and divisions in many parts of the world.

The promise of general system theory can be concisely stated in the words of Bertalanffy (1969), who summed up its aims in reference to the following points:

(1) There is a general tendency towards integration in the various sciences, natural and social.

(2) Such integration seems to be centered in a general theory of systems.

(3) Such theory may be an important means for aiming at exact theory in the nonphysical fields of science.

(4) Developing unifying principles running 'vertically' through the universe of the individual sciences, this theory brings us nearer to the goal of the unity of science.

(5) This can lead to a much-needed integration in scientific education.

The stated aims of the society created to promote general systems thinking, the Society for General Systems Research, include corresponding ideals.

(1) To investigate the isomorphy of concepts, laws, and models in various fields, and to help useful transfers from one field to another.

(2) To encourage the development of adequate theoretical models in fields which lack them.

(3) To minimize the duplication of theoretical effort in different fields.

(4) To promote the unity of science through improving communication among specialists.

The promise of general system theory is that it can capitalize on the emergence of parallelisms in different scientific fields and provide the basis for an integrated theory of complex organization *per se*. But there is still a significant gap between the promise of the theory and its present level of recognition. Let us assess this gap in reference to two sets of factors: those which favor the progress and recognition of general system theory; and those which block it.

## FACTORS FAVORING GENERAL SYSTEM THEORY

Factors favoring the development of general system theory operate both internally and externally to science. There is an intrinsic trend within science itself to maximize the scope of theories consistently with their precision. There are also extrinsic pressure on science to overcome traditional boundaries in producing multi-disciplinary theories applicable to societal problems.

Modern science has made great progress by adopting the analytical method of identifying and, if possible, isolating the phenomena to be investigated. If effective isolation is not feasible, e.g., in the life and social sciences, it is replaced by the theoretical device of averaging the values of inputs and outputs to the investigated object, and varying the quantities with the needs of the experiment. Thus influences from what has often been disparagingly called 'the rest of the world' can be disregarded. It appears, however, that the rest of the world is an important factor in many areas of investigation. The consequences of disregarding it are not immediately evident, for a good detailed knowledge of immediate phenomena in a short time-range can nevertheless be won. But the spin-offs, or side effects, of the phenomena will be incalculable, and such effects are not the secondary phenomena they were taken to be in the past. They are the results of the complex strands of interdependence which traverse all realms of empirical investigation but which science's analytical method selectively filters out. Hence we get much detailed knowledge of local phenomena, and a great deal of ignorance of the interconnections between such phenomena. The analytical method produced the explosion of contemporary scientific information, and the dearth of applicable scientific knowledge. It has also engendered wasteful parallelisms in research due to failures in the transfer of models and data between disciplines. Yet, to many scientists and philosophers of science, the advantages of specialization outweigh its disadvantages, and they are not discouraged by the prospect of further specialization and segmentation in the evolution of science.

However, there are factors operating within the scientific enterprise which correct for the deficiencies of overspecialization through the development of new, more integrated theoretical frameworks. Modern science has had long experience in dealing with explosions of data and proliferations of theory, and was quite successful in containing them in the past. Galileo, Kepler and Newton provided broad conceptual schemes for integrating observations in physics and astronomy; Darwin provided the master scheme for evolutionary biology; Schwann for cellular biology; Lavoisier for physical chemistry; and Mendel for genetics. When the Newtonian synthesis encountered anomalies, Einstein proposed a new framework for reinterpreting data in a more consistent and integrated manner. Scientists have always sought, in Einstein's words (1934), "the simplest possible system of thought which will bind together the observed facts". From Kepler, who had hoped to understand the Plan of Creation, to Heisenberg (1952) — who, despite the complexities of quantum physics, maintained that what the physicist seeks is to penetrate more and more reality as a great interconnected whole — we can perceive a search for theories that respond to the scientist's appreciation of elegance and accuracy combined with integral scope and extensibility to neighboring fields and as yet uninvestigated phenomena. Theories are required to be fertile not only in explaining and predicting already known observations and processes, but in generating specifying theorems which can deal with new observations and presently recalcitrant or anomalous processes. This requirement blurs the distinction between discovery and invention, and moves contemporary science beyond the traditional confines of classical empiricism and its neopositivist restatement.

It is instructive to review the contributions of great theoretical scientists in reference to the degree of integration, abstraction and generality they introduced in their fields (Laszlo and Margenau, 1972). Scientists value theory refinement as well as theory extension, although they do so to differing degrees. The routine experimentalist, mainly involved with puzzles that can be solved through a suitable application of existing theories and techniques, tends to disparage the philosophizing of colleagues bent on the revision and refinement of the theories themselves. But scientists who perceive internal inconsistencies in their frameworks of explanation are greatly concerned with overcoming them through the creation of new, more general postulates, embracing existing theories as special cases, or reinterpreting them in the light of new axioms. Although the emphasis changes from person to person, from scientific community to scientific community, and from period to period, depending on the problems encountered in the given field, it remains true that, on the whole, the progress of science involves the integration of loosely joined, lower level concepts and hypotheses in mathematically formulated general theories. As Conant (1952) said, we can view science as "a dynamic undertaking directed to lowering the degree of empiricism in solving problems; or . . . a process of fabricating a web of interconnected concepts and conceptual schemes arising from observations and experiments and fruitful of further experiments and observations."

The historical trend in modern science is to counterbalance segmentation and specialization in patterns of research and experimentation. However, when great progress is made by means of specialized research, corrective measures could be suspended for decades or even centuries; hope for a scientific synthesis might be dim if we had to rely on trends intrinsic to science alone. But a powerful ally of the theoreticians's dream of elegant and integrated theories has emerged in recent years in the guise of an extrinsic demand on science to deliver theories capable of societal application. This demand unfolds as a consequence of the excessive fragmentation of scientific data with respect to operational utility. For example, our knowledge of the environment is segmented into academic compartments, but the environmental factors themselves form an interdependent continuum. As a result there has been a marked shift in public support for scientific projects. The new patterns of allocation favor research that has social utility either by having direct applications, or by clarifying norms or techniques relevant to applications. At the same time the meaning of applied science has been greatly enlarged. It is no longer restricted to the kind of activity designed to produce labor saving energy conversion devices and processes for the manufacture of goods. Applied science now also includes the software of new social technologies, the fruit of research into human behavior, social organization, and the management of human and natural resources.

The new patterns of resource allocation reflect society's rising need for a scientific synthesis of its operationalizable bodies of knowledge. Such bodies of knowledge seldom result from research carried out within the compartments of traditional scientific disciplines. In almost every case, concrete societal problems call for interdisciplinary research and the integration of hitherto separately investigated variables. There are no problems that can be fully resolved without at the same time bearing on the resolution or aggravation of other problems — as Garrett Hardin said, we can never do just one thing. Disciplinary compartmentalization is useful only if it is coupled with transdisciplinary integration. This demand is not likely to eliminate specialized research for the sake of gathering knowledge independently of its potential of application, for such research continues to be an ideal of science and, beyond that, of human civilization. The scientific enterprise as a whole is likely to feel the effects of societal pressures for applicable knowledge. These effects will include a relative de-emphasis on specialized research for the sake of pure knowledge and a strong emphasis on all research that can produce socially applicable results.

Intrinsic trends to balance fragmentation in mathematically elegant general theories, and extrinsic trends to overcome the limitations in the application of fragmented knowledge, are factors which favor the evolution of any theory of integrative potential. They favor the development and acceptance of general system theory inasmuch as that theory is specifically designed to integrate theories of different fields of science, and to make possible the societal application of the integrated scientific knowledge. But general system theory is not thereby automatically elected as the paradigm of contemporary general theory in science. There is a great deal of scepticism that focuses on general theories as such, and on a general system theory especially.

## FACTORS BLOCKING GENERAL SYSTEM THEORY

The factors that block the progress of general system theory are due partly to intellectual and organizational inertia, and partly to confusions and suspicions centering on the general system concept itself.

### Intellectual inertia

Every theory innovation faces resistance due to intellectual inertia: the tendency of persons trained to work with earlier theories to fail to perceive, or perceive and fail to take seriously, or perceive, take seriously, but feel threatened by, the innovation. Such factors of intellectual inertia have created resistance for the acceptance of general theories within individual disciplines — they were experienced by Maxwell, Lavoisier, Pareto, Parsons, Skinner, to mention but a few. In some hard sciences effects of inertia eventually have been eliminated; such sciences are monistic and exclude rival theories from specific spheres of application — no Newtonian physics validated today except as a special case of relativity physics — no phlogiston or ether theories, and no theory of spontaneous generation. In the soft sciences theory innovations can be resisted because a plurality of theories may hold sway, e.g., behaviorism did not replace depth psychology, or Parsonian functionalism Marxian or positivistic social science. General theories have nevertheless gained a measure of acceptance in all fields. But such theories as so far have been accepted move within specific disciplines. There is as yet no accepted general scientific theory that moves *across* the disciplines.

Resistance to theories moving across disciplinary boundaries is stronger than resistance within the disciplines. It is due to several additional factors, including indifference and fear. A scientist confronted with a theory that did not originate in his field and is not confined to it can shrug off its meaning: it does not concern him in his professional capacity. Thus an ecologist taking a systems approach to information and energy flows in the ecologies he studies may disavow interest in and responsibility for a general theory of systems which would apply, in addition to ecologies, to economics or politics. *Mutatis mutandis,* with other scientists working with systems concepts in any of the sciences of complexity.

The other generic blocking factor is fear. Specialists rely on knowing more about their specialty than anyone else. They may not know, or even care, about theories and phenomena not directly connected with their specialties, as long as they feel assured that they are masters in their own corner of the scientific edifice. It is unsettling to them to find that some general theorists claim to know their field, and indeed offer interpretations of their findings with which they themselves are not familiar. Instead of welcoming such interest from other scientists and seeking to strengthen the linkages of their specialty with other fields, they feel threatened and tend to block overtures for collaboration. These are psychosociological factors which operate in science no less than in other organizations. General system theory is fully exposed to them. Persistent neglect in some quarters and isolation in others manifest their effects.

**Organizational inertia**

The organization of science in the Western world is centered in colleges and universities; in the socialist countries it is vested in the academies of science. The latter provide more flexibility for science policy but entail the risk of exposure to dogmatized ideology and the sway of powerful leading personalities. Western science, while decentralized in its administrative structure, is also more difficult to move from its present tracks. These are deeply disciplinary in nature. Monies and prestige are vested in academic departments, and the departmental structure of colleges and universities is almost exclusively disciplinary. There have been experiments with multidisciplinary departments, but outside of colleges of general studies, few have managed to survive. Department chairmen attempt to gather the best faculty and students to their department under the aegis of a single discipline. The discipline may be theory pluralistic in the softer sciences, but conflicts that arise due to this condition will be regarded as internal to the given department.

At a time when resources in higher education are scarce, funds for research outside the areas of societal application become scarce, the student body decreases in size, and competition among departments becomes sharper. Priority is given to filling the essential needs of each department, and these call forth the full authority of disciplinary expertise. The perceptions of departmental administrators tend to narrow proportionately to the tightening of the budget strings and the drop in enrollment. Only increasing opportunities of an inter- or multi-disciplinary nature, coupled with new shifts in the perspectives of influential department members could offset the lengthening of the departments' disciplinary tunnel vision.

This assessment is not as sanguine as that of Straus (1973), who predicts that "significant changes in the nature of departments are inevitable. Departments will either permit, or even seek, a realignment of their spheres of control over disciplinary activity or they will lose the power of control over basic academic decisions and rewards." Of course, in the long run Straus may be right, but current trends discourage short-run optimism.

Left to themselves, departments in general show unwillingness to stake their precious resources on new ventures leading beyond the known disciplinary boundaries. Administrators charged with curriculum tasks likewise show unease and unwillingness when faced with multidisciplinary proposals. While agreeing on the need for such programs, they are, for the most part, unfamiliar with the conceptual content of the required offerings. What, for example, are general systems? How much can one say about them? It would seem to many that, as soon as one goes into detail, one is constrained to speak about and conduct research on some *special* kind of system. What then is the point of institutionalizing a program based on *general* systems?

Furthermore, who is qualified to teach or investigate general systems? Those who claim such qualification include engineers, life scientists, social scientists, and philosophers. But are the engineers not merely talking about artificial systems, the life scientists about living systems, the social scientists about social systems, and the philosophers about conceptual systems? If so, they could well pursue their investigations and teaching programs within their existing departments.

The scientific and educational community is well aware of the proliferation of disciplinary specialties and is loath to add yet another, especially when the subject matter is something called general systems. The suggestion to spend money and step on toes just for the sake of teaching yet another abstraction seems downright frivolous. It would displace students now oriented in disciplinary tracks, confuse faculty, and generate a great deal of heat, possibly with little light. No wonder that few administrators are entertaining plans to create a general system department.

The problem lies (1) with the confusion of a cross-disciplinary general theory with a disciplinary specialty, and (2) with the novelty of a nondisciplinary academic teaching and research unit. General system theory is not another discipline, but a theory cutting across several, though not all, other scientific disciplines. It is meaningless if taught as a specialty. The reasonable way to handle it is to create new interdisciplinary units, institutes, centers, programs, for collaborative teaching and research by systems oriented faculty. The new academic units would include faculty from all relevant disciplines sharing a strong interest in the investigation of common elements, e.g., invariances in phenomena, isomorphies in theories. Thus, although members of the institutes or programs would have specialized competences, they would also have general interests; their work would not be the plumbing of specialty depths but the linking of specialized knowledge structures.

Fortunately, there are several counter-currents confronting organizational inertia in the academic world.

**Student interest.** The cry for relevance is also a cry for connection among scientific theories and the classification of an acceptable empirical world picture. A growing segment of the new generation of students seeks such connection and is frustrated for not finding it built into the instructional program. The hope that letting a student be successively exposed to different disciplines will make the whole body of scientific knowledge take shape in his head as a coherent and harmonious whole is just a pious hope, nothing more. The student moving from class to class in the various natural and social sciences does not spontaneously find strands of mutual relevance, and he is not encouraged to seek them. If he does seek them, he feels lonely and cut off from the main stream of academic life. He would be ready to enroll in a cross-disciplinary program devoted to the study of general theories of systems.

**Resource availability.** Private and public funding agencies — in the USA, the Ford, Rockefeller and Danforth Foundations, the National Science Foundation, the National Endowment for the Humanities, the Fund for the Improvement of Post-

Secondary Education, etc. — are becoming sensitive to the need for interdisciplinary education. They are aware, however, of the difficulties of giving content to such programs, beyond vague generalities and infighting between competing specialists. If those who propose interdisciplinary curricula based on general theories of systems could make clear the sound empirical and theoretical basis of their approach, they could obtain special purpose funds to launch experimental programs in systems studies. The emergence of some programs in this area would then act as a powerful force for the creation of further programs, demonstrating their legitimacy and ability to attract seed monies.

**Practical applications.** Systems modeling and systems approaches are used in a majority of projects dealing with societal problems. Those who are concretely involved with problem solving are aware that their problems cannot be confined within the bounds of any given discipline. The policy sciences are now pioneering a multidisciplinary systems approach, and are contributing to the level of awareness of the need for a general theory of systems. Such awareness in turn channels more funding and brainpower to this field.

Organizational inertia could be overcome if decision makers concerned with our educational system would realize that a program in general system theory is intrinsically sound, and can draw on growing student interest as well as on increasing financial and intellectual resources. At a time when student enrollments are sagging and budget problems plague private as well as public institutions, the counteracting forces favoring general system theory programs may be commensurate with the inertial forces working against them. If they are, we shall witness the emergence of an increasing number of systems science or systems studies institutes, centers, and programs in colleges and universities in many parts of the world. If they are not, general system theory will be a victim of what, paraphrasing Garrett Hardin, we may call the tragedy of multiple relevance.

In addition to generic inertial factors, there are important specific factors making for scepticism with respect to the cogency of general system theory. These fall under two categories: (1) confusions concerning the meaning and nature of general system theory, and (2) suspicions that it is guilty of some grievous fallacies.

**Semantic confusion**

The term general system theory is subject to basic misunderstandings. These often originate with the careless use of language but have a tendency to harden into metaphysical doctrines.

The practitioners of general system theory have an unfortunate tendency to speak of general systems as a subject that has predicates. They speak of general systems methods, models, education, and often refer to themselves as general systems people. There is now even a journal of general systems, *International Journal of General Systems,* and at least one writer wondered about presenting to students the gift of general systems (Rashkis, 1973). Current usage associates general with system instead of associating it with theory – and taking system as a predicate of theory. Thus we have general-system theory instead of general system-theory. This plays havoc with the legitimacy of the field. Elementary reflection discloses that there is no such real world entity as a general system. There is a kind of theory known as system theory, and there is a general form of this theory: *general* system theory. Assuming the contrary is nonsense. It is to assume that there is a theory of general systems. In fact, there is only a general theory of systems.

Let us try to sort out this semantic tangle. We can use Miller's distinction concerning three types of systems: conceptual, abstracted, and concrete. Conceptual systems are systems of concepts, such as the Aristotelian, the Hegelian, or the Newtonian systems. Abstracted systems refer to the real world but abstract elements of them and map these as components of the system model. Thus they mix empirical and conceptual factors. Cultures as systems constitute an example. Concrete systems, on the other hand, are space-time phenomena which process, store and balance energies, and/or matter, and/or information. It is evident that no empirical system can be general: real world things are always particular. Only models can be general, including their concepts, laws, principles and underlying theories. These, however, fall into the category of conceptual systems.

Now, at first sight it may appear that by general systems we mean conceptual systems. This, however, would fail to distinguish general system theory from any other system of thought, and would constitute a redundancy: general systems theory would merely mean general theories theory. We need a distinguishing feature to mark off general *system* theories from general *x*-theories. This we do by taking increasingly rigorous definitions of system. Broadest definitions include all varieties of systems, including conceptual ones. For example, take Miller's (1971): a system is "a set of interacting units with relationships among them". A similarly broad definition is first given by Hall and Fagen (1956): a system is "a set of objects together with the relationships between the objects and between their attributes". As one follows the definitions, one finds that they tighten up and progressively exclude conceptual and even abstracted systems. Hall and Fagen admit these but point out that terms such as static and dynamic refer to systems of which the concepts or equations are the abstract model. Conceptual systems themselves are always timeless; concepts of change are inapplicable to them. Concepts such as environment – which, according to Hall and Fagen is "the set of all objects a change in whose attributes affect the system and also those objects whose attributes are changed by the behavior of the system" – apply only to concrete systems, capable of change.

Some other well-known definitions of system make this quite clear. Take Weiss' (1971) definition of a system as a "complex unit in space and time so constituted that its component subunits, by 'systemic' co-operation, preserve its integral configuration of structure and behavior and tend to restore it after non-destructive disturbances". Obviously, this rules out conceptual and abstracted systems of all kinds. They do not exist in space and time, or do not entirely exist in that way, and they are not self-regulative. As we explore more rigorous definitions of system, we find that they define more precisely by excluding more of the erstwhile candidates for systemicity. What they fully exclude are sets of interrelated concepts, conjoined or not with real world events.

The more rigorous and technical definitions of system make it clear that only one variety of system can be meaningfully included in this definition, and that is the variety Miller terms concrete system. No theory or model is of this variety. It may well contain a set of elements in rigorous interrelation, such as a system of differential equations, in which a change in one term entails a change in all others. Yet models and theories do not process energy, matter or information, they do not modify their environment, and they are not changed by it. They are timeless sets of qualitative or quantitative concepts, which may include terms for such processes, but not the processes themselves. Hence in any rigorous definition of system they are not systems at all. They are models, maps, hypotheses, or theories. They may be models, maps, hypotheses, or theories of systems — or of anything else. But it is fruitless and higly confusing to speak of them as if they were systems themselves.

The semantic confusion discussed here is of more than academic interest. It impedes the development and acceptance of general system theory. Those who, seduced by the careless linguistic habits of its practitioners, believe that it is a theory of a curious entity called general system, view it with understandable scepticism. They are prevented from appreciating that general system theory is not the investigation of a mythological beast labelled general system but the investigation of the full scope of the phenomena conceptualized as various kinds of systems.

How did this unfortunate confusion arise? Indeed, it arises only in the English language scientific community and is due to the somewhat unsophisticated original translation of *allgemeine Systemlehre* by von Bertalanffy. Bertalanffy was very likely the first to give the name general system theory to theories of open organic systems which may have implications beyond biology. He spoke of general system theory at Charles Morris' seminar at the University of Chicago in 1937. Bertalanffy was then 36 years of age and his knowledge of English, never perfect, was rudimentary. From his writings of that period, it is evident that he was offering a direct translation of what he called *allgemeine Systemlehre*. Although this term first occurs in print in his *Das biologische Weltbild,* he spoke of the system theory of the developing organism in *Theoretische Biologie*. His writings specifically on the subject of *allgemeine Systemlehre* were destroyed in his Vienna home during the war, and we have only references to them in works dating from 1948 and later. It is clear that Bertalanffy meant by *allgemeine Systemlehre*, or, as he subsequently called it, *allgemeine Systemtheorie,* a Lehre or Theorie applicable in different sciences. It has probably never occurred to him that the English term general system theory could be read as a theory of an entity called general systems. In German one could not make such a mistake: the term would then read *Theorie der allgemeinen Systeme.*

Bertalanffy (1969) entitled his fundamental book on the subject *General System Theory*. In the current literature, however, the term is usually changed to the plural form: general systems theory. This change is justified by pointing to the fact that there are not one, but a significant number of theories in this field. If so, however, the plural should attach to theory and not system. Putting system in the plural suggests that we have several of the entities called general systems, and a theory that maps them. This of course is patently false.

## Metatheory confusion

If we observe what people who call themselves general system theorists are doing, we find that their activities fall into two broad categories. In one category, investigators focus on the common or general properties of systems encountered in fields such as cybernetics and computer science, electrical engineering, biology, ecology, economics, psychology, sociology, the management and policy sciences, and political science. They map and classify properties which some or all of these systems share in common, i.e., the general properties of systems. People in this category move on the level of empirical scientific theory but work with cross-level hypotheses.

In the second category we find investigators looking at the theories themselves that map the general properties of systems. Because general system theory is still in a relatively early phase of theory pluralism, there are a considerable number of general theories of systems. Some general system theorists attempt to sort out these theories, find common features, and thus build a higher level general theory, i.e., a general theory of the general theories. They move on the level of the history and philosophy of science, dealing not with empirical phenomena directly but with existing theories of empirical phenomena. They build metatheories of general theories of systems.

A common fallacy is to hold that all general system theorists are metatheorists. In that event, they would not be system theorists, but theorists of systemtheories. What they would be concerned with would not be systems, but theories of systems — and such theories themselves are not systems. Those who investigate existing general theories of systems are not system theorists, but historians or philosophers of science, specialized to the field of general system theory. Their relation to concrete systems is as indirect as the relation of the philosopher and historian of science is to the atom or to phlogiston. It matters not the least whether systems exist or not at this level; what matters is that there are theories of them. These are the objects of investigation, and they exist.

To claim that general system theorists are metatheorists is to claim that they have no direct relation to concrete systems, merely to theories of them. This fallacy makes the field comparable to the history and philosophy of science, and indeed into a special division of it. Inasmuch as the majority of general system theorists is very much concerned to investigate some variety of concrete system, the designation of the field as one of metatheory is false. As a source of confusion the designation is dangerous, for it subsumes general system theory within another field and thus removes its individual *raison d'être*.

## Fallacy of generalization suspicion

Frankl has pointed to the danger of specialized scientists using their specialty as a springboard for broad and unwarranted generalizations. When a scientists who is an expert in biology attempts to understand the phenomena of human existence in biological terms, he falls prey to biologism. When a sociologist attempts to explain culture in purely sociological categories, he is the victim of sociologism. What we have to deplore, Viktor Frankl (1969) told us, is not so much the fact that scientists are specializing, but rather that they are generalizing, i.e., indulging in overgeneralized statements. "We have for long been familiar with the *'terrible simplificateur'*; but now we meet more and more frequently another type, the *'terrible generalisateur'*." He turns biology into biologism, sociology into sociologism, and psychology into psychologism.

Some of the scepticism confronting general system theory is due to a (mistaken) belief that it is another terrible generalization. The most frequently heard opinions accuse it of being either a generalization of a theory of organism, or of a theory of automata, depending on whether the accuser has heard more of von Bertalanffy or of Ross Ashby, for example. Yet general system theory is innocent of such charges. It is not a generalized theory, but a general theory. We must not confuse the historical origins of a theory with its actual status and orientation. Every theory originates from somewhere; the original insight is usually suggested by some specific kind of phenomena. But this is not necessarily carried over into the theory. General system theory originated with the systems theory of organism, but does not infuse this now into a systems concept of society. There is a world of difference between an organismic conception of society and a systems conception. The former, of which social Darwinism is a good example, takes society as a superorganism, the individual 'writ large'. It assumes that what holds for individuals also holds for society, such as the struggle for survival, life cycles, senescence, etc. In its more primitive versions we find analogies such as head-government, heart-church, arms-army, and the like. By contrast a systems model of society does not borrow its concepts from organismic biology but takes a basically axiomatic position. Every complex organization must confront the challenge posed by the statistical prediction of the second law of thermodynamics. It must maintain structure and order by using available energies from its environment. If it is mainly an information, rather than a matter-energy processing system, it must maintain or optimize the ratio of information to noise in its channels. There are but a limited number of ways in which space-time systems can persist and grow in their environments. It should be possible to specify and catalogue the relevant processes, functions, and functional structures and components. Existing varieties of systems are likely to exhibit some selection from among the repertory of possible structures and processes. Their differences will be due to their level of complexity — measured in terms of entropy or information — the nature of their subsystems, and the nature of their environment. Sociocultural systems use social sanctions to maintain certain critical parameters in their organization; warm-blooded organisms use homeostatic processes controlled by the autonomic nervous system. We are not saying that political sanctions are nothing but societal homeostasis, any more than saying that homeostasis is nothing but the organic form of political sanctions. We are dealing with control processes operating on the principle of negative feedback. The manner of operations is independent of whether energy, matter or information is processed, and whether the parts are conscious human beings or cells in the animal body. Inputs, transformations, and outputs characterize each component in the system, and networks are formed among them with the noted control characteristics.

A general theory is a theory that is equally applicable throughout its defined range. A general theory in physics is applicable to all physical events of a certain kind; a general theory of biological evolution is applicable to all processes of speciation observed on earth. A general theory of multidisciplinary scope is equally applicable to certain specified kinds of phenomena in all the disciplines within its range. Its hypotheses are cross-level hypotheses, where each level correlates with one or more traditional specialized disciplines.

**Fallacy of generality suspicion**

The fallacy of generality charge differs from the fallacy of generalization in holding that what general system theory is doing is not so much generalizing from one field to another, but concentrating on the largest and most inclusive system it can investigate. For example, general system theorists are in the habit of criticizing specialists for concentrating on one set of variables and one type of system to the exclusion of others. It is said that general systems people consider the entire system in which the variables and subsystems figure as elements. It is natural to conclude from this that the entire system is what they regard as the general system. This, however, is simply false.

Take a concrete example. Let us say that we are dealing with the problems of a city and are attempting to map out the relevant factors and processes. Specialists produce models of the city's economic system, its energy system, transportation system, communication system, sewage and garbage disposal system, its political system, perhaps even of its educational and cultural system. Inasmuch as these system models are looked at in isolation, they represent special models. The general system model, it is said, is the model that integrates all these models.

Now, the point is well taken if by general system model we mean a general model of the system as contrasted with special or partial models. But if we use the term to denote a model of something called the general system, we make a deplorable, but indeed quite common mistake. The system that integrates the city's transportation, economic, energy, communication, etc., systems is not a general system but simply the city itself conceived as a system, i.e., the urban system. Not even the system formed by the city and its environment is the general system; that system is merely the regional system. And so on. The system formed by regional systems may be the state or provincial system, that formed by states and provinces the federal or nation-state system, and finally the international or global system.

If we insist on using a general system model, and mean by that a model which includes all other models, we merely move the level of inquiry to the next higher level of organization. On that level we can ask for a general system as well, and thus we are led to the following level. Ultimately we fail to grasp anything of real significance about the phenomena with which we started due to the awesome altitude of our vision. Levels of generality and levels of explanatory detail are inversely correlated: when we have characterized the most general phenomena, we have largely ignored all the concrete specifics.

But a general theory of systems is not the theory of the highest level system, just as a general system model is not the model of a general system. The general system model is a general model of certain kinds of systems; and a truly general system theory is a general theory of systems on all levels, insofar as they exhibit invariances in their structure and function. To claim the contrary is simply to push the field into high level but vague generalizations, short-circuiting the potential of a multidisciplinary theory with important cross-level hypotheses.

## PRINCIPLES OF GENERAL SYSTEM THEORY

General system theory is a new and at present explosively developing science. To state its principles is not, therefore, to produce a historical record of the classical tenets of an established discipline, but the attempt, always and necessarily tentative, to frame a body of concepts which is adequate to describe and define the main thrust of the work currently undertaken. Such attempts are salutary even if they may be shortlived, for after their appearance they force workers in the field to concentrate on fundamental issues and define their own standpoints. In the past, Bertalanffy, Boulding, Rapoport, Ashby and Miller have produced noteworthy essays stating basic factors and principles of this theory. Our own modest effort owes much to their work, and sets forth this type of attempt in the light of new developments in the field, viewed through the perspectives briefly discussed above.

### Definition

*General system theory is a general theory of systems.* A general theory of systems includes special system theories as special cases. The special system theories include the cybernetic system theories of Wiener and Ashby, the information system theories of Shannon and Weaver, the biological system theories of Bertalanffy, Weiss, and Miller, the mathematical system theories of Rapoport and von Neumann, the social system theories of Parsons, Merton, and Buckley, the political system theories of Easton, Taylor, and Deutsch, the management and organization system theories of Churchmann and Ackoff, the psychological and psychiatric system theories of

Grinker, Menninger, Arieti, and Gray, the human communication system theories of Cherry, Vickers, and Thayer, and others.

By implication, it follows that general system theory is not a theory of general systems; is not a generalized theory of some variety of systems; is not a theory of the most encompassing system; is not a metatheory.

## Specification

*The empirical objects of investigation of general system theory are concrete systems.* A system can be described as a set $\xi$ of parameters $X_i$ and a set $\eta$ of relations $Y_k$ among $\xi$ (Ropohl, 1973).

(1) $\xi = \{X_i\}$; $\quad X_i = \{x_{ij}\}$;

$\eta = \{Y_k\}$; $\quad Y_k < XX_i$.

Attributes $A_i$ constitute the set $\alpha$, which is an element in the system.

(2) $\{A_i\} = \alpha$; $\quad \alpha \in S$.

An attribute is a property, or characteristic, of the system $S$, and consists of values $a_{ij}$.

(3) $A_i = \{a_{ij}\}$.

Relations among the attributes $A_i$ of a system $S$ constitute functions $F_j$. $\phi$ is the set of functions $F_j$.

(4) $\{F_j\} = \phi$; $\quad \phi \in S$.

The set of attributes and the set of functions jointly describe the functional aspects of the system. These aspects apply equally to energy, matter and information processing systems.

Structural aspects of the system are described by part-whole and part-part relations among subsystems $S_*$, systems $S$, and suprasystems $S^*$. The set of subsystems $S_*$ is $\sigma$, taken from a basic set $\beta$.

(5) $\{S_*\} = \sigma$; $\quad \sigma \in S$; $\quad \sigma < \beta$.

Subsystems can be described as systems at level $(L-1)$. The set of their attributes is $\alpha_*$, and the set of their functions $\phi_*$. Subsystems consist of their own subsubsystems, and the set of which is $\sigma_*$, taken from the basic set $\beta_*$.

(6) $\quad\quad\quad \beta \;\; = \beta^{(L)}$;

$\quad\quad\quad\quad \beta_* = \beta^{(L-1)}$, etc.

$\quad\quad\quad\quad S \;\; = S^{(L)}$;

$\quad\quad\quad\quad S_* = S^{(L-1)}$, etc.

The difference between the basic set $\beta$, and the set $\sigma$ of subsystems defines the environment $\gamma$, of the system $S$.

(7) $\gamma = \beta - \sigma$.

The set $\sigma$ of the subsystems $S_*^{(L-1)}$ is a component in the system $S$; the set of systems $S^{(L)}$ is a component in the suprasystem $S*^{(L+1)}$.

(8) $\{S_*^{(L-1)}\} \in S^{(L)} \Rightarrow \{S^{(L)}\} \in S*^{(L+1)} \Rightarrow$ etc.

The relative subsumption of subsystems within systems, and systems within suprasystems defines a hierarchy of systems. Such a hierarchy consists of concrete systems when the set $\alpha$ of attributes is not empty, and when the set $\sigma$ of subsystems is not empty and consists of energy, matter and/or information processing entities.

In a system $S$, each subsystem $S_*$ has at least one attribute $A_{*i}$. Relations $P_q$ among the attributes $A_{*i}$ give the cartesian product

(9) $P_q < XA_{*ki}$.

The set $\pi$ of relations $P_q$ is the structure of the system $S$.

(10) $\{P_q\} = \pi$;   $\pi \in S$.

A concrete system can now be defined as

(11) $S = (\alpha, \phi, \sigma, \pi)$

where $\alpha$ is the set of attributes $A_{*i}$; $\phi$ is the set of functions $F_j$ among the set $\alpha$ of attributes, $\sigma$ is the set of information, matter, or energy processing subsystems $S_*$ derived from the basic set $\beta$, and $\pi$ is the set of relations $P_q$ among the set $\sigma$ of subsystems.

A temporal state of $S$, characterized by definite numerical values for $\alpha$, $\phi$, $\sigma$, and $\pi$, is $S_{ti}$.

*States of concrete systems are determined by interaction with the environment.* Concrete systems of all types are relatively open systems, i.e., such a system $S$ has semipermeable boundaries which filter energy, matter and information passing to and from the system and its environment $\gamma$. Matter, energy or information originating in the environment and affecting system structure and function are inputs $P_i$. Matter, energy or information originated by the system and affecting the environment are outputs $P_j$. $P_i$ is in part determined by $P_j$ since $P_j$ acts on $\gamma$, which originates $P_i$. This and the factors immediately following are negligible for simpler varieties of technical systems.

(12) $P_i = P_j \gamma$.

$P_j$ in turn is a joint product of $P_i$ and the given system state $S_{ti}$.

(13) $P_j = P_i S_{ti}$.

In accordance with Eq. (13), the given system state $S_{ti}$ is

(14) $S_{ti} = P_j/P_i$.

Hence the output is more fully described as

(15) $P_j = P_i(P_j\gamma) S_{ti}(P_j/P_i)$.

Any given variable is jointly determined by the circular flow

(16) $S_{ti} \to P_j \to \gamma \to P_i \to S_{t+1} \to P_j$ etc.

## Categories

*There are seven principal types of systems distributed on three major levels.* The seven principal types of systems are the physicochemical, the biological, the organ, the social-ecological, the sociocutural, the organizational, and the technical. The systems of these types are distributed over three major levels of hierarchical organization in the biosphere: the suborganic, the organic, and the supraorganic.

Table 1 of concrete systems shows the level-type correlations.

TABLE 1

|  | Supraorganic | Level Organic | Suborganic |
|---|---|---|---|
| Type: |  |  |  |
| Physicochemical |  |  | X |
| Biological |  | X |  |
| Organ |  | X |  |
| Social-ecological | X |  |  |
| Socio-cultural | X |  |  |
| Organizational | X |  |  |
| Technical |  |  | X |

*Physicochemical systems* include the atoms of the elements, chemical and organic molecules, molecular and crystalline complexes, up to and including nucleic acids and viruses detached from their host.

*Biological systems* include viruses coupled with a host, and unicellular and multicellular organisms of all existing species.

*Organ systems* include the specialized organs of all more complex multicellular organisms.

*Social-ecological systems* include all systems formed by the niche structures, energy and mass transfers of organisms within a geographic region. They include interspecific ecosystems and intraspecific (non- or pre-cultural) social systems.

*Sociocultural systems* include all forms of (human) social systems distinguished by a culture, i.e., a symbolic communication system, extraskeletal memory stores and the associated capacity to acquire, code and hand down empirically gathered information.

*Organizational systems* include all specialized role structures formed by human beings within their sociocultural systems to carry out specific tasks and realize particular objectives. They may be private or public, business, educational, political, social service, or other in nature.

*Technical systems* include systems made of suborganic components by organizations to carry out special purpose tasks within sociocultural systems. Technical systems may be mechanical, thermal, hydraulic, chemical, electric, electronic, atomic or other, and they may process matter, energy or information. Simpler technical systems are relatively closed and have zero or negligible feedback built into them. More sophisticated technical systems are open to wide channels of inputs, mainly in the form of information, and have sensitivities to their own performance analogous to non-technical varieties of systems.

**Intertype relations**

*Systems on each lower level jointly form systems on the next higher level.* Physicochemical systems in specific structural forms constitute biological systems. Biological systems, for the most part equipped with organ systems, in specific structural forms constitute social, ecological, sociocultural, and organizational systems. The latter produce technical systems of suborganic components.

*Systems on each level produce their own differentiated subsystems.* Complex biological systems evolve their own subsidiary organ systems: social systems, in the case of humans, evolve sociocultural systems; socio-cultural systems evolve organizations, and organizations evolve technical systems. Physicochemical systems do not evolve their own differentiated type of subsidiary systems.

**Evolution**

*The evolution of systems of each type is the precondition, or template, for the evolution of systems of each further type.* Physicochemical systems, such as thymine, adenine, cytosine and guanine, built into nucleic acids form the precondition of the evolution of biological systems. Populations of biological systems acted upon by selection pressures and endowed with the capacity of mutating a quasi-stable genotype are the precondition for the emergence of differentiated organ systems. Biological organisms, with and without organ systems, are the precondition for the emergence of interspecific ecological and intraspecific social systems. Intraspecific human social systems in their ecological environment are the precondition for the development of sociocultural systems. Sociocultural systems are the template on which evolve organizations, and organizations are the template for the creation and propagation of technical systems.

*The rate of evolution of different types of systems accelerates progressively.* Physicochemical systems evolve in nuclear transmutation processes in stars and the surrounding space over many billions of years. Biological systems possibly date back over five billion years on the earth's surface. Organ systems had to wait for the emergence of relatively complex multicellular forms of life. Social-ecological systems

TABLE 2

| Approach | Level | Type | Classical Discipline |
|---|---|---|---|
| Systems Sciences | suborganic | physicochemical | solid state physics<br>plasma physics<br>quantum physics<br>nonequilibrium thermodynamics<br>physical chemistry<br>organic chemistry<br>biophysics<br>biochemistry<br>molecular biology |
| | organic | biological | zoology<br>botany, plant biology<br>embryology<br>organismic biology<br>physical anthropology<br>individual psychology |
| | | organ | physiology<br>neurophysiology<br>experimental psychology (sensory functions) |
| | supraorganic | social-ecological | population biology<br>ecology<br>insect and animal sociology |
| | | sociocultural | social and cultural anthropology<br>sociology<br>human ecology<br>economics and related studies<br>political and policy sciences<br>international and world order studies |
| | | organizational | organization theory<br>management science<br>planning and forecasting<br>organizational psychology<br>microeconomics and sociology<br>efficiency systems analysis |
| Systems Technology | suborganic | technical | engineering sciences<br>computer science<br>information and communication sciences<br>cybernetics<br>applied mathematics |
| Systems Philosophy | organic | biological/homo | axiology, value theory<br>ethics, moral theory<br>epistemology |
| | supraorganic | sociocultural | social ethics<br>social and political theory<br>theory of justice<br>human communication theory<br>culturology<br>technology assessment |

emerged simultaneously with organ systems on their own, supraorganic level. Sociocultural systems date back about 28,000 years, although stone age agriculture and its system of communication and village-type social organization emerged only 7000-8000 B.C. Organizations have been known in rudimentary forms in classical civilizations, e.g., mercenary armies, political bureaucracies, religious institutions, academies, but evolved in their present form only since the first industrial revolution in the middle of the 18th century. Technical systems, while tracing their origins to the tools of Stone Age man, have evolved to great sophistication within the span of the present century.

### Research approaches

*Concrete systems are investigated through three distinct approaches: systems technology, the systems sciences, and systems philosophy.* Physicochemical, biological, organ, social-ecological, sociocultural, and organizational systems are investigated by the various branches of the systems sciences. Technical systems are investigated through systems technology, and systems philosophy considers special problems connected with human beings and human society, as well as with the other systems approaches themselves.

Table 2 is a general matrix of the three basic systems approaches, the seven principal system types, the three major system levels, and their relation to classical scientific and philosophic disciplines.

### REFERENCES

Bertalanffy, L. von. *General system theory: Essays on its foundation and development* (rev. ed.). New York: George Braziller, 1969.
Conant, J. B. *Modern science and modern man.* New York: Doubleday-Anchor, 1952.
Einstein, A. *The world as I see it.* New York: Covici-Friede, 1934.
Frankl, V. Reductionism and nihilism. In A. Koestler and J. R. Smythies (Eds.), *Beyond reductionism.* New York: Macmillan, 1969.
Hall, A. D. and Fagen, R. E. Definition of system. *Gen. Systems*, 1956, 1.
Heisenberg, W. *Philosophical problems of nuclear science.* London: Faber & Faber, 1952.
Laszlo, E. and Margenau, H. The emergence of integrative concepts in contemporary science. *Phil. Sci.*, 1972, 39, 252-259.
Miller, J. G. The nature of living systems. *Behav. Sci.*, 1971, 16, 277-301.
Rashkis, H. A. General systems research as a constructive channel for student aggression. In M. Rubin (Ed.), *Systems in society.* Washington, D.C.: Society for General Systems Research, 1973.
Ropohl, G. *Einführung in die allgemeine Systemtheorie.* Karlsruhe: 1973 (mimeographed).
Straus, R. Departments and disciplines: Stasis and change. *Science*, 1973, 182, 895-898.
Weiss, P. A. *Hierarchically organized systems in theory and practice.* New York: Hafner, 1971.

# 2

## A SYSTEMS VIEW OF EVOLUTION AND INVARIANCE*

### THE EVOLUTION OF COMPLEXITY

Evolutionary thinking is characteristic of process metaphysics and of the newer theories of the empirical sciences. But whereas process metaphysics saw evolution as a cosmic process, embracing all empirical phenomena in a continuous if specifically differentiated sweep, the modern empirical sciences developed special laws of evolution, applicable only within limited domains. Thus there is a law of the evolution of matter in the universe, stated in the equations of astrophysics; there is a law of the evolution of the macro-structure of the universe itself, based on the calculations of astronomy; there is also a law of the evolution of biological entities, from macro-molecules and protocells with replicating capability to complex and integrated multicellular organisms; there are other laws applicable to the evolution of ecosystems, still others to sociocultural evolution (the controversial 'laws of history'), and laws or principles of the evolution of science, art, and religion. The unitary vision of a continuous evolutionary process is upheld only by metaphysicians, divorced from the main streams of scientific thought.

With the rise of the systems sciences, however, general system theory can now reaffirm the concept of a continuous, if internally highly differentiated, evolutionary process on a scientific basis. Its concept of evolution is the offspring of two, initially opposing, currents of thought within 19th century science. One was the Darwinian theory of the origin of species; the other, the early formulations of the laws of thermodynamics.

In 1862, Spencer argued that there is a fundamental law of matter, called the law of persistence of force, from which it follows that nothing homogeneous can remain as such if it is acted on by external forces, because such forces affect different parts of the system differently and, hence, cause internal differentiation in it. Every force thus tends to bring about increasing variety. The cosmos develops from an

---
*Reprinted from *General Systems*, Vol. XIX, 1974.

indefinite and incoherent homogeneity to a definite and coherent inhomogeneity, representing the emergence of better and better things. Evolution, said Spencer, can only end in the establishment of the greatest perfection and most complete happiness.

Spencer's *First Principles* followed (after an interval of three years) the publication of Darwin's *The Origin of Species* (1859). Both placed emphasis on progressive evolution, with complexity and differentiation generally associated with goodness and value. However, parallel developments in physics came to the fore at about the same time. Carnot developed the basic principles of what came later to be known as the second law of thermodynamics (1824), and William Thompson stated them more forcefully in his treatise "On the Universal Tendency in Nature to the Dissipation of Mechanical Energy" (1852). On the continent, Helmholtz published his essay on the preservation of energy (*Über die Erhaltung der Kraft*[1], 1847), and in 1865 Clausius introduced the concept of entropy. A year later Boltzmann offered a new formulation of the second law, in which it is linked with probability theory and statistical mechanics. The status of the law appeared unquestionable. And its thrust was that, instead of building up, the universe as a whole is inevitably running down. Every process dissipates energy and renders it unavailable for performing work.[2] The great arrow of evolution points, therefore, not toward increasingly differentiated and complex things, but toward progressively disorganized, simple, and random aggregates.

The effect of the advent of thermodynamical laws on thinking about evolution in the universe was profound. The optimistic sentence, concerning evolution leading to perfection and happiness, included in the first edition of Spencer's *First Principles*, is lacking in the sixth.

Despite the arguments of the physicists, it remained evident that, at least on the surface of the earth, many things continue to build up instead of running down. More recent work in astrophysics showed that, even in the wider cosmos, matter is constantly building up in the course of the chemical evolution of stars and in interstellar processes associated with quasars, supernovae, and gravitational contraction of interstellar dust. Science had to wait for the development of the thermodynamics of irreversible processes in the 20th century, and its application in astrophysics, biophysics and biochemistry, to perceive that there is no contradiction between the laws of thermodynamics and the observed direction of evolution in some regions and aspects of the universe. Evolution, it turned out, exploits energy flows which possess inherent stability in certain highly specific configurations. It takes place in open systems with inputs and outputs, whereas the laws of thermodynamics apply to closed systems. Hence the universe, as a theoretically closed system, may tend on the whole toward entropy and equilibrium; enclaves can nevertheless form within it, given large enough flows and suitable energetic conditions, which locally and temporally reverse this trend. There is no conflict with the second law — but there is no explanation by it either. We have to add further laws of the natural universe before the second law can be used to predict the evolution of complexity.

By and large, we can understand the nature of such laws at present, even if we do not have quantitative formulations beyond the first few stages of their operation. The understanding comes from the concept of 'dissipative structures' advanced by scientists working in irreversible thermodynamics (Prigogine, Katchalsky, Onsager, De Groot, and others), and from the conclusions drawn by Jacob Bronowski.[3] Dissipative structures are systems which dissipate energy in the course of their self-maintenance and self-organization. Complex entities cannot arise in nature unless there is a flow mixing the existing elements in random configurations. If all configurations had equal intrinsic stability, the probability of their being maintained would be equal and described by the second law in its Boltzmannian formulation. Eventually all configurations would break down and the average pattern would bunch around the thermodynamic equilibrium state. But it appears that the flows have intrinsic stability in specific configurations. For example, protons and neutrons build enduring, stable nuclei. They can be balanced by shells of electrons, giving stable atoms. A helium atom is stable, but the configuration resulting from the thermal collision of two helium atoms is not. The structure would disintegrate in about a millionth of a microsecond. But, if during that time a third helium atom enters the configuration a stable structure results: the nucleus of carbon. This serves as a simple physical model for the understanding of how increasinly complex structures can come about through the chance rearrangements of components in a flow. Atoms make molecules and crystals, macromolecules are composed of simpler molecules and of crystalline elements, and the simplest forms of life are composed of relatively stable configurations of the already established macromolecular aggregates. For example, the base molecules of living things, i.e. thymine, adenine, cytosine and guanine, are stable configurations of macromolecules built into likewise stable configurations of nucleic acids. Nucleic acids in recurrent patterns code the build-up of organic phenotypes. Cells are stable configurations as self-contained units, capable of self-maintenance (metabolism) and continuity (reproduction). But they, in turn, can be structured into complex multicellular organisms having the basic properties of life on their own level of organization. We can carry the process still further and discover that self-contained populations find coordinations of relatively stable sorts in inter-specific structures (known as ecosystems) and that local structures of this kind are coordinated in more encompassing ones, leading to the concept of the ecosphere as a complex, interdetermined system. Man is a system on one level of this emergent hierarchy; his environment is composed of its other levels.

Two general conditions make for the build-up of systems, notwithstanding the validity of the second law. The first is a flow of energy entering the evolving region as a whole (in our case, from the sun); the second, the natural selection which hits upon, through chance variations, intrinsically stable configurations of energy flows and matches one such configuration against and with another. If we allow that there are actual or potential configurations of energy flows in the universe which are intrinsically stable, we get a bonafide explanation of the build up of complexity. The second law becomes a law of evolution if we add to it the repertory of configurations which, when hit upon, manifest a degree of stability. Such configurations bias the statistics upon which the second law is based: random fluctuations induced by energy winds will not have thermodynamical equilibrium as their average, but the stable configuration. Hence we get a new average which serves as the starting point of fluctuations that involve the chance that further configurations of stability are hit upon, made up of the existing stable configurations as their components. Thus atoms can build into molecules, and molecules into the building blocks of life. Living species can build into ecosystems, and ecosystems into the system of the ecosphere.

A new general system concept of evolution allows that the second law of thermodynamics is an adequate description of the real universe only if it is integrated with the concept of 'hidden' or 'potential' strata of stability upon which the flows can be hit. Every system we encounter in nature is the actualization of some such stratum of stability. This includes man, the organs and cells in his body, the molecules in the cells, and the atoms in the molecules. It includes any and all naturally constituted multi-organic systems, such as ecologies. In this class come some varieties of social systems and the world system. The result of evolution on earth is a multilevel hierarchy which encompasses atoms on the one end and large-scale multiorganic systems on the other. The higher systems are composed of integrated sets of lower-level systems. Systemic interactions among them yield higher systemic units; other types of interactions produce differentiation and lead to speciation. The processes of evolution proceed from a state of partly ordered chaos—energy fluxes interacting with some relatively stable configurations of flows. Given a matrix with such types of order, evolution tends to produce higher levels of organization in structures of greater complexity. Disturbances affecting existing systems lead to the merging of some dynamic properties, the differentiation of others, and result in the selective evolution of systems progressively fitted to their environment. Systems evolve by adding weaker bonded components to the already strongly bonded ones, as atoms are electronically bonded in molecules; molecules, in complex polymers and macromolecular structures; these, in turn, in cellular units; cells, in tissues and multicellular systems, and multicellular individuals, in ecological and social systems.

## SYSTEMIC INVARIANCE

The dissipative structures which emerge in the process of evolution in the ecosphere of the earth exhibit basic invariances of structure and function, notwithstanding the fact that they are diverse in appearance and seem to differ greatly in behavior. The invariances are due to the shared situation and common origin of the systems; they are dynamic open systems that maintain themselves in an energy flow by dissipating organized energies and using the energies thus freed to counteract statistical tendencies toward energy degradation in the physical universe. Whether a system is relatively simple, composed directly of atoms or molecules, or highly complex, constituted of multiple strands of ordered relationships among already complex multicellular organisms, it must respect the universe's general conditions of self-sustenance. The manner in which particular systems do so is very different, and at first sight no comparison seems possible between them. Yet, when we reconstitute the structural characteristics and functional dynamics of the various manifest properties, we find that they exhibit the invariances associated with systemic existence. Four such basic systems invariances are discussed here; they are basic factors in our understanding of the unity which underlies phenomenal diversity. They offer fresh insights also for our understanding of that most diverse and complex system, the global system and its own patterns of world order.

1. *Order and irreducibility*. 'Order' in a system refers to the invariance that underlies transformation of state, and by means of which the system's structure can be identified. A stable atom manifests order in the relation of its electrons to its nucleus; a social system manifests it in the relations of its members. These relations, in atoms as well as societies, can undergo transformations: a hydrogen atom can undergo fusion and become part of a helium atom minus a radiated surplus of energy; an independent state can become federated with or assimilated into larger polities, with or without eliciting a stream of emigrants or immigrants. Inasmuch as we can speak of a system as a "something" that endures long enough to identify it and recurs often enough to have a name, we are speaking of some elements of order that are characteristic of it. We can speak of *this* world order or *that* but, inasmuch as we can identify different varieties of world order, we speak of a (real or imagined) system that has invariant structural features. The opposite of order is chaos and the total lack of determination informing a set of elements. Absolute chaos, as well as absolute order, are abstractions; real-world systems manifest some finite degree of order, ranged between a state of minimum determination and maximum (but not complete) chaos (typified by the motion of molecules in a gas) and a state of maximum (but not complete) determination and minimum chaos (e.g., the behavior of a well-built machine). Systems are not necessarily "better" the more ordered they are; there is no correlation between positive value judgments and degrees of order. The concept of order is significant for our purposes as a way to identify systems by reference to their invariant structural features, i.e., by the order of their parts. A system that has small degrees of determination will tend to undergo a rapid sequence of possible complex transformations and poses more difficulties for the investigator than one that is highly determinate and produces few, or simple and thus highly predictable, transformations. Yet, a system composed of many relatively indetermined systems does not become that much less determined itself: degrees of indeterminacy are not simply additive. In fact, any whole system we examine in the natural world is likely to be significantly more determinate as a whole than the sum of the determinacy of its parts. In other words, whole systems are more ordered than the sum of the relative disorders of their parts.[4] Indeed, unless this was the case, evolution would result in increasing chaos. As system interacts with system and forms a suprasystem, the individual degrees of freedom of the parts would make the whole system chaotic. However, in the real world, even highly indeterminate systems

can jointly compose systems with ordered characteristics. For example, in the organic body there is a constant chemical flux of complex reactions which, nevertheless, yields a total organism that obeys the laws of physiology. And in a complex sociocultural system invidivuals may have a great deal of personal autonomy, yet the complex patterns of their interactions produce a total structure that can be grasped by the principles of the social sciences.

This takes us to the concept of irreducibility. The concept refers to certain properties of a whole system which are specific on that level, and are not the simple additions of the properties of its parts. The order of a whole system is one such property, and there are others as we shall see. However, claiming that certain properties of whole systems are not equal to the sum of the properties of their parts is not to reaffirm a mystical belief in the old adage, "The whole is more than the sum of its parts". In fact, wholes can be mathematically shown to be other than the simple sum of the properties and functions of their parts.[5]

Let us consider merely the following basic notions. Complexes of parts can be calculated in three distinct ways:[6]

(i) by counting the *number* of parts,
(ii) by taking into account the *species* to which the parts belong, and
(iii) by considering the *relations* between the parts.

In cases (i) and (ii), the complex may be understood as the sum of the parts considered in isolation. In these cases the complex has *cumulative* characteristics: it is sufficient to sum the properties of the parts to obtain the properties of the whole. Such wholes are better known as 'heaps' or 'aggregates', since the fact that the parts are joined in them makes no difference to their functions — i.e., the interrelation of the parts do not qualify their joint behavior. A heap of bricks is an example. But consider anything from an atom to an organism or a society: the particular relations of the parts bring forth properties which are not present (or are meaningless in reference to) the parts. Examples range from the Pauli exclusion principle (which does not say anything about individual electrons), through homeostatic self-regulation (which is meaningless in reference to individual cells or organs), all the way to distributive justice (likewise meaningless in regard to individual members of a society). Each of these complexes is not a mere heap, but a whole which is *other* than the sum of its parts.

The mathematics of non-summative complexes apply to systems of the widest variety, including physical, biological, social, and psychological systems. These systems form ordered wholes in which the law-bound regularities exhibited by interdependent elements determine the functional behavior of the totality. The fallacy of reducing the whole atom to the sum of the properties of its parts is well known to atomic physicists; the analogous fallacy of reducing the whole organism to biochemical reactions and physical properties manifested by particular components is also becoming recognized, and so is the fallacy of reducing the properties of human multi-person systems to the psychological and physiological properties of the participating members.

The irreducibility of the properties of social systems formed by human beings has been stressed by the functionalists and is acknowledged by most social scientists, with the possible exception of a few radical phenomenologists and empiricists. The holistic nature of social phenomena is evident in the study of group behavior and runs through the gamut of social entities up to and including the international level. The reductionist-mechanistic concept is inapplicable to social systems, since mechanistic systems behave in an exactly identical fashion whenever their members are disassembled and put together again, irrespective of the sequence in which the disassembling and reassembling took place. But it is *not* the case that the members of social systems are never significantly modified by each other, their own past, and remain interchangeable in terms of their precise function. Moreover, the characteristic properties of social systems are not characteristics of the individual humans who participate in them, but arise out of their strands of interaction. Thus it is nonsense to speak of 'government', 'justice', 'economic structure', 'legal system', 'political order', (etc.) in terms of individuals, except perhaps in a loose, metaphorical sense. Yet, individuals collectively form systems to which such concepts clearly apply. The characteristics of structure and function, which render such concepts applicable to social systems and not to their individual members, constitute the irreducible properties of social systems. They are as irreducible as the properties of organisms (e.g., homeostasis, adaptation, purposive behavior, etc.) and even of atoms (such as chemical valence).

2. *Self-stabilization.* Real-world systems are exposed to environmental perturbations, yet they depend on their environments to obtain the energies needed for the coherence of their structure. Consequently, viable systems exhibit a repertory of self-stabilizing functions, by means of which they counteract non-lethal perturbations produced by their milieu. Self-stabilization involves a temporary (forced) departure by the system from its characteristic set of internal relations, coupled with a pronounced tendency to return to the characteristic relations when the perturbation is over. The characteristic states of the systems are its 'steady-states' — they are not static states, but ones which represent a level of equilibrium between the internal constraints among the system's components and the forces acting on it from its environment.

Katchalsky and Curran have shown that systems characterized by fixed internal constraints and exposed to unrestrained forces in their environment tend to produce countervailing forces that bring them back to the stable states, since the flow caused by the perturbation has the same sign as the perturbation itself.[7] Hence, the effect of the flow is to reduce the perturbation and permit the system to return to its steady-state. If the perturbations vanish, the system is again characterized by the parameters of its fixed constraints. If both the fixed and the unrestrained forces vanish, the system reaches a state of thermodynamic equilibrium — it becomes a heap, rather than a dynamically ordered whole.

In the steady state the systems are the most economical from the energetic viewpoint, since they lose the minimum amount of free energy. (A still more economical state is the state of thermodynamic equilibrium; in that state, however, the systems are no longer ordered wholes.) Minimum entropy production characterizes the complex systems we term 'living', which slow down the process of thermodynamic decay during their lifetime and remain in a sequence of time-dependent steady states characterized by the typical constraints making up the species-specific organization of the individual. Such systems possess regulating mechanisms that preserve the steady-state and bring the organism back to its unperturbed condition in a way which resembles the action of a restoring force coming into play in any fluctuation from a stationary state in a physical system. Inasmuch as both physical and biological systems maintain themselves in steady-states characterized by the parameters of their internal forces, life as a cybernetic process is analogous to any physical system describable, by our definition, as endowed with the dynamics of self-stabilization.

Self-stabilization occurs by means of stereotyped function performance in relatively mechanistic systems, and through synergistic, simultaneous mutual regulation of the parts in most other varieties of systems. The paradigm of stereotyped self-stabilization is the negative-feedback mechanism consisting of sensor, effector, correlator, and regulator components with a unidirectional circular flow among them. The exact nature of the causal dynamics responsible for synergistic simultaneous regulations of parts in a non-mechanistic system is not fully known, but recent investigations suggest that continuous fields rather than atomistic causal chains may be involved, and that the phenomenon known as inductive resonance may have a role to play.[8]

In most kinds of natural systems, relatively stereotyped negative feedback mechanisms and relatively spontaneous and holistic simultaneous self-regulations are intertwined, although one mode of operation may be vastly more important than the other. For example, in the regulation of cellular activity in simpler species of organisms (lacking an evolved nervous system), resonance induced by the biochemical locking or entrainment of oscillators may be the principal mechanism of self-regulation, whereas in formally organized human societies the institutionally performed negative-feedback control of all relevant inputs and outputs (manufacture and dumping of products, demands and decisions, energy sources and sinks, etc.) is the decisive agency of control and stability.

Systems stabilize themselves around dynamic steady states by means of a variety of mechanisms and processes, the possibilities for which are determined by the nature of their components and the level of their integration within the systemic whole. But, regardless of what process or mechanism is used to perform the stabilizing functions, we may note that self-stabilization is effectively accomplished by systems on all principal levels of organization. On the supraorganic level it is manifested by systems that may be inter- or intra-specific. Most ecosystems are interspecific, whereas social systems are intra-specific. Intra-specific social systems occur among various species, but the complex forms obtain among the higher vertebrates. The most complex and sophisticated social systems are produced by our species; these are distinguished by the *sui generis* elements of language and culture.

Regardless of the differences, however, all such systems maintain themselves over time and, inasmuch as their structural characteristics do not change despite variations in their environment, they manifest the dynamics of steady-state self-stabilization in one form or another.

Functionalist sociologists use the concept of 'equilibrium' to define the stabilized states in human sociocultural systems. (By this they do not mean *thermodynamical* equilibrium, however.) They view human societies as open systems with self-regulating mechanisms maintaining the equilibrium states of the system within definite limits. In order to survive, the system has needs which are fulfilled by its parts or components. These define their 'function'. According to functionalists, every part of a social system should be interpreted and analyzed from the perspective of the contribution it makes to the survival and adaptation of the whole system.

Because of its emphasis on self-stabilization, functionalism has been criticized for leading to a conservative bias: if all existing institutions contribute towards the survival needs of a social system, they are all valuable on that account. Regardless of the warrant for such criticism (which has been partially answered by general system theorists, who have also described social system processes of *self-organization*), it is clear that the phenomenon of self-stabilization is manifested in social as well as in biological systems and that, in the social realm, it is manifested through mechanisms that conserve established patterns: rituals, mores, law enforcement, political conservatism, traditionalism, and so on.

3. *Self-organization.* A number of different cybernetic and systems models have been produced to account for the phenomenon of self-organization.[9] It is fair to say, however, that except in the case of relatively simple systems (mainly artificial ones), the principles of self-organization are not understood in detail. How, for example, the very information which codes a genotype is generated in the course of phylogenetic evolution is still not satisfactorily explained. Nevertheless, some general principles did come to light. First, it now appears that self-organization necessarily involves an open system (or a system coupled with another system) and can never take place in an isolated system. Second, self-organization presupposes some inputs from the system's environment which stress or stimulate the system in some way, i.e., have the overall effect of perturbations. However, if a system has experienced a long and complex series of perturbations in its evolutionary history, it may develop random or residual innovative activity (such as mutations in a genotype or sponaneous innovations in a culture) which diversify populations of systems and keep them adapted to a wide range of possible environmental perturbations. Third, it is now understood that self-organization occurs in systems that have multiple equilibria or, what is the same thing in different words, several strata of potential stability. In view of these general principles, self-organization can be explained on the general evolutionary principle of fluctuations induced either by energy-flows in the milieu acting on systems, or by spontaneous activity by the systems themselves inducing chance variations of states, some of which hit upon levels of stability. This principle makes self-organization a non-random, yet non-teleological, process

governed by the interplay of chance fluctuations of state and determinate levels of potential stability. It respects the characteristic principles of self-organization: openness in the systems, perturbing environmental inputs or self-induced variations, and multiple levels of potential stability.

The fact that self-organization occurs in a system does not conflict with the laws of thermodynamics, as previously shown. It can even be expressed in the language of irreversible thermodynamics.[10] Consequently there is nothing mysterious or supernatural about the fact of systemic self-organization, even if its detailed workings in complex real-world systems are not yet adequately understood. It is the system property which permits populations of systems to evolve, and to create the rich diversity of phenomena in the world. Without self-organizing systems the universe would still not have progressed beyond its chemical elements — and even the build-up of the elements is an instance of progressive self-organization, on the most basic physical level.[11]

The particular mechanism through which self-organizing expresses itself varies with the level of complexity and evolutionary history of the systems. In biological systems, the principal mechanisms of self-organization is mutation in the genotype, coupled with environmental selection acting on the phenotype. In sociocultural systems, self-organization occurs by means of innovative changes induced by members of a society, either to better cope with internal or external perturbations or to extend their control capacity over the rest of the social system or its social and natural environment. The development of new technologies, both hardware and software, calls for a modified social structure that is more adapted than previous structures for handling the new system-environment relations. Threats to the safety or identity of a social system likewise trigger a defensive reorganization of structures and functions. Sociocultural evolution occurs because of the capacity of viable social systems to respond to external challenges and to internal innovations through self-organization, much as biological evolution is rendered possible by the ability of the genotype to undergo adaptively advantageous mutations.

Independently of the local mechanisms responsible for the processes, we can say that, in general, self-organization conduces systems toward more negentropic states while self-stabilization maintains them in their pre-existing level and state of organization. If the systems have some residual innovative capacity, or if perturbations are continuously operating on them in their environment, systems not only survive but also evolve. The evolution of systems can then be conceptualized as a sequence of parallel, or irregularly alternating, stabilization around the parameters of their existing fixed forces (defining the steady-states) and the reorganization of the fixed forces for increasing adaptation to changes in the systems' internal or external environment.

4. *Hierarchization.* Whenever a set of self-stabilizing and self-organizing systems share a common environment, their patterns of evolution crystallize some strands of mutual adaptations. Some varieties of system may evolve specialized functions within cooperative networks of relations. The network formed by the

mutually adapted functions may likewise represent the realization of a potential level of stability, though on a superordinate level, and may be conceptualized as a system in its own right. Such a system can interact with other systems on its own superordinate level and form still higher-level suprasystems through the evolutionary crystallization of their own mutual adaptations. Systems on every level may exhibit the general properties of order, irreducibility, homeostatic self-stabilization, and evolutionary self-organization. The apex of any such hierarchy is itself a system, of which all other systems are subsystems.

That evolutionary development proceeds in a hierarchical fashion can be clearly understood by reference to Simon's calculations.[12] These show that a system composed of independently stable subsystems can withstand perturbations to a significantly higher degree than systems built directly from their components. Hence, hierarchical systems are more stable in a changing milieu, and there is an overwhelming probability that surviving real-world systems possess a hierarchical structure. Indeed, such structure is exhibited by existing systems in the biological as well as the social realm. Whatever living system we analyze, we find hierarchical order in descending steps, from the whole system down to the most basic subsystem. For instance, complex whole organisms are composed of major parts (such as limbs) and principal organ system (such as the respiratory system). Each of these systems is further composed of relatively stable subsystems. Limbs are not built directly from their contingent of cells, but cells in groups establish unit sub-limb structures, such as a skeletal element or a muscle. These, in turn, constitute limb parts (such as toes), and all such parts in concert yield the unit limb. One can further go beyond the cell down to its parts: the organelle, the macromolecular system, the macromolecule, the constituent chemical molecules, and atoms themselves. Although the higher units cannot exist outside the context of the integrated whole organism, the lower units can. Moreover, the morphogenesis of the organism follows the paths of unit-construction and assembly, capitalizing on the coherence and integration of the already constituted subunits.

We can also analyze a social system and find that its many subsystems form relatively stable assemblies. Political systems, for example, are composed of principal institutional structures with established, relatively stable functions. The institutions themselves are segmented into bureaus and departments, each with distinct responsibilites and resources. Although here, too, the higher substructures may depend on the whole system for viability, lower level bureaucratic units are independently stable: they are maintained regardless of changes at the top. Hierarchical organization assures continuity and, therewith, stability in a political system. Similar observations hold, *mutatis mutandis*, for the economic, cultural, military, industrial, agricultural, and other domains of sociocultural systems.

That development generally proceeds in a hierarchical fashion explains many otherwise puzzling phenomena. It tells us that, in complex systems, different descriptions will apply to different levels of structure and function. For example, we get different descriptions when we concentrate on the organ, the cell, the organelle, the macromolecule, and the atom in an organism. We get different descriptions when we examine an entire political system, its particular institutional components, and its specialized bureaus and departments. The hierarchical nature of development also tells us that there will be greater diversity of structure and function at the higher levels than at the lower ones. The higher levels are made up of many lower level systems, plus all their interrelations. New functions and structures can thus emerge at each higher level, and these are specific transformations of basic invariances found on all levels. For example, homeostasis as well as ethical conservatism are self-stabilizing functions in systems, but are expressed in qualitatively different forms. Revolutionary movements and mutations are both elements in processes of self-organization, exposed to the test of natural selection; but they, too, assume very different manifest forms. The properties emerging at successive levels in hierarchical systems are irreducible transformations of the systems invariances which hold true on all levels.

Last, but not least, we understand that greater diversity at higher levels goes hand in hand with smaller populations. There are fewer cells than molecules, fewer organisms than cells, and fewer societies than organisms. Ultimately, there is but one global ecosystem which, together with its human components, forms the world system which is the object of principal concern in the present volume.

## REFERENCES

1. It is important to recall that Helmholtz still used 'Kraft' (now meaning 'force' ) in the sense of 'energy' .

2. The reasoning behind the experimental evidence that led to the various formulations of the second law is complex and has varied throughout the 19th century. In its most general form, it may be summed up in the argument that perpetuum mobile machines fail necessarily i.e., no cyclic heat engine can extract internal energy (the force capable of changing an adiabatically enclosed system from one equilibrium state to another) from a system and use it without loss in performing mechanical work. (Alternatively, without compensating changes heat cannot flow from a colder to a hotter body; according to Joule's calculations, a unit of heat is equivalent to a corresponding unit of mechanical work [e.g., 778 foot-pounds = 1 B.T.U.].) For any change in a system from one equilibrium state to another, the heat absorbed by it (dQ) may be written $dQ \leq TdS$, where the equality holds only for a reversible process (T stands for absolute temperature and S for entropy). Thus, for a natural adiabatic process, where dQ = 0, dS becomes positive: entropy increases. In any thermodynamic (adiabatically closed) system, dS can either remain constant or increase; it can never decrease. Since maximum entropy (in thermodynamical equilibrium) is the state of highest probability in Boltzmann's statistical mechanics, and it is a state of maximum randomness or disorganization, the broader philosophic consequences of the above simple equation are considerable.

3. Cf. T. Prigogine, *Etude Thermodynamique des Phenomènes Irreversibles*, Paris, 1947; A. Katchalsky and P. F. Curran, *Nonequilibrium Thermodynamics in Biophysics*, Cambridge, Mass.: Harvard University Press, 1965; A. Katchalsky, "Thermodynamics of Flow and Biological Organization", *Zygon*, Vol. 6(2), June 1971, pp. 99-125; Jacob Bronowski, "New Concepts in the Evolution of Complexity", *Zygon*, Vol. 5(1), March 1970, pp. 18-35.

4. This proposition is expressed by the formula
$$V_S \ll (v_a + v_b + v_c \ldots v_n) \quad (1)$$
where S denotes the whole system; a, b, c, ... n the parts, and v stands for their degrees of variance from some given state that gives a measure of the system's order. See Paul A. Weiss, "The Living System: Determinism Stratified", in *Beyond Reductionism*, A. Koestler and J. R. Smythies, eds., London: Macmillan, 1969.

5. A non-summative complex of interdetermined elements may be represented thus:

$$\begin{aligned} \frac{dQ_1}{dt} &= f_1(Q_1, Q_2, \ldots Q_n) \\ \frac{dQ_2}{dt} &= f_2(Q_1, Q_2, \ldots Q_n) \\ &\vdots \\ \frac{dQ_n}{dt} &= f_n(Q_1, Q_2, \ldots Q_n) \end{aligned} \quad (2)$$

In this system of simultaneous differential equations, change of any measure $Q_i$ is a function of all Q's, and conversely. An equation governing a change in any one part is different in form from the equation governing change in the whole. Thus the pattern of change in the whole complex is different from (is not reducible to) the patterns of change in any of its parts. However, by developing the complex into Taylor series, and assuming that the coefficients of the variables $Q_j$ become zero, it becomes summative: change in each element is unaffected by its relations to change in other elements, and the sum of the changes precisely equals the change in the whole. (Such transformation of a non-summative into a summative complex is not possible in real-world systems without "killing" the system, i.e., destroying the dynamics which maintains it.) See L. von Bertalanffy, *General System Theory*, New York: George Braziller, 1968, Chapter 3.

6. Cf. Bertalanffy, op. cit., pp. 54 ff.

7. A. Katchalsky and P. F. Curran, *Nonequilibrium Thermodynamics in Biophysics* (n. 3), Ch. 16.

8. Weiss points out that whenever one group of components in a system deviates from its standard course, the rest automatically change course so as to counteract the distortion of the pattern of the whole. But how do the components know what happens elsewhere in the system, and how to act appropriately? Since the number of possible departures from an ideal standard course is infinite, the number of corrective responses potentially called for from each component is likewise infinite. It is further compounded by the number of subunits involved in the collective response. Faced without hedging, says Weiss, this problem patently defies solution in terms of the "cooperation" of atomistic, free, and independent components. Instead, we must switch to the concept of *field continua*. "The Basic Concept of Hierarchic Systems", in *Hierarchically Organized Systems in Theory and Practice*, Paul A. Weiss, and others, New York: Hafner, 1971.

Although the question of stabilization around dynamically stable integral configurations in complex systems is still not clearly answered, one possible solution may lie in an extension of the phenomenon of inductive resonance. Inductive resonance was discovered by Huygens in the 17th century when he observed that two clocks which were slightly out of phase when fixed to a solid wall became synchronized when attached to a thin wooden board. The finding was ignored until Van der Pol explained it in 1922 as inductive coupling due to heteroperiodic resonance. The principal effect is the synchronization of slightly out-of-step oscillators under mutual influence. It is found to occur in the energy transfer in photosynthesis between chlorophyll *a* and *b*, in the synchronization of the flashes of fireflies, in the action of electronic pace-makers on the heart, in the adjustment of alpharhythms to stroboscopic flashes perceived through the eye. Some investigators now suggest that it may be basic to the self-regulation of complex biochemical systems. (See Brian C. Goodwin, "A Statistical Mechanics of Temporal Organization in Cells", *Towards a Theoretical Biology*, C. H. Waddington, ed., Chicago: Aldine, 1969, pp. 141-63; A. S. Iberall, S. Cardon, A. Schindler, F. Yates, and D. March, "Progress Toward the Application of Systems Science Concepts to Biology", Arlington, Va.: Army Research Office, September 1972, pp. 65-68.

9. See, for example, *Principles of Self-Organization*, Heinz von Foerster and George W. Zopf, eds. New York: Pergamon, 1962. Also consult Norbert Wiener, *Cybernetics*, Cambridge, Mass.: MIT Press, 1961; W. Ross Ashby, *An Introduction to Cybernetics*, New York: Barnes & Noble, 1956, and *Design for a Brain*, London: Chapman and Hall, 1952.

10. The Prigogine equation states that entropy change in a system is governed by the relative values of the terms in the equation, $dS = dS_e + dS_i$, where $dS_i$ denotes entropy change through the input and $dS_e$ entropy produced through irreversible processes within the system. Whereas $dS_e$ is always positive, $dS_i$ may be positive as well as negative. If it is negative, the dissipation function of a system ($\Psi = dS/dt$) is negative; i.e., $\Psi < 0$. In that case the system decreases its net entropy or, what is the same thing, gathers information ($\Psi < 0$) = (d info/dt > 0).

11. Cf. Ervin Laszlo, *Introduction to Systems Philosophy*, New York: Harper Torchbooks, 1973, pp. 63-66.

12. Herbert A. Simon, "The Architecture of Complexity", *Proceedings of the American Philosophical Society*, p. 106 (1962).

# 3

## BASIC CONSTRUCTS OF SYSTEMS PHILOSOPHY*

This writer has frequently argued for the importance and feasibility of a synthetic kind of philosophy based on an integration of the current findings of the empirical sciences. Systems philosophy is predicated on the assumption that thinking in terms of systems about man and the world is not to force the facts of experience into the Procrustean bed of a preconceived abstract scheme, but is warranted by the currently much dicussed applicability of systems concepts to many spheres of inquiry. We perceive and understand in systems terms because phenomena are perceivable and constructable as systems. (Whether they *are* systems independently of our knowledge of them is a moot question, to be answered only by a God.) The ways we perceive and conceive of phenomena can be integrated in a general conceptual framework called Systems Philosophy. Of course, systems philosophy has practical applications, as well as areas of formal specification, and thus crosses the divide between formalism and empirical theory and practice. In this study we shall concentrate on the pure or theoretical aspect of systems philosophy, and suggest some constructs which are basic in the formulation of a general theory of systems. These constructs can then be used as the premises of a general philosophical theory having the required properties of synthesis and empirical relevance.

All theory construction of the empirical world presupposes that the world beyond human knowledge and experience is in some respects rationally ordered. There can be no theory of a chaotic universe, and inasmuch as we do have theories of the universe we hold them on the expectation that the universe is not — or not entirely — chaotic. Once this assumption is made, we confront the dilemma of special methods and special constructs to deal with particular phenomena with optimum fidelity, or using some general conceptual tools and frameworks to attempt to understand the interconnection of diverse phenomena. The specialist is motivated by a desire to achieve optimum adequacy to the phenomena in his constructs, and

---

*Reprinted from *Systematics*, 1972, 10(1), pp. 40-54.

builds models and proposes theories with an eye solely on the accuracy of the match with nature. The generalist believes, on the other hand, that one does not adequately understand any phenomenon unless one knows its interconnections with other phenomena, and he seeks to produce those general concepts and frameworks which may prove to be adequate for the understanding not only of isolated events, but of general patterns of relationships. The methodological supposition of the specialist would be superior to that of the 'generalist' if phenomena would indeed lend themselves to accurate mapping only through specific laws and concepts. But phenomena do not impose their own categories with finality, and a number of different (and according to Kuhn and Feyerabend, even incommensurable) theories can be confirmed in regard to any set of phenomena. The selection between theories depends in the last analysis on the preferences of the investigators. These preferences are not 'merely' psychological quirks, however, but underlie all rational modes of thoughts. They are the values of thinking with empirical accuracy and yet with heuristic power conferred by economy, internal consistency, and wide range of applicability. Theories which combine empirical ideals of accuracy with the rational ideals of economy, consistency and generality have the edge over theories that sacrifice one component for the sake of others. Those that sacrifice the rational factors become *ad hoc* and their scientific status is corresponding lower (as Pepper, among others, clearly noted). Others, which sacrifice empirical accuracy for the rational component's elegance and heuristic, strain credulity and belong to the realm of rationalist theology and metaphysics. Somewhere between these extremes lies the ideal of a scientific theory, where empirical and rational ideals are optimally combined. Systems philosophy belongs to this range.

The foundation of systems philosophy is the recurrent applicability of empirically precise systems concepts in diverse fields of investigation. Cybernetics, general system theory, information and game theories, and an entire constellation of mathematical and empirical disciplines emerged with striking rapidity since the 1950s. They are not unprecedented in contemporary or even classical thought, of course ('organistic' thinking was characteristic already of Greek cosmologies and reappeared in the modern age in the works of Lloyd Morgan, Henri Bergson, Alfred North Whitehead, Samuel Alexander and John Dewey — to mention only the key proponents), but the empirical accuracy which this mode of thought could now achieve is unparallelled by earlier attempts. The insights of past generations of thinkers may have been as great or greater than those of systems thinkers at present, but they lacked the empirical base of the contemporary natural and social sciences. These sciences give us not only more sophisticated theories, but qualitatively different ones: they are, on the whole no longer atomistic, mechanistic and reductionist, but tend toward the appreciation of wider contexts, general theories, and irreducibilities. Classical concepts and methods still hold their own in contemporary science, but the spotlight is increasingly taken by the sciences which supplant them with systems concepts. We need only to consider such recent and still rapidly rising 'stars' as ecology and world-system modelling, to appreciate this trend.

Systems philosophy is envisaged as a general philosophy of man and nature, using the invariant constructs which recur in isomorphic transformations in the various systems-oriented sciences. The scientific theories are used as anchor points for constructing an embracing philosophy which is no less empirically relevant than the systems models upon which it is built, but is considerably more general in scope. Hence it responds to the *rational* ideal of contemporary science without losing sight of its *empirical* ideal.

Empirical sciences map phenomena from their own particular disciplinary perspective. For example, man, perhaps the most complex of all phenomena, is mapped from the perspectives of biology, psychology, the social sciences, and diverse philosophies, e.g. existentialism, idealism, spiritualism, etc. Each strand of order elucidated by inquiries from these different perspectives tells us something about man. But none does him justice, for man is a biological, as well as a psychosocial entity. In an integrated systems philosophy he can be recognized as such, by taking the ismorphies appearing in the different perspectives as starting point, and finding the invariance which underlies them. That invariance defines man.

When we look for invariant orders we simplify and organize the stream of sensed phenomena. If this process permits us to recover the wealth of empirical diversity by derivation from our model, its simplification and organization confers meaning without essential distortion. If systems concepts do indeed apply to a wide realm of empirical phenomena, the invariances which they code are empirically adequate through detailed application. For example, although the concept of negative feedback control is a simplification and organization of a wide variety of data, it helps us to comprehend the principle of control in phenomena as diverse as the ordinary room thermostat, the sonar-guided underwater torpedo, the instrument landing system of modern airplanes, and the homeostasis of the human body. There is no mechanistic — or even essentialistic or spiritualistic — explanation which would have comparable integrative power without loss of empirical accuracy.

The methodological principles of systems philosophy are represented in the following graph, where the overarching unity of nature within its manifest diversity is heuristically assumed, and the capacity of particular empirical systems sciences to grasp such orders under specific aspects accounted for.

$X_s$ — systems philosophy

$X_1$, $X_2$, $X_3$, $X_4$, $X_5$, $X_6$ — empirical systems sciences

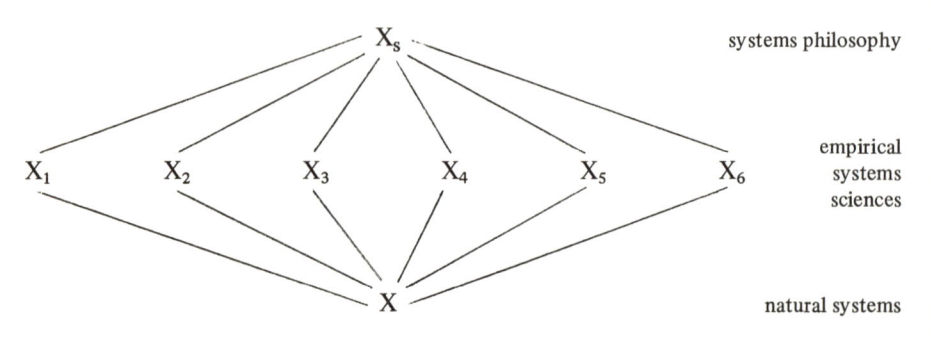

$X$ — natural systems

*Fig. 1*

We suggest four basic constructs of systems philosophy. These were found to be extremely fertile, in enabling investigators to construct a general model of systems, which finds detailed empirical application in empirical fields as diverse as physics, biology, psychology, and the social sciences.

The four constructs jointly define the system's attributes. The set of basic systems we are dealing with are those called 'natural systems', i.e., systems which arise independently of conscious human planning and execution. (Since almost all social and cultural systems arise in this way, they, too, are included in this definition. The primary set of excluded systems are the *technical* systems.)

Let the general class of natural systems be defined by the symbol R. Each of the four properties is given a symbol: $\alpha$, $\beta$, $\gamma$, $\delta$. Then any natural systems can be defined by one particular combination of transforms of the basic equation,

$$R = f(\alpha, \beta, \gamma, \delta).$$

An identification and brief discussion of each of the constructs follows.

## ORDERED WHOLENESS – $\alpha$

An ordered whole is a non-summative system in which a number of constant constraints are imposed by fixed forces, yielding conditions with enduring mathematically calculable parameters. A system of this kind always contains an element of order; complete randomness is excluded from it.

Wholeness defines the character of the system as such, in contrast to the character of its parts in isolation. A whole possesses characteristics which are not possessed by its parts singly. Insofar as this is the case, the whole is other than the simple sum of its parts. (For example, an atom is other than the sum of the component particles taken individually and added together; a nation is other than the sum of individual beings composing it, etc.). However, no mysticism is implied or involved in this assertion. Traditionally, wholes were often considered to be qualitative and intrinsically unmeasurable entities because they were seen as "more than the sum of their parts". This conception is spurious. Wholes can be mathematically shown to be other than the simple sum of the properties and functions of their parts.

The mathematics of non-summative complexes apply to systems of the widest variety, including physical, biological, social and psychological systems. These systems form ordered wholes in which the law-bound regularities exhibited by interdependent elements determine the functional behavior of the totality. The fallacy of reducing a whole atom to the sum of the properties of its parts is well known to atomic physicists; the analogous fallacy of reducing the whole organism to biochemical reactions and physical properties manifested by particular components is becoming increasingly recognized too, and social scientists, as well as social and individual psychologists accumulate evidence every day concerning the unfeasibility of explaining either social or psychological events by reference to the qualities of the individual components, e.g. the motivations, wishes and habits of individuals, and the properties of particular cognitive or emotive factors. One need not embrace a metaphysical holism and radical emergentism to subscribe to the proposition that the concept of an ordered whole which is other than the sum of its parts is not a mystical and unverifiable concept but one which is generally used in the natural, psychological and social sciences today.

## SELF-STABILIZATION – β

A whole is an entity that forms a dynamic balance between internal fixed constraints, which impose its enduring structure, and external unrestrained forces, which mold the structure and evolve the entity. The presence of fixed forces brings about a steady, or stationary, state when all flows induced by unrestrained forces vanish. When unrestrained forces are introduced into a dynamically balanced system disposing over fixed constraints, the system will tend to buffer out forces which perturb its stable configuration.

Inasmuch as both physical and biological systems maintain themselves in stationary states, characterized by the parameters of the fixed forces within them, life as a cybernetic process is analogous to any physical system describable, by our definition, as an ordered whole. But we must recognize that in a biological system the stationary states are not fully time-independent: they are *quasi*-stationary.

The here discussed general system property abstracts from the many varieties of regulatory mechanisms and generalizes the concept of adaptation to the environment through the self-maintenance of systems forming ordered wholes. The generalized conclusion may be stated thus: within a limited range or perturbation, an ordered whole will tend to return to the stationary states characterized by the parameters of its constant constraints. Inasmuch as the systems reorganize their flows to buffer out or eliminate the externally introduced perturbations, they *adapt* to their environments. This is adaptation in a limited sense – a more striking form of it, involving the reorganization of the fixed forces themselves, will be discussed next.

## SELF-ORGANIZATION – γ

We have shown that ordered wholes, i.e. systems with calculable fixed forces, tend to return to stationary states following perturbations introduced from their surroundings. It is likewise possible to show that such systems *reorganize* their fixed forces and acquire new parameters in their stationary states when subjected to *constant* perturbation (the action of a physical constant) in their environment.

This conclusion follows if we consider Ashby's principle of self-organization with some modifications. The latter concern the substitution of 'ordered stationary state' for Ashby's 'equilibrium state' in reference to *natural* systems. Undertaking the pertinent substitutions, Ashby's principle of self-organization reads as follows.

We start with the fact that natural systems in general go to ordered stationary states. Now most of a natural system's states are non-stationary. So in going from any state to one of the stationary ones, the system is going from a larger number of states to a smaller. In this way it is performing a selection, in the purely objective sense that it rejects some states, by leaving them, and retains some other state by sticking to it. Thus, as every determinate natural system goes to its stationary state, so does it select.

The selection described by Ashby involves not merely the re-establishment of the parameters defining a previous stationary state of the system after perturbation, but the progressive development of new stationary states which are *more resistant* to the perturbation than the former ones.

Ashby suggests the following example. Suppose the stores of a computer are filled with the digits 0 to 9. Suppose its dynamic law is that the digits are continuously being multiplied in pairs and the right-hand digit of the product is going to replace the first digit taken. Since even x even gives even, odd x odd gives odd and even x odd gives even, the system will 'selectively evolve' toward the evens. But since among the evens the zeros are uniquely resistant to change, the system will approach an all-zero state as a function of the number of operations performed.

Ashby concludes that this is an example of self-organization of the utmost generality. There is a well-defined operator (the multiplication and replacement law) which drives the system toward a specific stationary state (Ashby's 'equilibrium state'). It selectively evolves the system to maximum resistance to change. Consequently all that is necessary for producing self-organization is that the 'machine with input' (the computer—dynamic-law system) should be isolated. Adaptive self-organization inevitably leads toward the known biological and psychological systems.

The above argument applies to the present thesis with the suggested two modifications: (a) it is restricted to natural (as opposed to technical) systems, and (b) the operator drives not toward a state of equilibrium in the system, but toward stationary or quasi-stationary *non-equilibrium* states. The reasons are potent for discarding the concept of the equilibrium state in favor of that of a non-equilibrium stationary state in *natural* systems: (i) equilibrium states do not dispose over usable energy whereas natural systems of the widest variety do; (ii) equilibrium states are 'memoryless', whereas natural systems behave in large part in function of their past histories. In short, an equilibrium system is a dead system — more 'dead' even than atoms and molecules. Thus, although a machine may go to equilibrium as its preferred state, natural systems go to increasingly organized *non*-equilibrium states.

The modified Ashby principle shows that in any sufficiently isolated system-environment context, the system organizes itself in function of maximal resistance to change in the environment. Its new level of organization is measurable both as negative entropy, and as the number of 'bits' necessary to build the system from its components. Every system produces entropy relative to time. Disorder in systems grows at a rate $ds/dt$. This is the dissipation function, $\psi$. $\Psi$ may be positive, negative, or zero. If $\psi$ is zero, the system is in a stationary state. If $\psi$ is positive ($\psi>0$), the system is in a state of progressive disorganization. But if $\psi$ is negative ($\psi<0$), the system is in a state of progressive *organization*, that is, it actually decreases its entropy or, what is the same thing, gathers information

$$\psi < 0 = (d\ info/dt) > 0.$$

Self-organization conduces systems toward more negetropic states; self-stabilization maintains them in their pre-existing state of organization. In an environment in which constant forces are operative, and the perturbations they occasion are beyond the range of correction by self-stabilization, systems not only survive, but evolve. The development of systems in such environments can be conceptualized as a sequence of parallel, or irregularly alternating, stabilization around the parameters of existing fixed forces and re-organization of the fixed forces in function of increasing resistance to the constant forces in the environment.

## HIERARCHIZATION – $\delta$

Self-stabilizing and self-organizing ordered wholes (systems constructs $\beta$, $\gamma$, $\alpha$) sharing a common environment impose systemic order on that environment. Sets of mutually interacting systems form suprasystems and organize themselves as parts within the emerging whole. The thus formed system can interact with other systems on its own level, and form still higher level suprasystems. Each of these systems exhibits the properties of irreducibility, temporal and spatial order, homeostatic self-stabilization and evolutionary self-organization. The coexistence of systems on multiple levels results in a highest-level system which is hierarchially organized. That structure is the totality of all systems, welded into systematic unity by means of the mutual self-stabilizations and self-organizations of its parts.

The concept of a multilevel hierarchy can account for the manifest diversity of phenomenal properties as well as the multiplicity of structures and functions consistently with the invariant framework of a general system theory. Fresh qualities and properties can emerge in the form of new transformations of invariant systems attributes. The diversity of structures and functions can be shown to be the consequence of the manifestation of some recurrent basic function in particular variations corresponding to the hierarchic level of the system. Such *nova* are explained by the fact that systems at each level contain systems at all lower levels plus their combination within the whole formed at that level. Hence the possibilities for diversity of structure and function increase with the levels, and one need not reduce the typical characteristics of higher-level entities to those of lower levels but can apply criteria appropriate to their particular hierarchical position. The higher we raise our sights on the hierarchy, the more diversity of functions and properties we are likely to find, manifested by a smaller number of actualized systems. Thus atoms exist in greater numbers than molecules but have fewer properties and variations of structure; organisms exist in smaller numbers than molecules but have an enormously wide repertory of functions and properties and are capable of existing in untold variety of structural forms (the roughly one million existing species of plants and animals are but a fraction of all the possible species which *did* exist and *could* exist), and the number of ecologies and societies is smaller than that of organisms but already within their small population manifest greater diversity and flexibility than biological phenomena. It is evident that both the numerical and the functional differences are due to the hierarchical position of the systems on the various levels: many systems on one level constitute one system on a higher level; consequently higher level systems are less abundant and have a wider repertory of functional properties than systems on lower levels. Thus to claim that all systems exhibit invariant properties and types of relationships does not entail reductionism: the invariances express themselves in specific non-reducible transformations corresponding to the degrees of freedom proper to each level of the hierarchy.

Now, the concept of 'hierarchy', while much used in the contemporary natural scientific and philosophic literature, is seldom defined rigorously, and when it is so defined, it is often inapplicable to the phenomena for which it is most often used. A rigorous definition implies a governing-governed or 'bossing' relation between levels, so that a diagram of a hierarchy becomes a finite tree branching out of a single point, without loops. Such hierarchies apply at best to military or quasi-miliary organizations with established non-reciprocal chains of command. But hierarchies have found their most fruitful application in nature, where rigorously unidirectional action is hardly ever the case. Hence in the present use the concept of 'hierarchy' will not be given its rigorous meaning but will denote a 'level-structure' or a 'set of superimposed modules', so constituted that the components of modules at one level are modules belonging to some lower level. Using the term 'system' for 'module', we can speak of a hierarchy as a level-structure in which the systems functioning as wholes on one level function as parts on the higher levels, and where the parts of a system on any level, with the exception of the lowest or 'basic' level, are themselves wholes on lower levels.

Systems belonging to a level below that of any chosen level are called "subsystems" in relation to the system of the chosen level, and the system belonging to the next higher level is a "suprasystem" in relation to it. The relativity of these terms is evident: a given system **a** may be a subsystem in relation to **b** and a suprasystem in relation to **c**. Merely that $(c \in a) \in b$ is required. In this structure of relationships **b** is a suprasystem in relation to **a**, and **c** a subsystem in relation to **b**. We can readily see how a theoretically infinite hierarchy may be constructed in this way. But if our postulates take account of the empirical world as their sphere of applicability, our hierarchy will be finite: although there may be a large number of levels of systems in the observable universe, there is no serious warrant for believing that the series is infinite. (Unless, of course, the universe itself is both infinite and hierarchical — but such an endless series of universes within universes boggles the mind.) Thus a more realistic task is to propose a finite-level hierarchy and identify each of its rungs with one predominant type of observable.

Attempts of this kind have been often made and, until relatively recently, came under the heading of an ontological category scheme (one of the best major systems of this kind being that of N. Hartmann). More recently, this type of endeavor has been taken over by general system theorists, who wish to establish similarities as well as differences between systems encountered in various empirical domains. Thus Boulding supplied key notions of a "hierarchy of systems" which Bertalanffy formalized into a table of system levels, theories and models, and empirical descriptions. It includes both natural and technical systems, e.g. both atoms, molecules and organisms; and clockworks and control mechanisms. The hierarchy we are concerned with here is less inclusive than this, dealing only with *natural* systems, and more rigorous in one basic regard: its levels follow the hierarchical scheme of relative inclusion without gaps or redundancies. Thus we seek to order natural phenomena into a 'vertical' order wherein any given system, with the exception of those on the lowest or *basic* level and that (one) on the highest or *ultimate* level, is both a suprasystem in regard to its hierarchical parts and a subsystem with respect to the system(s) which it forms together with other systems in its environment. Hence, from the viewpoint of a system of level **n**, there is an *internal hierarchy* of its structure-functional constitution, made up of the hierarchically ordered series ... [(a $\epsilon$ b) $\epsilon$ c] $\epsilon$ n, as well as an *external hierarchy* consisting of the structure-functional wholes constituted by its environmental coordinations with other systems, [(n $\epsilon$ x) $\epsilon$ y] $\epsilon$ z ... Since n is situated at the intersection of the internal and the external hierarchies, the number of levels in each defines n's specific position within the objective level structure in nature, ranging from atoms to ecologies and beyond.

If a hierarchy of this kind could be confirmed by empirical data, a basic ideal of science would be realized: the many entities investigated by the diverse empirical sciences would be plotted on a map of hierarchical organization and the theories applicable to them could thereby be interrelated. Such confirmation encounters serious difficulties at this stage of scientific development, as the uncertainties concerning relationships of wholes to parts emerge in all disciplines (e.g. is the 'particle' itself a system of more primitive units such as quarks; is a tissue a level below the organ, or above, or equal to it; is a community of people on the same multiorganic level as a beehive or above it, etc.). But empirical difficulties of identification do not adduce evidence for the inapplicability or falsity of the concept of a hierarchy of natural systems, only for the methodological and observational problems of confirming any given hypothesis about it. The hierarchy concept remains valid as a general system-concept in virtue of the part-whole relations that hold true in whatever area of natural phenomena one investigates. Nature, rather than resembling a machine with all its parts on a par, grinding out the observed phenomena, appears to create self-maintaining and self-organizing systems which, in mutual relationships, jointly constitute progressively higher levels of self-maintaining and self-organizing systems.

Atoms and organisms, molecules, cells and societies — units of investigation which appear ordered in their own special way when approached within the framework of the special empirical sciences, reappear as units of the same general class in a recurrently ordered realm of nature when the special theories are integrated within the framework of systems philosophy. We may never know whether the 'real' world, that ultimate reality which surely underlies all our observations and constitutes our very existence, is truly ordered, and if so, whether it is divided into distinct types of special orders or manifests one overarching type of systematic order. What we do know is that the human mind seeks order and that the more general and simple the order it perceives the more meaning it confers on experience. As long as no direct metaphysical insights into the nature of reality are available, we must reconstruct reality through rational theories with empirical applications. If our theories are optimally simple and general, and yet have optimal empirical accuracy, they are the most acceptable and deserving of the coveted title 'scientific'. Systems philosophy should thus be the appropriate instrument for the development of our understanding of man, experience, and the world in general. Such understanding is elicited by the integration of the findings of the empirical sciences by means of the invariances exhibited by their respective systems models. The here described basic constructs of systems philosophy provide the conceptual reference points for the discovery of such invariances, and the consequent integration of empirical scientific findings. Every set of enduring entities that comes about in the natural world must exhibit the basic properties of ordered wholeness, self-stabilization and self-organization, and hierarchization: these are the very conditions of systematic endurance in a dynamic universe. If we take them as our conceptual gestalt, invariant orders are revealed to us across a wide range of transformations. Atoms, organisms and societies share these invariant orders, and man finds himself in a world which is no longer a stranger to him. The implications of this new way of organizing experience and integrating scientific knowledge are tremendous. A broad and rich field of philosophic-scientific investigation opens up. Its exploration is among the most exciting challenges available to us today.

# 4

# A SYSTEMS PHILOSOPHY OF HUMAN VALUES*

## SYSTEMS SCIENCE AND SYSTEMS PHILOSOPHY

Work in general system theory currently progresses in several conceptual modes, as well as within different disciplines in any given conceptual mode (Laszlo, 1972a). Following von Bertalanffy's (1972) assessment of trends in general system theory, we distinguish two principal modes of theory formulation in systems research. These modes are measured against a scale of quantitative formal mathematical approaches shading into general conceptual explorations. The scale can also be stated as encompassing science on the one end and philosophy on the other. Hence we have systems science culminating in formal mathematical approaches, and systems philosophy symbolizing broader conceptual explorations. Both are indispensable for the progress of work in any field, and especially in a relatively new one.

On the science end of the scale, work progresses in both pure and applied general system theory. In pure systems science, mathematicians and logicians specify axioms, rules of deduction, and theorems applicable to systems as such, abstracted from further empirical considerations. Manipulation of the models permits the derivation of dynamic processes in the form of temporal transforms, which yield a spectrum of possible systemic states. Empirically oriented pure systems science can use such models to map observed or reconstructed empirical phenomena in the light of the concepts, instruments and knowledge systems already accumulated in the given field. Through the use of formal mathematical systems models, both the scope and the problem solving capacity of a science may be enlarged, the latter through the ability of scientists to formulate problems in a resoluble manner in reference to systems models, and the former by leading them to new phenomena, suggested by the application of the models. Moreover, the concepts and theories of empirical systems science become readily extensible to different fields, since the language and its grammar are isomorphic, regardless of the genus of

---
*Reprinted from *Behavioral Science*, Vol. 18, No. 4, July 1973.

empirical fact to which they are applied.

Applied general system theory constitutes systems technology. Here a distinction can be made between the application of a formal mathematical system theory to *map* states and processes in the domain of the empirical world, and to *bring about* new kinds of states and processes in the light of the investigators' goals. The latter kind of effort constitutes the basic characteristic of technology, as contrasted with science where experimental situations may create new conditions but do so only to map the full scope of empirical possibilities rather than to produce novelty in accordance with human goals. In systems technology, theories are translated into operations, and instrumental hardware and software are specified. In order to allow for operationalization, the concepts have to be stated in some formal mode, e.g., in a language which is understood by computers. Formalization is pursued here not as an ideal in itself, subserving the scientific values associated with precision, integration and elegance, but as an instrumental means of achieving the designated goals.

On the philosophy end of the spectrum of general conceptual orientations, rigorous formalization is a limiting case where a theory is already sufficiently well worked out to allow the restatement of its principles as quantifiable axioms. It is evident that before this stage is reached, the principles themselves must be postulated, and their relevance and trustworthiness discussed. It is often a temptation to formalize relatively trivial notions and then mistake the complex logicomathematical apparatus for sophistication and depth of insight. In general, it may be said that the birth cycle of theories includes an initial phase where a basic reordering of fundamental concepts is undertaken in the hope of some expectation that the new structure of ideas will be more fruitful than previously existing ones. Such reordering of fundamental concepts has preceded every major scientific revolution from Galileo to modern genetics (Kuhn, 1962). New ways of thinking are required to confront the challenge of stubborn anomalies or theory failures. The initial task is to free the mind from the shackles of established concepts and theories and explore new concepts and new ways of structuring existing ones. The importance of this preparadigmatic footwork is illuminated particularly clearly in the history of recent physics, where it was exemplified in Einstein's thought processes, as well as in the full range of innovations which led microphysicists to move from the Rutherford atom through the Bohr atom to the modern quantum mechanical principles. A similar revolution took place in genetics, biology, and psychology, and is presently shaping up in the social sciences. Since the reshuffling of fundamental concepts and relations often results in the espousal of systems theories, it is important to keep alive pioneering work in the conceptual arena of systems theory. Such work can have as consequence the emergence of new systems theories in a wide range of empirical systems sciences. Moreover a continued high-altitude mapping of existing and evolving systems theories can facilitate the transfer of information between them and produce a general scientific world picture which is conducive to the exploration of new problems and the formulation of further theories (von Bertalanffy, 1968; Laszlo, 1972b).

Systems philosophy is both a propaedeutic to systems science and a linker of systems sciences. It is a new philosophy of science that preserves the traditional role of philosophy, as integrator and elucidator of scientific theories and world pictures, alongside the new role of philosophy of science, as a critic of fundamental assumptions in the sciences. Hereby the role of systems philosophy is specified: it is not to produce mistakenly rigorous formalisms of trivial assumptions, but to bring to the surface problems and conceptual frameworks which could, in time, pass into the realm of systems science and find quantitative expression. Systems philosophy is the growing edge of systems science, and it must remain diversified and flexible enough to fulfill this function. The aging of scientific paradigms is accompanied by an ailment one may characterize as a hardening of the categories, but this ailment must not afflict the growth potential of a new science. If it does, that science is doomed.

## VALUE THEORY: SUBJECT-ENVIRONMENT INTERACTION

The area of value theory is one of the most important branches of contemporary philosophic and scientific thought, given the widespread breakdown of traditional values and the need for new and more viable value systems. Here we must urgently seek the development of new approaches, and we may look to systems concepts for a more adequate theory. As in other areas involving a major rethinking of problems and solutions, we must abandon useless notions from the past, and learn to look at the phenomena through the spectacles of a potentially more fruitful body of concepts.

Traditionally, values were considered furnitures of objective reality — in fact, Plato's thought can be interpreted as a value theory which places values (such as 'the Good') above the plane of empirical reality. Objectivism in value theory was placed in a more cautious empirical context by Aristotle, was subsequently elevated to a transcendental sphere by the great scholastic thinkers of the Middle Ages, and led in modern times to a complete scepticism concerning the ontological status of values. Contemporary philosophers tend to approach value problems by analyzing the language of moral discourse, and disclaim truth value and correspondence with objective reality for such statements. In its extreme form, contemporary value theory offers little more than a diagnosis of the nature of moral utterances, and is helpless when it comes to distinguishing between values such as good or bad, right or wrong. It analyzes the meaning of such moral words, and the states of affairs, to which these words refer — e.g., wisdom, pleasure, stealing, polygamy, etc. — but can no longer distinguish what values the wise or reasonable man holds, as the Greeks did. Indeed, it often appears that the paragon of the reasonable man of contemporary philosophical value theory is one who does not value anything at all, having realized that all such valuations are but subjective and cognitively worthless expressions of emotive states.

The case for confining philosophical studies of value to analytical and logical inquiries into moral discourse is sometimes held to rest on the insight that value theory is a part of philosophy, and the task of philosophy is mainly the criticism and analysis of presuppositions rather than the construction of cosmologies and prescriptions for human behavior. Thus contemporary value theory stands in much the same relation to the field of individual and social morals as does the (analytic) philosophy of science to science. Unfortuntely, this argument begs the question: it presupposes the kind of inquiries which it perceives as being included in philosophy as the premise which proves the conclusion. Yet there was a main stream of thought in the history of philosophy which sought reasoned conclusions about goodness, rightness, and reasoned speculation about the nature of the world and of man. An analysis of manifest discourse in everyday contexts is a relatively new phenomenon in philosophy — even Aristotle, though he paid much attentnion to the words of his contemporaries, used his observations within the framework of his theories, and used his theories to judge the behavior and utterances of his contemporaries.

Linguistic philosophy, Russell is once said to have remarked, tends to be the analysis of what silly people mean when they say silly things. When we consider the crisis of values today, and contrast the seriousness of the situation with the odd and misguided notions people often entertain about themselves and their world, it appears questionable whether a rigorous analysis of their utterances is the fruitful way to approach our problems. It appears more indicated to abandon the idea that the task of value theory is to analyze the logic of moral discourse and to concentrate on the *context* in which value judgments are made.

Here systems philosophy can offer a heuristic framework of highly applicable concepts. Value judgments can be understood as expressions of the states of the evaluator. As such they become indices of factual events about which meaningful discourse is possible. Attributing value expressions to states of the subject does not mean that we make values subjective. Judgments are *about* objects, even if they are *by* the subject; they express the relationship of objects and subject from the perspective of the latter. Only if we erect an artificial gap between object and subject does this assessment become problematic. In reality, object and subject form a single if complex loop of perceptions, interpretations, memory storage and retrieval, and responsive action. The content of the subject's value-relevant states is the object valued. Subject and object cannot be separated in the valuational act. This means, then, that value judgments are neither purely subjective nor purely objective. They do not necessarily tell us anything about the object valued that could be upheld as valid independently of the subject's relations to it. Value judgments express interactive states. They are human expressions of how human beings relate to the world around them.

The content of value judgments is not significantly analyzable into synthetic or analytic statements. The significant factor about value judgments is not the verbally expressed content, but what the verbal expression signifies. It is an index, or a symptom, of a relational state linking evaluating subject to the evaluated object. In itself it is no more meaningful than the feeling of unusual warmth is in our fingertips when we lay our hands on the forehead of a sick child. Even the instrument-reading of the sensation on the fever thermometer is not meaningful in itself. It acquires meaning and significance only in the context of an interpretation whereby what is perceived is related to the inferred states, as consequence to ground. The concept of fever is not a perceptible datum – it is a theoretical construct. All we can perceive is felt or instrument-read heat emanating from the body. But this perception becomes significant because it is taken as an index of a causative state which is construed to be one of inflammation, somewhere in the body, triggering the defense mechanisms of fever.

Values are likewise indices of subject-environment interactive states in the evaluator. They assume paramount importance when we remember that human evaluators depend on environmental interactions for all their life functions. They are dynamic open systems which must maintain the constancies of their physiology and psychology amidst continual series of fluxes in the surroundings. Their manifest value judgments are indices of how successful they are, in particular cases, in maintaining such constancies through the purposive use of environmental objects.

Despite the many specificities of man, the most important of which are reflective consciousness, language, and culture, he is an adaptive – adapted and further adaptable – system who has traded the structural stability of protozoan forms of life for the flexible cybernetic ultrastability of higher mammals in the long processes of trial and error of phylogenetic evolution. Human beings are cybernetically ultrastable dynamic open systems, dependent for their persistence and development on coping with an extremely wide range of environmental circumstances through consciously guided flexible adaptive and manipulative activities. Their basic goal, upon which rests an entire array of other goals, instrumental and intrinsic, remains the persistence of the organism amidst the multiple adventures of biological, social and cultural existence. Because the cohesive forces which bind the components of the human organism into a single body are relatively weak – compare it to the nuclear exchange forces binding the elements of the atomic nucleus, or even the forces of electronic bonding existing between the atoms of a molecule – the human being, as indeed all complex multicellular organisms, relies on cybernetic self-maintaining and self-organizing functions to assure its endurance. Such self-stabilizing processes range from the homeostatic loops controlled by the autonomic nervous system (which maintains the body's vital constancies), through the feedback processes by which the perceptual form-world is constituted (which in turn has constancy maintaining properties in regard, e.g., to shape, size, relative motion, color, etc.), all the way to the highest expressions of the human mind. As Piaget (1971) affirmed on the basis of his research, even abstract logicomathematical operations are expressions, as well as highly differentiated organs, of organic autoregulations.

## SYSTEMS ORIENTED VALUE THEORY

Values can now be understood in cybernetic terms as objective factors in the dynamic behavior of systems. Wiener, Rosenblueth, and Bigelow have shown in their classic 1943 paper that concepts such as purpose and teleology are *bona fide* elements of certain varieties of systems, those namely which command an internal energy source, in the form of stored and activable energy, that motivates behavior corresponding to a program built into the system. Systems of this kind include artificial servomechanisms, such as radar guided antiaircraft guns, sonar guided torpedoes, automatic pilots, and even the ordinary heating system controlled by a thermostat. These systems are not value free; they incorporate the norms or values which their behavior is deployed to realize. Such behavior can be remarkably human-like in some cases, e.g., in *M. speculatrix*, which is endowed with both positive and negative tropisms, discernment, self-recognition, the recognition of others of its species, and internal stability (Walter, 1953).

The usual objection, that such goals or values are built into the systems by their engineers and hence are projected human values, misses the point. It is not the causal origin of the value manifesting program that is significant, but its actual locus within the system. No system is entirely self-created — human beings are likewise endowed with genetic programs without which they could not exist. In the sense in which human beings program artificial systems to seek certain physical states, the genotype and the culturetype program human beings to manifest certain types of values and preferences. Even the large degree of autonomy of human beings in evolving further values and choosing among those available in their culture can be built into artificial systems of the self-organizing variety. That such systems do not yet exist in sophisticated forms does not preclude that they could exist if sufficient engineering know-how to construct them could be assembled.

The fact is that, regardless of other artificial, biological, ecological and social systems, human beings themselves are goal directed, program pursuing systems. They have a foundation of genetic programs upon which are superimposed multiple layers of cultural programs in constellations determined by the individual and his adventures in the empirical world.

The goal-orientedness of human beings has been recognized by many scientific investigators of values and several philosophers. Among the latter we should note R. B. Perry, John Dewey and Stephen C. Pepper. Pepper's (1969) own value theory makes the decisive step to a systems theory of value, as the following passage indicates.

> Purposive behavior furnishes an excellent example of a selective system. Here a dynamic agency (call it a need, a drive, a desire, or an interest, arising either from changes within the organism, like hunger or thirst, or from external stimulation, like a sudden downpour of rain or a nail in your shoe) presents a pattern of tensions with accompanying conditions of satisfaction. In appetitions these acts lead to instrumental and terminal goals and often a consummatory act yielding pleasure.

In aversions there are acts of avoidance of objects of apprehension and actual pain terminating when there is relief from these tensions.

Here is a dynamic structure of activities. The structure institutes a norm on the basis of the conditions of satisfaction intrinsic to the specific need or drive or desire. Acts and objects are selected as correct or incorrect in proportion as they serve toward the attainment of the conditions of satisfaction for the dynamics of the purposive structure. It is a selective system. And values of various kinds spread out along the route of these transactions. There are positive and negative conative values — and as goal objects are anticipated these are potential objects of value — and there are also objects of potential value instituted in the environment. There are frustrations and achievements and pains and pleasures, all closely bound up with the intensification or relaxation of tensions in the patterns of the purposive transactions. And in the process of achievement the purposive dynamics selects toward the shortest path.

There is no question that such a selective system institutes values and sets up norms for the good and the bad, the better and the worse, within its range of application.

In a systems oriented value theory, where the interaction of object and subject is the decisive element in the determination of value, the specious dichotomy of facts and values disappears. The subject himself is known to be a highly motivated, goal seeking entity, rather than an abstract observer perceiving facts in pristine purity and offering pure descriptions of them. Psychologists have effectively destroyed the concept of immaculate perception and therewith the categorical disjunction of facts and values. In a paper appropriately entitled "Fusion of Facts and Values", Abraham Maslow (1963) proposed the "inclusive generalization, namely that increase in the factiness of facts, of their facty quality, leads simultaneously to increase in the oughty quality of these facts. Factiness generates oughtiness, we might say." This striking statement is backed by analyses from the realm of human personality and organismic as well as cognitive functioning. For example, Maslow refers to Goldstein's assertion that a damaged organism is not satisfied just to be what it is, namely damaged, but strives, presses and pushes — it fights and struggles with itself in order to make itself into a unity again. It governs itself, makes itself, recreates itself. Likewise with the cognitive aspects of perception. Perceived facts are not static; they are not scalar but also vectorial, having not only magnitude but also direction. "Facts don't just lie there, like oatmeal in a bowl; they do all sorts of things. They group themselves, and they complete themselves; an incomplete series 'calls for' a good completion.... Poor gestalten make themselves into better gestalten and unnecessarily complex percepts or memories simplify themselves." From these considerations Maslow (1963) concludes that "Gestalt and Organismic psychologies are not only is-perceptive but they are also vector-perceptive... instead of being ought-blind as the behaviorisms are, in which organisms only get passively 'done-to', instead of also 'doing', 'calling for'." These dynamic characteristics of facts, 'vectorial qualities', fall within the semantic jurisdiction of 'value' and bridge the dichotomy between fact and value, conventionally held to be a defining characteristic of science itself.

The above propositions, coming from a psychologist, include reference to 'facts' as they are perceived and interpreted by cognizant human beings. But it is the human beings themselves who make the facts dynamic, endowing them with their vectorial character. Thus the fusion of facts and values, described by Maslow, resides in the last analysis in the dynamic vectorial quality of organismic, gestalt perceiving and cognizing human beings. Which is precisely what a systems theory of value maintains.

The basic concepts of a systems philosophy of value were mapped out by James Miller (1965a, 1965b). He describes organisms as open systems in steady state, and defines the range of stability of the system as "that range within which the rate of correction of deviations is minimal or zero, and beyond which correction occurs. An input or output of either matter-energy or information, which by lack or excess of some characteristic, forces the variables beyond the range of stability constitutes a *stress* and produces a *strain* within the system" (Miller, 1965a, p. 224). Stresses and strains may or may not be capable of being reduced; this depends on the adjustment resources of the system. The existing strains are called the values or utilities of the system, and the relative urgency of reducing specific strains represents the system's hierarchy of values.

## LEVEL OF ADAPTATION

The here espoused approach to the problem of values agrees with the Pepper-Miller framework in locating the determination of values in the organism-environment interaction. It, however, defines values in positive terms as states of the system specified by its incorporated program and realized through normative interaction with the milieu. Hence we take normative values to be correlates of states of adaptation of the human being to his biological and cultural environment. [One should point out that Miller uses value in a descriptive rather than a normative sense. However, in suggesting that values are defined by the consistency of the system's goals with norms established in the environing social and other systems, his definition of value harbors a normative element as well.]

It is important to note that normative value correlates with states of adaptation and not necessarily with states of increasingly complex organization. Adapted states may, but need not in every case, be the optimally complex, or the most highly organized states. This theory differs from the Spencerian evolutionary ethics, which underlies even a systems oriented theory offered by Boulding (1962) where the trend toward higher organization is also the trend toward the higher good, and avoids some of the difficulties attendant upon the biological approach. These have been summarized by Russell (1949).

> What might be called the biological theory is derived from a contemplation of evolution. The struggle for existence is supposed to have

gradually led to more and more complex organisms culminating (so far) in Man. In this view survival is the supreme end, or rather survival of one's own species. Whatever increases the human population of the globe, if this theory is right, is to count as good and whatever diminishes the population is to count as bad.

Given the contemporary realization of the finitude of the planet and its resources, the logical conclusion of a value theory which identifies value with higher levels of organization and greater complexity is a travesty of the real goals of contemporary humanity. We cannot seek the good in the form of a larger human population of more complex socioeconomic and cultural networks of organization, for human welfare and the absolute size of the human population are inversely related beyond a given point. We can say with Russell (1949), "what humane person would prefer a large population living in poverty and squalor to a smaller population living happily with a sufficiency of comfort?"

Beyond pragmatic considerations of the immediate future, it may also be pointed out that the goal of long-term evolutionary processes is never complexity or greater numbers *per se*. There are regulatory dynamics of various kinds built into populations and ecosystems which keep the growth of complexity within thresholds of stability, and restrain also the absolute growth of the whole system as well as of each of its subsystems. Long-term processes have adaptation as their focal point, and seek the type of organization which is most appropriate for the environmental conditions of the system. That appropriate organization of higher adaptative value often involves a *de facto* increase in level of organization — measured by some standard such as negentropy or information content — only argues for the instrumental utility, in certain widely recurring circumstances, of more complex forms of organization, e.g., for performing receptor, decision, and effector functions. But the level of organization achieved by viable systems is a *product* of their evolutionary adaptation and not their *goal*. Even if adaptation and higher organization often go together, organization level cannot be viewed as a goal of the process. The goal appears to be persistence, which means adaptation to the conditions under which the system can obtain its required supply of information and utilizable energy from its environment. It follows, then, that an amoeba is not necessarily less good than a human being for persisting in a less complex state of organization. If it is well adapted to its own milieu, it realizes as much value as the human being adapted to *his* milieu does — and it remains entirely possible that some human beings are less adapted to their milieu than many amoebae are to theirs. In this systems value theory it is the level of adaptation, and not the absolute level of organization, that correlates with value, and value is always relative to the context of the system-environment interaction. Since such interactions can be evaluated in reference to the intrinsic requirements of open self-regulating systems for energy and information, the contextual relativity of the value criteria does not mean vagueness and subjectivity.

## CULTURAL UNIVERSALS

Adaptation means adaptation to all features of the milieu which are relevant to the persistence oriented programs of the system. If the system relies primarily on the import of negentropy in the form of nourishment, the biological features of the environment are the focus of its values. But if the system requires information related to, but transcending in some respects, the range of biological satisfactions, additional features of the environment emerge into prominence. This is the case of contemporary man, who is a biosociocultural, and not merely a biological system. A human being realizes values if he adapts to the biological, as well as the sociocultural, features of his milieu.

We know of determinate universals of biological adaptation, defined by the physiological capabilities of a viable organism relevant to its growth, persistence and reproduction. But that cultural universals exist in the analogous sense has been contested by the school of cultural relativism championed by Boas, Benedict, and their associates. Yet lately some cross-cultural universals have come to light which define basic features of social adaptation in individuals. Linton (1954) as well as Kluckhohn (1951, 1953) have discovered a number of such universal features of social organization. Firth (1963) summed up the new position in saying, "Some common factors are discernible in the basic requirements of all societies, so certain moral absolutes exist... Morality, then, is not merely subjective. It is objective in the sense of being founded on a social existence which is external to the individual, and to any specific social system..."

Attributes such as courage and self-control, deference of children to parents, observance of incest taboos and of the regulation of kinship relations, and similar factors are found to be universal in human societies; they define the conditions under which individuals are not merely biologically but also socially well adapted. Only if a group of individuals manifest these states of social adaptation is social organization possible. Larger, more complex literate societies codify these states in their laws and regulations, and enforce conformance to them. A socially maladapted individual is thus recognized to be a deviant, subject to publicly approved sanctions.

## ADAPTIVE TRANSFORMATION

Adaptation to the natural and social environment is not a passive process of fitting oneself to the best of his ability to existing conditions. Rather, adaptation is a dynamic activity through which the system fits itself to its environment and fits the environment to its needs and expectations. Adaptation often requires the restructuring of some part of the environment, as a precondition of achieving more complete adaptation to the whole environment. If a university is alienated from the rest of society, for example, through offering outdated programs and a restrictive general learning environment, it imposes alienation on all faculty, students and staff who accept its standard. These individuals will find themselves maladapted to the larger society within which the university functions. It is therefore in the interest of all members of such an institution to make their institution well adapted to contemporary society on all its multiple levels. Only by so doing can their own social adaptation to the institution signify adaptation to society in a wider context.

The same applies, *mutatis mutandis*, to other social systems and subsystems, including economic, political and legal systems. In every instance it is in the interest of the participating individuals to reform the institutional systems and make them adapted to the wider contexts of sociocultural organization. Obviously, individuals who have a conscious knowledge of adapted states on the multiple levels of the social hierarchy of organization have a selective advantage over those who trust to intuitions or espouse arbitrary standards of reform.

The adaptive transformation of sociocultural systems is particularly vital at times like the present when, due to the scale of the social and technological processes, error tolerance in the systems is greatly reduced. It becomes imperative to understand the state of adaptation of the entire array of human social systems to the basic life support systems of the planet as well as to its energy sources and sinks. These global states provide the norms against which the adaptation of particular social, economic and legal systems can be measured (Forrester, 1971; Meadows, Meadows, Randers and Behrens, 1972; Laszlo, 1973).

## ERROR TOLERANCE

We appear to be heading toward an environmental, energy and resource crisis of global proportions. Yet human populations are both genetically and culturally programmed to maintain themselves amidst changing circumstances in their environment. How can we explain the breakdown of humanity's biological and cultural values in our day?

The problem of value mistakes, as that of error in general, is a complex issue, requiring that we take into account the structure of the cognitive activity which is responsible for them. Systems with simple cognitive structures — i.e., those where the linkage between receptors and effectors is programmed by relatively fixed codes — do not make significant errors. Their behavior approximates that of a conditioned or unconditioned response arc with the dependability of the response for purposes of survival being the fruit of trials and errors in the course of phylogenetic evolution. Complex natural systems interconnect the signals that inform them of states of their environment with the signals that activate their motor centers through complex information processing circuits, and these are prone to error. Such systems are endowed with empirical learning capacities, and the freedom to choose between alternative pathways of learned behavior. They thus have the freedom to choose not only the correct, but also the incorrect behavioral pathway, the one which does not lead to the intended and valued state but to another, detrimental one.

Human beings construct maps not only of the states of their environment that are relevant to their purposes, but also of their own goals and purposes. Representations of environmental states, as well as of states of mind, can be more or less faithful. Sometimes they may be entirely mistaken. If the goals are properly represented but the environmental conditions required for their realization are mistaken, basically healthy strivings turn out to have unhealthy consequences. If the goals themselves are misconceived, the very structure of the activities pursued by the system is transformed. Sound value optimizing motivations transfigure into pathological, counterfunctional purposes. The textbooks of psychology are filled with relevant examples.

Value mistakes in individual goal settings bias value dynamics on the level of sociocultural systems. When technology is highly evolved, individual goal setting has rapid and intense impact on the states of larger societal systems. A Baconian view of the role of man vis-à-vis nature, coupled with advances in modern science and supported by a protestant work ethic, can lead to the use of technology to exploit the natural environment in the interest of satisfying short-term human wants. The ideology of a laissez-faire economy, à la Adam Smith, encourages individual profit seeking and likewise leads to pernicious results, i.e., suboptimization on the level of social subsystems at the cost of crises on the level of the whole system. Pursuing goals of national interest, narrowly defined and without regard for long-term consequences, produces still other forms of societal maladaptation, and can lead to tensions erupting in domestic violence and international war.

Human options are large, but the error tolerance of the systems affected by exercising the options is decreasing. It becomes imperative to exercise options in the light of sound information, implementing the basic genetic and cultural goals of human survival and sociocultural development. Pursuing mistaken values, as well as pursuing sound values but through mistaken pathways of realization, becomes critical, not only on the level of the individual, but on that of human civilization as a whole.

## CONCLUSIONS

Manifest values are expressions of the states of adaptation reached by the system in the course of its interactions with its relevant environment. Normative values underlie the manifest values as the values programmed into a thermostat underlie the thermometer readings registering the real world temperature of the air. In a well functioning heating system the readings will fluctuate around the programmed norms. Likewise in a well-functioning human being, the manifest values actually held by him will converge upon the normative values which specify the conditions under which he is optimally fitted to the world around him. But these norms cannot be read off the manifest values anymore than the norms of a thermostat can be read off by temperature readings. We could infer some norms in both cases, but could not tell whether the inferred norms represent viable conditions in the system or aberrations. Psychotic persons and decadent societies have norms too, but to stabilize them around their norms is to reduce their viability. Hence we must look beyond existing, manifest values, to the realm of normative values. In the past, such values were advocated on the basis of personal insight, or speculative reconstructions of the evidence. Today, we can pinpoint norms of functioning in the psychophysical human being on multiple levels, biological, social and cultural. To do so we have to model the human being as a complex multilevel adaptive system, embedded in a likewise complex hierarchy of natural and sociocultural organization. By understanding the patterns of persistence traversing the hierarchy, and the relations of the ecological and societal systems to the physiological as well as psychological growth patterns of the individual, we can define what sets of environmenal interactions represent states of true adaptation for him. This is a highly complex task which for the time being must be pursued on the exploratory level of systems philosophy. But if we succeed in identifying the relevant variables of human biosocial-cultural fulfilment in reference to ecosystems and sociocultural systems, we can realize a perennial ideal of rational thought: the specification of the valuable life, worthy of the human potential. Systems value theory has still a long way to grow, but in mapping out its basic conceptual framework we can take the first step on a road which, while arduous, is also full of promise and humanistic significance.

## REFERENCES

Bertalanffy, L. v. *General system theory.* New York: Braziller, 1968.
Bertalanffy, L. v. The history and status of general system theory. In G. J. Klir (Ed.), *Trends in general systems theory.* New York: Wiley, 1972.
Boulding, K. E. Some questions on the measurement and evaluation of organization. In H. Cleveland and H. D. Laswell (Eds.), *Ethics and bigness.* New York: Harper, 1962.
Firth, R. *Elements of social organization.* Boston: Beacon, 1963.
Forrester, J. W. *World dynamics.* Cambridge, Mass.: Wright-Allen, 1971.
Kluckhohn, C. Values and value-orientations in the theory of action. In T. Parsons (Ed.), *Toward a general theory of action.* Cambridge, Mass.: Harvard Univ. Press, 1951.
Kluckhohn, C. Universal categories of culture. In A. L. Kroeber (Ed.), *Anthropology today.* Chicago: Univ. Chicago Press, 1953.
Kuhn, T, S, *The structure of scientific revolutions.* Chicago: Univ. Chicago Press, 1962.
Laszlo, E. (Ed.) Introduction. *The relevance of general systems theory.* New York: Braziller, 1972 (a).
Laszlo, E. *The systems view of the world.* New York: Braziller, 1972 (b).
Laszlo, E. (Ed.), *The world system.* New York: Braziller, 1973.
Linton, R. The problem of universal values. In R. Spencer (Ed.), *Method and perspective in anthropology.* St. Paul: Univ. Minnesota Press, 1954.
Maslow, A. H. Fusions of facts and values. *Amer. J. Psychoan.*, 1964, 23, 117-131.
Meadows, D. H., Meadows, D. L., Randers, J. and Behrens, W. W., III. *The limits to growth.* New York: Universe Books, 1972.

Miller, J. G. Living systems: Basic concepts. *Behav. Sci.*, 1965, 10, 193-237 (a).
Miller, J. G. The organization of life. *Perspect. biol. Med.*, 1965, 9, 107-125 (b).
Pepper, S. C. Survival value. In E. Laszlo and J. B. Wilbur (Eds.), *Human values and natural science.* New York & London: Gordon and Breach, 1969.
Piaget, J. *Biology and knowledge.* Chicago: Univ. Chicago Press, 1971.
Rosenblueth, A., Wiener, N. and Bigelow, J. Behavior, purpose, and teleology. *Philos. Sci.*, 1943, 10, 18-24.
Russell, B. *Authority and the individual.* Boston: Simon & Schuster, 1949.
Walter, W. G. *The living brain.* London: Duckworth, 1953.

# 5

## BIPERSPECTIVISM: A UNIVERSAL SYSTEMS APPROACH TO THE MIND-BODY PROBLEM*

The universal systems approach to the mind-body problem derives from the general theretical framework known as systems philosophy. This conceptual framework associates reality with function and organization, and not with matter or substance. It builds on the foundation of contemporary scientific theories and attempts answers to perennial philosophical questions by integrating scientific theories within an internally consistent theory of the nature of reality; physical, human, as well as social.

The answers derived from systems philosophy with respect to the mind-body problem differ from traditional answers as well as from attempts to produce satisfactory accounts in reference to common-sense and everyday language. The systems philosophical account does not take the 'facts' of everyday experience and of language as given, although it does take recourse to empirical experience in the testing of the scientific theories upon which it builds. It also does not acknowledge traditional philosophical or theological doctrines as valid beyond dispute but starts with a philosophically clean slate, gathering scientific evidence for the most rational and complete explanation of the phenomena regardless of whether or not the evidence accords with any particular philosophical preconception. Systems philosophy proceeds in this regard as genuine systematic philosophy has always proceeded: by building on the most reliable elements of the contemporaneous knowledge system, and thinking through their implications for the problem at hand in an integral fashion.

---

*Reprinted from *Epistemologia*, 1982.

## THE PROBLEM

The problem of mind and body can be stated as the problem of accounting for 'lived' or 'immediate' experience consistently with the sometimes elaborate conceptualizations of the nature of reality produced *par excellence* by science. Direct experience is qualitative and consists of feelings, sensations, volitions, images, thoughts, and the like. Conceptual constructions, especially of the scientific variety, are usually quantitative and describe the world in terms of abstract 'constructs' such as mass, velocity, temperature, position, relation, entropy, and so on. These constructs are not *derived* from immediate experience (there does not seem to be any way of deriving quantitative and abstract symbols from qualitative 'felt' experience), and it is often the case that the meaning attached to a system of constructs actually *contradicts* the commonsense interpretation of direct experience. (The world, the scientist would say, is neither always the way it appears to our senses nor necessarily the way we would infer it to be from its everyday appearance.)

Thus we face a problem of bifurcation and inconsistency in the accounts given of the nature of reality by science and by ordinary commonsense. It does not help to account for science as a logical consequence of everyday experience since, as Bertrand Russell said, if we assume that commonsense gives rise to physics and physics shows commonsense to be false, then we must conclude that commonsense, if true is false. Therefore it is false. Physics — and all other more rigorous and quantitative conceptualizations of the furnishings of experience — is not simply derived from everyday experience but is built 'from above' through a relatively unconstrained play of the scientific imagination, and is only tested with reference to carefully chosen critical factors of experience, often mediated by readings of instruments. Must we admit, therefore, that there are two disjoined universes: a qualitative sensed universe, and a quantitative constructed (even if empirically tested) one? The answers to this question usually involve a recourse to human nature: the human mind and brain, and the nature of thinking. While it is true that only human beings, in our experience and to our knowledge, conceive of two disjoined kinds of universe, from this it does not follow that to resolve this problem it is sufficient to analyze the nature of human beings. The problem, after all, refers to the nature of reality, regardless of by whom or what it is experienced. The standard formulations of the mind-body problem entail an ontological dualism whether or not they opt for the epistemological one. The ontological dualism results from the implicit or explicit separation of man from nature: it is almost always *man* who experiences, *man* who has a spirit, a mind, a language, a science, a commonsense, or whatever. That man could be one, even if highly evolved, instance of a wider pattern recurrent in nature and relevant to the understanding of the unity or duality of reality, is very seldom seriously considered.

Yet such ontological dualism becomes less and less warranted in the light of what may be loosely termed 'the progress of science'. If there is one seemingly inexorable trend in science in the twentieth century it is the advance of evolutionary theories wich show man to be an emergent 'product' of vast evolutionary trends: not even a final product or an ultimate end but something that arises under specific circumstances and may perish again in time. The human phenomenon exhibits several specificities — such as the use of a highly evolved symbolic language, highly evolved tool-using ability, highly evolved social organization, highly evolved capacity for abstract or conceptual thinking, among others — but these specificities do not imply unique and irreproducible qualities in nature but merely the exceptional development of certain general capacities which exist in potential in all species. Indeed, there is increasing evidence that other species, notably the primates, are capable of grasping and using symbols, using tools, making use of abstract concepts and creating complex forms of social organization (the latter extends over a wide array of species since it can also be genetically programmed).

It is strange, therefore, to witness the survival of human-centrism, and indeed anthropo-chauvinism, in philosophical domains, especially in the debates on body and mind. To consider this problem as applicable to humans alone is a throw-back to Cartesian times when animals could be viewed as mere robots. If humans may have 'minds' as well as 'bodies' may not other species? If 'minds' and 'bodies' are in some sort of correlation, may it not be reasonable to assume that just as the physical-biological organism evolves, diversifies, complexifies and comes to possess a nervous system in the tortuous processes of mutation and natural selection, so mental capacities might also evolve and crystallize in the course of evolution?

In all fairness to philosophers, some did indeed accept such a thesis, perhaps most notably in recent times Teilhard de Chardin (other examples exist, from earliest Ionian nature philosophers to Leibnitz and Spinoza, but they did not have the scientific evidence of the 20th century to back them up and orient them). In any case, acceptance of the evolutionary thesis does not entail an acceptance of the physicalist-monistic position often espoused by scientists themselves. Inasmuch as scientists refuse to deal with 'lived' experience — although they may be constrained to do so, as even Skinner's example shows — they can ignore the intimate universe of immediate sensation and mental activity. But if one builds a philosophical theory based on the integral meaning of contemporary science, with due regard for its evolutionary thrust, one is obliged to integrate the data of immediate experience with the evolutionary evidence, and liberate onself from the anthropo-chauvinism of assuming that the body-mind problem is solely, or even primarily, a human problem. It is, indeed, a problem for all nature, although it may emerge into prominence in certain of its sectors, notably those of the more highly evolved biological, and especially biological and socio-cultural species of which man is the best, but not the only, example.

The position advocated here resembles traditional pan-psychism but is considerably more sophisticated. It does not attribute 'mind' or 'spirit' to all things indiscriminately, nor does it attribute to the selected class of things the same kind of mind without regard to level of evolution, and for the function that the possession of mental faculties signifies for the entities possessing them. Mind becomes a functional manifestation in certain phases of evolution, and not a rigid phenomenon which either is, or is not, present. Moreover it is not something that is created or generated by some external fiat at a given evolutionary moment but something that exists in parallel with what we ordinarily conceive as 'matter' or 'physical substance'. In this way we preserve the basic unity of man and nature, for which we have good independent reasons, without sacrificing the seriousness of the two-universe phenomenon and the array of questions which constitute the heart of the mind-body problem. A science-based philosophy need not deny the reality of mind to man, but can, on the contrary assume its reality throughout nature. That this need not imply panpsychism has already been discussed; that it also need not imply a traditional and rigid dualism will become clear subsequently.

Mind in nature? To the person versed in the history of philosophy a number of fallacies come to mind. Panpsychism is only one. The very concept of 'nature' as conceived in science smacks of materialism. Can we really put 'mind' inside 'matter' without committing the sins of physicalist or materialist reductionism? — or committing, even worse, the sin of self-contradiction, for does not the very concept of 'matter' exclude the concept of 'mind'?

Such worries prove to be exaggerated, to say the least. We first create a concept and then proceed to defend it as though it was a pillar of reality. The traditional concept of matter is one of the most striking examples. As 'inert substance' (more commonly as 'dead matter') it has long been discarded by scientists, but this has not been noticed by the majority of philosophers who continue to use it to denote some kind of physical stuff that resembles Newton's mechanically moving mass and Hume's billiard balls. Yet the concept of dead matter is itself dead. The current concept of matter has little if any of the traditional attributes of substance, and no attribute of deadness or inertness. It comes closest to being grasped as a wave packet or a particle-wave propagation, or as a singularity in a dynamic force field. That such esoteric entities can nevertheless produce seemingly solid and enduring 'material-like' bodies may be due more to the organization of our sense-organs and conceptual apparatus than to the nature of reality itself. An apparently hard and material body may, in fact, be a highly complex and integrated array of force fields with enduring patterns of which some reflect light (itself a form of wave-particle propagation) and resist penetration by equally or less strongly integrated force-fields (such as our fingers). Even such esoteric descriptions as the above do not imply, in a rigorous sense, the presence in nature of anything we could call 'mind'. But they clearly do not exclude it as the 'inert substance' concept of matter appears to do: a dynamic evolving universe can well have 'mental' qualities in addition to more 'physical' attributes.

Yet other minds are never accessible to observation, whether by sympathetic humans or by dispassionate physicists. If this is true even with respect to other human beings (a point that will be stressed below), it is clearly true in regard to other species and the so-called inorganic realms of nature. The question of whether or not there is a mental aspect or correlate in nature is not a question open to verification by simple inspection. It is one for logical theory-construction and due regard for the basic data of the seemingly separate two universes: the qualitative and lived, and the quantitative and constructed.

The philosopher's mind is still dominated by antiquated notions of man and nature, and mind and matter. It still boggles at the suggestion that mind is not the privileged domain of our species. It prefers to separate man from nature to assuming that nature could share at least the potential of mind. This choice is emotional, not rational. It is not shared by all philosophers, and it may be that it will be less popular with the next generation of thinkers. In any event it is worth challenging, and re-examining the mind-body problem from the viewpoint of a universal systems approach. The attempt that follows constitutes but an early and tentative exploration of this field, which holds vast challenges for philosophical speculation and vast promises of clarification of a traditionally vexing philosophical issue.

## THE SYSTEMIC INTERPRETATION OF MIND

The integrated world picture of the systems sciences perceives an orderly sequence of natural systems arising in varied evolutionary processes from the relatively simple and small to the relatively large and complex. This view does not, and indeed cannot, say anything directly about the existence or prevalence of mind in nature. Mind is not a scientific observable: it is not something that can be reduced to sense-data, or instrument-readings, or dependably recurring sequences of sensations — and this despite the strenuous endeavors of existential philosophers who seek to assure themselves of the existence of other minds through recourse to such concepts as communication, empathy, and the like. The sceptic, if he presses his case, can always have the last word: in the last analysis we have direct empirical evidence only of our own minds.

This, however, does not stop us from assuming that we are not alone in the world to possess a mind. The solipsist may win his logical point but he cannot (and indeed should not wish to) stop philosophical inquiry into the nature and prevalence of other minds. Such inquiry must proceed, then, on the basis of assumptions and inferences rather than direct and incontrovertible evidence. Now, the most reasonable assumption is one that is based on analogy: like bodies and behaviors suggest like minds and mental experiences. It is such reasoning which has led to the earlier-noted anthropo-chauvinism that allows other minds only for humans. On the common-sense premiss only other humans behave like we do; therefore only other humans have minds.

But the premiss no longer holds true when viewed in the light of current scientific evidence. All natural systems, in the entire evolutionary sequence, share some fundamental analogies of function and behavior. These are due to the very conditions of existence of such systems: the need to obtain a constant and dependable supply of negentropy from the environment to replenish the energies used up in irreversible processes within the system, i.e. to balance their own inescapable entropy-production. The identification and in-gestion of sources of negentropy (oxygen, nutrients, etc.) entails certain universal functional solutions: sensitivity to certain aspects of the environment, feedback control of one's own behavior vis-à-vis such selected portions of the milieu, the capability of revising mal- or nonfunctioning behavioral routines (whether in the lifetime of the individual by processes of learning, or through the evolutionary sequence of genetic mutations and consequent differential reproduction rates), and the constant control of the exchange of information and energy with others of one's species as well as with other species making up the relevant environment. The universal character of these solutions extends the analogies of function and behavior way beyond the members of our own species to the entire realm of the living, and even beyond, to the inorganic but evolutionary realm which has built up in processes of chemical evolution from physical components and has furnished the template on which biological evolution has taken off.

In light of the above, there are only two acceptable alternatives for the philosophical interpretation of mind. The first is the solipsist's alternative: only *my* mind exists, and all other minds are but hypothetical constructions of my mind (possibly with the mediation of Berkeley's universal mind of God). The second alternative is to assume that mind is associated with all entities in the world that exhibit the same basic kinds of functional-behavioristic characteristics that my body does.

The second alternative is the one espoused in the systems philosophical interpretation of the scientific evidence with respect to the mind-body problem. Its logic is simple but far from simple-minded. I am a natural system and I know from immediate experience that I have a mind. To be a natural system is to satisfy certain criteria (e.g. being a resultant of evolution, being an open system, being a self-maintaining and self-evolving system balancing internal entropy-production with the import of negative entropy, and having the necessary functional attributes to persist, namely sensitivity vis-à-vis the external environment, feedback control over one's critical environmental interactions, and capacity to adapt to, as well as reshape, the immediate and immediately relevant milieu). Thus all entities which qualify for inclusion in the class of natural systems have minds. 'Natural systemicity' is the fundamental criterion of the possession of mental characteristics.

The argument cannot satisfy the sceptic, who can always opt for solipsism and the denial, *inter alia*, of other minds. But it is superior to other arguments based on ampliative inferences, e.g. arguments using similarity of form or appearance, or similarity of substance as criterion. The systems philosophical criterion is similarity of functional behavior deriving directly from the very nature of the entities in question. It is not 'accidental' in an Aristotelian sense, that I am a natural system: it is a basic and essential characteristic. The same can be said of all other systems which satisfy the requirements for inclusion in this class. Thus what unites me with other entities in the world is our belonging to the class of natural systems. Not all entities in the world do, but a significant number and variety qualify. This special class of entities is endowed with mind.

But there is more to the argument than this simple statement. 'Mind' is not a fixed quality which either exists or does not exist. It has myriad manifestations and levels of specification and development. Mind is a correlate of a function: the function of persistence in natural systems. This function calls for an almost constant monitoring of one's own states and conditions vis-à-vis the relevant conditions and events in the environment, and for assuring access to the necessary types and amounts of free energies to offset the constant and irreversible entropy-production within one's own system. This constant activity is mirrored in and for the system in mental terms, i.e. the sensitivity to the environment is 'felt', rather than depicted in terms of electric or chemical discharges and neural transmission patterns. Such primitive 'feeling' (used in its Whiteheadian sense as the primal component of all experience) is how the natural system registers the crucial factors of its environment; and the primitive types of repulsion and attraction are those first specifications of feeling which orient the natural system *away* from dangerous and non-functional, and *toward* beneficial and functional events and energy sources in its milieu (these are the basic tropisms observed already in primitive organisms).

Mental characteristics are built up in complex evolutionary sequences over eons of time, as the internal aspects of the slow yet occasionally radical transformation and complexification of functions in increasingly large, complex and hence negentropy-hungry natural systems. The more precise orientation requirement on these evolved systems calls for additional cybernetic information processing loops and higher levels of codes for storing and evaluating sense perceptions. The systems perceive an always broader spectrum of the environment as more and more things become relevant — though often indirectly — to their persistence in the milieu. In time certain species of natural systems may evolve additional information processing loops which function to analyze sensations and compare them to codes stored in the system. This gives the system the capacity to 'reflect' on its experience, i.e. not only to sense, but to know that it senses. Higher levels of this kind of loops can always be evolved, so that systems can emerge that know that they know that they sense, and so on. Thus we encounter the phenomenon of 'consciousness' as distinct from the more general phenomenon of 'feeling' the world and reacting to it.

It is fallacious to reduce the entire wealth of human cultural accomplishment made possible by consciousness to basic functions of natural system persistence. But this reduction is not necessary to maintain the argument. The genetic origin of a capacity is not to be confused with its existing status and functioning — the contrary would be to commit the 'genetic fallacy'. Consciousness could — and in the light of this argument did — have a persistence-enabling (i.e. survival-oriented) function when it appeared: natural selection favored those individuals who selectively evolved reflective capacities and could make use of them in perfecting food-gathering, hunting and social routines. But the capacities, once developed, could serve — and indeed have served — purposes not directly related to physical survival. This self-liberation of humans from the bondage of immediate survival functions was probably a slow process: the cave paintings in Lascaux had most likely elements related to survival (as rituals connected with hunting) but they also had aesthetic elements. The same goes for the gradual emergence of utilitarian objects with embellishments: their early forms were more directly associated with survival functions while the later forms occasionally moved entirely into the sphere of the decorative or the artistic. *Mutatis mutandis* in the case of language, architecture, social and even moral rules and intercourse, and so on.

The gradual emancipation of culture from the realm of physical survival brought with it the emergence of a culturally specified mind. The latter, endowed with the capacity of consciousness (i.e. having self-monitoring feedback loops) could not only perceive the world but could reflect on it, and could thus undertake activities which had other ends than day-to-day survival. Cultural mind in its evolved form may thus be uniquely human (at least on earth), but the kind of mind of which cultural mind is a specification is not. It is possessed by all natural systems, though in variously evolved form. Chimpanzees, for example, duplicate in more primitive form most of the attributes of the human mind, and there is no reason to doubt that if a sequence of apt mutations would evolve their forebrain they could be capable of speech, the appreciation of beauty and form, the mastery of more complex symbols, and the rest. The same capacity cannot be denied *in potential* to any natural systems, whatever its level of evolution. Mind is not an insertion of absolute novelty into the chain of being at a given point in time or at a given level of complexity: it is there in potential on all levels and comes merely to be specified and evolved as the system itself requires more accurate and complex orientation capacities to assure its persistence. (It is thus far from committing a 'category mistake' to speak of 'feelings' with respect to the atoms of the elements and the chemical and organic molecules and compounds which make up the building blocs of life.) It should be possible to identify levels of mental evolution together with physical evolution in reference to the functional requirements posed by the latter. It should also be possible to understand when and how a complex system, endowed with internal monitoring loops (and hence with the capacity of consciousness) can emancipate itself from the bounds and functions of immediate survival and 'take off' into the cultural realm.

The possession of a mind capable of consciousness, language and culture does not cut man off from the rest of nature, although it does differentiate him within the evolutionary scale from others. This differentiation, joined with the underlying unity, allows one to assert that the human mind is a specific elaboration of a more universal mental capacity found in all natural systems. For all systems a basic postulate holds true: the mental aspect (i.e. the 'feeling' of the world, including on higher levels more differentiated perceptions, emotions, thoughts, introspections, memories, volitions, abstract concepts and constructs, etc.) is an *internal read-out* of the system of some of its critical system-environment interactions; whereas the physical aspect (the energy flows, chemical and bio-chemical chains and reactions and the organic and higher homeostatic feedback processes) is how the system interprets its own body as well as other systems, in its capacity as an *external observer*.

Put more simply, natural systems have two aspects or perspectives: one internal and qualitative, the other external and capable of quantification. In human culture the external aspects have become highly abstracted and rigorously conceptualized, and thus removed from the intimate experience of the internal readout. Hence the two universes. They are in reality the consequences of the biperspectival nature of all systems, dichotomized in human culture into two seemingly disparate and even opposing spheres.

## CONCLUSIONS

Much more can be, and has been, said of the systems philosophical interpretation of mind and the mind-body problem in the literature, but a few observations can already be offered to conclude this overview.

The systems approach to the mind-body problem, joined with the heuristic but necessary assumption of dual perspectives, constitutes the simplest and most consistent account of the manifest facts. Its basic premises can be restated in the following terms.

1. Mental events exist (these are indubitable elements of immediate experience).
2. Physical events are assumed to exist (we allow that the qualitative sensations of our immediate experience refer to 'objective' events which may be grasped in non-mental terms, e.g. through the constructs of science).
3. Mental and physical events are not identical (in the sense of the stronger version of the identity thesis) since they are qualitatively different at all times and circumstances and cannot be transformed or collapsed into each other.
4. Mental and physical events are not causally correlated: there is no 'mental component' within a causal chain that starts and ends with physical energy or matter propagations (e.g. a 'soul' switched into a network of material events).
5. Mental events and physical events are correlated as two aspects or perspectives of the functions of self-maintaining and evolving natural systems. The physical events are never the same as the mental events: they constitute two distinct perspectives. But the natural system *of* which they are the perspectives is a single, physical-mental, or natural-cognitive system.
6. The correlation of mental and physical events is one-to-one but not co-extensive. The range of physical events is wider: not all physical events have mental perspectives, although all mental events have physical perspectives. (There are organic functions which are not perceived or registered in the form of feelings and sensations, while all perceptions and feelings are assumed to have physical correlates in the organism.)
7. Biperspectivism does not reduce, or collapse, mental events into physical events or vice versa, as physicalist and mentalist versions of monism do; yet it does not separate the mental from the physical as dualism does.
8. Biperspectivism applied to the integration of evolutionary scientific theories in the theory of natural systems does not separate man from nature, nor does

it commit the opposite fallacy of reducing man to a mindless organism or robot. It establishes an integral link between theories of man and theories of nature. The mind-body issue is an issue not only for humans but for all entities that arise in the course of evolution in the universe.

Thus, while we started with the intent to analyze one specific problem, that of body and mind, we ended by constructing the outlines of a theory of man and nature, more exactly, of man-in-nature. If the basic premise of such a theory is true — namely that man is not a categorically separate creation but an integral part of nature and product of its evolution — then such expansion of horizons is uneliminably necessary. Suspecting strongly that the man-in-nature thesis is basically justified, it remains to express the sincere hope that subsequent discussions of the mind-body problem break away from the limitations of traditional views of man, and let in the fresh air of the contemporary conception of an evolving universe which contains within its rich domain the potential for all that we experience, the mental as well as the physical.

# 6

## THE RISE OF GENERAL THEORIES IN CONTEMPORARY SCIENCE*

As we trace the evolution of any theoretical science, we come across a noteworthy phenomenon: the level of generality of the theories seems to increase with time. New theories not only overcome anomalies in pre-existing conceptions but become empirically richer: they are interpretable for more phenomena than the old. One way to express this process is to say that the range of invariance of basic theoretical constructs becomes extended (that is, the number of different phenomena with respect to which theoretical entities remain invariant grows). The question we shall raise is whether such theories come about through a psychological preference of contemporary scientists for abstract-general concepts, or through some possibly law-like progression in the development of science.

It has become clear in the 20th century that science does not progress in a simple linear fashion. Scientific growth is not prescribed by nature, as classical empiricists tended to assume. Science does not grow by piecemeal accumulation, as one bit of carefully researched and tested knowledge is added to others. Rather, the axiomatic bases of scientific theories are, as Einstein said, freely invented; only their deduced consequences are tested against experience. And the overthrow of theories occurs not on the grounds that they are not good pictorial representations of objective reality, but that new theories become available which offer corroborable consequences in more respects than the old. As Northrop observed, science progresses from an early 'natural history' period, where emphasis is on field work and there tend to be as many independent propositions and assumptions as there are naively observed facts, to a mature deductively formulated theory stage, where the already gathered facts are analyzed, and then described in terms of the smallest possible number of primitive concepts and elementary propositions. The primitive terms of mature theories are thus significantly more general and integrative than the theoretical concepts of early phases. Because of the propensity of abstract mathematical models and definitions to remain invariant under a large number of

---
*Reprinted from *Journal for General Philosophy of Science* IV/2 (1973).

transformations, there is no trade-off between generality, and empirical accuracy and adequacy. A law, such as that of Galileo, applies to all falling bodies on the earth's surface; Newton's law generalizes this law without loss of adequacy. And the relativity equations yield simple equivalences which are conserved (such as mass-energy relations, and the Einsteinian interval) where previous formulas broke down. The very attraction of systems concepts in contemporary biology, economics, ecology, psychology, political and computer science, management theory and other fields, is due to the conservation of the same (or analogous) open system model under diverse transformations (Laszlo and Margenau, 1971). The significance of formal methods in contemporary sciences lies in the capacity of axiomatically formulated, mathematically stated theories to combine generality with empirical adequacy. Such theories contain relatively few primitive postulates and can be stated with remarkable economy. Compare the physics of Aristotle and Newton. Aristotle required a treatise to describe the several disjunctive motions and natures of the various elements, whereas Newton's primitive concepts and postulates can be put on one page, and the definition of his eight most important defined concepts takes up but sixteen lines. Yet such a simple minimum generates rigorous explanations for empirical phenomena as diverse as the motion of the planets, the swing of the pendulum, the falling of an object to the ground, the lever, the balance, and the gyroscope. Hence the trade-off is not between generality and empirical adequacy, but between generality and common-sense. The mature theories of a science use more abstract mathematical concepts than the early theories, and are further removed from the concrete realities of everyday experience.

Does science evolve this way because scientists prefer, due to some inscrutable psychological disposition, abstract-general theories to concrete-particular ones? Are conversions from one paradigm to another a matter of persuasion to share a valuation for a higher level of generality? Or are there law-like factors at work, which guide science toward reliance on increasingly high-level integrative concepts?

This is the problem to consider. Philosophers of science have not posed it in just this way but have argued instead the reasons which prompt scientists to accept one theory rather than another. In the course of their arguments they have realized that factors such as 'unity', 'elegance', 'heuristic power', 'simplicity', and related criteria play a significant role (cf. Kuhn, 1970, postscript). But they have not singled out the question, whether the growth of science toward higher levels of integrative generality is governed by law or by chance. To ask whether integrative concepts arise due to chance or law is to ask whether they are personal and subjective, or have roots in those basic processes which govern the evolution of science itself.

Our thesis is that the emergence of integrative concepts in science is not due to an unanalyzable psychological preference of contemporary scientists but is an expression of dynamic developmental laws in the scientific enterprise itself. In assessing the nature of this enterprise, we have to take two fundamental factors into account. One is *empirical*, and has to do with the number of different observations taken into account, as well as with the accuracy of their explanation and prediction. The other is *rational* in character, and comes under the heading of what Margenau calls "metaphysical requirements" on scientific constructs. (Non-empirical criteria have been identified by most contemporary philosophers of science, most explicitly by Northrop, Popper, Feyerabend, Lakatos, Harris, and Kuhn. The combination of the empirical with the rationalistic factor accounts for the general trend of development in science, and displays its growth toward higher integrative generality as a law-like process. Let us first discuss the empirical factor, and then go on to consider the rationalistic factor in more detail.

Envisage the structure of science as an edifice built on a horizontal two-dimensional plane, and rising above it in the third dimension. The two-dimensional foundation is "nature" as it is presented to science in observation and experiment. The structure rising above it is the body of concepts, principles, theories and laws evolved in a given science. We shall call 'empirical adequacy' the factor which requires science to make contact between the theoretical structure and nature at all points where such contact is possible (i.e. where the constructs have 'epistemic correlations' [Northrop], 'rules of correspondence' [Margenau], or 'operational definitions' [Bridgman]). Such coupling of theory and nature is to be as extensive and intensive as currently feasible, given the existing theoretical structure. That is, theory should eventually match all relevant observations with quantitative and predictive accuracy. We can picture work designed to bring about such match as extending the structure of science *horizontally*, exploring the two-dimensional field of 'nature' in all directions, and driving down pillars from the theoretical structure above. Experimental scientists are those typically involved in such work, and the period Kuhn calls 'normal science' is the phase where growth of this kind is usually manifested.

In contrast to growth in terms of empirical adequacy, the operation of the rationalistic factor produces growth in the *vertical* direction, adding to the unity and level of generality of the theoretical structure. Work of this kind is typically performed by theoretical scientists, and is most evident at times of 'scientific revolutions', since new paradigms are not only empirically more adequate than old ones, but move at the same time on a higher level of generality.

Development in the vertical direction integrates existing theories and hypotheses within a field of science, or integrates theories on one field with those on others. Such integration is not due to a psychological preference: it is objectively needed when compartmentalized research leads to the development of independent, and perhaps incommensurable, conceptual frameworks. Communication between different specialists in one field, as well as communication between investigators on diverse fields, becomes tenuous and can only be safeguarded or restored through unification of the constructs by reinterpretation in a general theory. In contemporary science, the need for such theory is felt by many investigators on different fields. Wigner (1972) writes, "If we want to maintain the unity of science, physicists and chemists must learn to understand one another, and must understand each other not only in a half-hearted way. The same applies even to the relation between biologists and physicists, and to unite their thinking now appears an even more arduous, though *perhaps* not entirely hopeless task". In a similar vein, Whyte (1949, p. xiii) points out that "Science is in need of a new foundation establishing unity and order in knowledge. Specialized research has long outrun synthesis and during this century has entered realms lying outside the scope of earlier fundamental principles". General theories serve to order existing scientific knowledge, guide further research, and control biases that may evolve in specialized research teams. These points are emphasized by Parsons and his collaborators in their introduction to a general theory in social science (Parsons and Shils, 1962, p. 3). These and similar functions establish the objective need for the work of theoretical scientists in every field of science that, in the course of its development, accumulated empirical findings and independently formulated constructs. Without a logical unification of these components in a theory on the next higher level of generality, development in the science, or cluster of sciences in a domain, would be impeded: the data could not be adequately ordered, communication between research groups would break down, and biases acquired in isolated investigations could not be cancelled by reduction to accepted standards in the scientific community.

The claim that general theory functions to integrate empirical findings and lower-level theories and principles within a given field of science, and/or to integrate the construct framework of a science with that of others, may be illustrated by an example for each case. First, take the thrust of Einstein's work. An internal inconsistency arose in physical theory due to the interpretation of the results of the Michelson-Morley experiments of 1881 and 1887. A combination of Newton's laws of motion with wave optics gave rise to the prediction that the absolute motion of the earth through a medium at rest is measurable by means of the effect of the motion on the velocity of light. Light, however, turned out to have constant velocity regardless of the direction of motion of the body in reference to which it is measured; no movement through a 'luminiferous ether' was observed. That concept became redundant and was eliminated. Theory was left with a wave propagation concept of light without a medium of propagation. If light is a disturbance in a medium, but there is no medium, light is like the grin of the Cheshire cat (Radnitzky, 1971, p. 171). The inconsistency was resolved by Einstein's postulation of a space-time continuum having sufficient structure to account for the interaction of matter and space. In place of an isotropic ether, he substituted a non-isotropic space-time matrix which, as Törnebohm (1970, p. 55) emphasized, shows enough family resemblance to be considered its rightful heir. In subsequent formulations Einstein attempted to construct a unified field theory which would not only incorporate the gravitational field into the structure of four-dimensional space-time, but integrate within this manifold electromagnetic and nuclear forces as well. Thus in place of physical reality consisting of particles and field of force, a single non-isotropic continuum was envisaged, in which particles are 'electromagnetic condensations', i.e. singularities due to high field intensity.

Thus, in providing a continuous medium for light, gravity and energy transport, Einstein overcame the inconsistency left in the wake of the rejection of the classical ether concept; and in attempting (even if unsuccessfully) to produce a unified field theory he gave evidence of a persistent search for further logical unification within physics.

The second example concerns von Bertalanffy's theory (or 'research program'), general system theory. As Warren Weaver, among others, pointed out, classical physics was highly successful in dealing with phenomena of "unorganized complexity", for example, the behavior of a gas in reference to the individually random movements of its molecules. Such theories are based on the second law of thermodynamics, which is essentially a 'law of disorder'. Boltzmann showed that this law could be derived from a combination of the laws of mechanics, applied to the motion of atoms, with the theory of probability. Hence the second law is statistical in character, and postulates that a system will approach a state of thermodynamical equilibrium (or maximum disorder and randomness) because such a state is the most probable one. But in contrast to predictions flowing from this law, phenomena in many sectors of nature show increasing order and organization (and hence decreasing states of entropy). Development in the biological, ecological, social, and cultural sectors is unintelligible in exclusive reference to the second law. To resolve this inconsistency between theories in classical physics, and the contemporary life and social sciences (investigating what Weaver called *"organized complexity"*), von Bertalanffy and his co-workers proposed an inquiry into problems of organization as such, regardless of in what sector of nature they may occur. They called for a general system theory whose subject matter is the formulation of 'systems' in general, whatever the nature of their component elements, and the relations or forces between them (von Bertalanffy, 1968, p. 32). Heeding the call, systems theorists in biology, social science, mathematics, and computer theory now investigate the properties of complex entities which form ordered wholes and appear to be endowed with properties such as self-regulation, adaptation, and growth. Systems of this kind turn out not to contradict the second law, but to constitute special subsystems where Boltzmann's statistical probability is locally reversed. At the same time such research significantly integrates parallel research programs in fields dealing with organized complexity, and provides communication between, and possible unification of, hitherto separate investigations.

Einstein's theories represent an attempt to achieve logical unification through theories of high level of generality within a single field: physics. Von Bertalanffy's theories and program constitute an attempt to achieve logical unification among the sciences themselves, by developing a theory which is more general than any in the particular sciences. The integrative thrust is intra-science in one, and inter-science in the other; in both it makes use of theory of higher level of generality than anything existing previously.

Let us now look briefly at the first three postulates of von Bertalanffy to see whether there are processes in contemporary science which exemplify them. The postulates are that there is a general tendency towards integration in the sciences; that such integration is centered in a general theory of systems, and that such theory may be an important means for aiming at exact theory in the nonphysical sciences.

An important example concerns current research in ecology. This is a field which is intensely worked at present; boasts a high number of findings of the most diverse kinds, and is still in search of a general theory to organize the findings and produce predictions. At present it is not clear whether ecological observations should center on entities, or processes between entities, and if the latter, what their scope should be. If observations are conducted on the interactions between individual organisms, the findings become too complex to permit handling in terms of an entire ecosystem. Alternatives would be interactions between species, or groups of similar species. Further it is not clear what kind of interactions should be singled out as relevant. There may be biochemical, social, genetic, competitive, food-chain types of interactions available to observation in regard to any desired research focus. What types of observations should the investigator select, and how should he organize them? Classical biology gives no decisive answer, since it deals either with the relation of an individual organism or species to its environment, or with the evolution of species through genetic mutation, recombination and natural selection. Just how a set of organisms, or species, functions interactively, and (as it appears) interdependently, is not answered by received biological theory. Hence if ecology is to develop into a fullfledged science it must produce its own theory, to select and organize data, and predict future events. Rather than de-aggregating into a number of vaguely related, and possibly inconsistent low-level hypotheses and theory-fragments, ecology appears to be in process of feeling its way toward a general theory of the ecosystem.

Ecology has become 'big science': the US participation in the International Biological Program receives some six million dollars in federal funding a year (Hammond, 1972). It employs more than 600 scientists, coming from diverse fields in biology, hydrology and meteorology, as well as systems engineers. Research is conducted on five major habitat types ('biomes'): grasslands, deciduous and coniferous forests, deserts, and arctic tundra. A sixth biome, tropical forest, is now added to the program. Headed by different scientists, the research teams formulate the theoretical models which appear to them to have the best chances of leading to the desired goal: understanding and predicting long-range processes in the ecology. Two research groups (working on the grasslands and tundra biomes, respectively) chose to construct a systems model of the entire ecosystem. More detailed submodels for components are fitted into the general model subsequently. Researchers working on the deciduous forest biome work in the contrary direction, from constructing models of finer resolution for fundamental processes (such as primary production by photosynthesis in relation to light, temperature and available moisture, and the carbon cycle in a forest), toward more general models. A third method is used by the desert biome team: the models are designed to answer specific questions and deal with particular problems, selctively ignoring facts which do not directly relate to them. These are fine-resolution models, of limited scope.

Now, some general findings concerning this program have already come to light and serve to illustrate the situation of the science as a whole. First of all, the research programs are found to change the type of observations, and the way they are reported. Increasingly, observational studies are focusing on the material and energy flows within an ecosystem, and on the basic processes which control these flows, rather than on the component entities themselves. Due to the research program, emphasis is on identifying the factors that control the dynamics of a biome, and measuring the flows throughout the system. Obviously, without a prior hypothesis concerning the systemic interdependence of phenomena within a biome, i.e. without a conceptual reconstruction of the biome *as a system*, such observations would not be undertaken. Hence one of the functions of the work toward general models of ecosystems is the channeling of field work emphasis from *entities* to systemic *flows*. Second, problems have arisen in the deciduous forest biome group (which attempts to build its model 'from the bottom up') on the score of coordinating the research program. Fieldwork concerns a number of different models at five different sites, and results in a great diversity of findings. Due to the method of procedure, however, there is no general model to unify and coordinate these findings. The problem of selection from diverse data has been raised from the level of descriptive observations to limited scope models. Its solution could only be effected, however, at the level of a general model of the ecosystem as a whole. Such models cannot, at this time, be adequately tested, and many scientists estimate that several more years of research will be needed to produce tested general models having predictive capability. In the meanwhile, work proceeds either through more loosely constructed general models, or through subsidiary models proposed as components of a yet to be constructed general one. Regardless of the diversity of the specific approaches, however, the overall thrust of the research program unmistakably demonstrates that von Bertalanffy's assessment is correct: there is a general tendency toward integration; such integration is centered in a systems theory, and such theory proves itself to be an important means of achieving exact theory in the nonphysical sciences. Similar examples could be drawn from current work in sociology (functionalism), psychology (personality theory), cultural anthropology (structuralism), economics, organization and management theory, and related fields.

Consequently the dynamics of scientific development includes gains in levels of integrative generality as a law-like, rather than as a random or chance-governed factor. Such gains come about at all times, but are relatively insignificant in magnitude in periods of normal science. It is when persistent anomalies pulverize the integrative heuristic of an existing theory, and when research centers on relatively new types of phenomena (such as 'ecosystems') that scientific theory is vertically extended to those higher levels of generality where the bits and pieces of lower-level theory can be integrated. The overall dynamics of such progression is illustrated in Figures (i) to (v).

The level of integration and generality explored in the past by speculative metaphysicians from their armchairs is now becoming the domain of mathematical natural and social scientists. In the second half of the 20th century, seeking integrative concepts of high generality is not just indulging one's metaphysical fancy, but a valid scientific research program. Maslow points out that holistically thinking persons are healthy, self-actualizing individuals, while persistent atomistic thinking may signify a mildly psychopathological state. At the present time in history holistically thinking people are not just healthy as individuals; they may also be good theoretical scientists. While holistic thinking is not a sufficient condition of

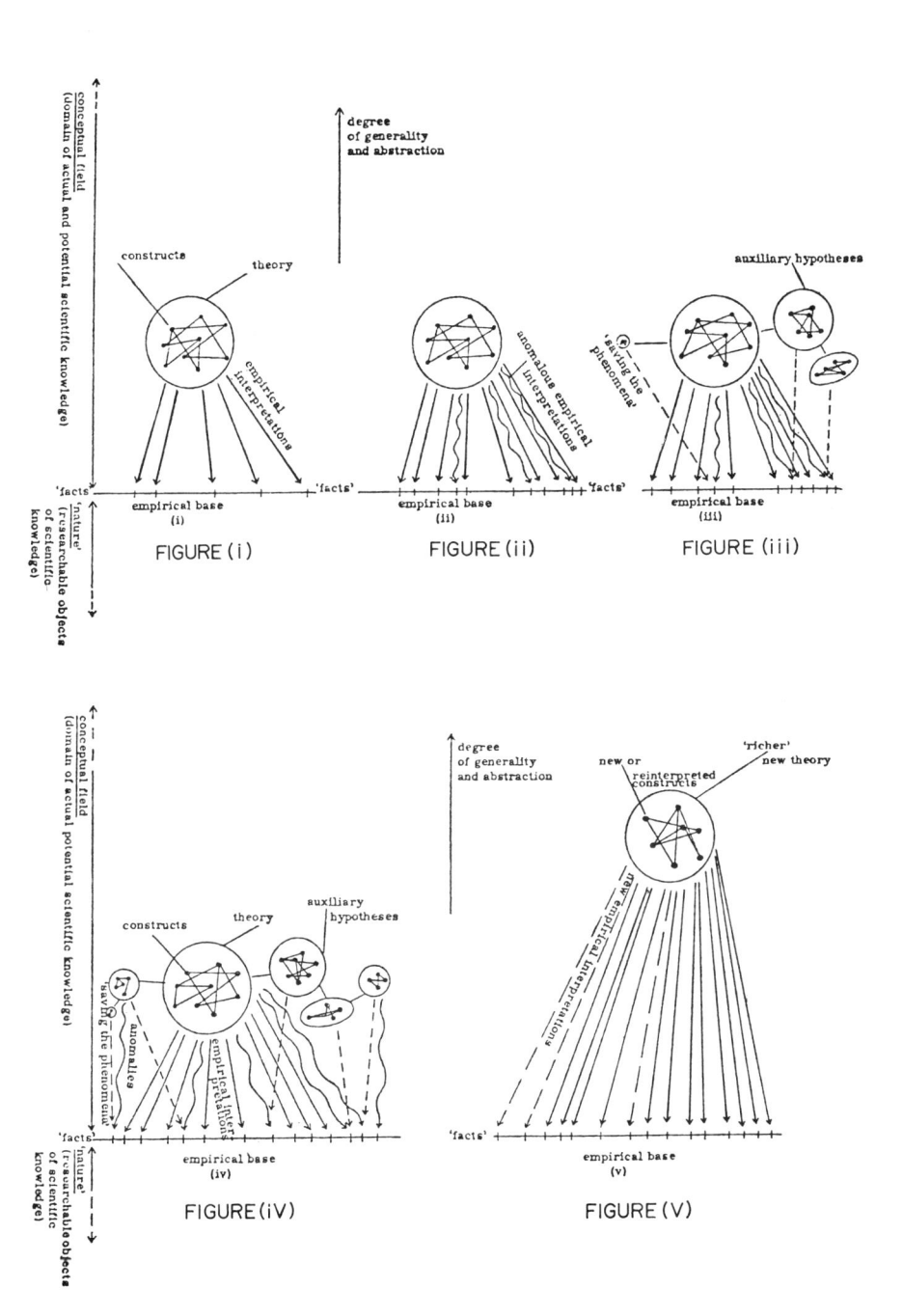

*The Rise of General Theories in Contemporary Science* 79

FIGURE (i)

FIGURE (ii)

FIGURE (iii)

FIGURE (iv)

FIGURE (v)

being a great scientific theoretician, it does appear to be its necessary condition. And this conclusion is directly contrary to the assertions of positivists and 'careful' analysts, who have ruled integrative concepts out of science as meaningless metaphysics, and referred persons seeking unity and wholeness in phenomena to psychoanalysis.

## REFERENCES

von Bertalanffy (1968): *General System Theory. Foundations – Development – Application, op. cit.*
Einstein (1934): *The World As I See It.* Covici-Friede, 1934.
Hammond (1972): 'Ecosystem Analysis: Biome Approach to Environmental Research. *Science* 175, No. 4017, 46-48.
Kuhn (1970): *The Structure of Scientific Revolutions* (2nd edition), *op. cit.*
Lakatos (1970): 'Falsification and the Methodology of Scientific Research Programmes, in Lakatos and Musgrave (eds.): *Criticism and the Growth of Knowledge.*
Laszlo (1973): *Introduction to Systems Philosophy: Toward a New Paradigm of Contemporary Thought, op. cit.*
Laszlo (1972): 'A General Systems Model of the Evolution of Science', *Scientia*, May-June.
Laszlo and Margenau (1971): 'The Emergence of Integrative Concepts in Contemporary Science', *XIIIth International Congress of the History of Science* (in Russian); *Philosophy of Science*, June (in English).
Margenau (1950): *The Nature of Physical Reality.*
Margenau (1961): *Open Vistas: Philosophical Perspectives of Modern Science.*
Northrop (1950): 'The Problem of Integrating and the Method of Its Solution', in *The Nature of Concepts, Their Interrelation and Role in Social Structure.*
Northrop (1962): 'Towards a Deductively Formulated and Operationally Verifiable Comparative Cultural Anthropology', in: *The Determination of the Philosophy of a Culture; Burg Wartenstein Symposium No. 21.*
Parsons and Shils (1962): *Toward a General Theory of Action*, Parsons and Shils (eds.).
Popper (1959): *Logic of Scientific Discovery.*
Popper (1963): *Conjectures and Refutations.*
Radnitzky (1971): 'Theorienpluralismus – Theorienmonismus: Einer der Faktoren, die den Forschungsprozess beeinflussen und die selbst von Weltbildannahmen abhängig sind', in: Diemer (ed.): *Der Methoden- und Theorienpluralismus in den Wissenschaften.*
Rapoport (1972): 'The Search for Simplicity', in Laszlo (ed.): *The Relevance of General Systems Theory.*
Törnebohm (1970): 'Two Studies Concerning the Michelson-Morley Experiment', *Foundations of Physics*, 1, 47-56.
Whyte (1949): *The Unitary Principles in Physics and Biology.*
Wigner (1972): 'On Some of Physics' Problems', in Laszlo and Sellon (eds.): *Vistas in Physical Reality: A Festschrift for Henry Margenau Margenau.*

# 7

# THE APPLICATION OF GENERAL SYSTEM MODELS IN THE THEORY OF SCIENTIFIC DEVELOPMENT*

## THE PROBLEM OF PREDICTABILITY OF SCIENTIFIC DEVELOPMENT

The predictability of the future course of scientific development is contested today on the grounds that the growth of science is neither a fully rational process, nor do we have any knowledge of nature independently of science for use as a standard in comparing successive scientific theories. Popper emphasizes the unavailability of objective truth but believes in the logic of scientific development. Kuhn contests both the availability of objective truth and the rationality of scientific progress. Lakatos softens the Popperian logic of testability by showing that no single observation or lower-level hypothesis ever falsifies a theory. Feyerabend deepens Kuhn's irrationalistic relativism by denying that scientific development even lets itself be categorized into 'normal' and 'extraordinary' phases of development. Phenomenologically oriented philosophers search for the explanation of scientific development in the heuristic structure of science resulting upon the intentionality of scientists vis-à-vis their objects of investigation. In the process of contemporary theorizing, nature as criterion of science recedes increasingly further into the background, and logic and reason are pressed into progressively more restricted corners.

Contemporary Marxist philosophers of science, on the other hand, affirm their belief in the rational and discoverable laws which guide the progress of science. Kedrov suggests that there are genuine laws of scientific development although we are not yet in possession of them. These laws are not simply laws of nature but are specific to science itself. One such law is that science progresses over three stages: an empirical stage, in which information concerning the HOW of processes is gathered; a theoretical stage of interpretation aimed at learning WHY concrete processes evolve along specific lines; and a prognostic stage where the prediction of future events becomes possible. In the theory of science — a 'science of science' —

---

*Reprinted from *Advances in Cybernetics and Systems Research*, 1973.

the highest stage is that in which valid predictions of the future growth of science are offered.[1]

The desirability of predicting the future course of science is evident. But on what grounds can such predictions be produced? Marxists take an essentially realist position and speak of the accumulation of objective knowledge in the history of human praxis. Non-Marxist thinkers do not believe themselves possessed of absolutely true knowledge concerning the nature of reality. They seek therefore to exhibit the past history of science as a process somewhat analogous to biological evolution in the classical Darwinian view. Conscious rationality is not called upon in the explanation of the evolution of species and yet such evolution discloses recognizable patterns. If the choice among alternative, and perhaps incommensurable, theories whereby science evolves is not based on conscious rationality, it can nevertheless disclose regularities similar to those of biological evolution. It is not necessary that scientists should be in possession of the truth about reality to evaluate their theories, nor is it needed that they base their choices on logical reasons. It is enough that alternative theories be produced by them, and that they select from them those that 'survive'. But, although such evolutionary models can explain why science progressed the way it did in the past, they cannot predict how science will progress in the future. The failure is intrinsic to the Darwinian evolutionary model itself.

## THE FAILURE OF CLASSICAL EVOLUTIONARY MODELS

Holton writes concerning 'mutations' in science: "In the case of biological species ... the process of mutation is made possible by various chemical and physical influences on the genes, and on chromosome partition and recombination; in science mutations are assured by its essential freedom and by the boundless curiosity of the human mind ...". Natural selection takes place in science no less than in biology: "The survival of a variant under the most diverse and adverse conditions is mirrored in science by the survival of those discoveries and concepts that find usefulness in the greatest variety of further applications – of those conceptual schemes that withstand the constant check against experience."[2]

A wide variety of otherwise dissimilar points of view converge under the concept of classical evolution theory. Popper agrees that the concept of natural selection is applicable to the growth of science. The aim of scientific method is "to select the one (theory) which is by comparison the fittest, by exposing them all to the fiercest struggle for survival". "We choose the theory which best holds its own in competition with other theories; the one which, by natural selection, proves itself the fittest to survive."[3] Popper's concept of 'conjectures' offers a close parallel to the process of mutation. Conjectures are relatively 'blind' – Popper speaks of them as 'guesses', 'anticipations, rash and premature' and even as 'prejudices'. The test of a theory is not the meaningfulness of the conjectures, but the degree to which they can be corroborated. This makes the growth of science a quasi-biological process of relatively random variation and fierce competitive selection.

Kuhn likewise subscribes to the classical biological model in general terms. He describes 'verification' as "natural selection: it picks out the most viable among the actual alternatives in a particular historical situation".[4] Selection is undertaken by a sociological community of scientists with predominant shared values and standards. Some of these are widely shared, such as accuracy of prediction, the balance between esoteric and everyday subject matter, and the number of different problems solved.[5] Through the application of values of this kind, members of scientific communities pick out the mutants which they prefer and adopt them as their new framework for experimentation and exploration. Successive frameworks may be incommensurable and be chosen not by a comparison (which is logically impossible) but by reference to preferences dictated by the dominant values.

Toulmin criticizes Kuhn for exaggerating the discontinuities in science and proposes instead to treat revolutions as units of *variation* in the development of science. Thus the question 'How do revolutions occur in science?' has to be reformulated as two distinct groups of questions. "On the one hand we must ask, 'What factors determine the number and nature of theoretical variants proposed for consideration in a particular science during a period?' — the counterpart, in biological evolution, to the genetical question about the origin of mutant forms. On the other hand we must ask, 'What factors and considerations determine which intellectual variants win acceptance, to become established in the body of ideas which serves as the starting-point for the next round of variations?' — the counterpart to biological questions about selection."[6]

The above cluster of theories constitutes samples of contemporary attempts to fit the past development of science into a theoretical framework without calling upon either rationality as a motive force of the process, or on nature as its yardstick. The failure of the theories lies in their inability to predict future developments in the sciences. This is a failure of the model itself: classical Darwinian theory is intrinsically incapable of generating predictions concerning the future course of the processes it explains. Statistical laws based on this theory cannot predict the actual occurrence of mutation, selection, or of any given factor in the developmental process relative to specific points in space and time. The occurrence of mutations is not subject to any laws formulated in the theory, and the coincidence of the chance mutations with environmental factors, which confer selective value on the mutants, is free from discoverable correlations. Mutations are entirely random with respect to natural selection, and the dynamics of the environmental factors which select for the fittest mutants are random with respect to the occurrence of the mutations. Since all relevant factors are randomly coordinated, the course of evolution in any particular case is governed by chance. Although causal explanations of past events can be given, extrapolations to future events are blocked by the structure of the theory.

However, at least two basic considerations are overlooked in the application of classical Darwinian theory to the process of scientific development.

One consideration comes from within biology itself: advanced theoreticians question the adequacy of Darwinian theory and are gradually replacing it with some form of organismic or systems theory. The clash of the classical and new viewpoints comes clearly to the fore in Dobzhansky's review of Monod's *Chance and Necessity*[7]. Dobzhansky, a pioneer of the organismic viewpoint, disagrees with Monod's conclusion that evolution is the result of pure chance — a conclusion reached on the basis of the mechanistic-materialistic philosophy still shared by many members of the present establishment in biology. In Dobzhansky's words, "Mutation and recombination link with natural selection to form a cybernetic system that maintains or enhances the internal teleology, that is, the harmony between a living species and its environments". Neither mankind nor any biological species evolved by pure chance, although from this it does not follow that they were the result of predetermination in nature. But the concepts 'chance' and 'necessity' are not applicable concepts in biological evolution: they fuse into what Dobzhansky calls a "unique creative system" based on the systematic relatedness of 'blind' mutation with recombination and natural selection in a self-directed (but not predetermined) evolving system.

The second factor overlooked in the application of classical evolutionary theory to scientific development is that developmental factors in science are neither random, nor unconnected. Even more clearly than in the still contested domain of biological evolution, scientific evolution is not the domain of pure chance resulting from the operation of random processes. Mutations themselves may be blind with respect to the needs of the species on which they operate, but theory innovations in science are not blind in regard to the needs of the science wherein they are proposed. To call such innovations 'random' is to exaggerate beyond bounds what Holton calls science's "essential freedom and ... the boundless curiosity of the human mind". If theory innovation was due to such factors, the development of science would be as unpredictable and chance-governed as Monod's view of biological evolution. However, while curiosity has its place in scientific research and some breakthroughs have been due to 'serendipity' (e.g. the discovery of X-rays and of the photoelectric effect), on the whole innovations have not been disconnected from the problems and accomplishments of pre-existing theories. The latter define both the problems and the likely solutions, and it is the breakdown of such solutions that brings forth attempts at theory innovation. Thus, unlike in biological evolution, there is a relatively direct causal connection between the field of theory testing and specification, and the process of changing the theories themselves.

The reason for the close coupling of 'selection' and 'mutation' in science is not hard to find, although it has been ignored by most investigators. In organic evolution it is the genotype that mutates while the phenotype is exposed to natural selection and the genotypic and phenotypic space is interconnected by a complex transmission field which Waddington calls the "epigenetic landscape". However, in science it is the theoretical structure which 'mutates', and it is likewise the theoretical structure which is exposed to 'natural selection' in the form of testing, specification, and criticism. Hence selection pressures are exerted directly on the source of the mutations. This changes the mechanism of scientific development from a direct parallel to biological evolution: it eliminates the possibility that theory-innovation (the scientific equivalent of mutation) is 'blind' or 'random' with respect to theory testing. Of course, the organismic view of evolution acknowledges that mutation and selection are not entirely disconnected even in biological evolution. Every population of organisms has to solve the problem of maintaining an information store which is sufficiently unreactive to be reliable, and yet remains responsive to changes in environmental conditions. The biological solution is to endow the genetic material with a residual activity that is independent from selection pressures. Thus the genotype can constantly bring forth new mutations which are tested on the phenotype. This, as biologists point out, is a most efficient mechanism for ensuring adaptability coupled with continuity in species. In science the link between the source and the testing of mutations is much closer. Science solves the problem of continuity coupled with adaptability by combining what Feyerabend calls the 'principle of tenacity' with the 'principle of proliferation'.[8] Established theories are defended even in the face of adverse criticism, but alternative theories are at the same time produced by other members of the community. The processes of theory-proliferation and theory-adherence are closely linked. There is a direct interaction between the tenacious champions of dominant theories and the audacious proliferators of alternatives. The causal interaction is by no means simple, but it is clearly different from the dynamics of biological evolution as conceived in classical Darwinian theory.

## A GENERAL SYSTEM MODEL OF SCIENCE

General system models achieve increasing importance in contemporary biology and are likewise applied to analogous processes of development in economics, psychology, sociology, international relations, anthropology, and philosophy. Such models conceive of their subject matter as constituted by complex open systems interacting with their environment. Their applicability to the phenomena of scientific development has not been exhaustively investigated, although some beginnings have already been made.[9]

The evolutionary hypothesis outlined here constitutes another attempt to use general system models to explain and predict the overall dynamics of scientific growth. Models of this kind conceive of growth as the interaction of system and environment, determined by potentials inherent in the system and actualized to various degrees by inputs from its environment. Hence if the principal factors controlling the system's parameters and their reactivity to environmental inputs are known, systems models can not only explain the past patterns of development of the system *ex post facto*, but predict the general characteristics of its future states. The intrinsic limitations of the classical Darwinian model do not apply to general system models.

At first glance the notion of science as a system seems far fetched. It may arouse the suspicion that here is another area in which phenomena are forced into the Procrustean bed of systems analysis. On reflection, however, systems models of science are no more (and no less) arbitrary than organismic theories in biology, functionalism in sociology, personality system theory in psychology, and systems models of a wide range of economic, societal and cultural phenomena. Systems models are high-level general theories to be tested by their deduced consequences, and their validity is determined by the precision with which they account for phenomena, past, present, and future. Their intrinsic elegance, as highly integrated general frameworks, recommends them for serious consideration. If they surpass other, non-system theories applied to the same set of phenomena in empirical adequacy, no further warrant is required for embracing them, at least until such a time as a more general, or empirically more adequate, theory appears on the scene.

We first choose a general system model for consideration, and then interpret it specifically for science.

## PREMISES OF THE SYSTEMS MODEL

The model we choose is that of a self-organizing system. Such systems are necessarily open since they require a means to import negentropy (or information) to offset the statistically irreversible tendency of closed systems to maximize disorder (in the thermodynamic sense). Self-organizing systems in the physical world process energy and counteract the second law of thermodynamics in locally reversing the increase of entropy. Non-physical self-organizing systems (such as systems of personality, cognition, culture and, *inter alia*, science) process, store, and retrieve information, rather than energy. In such systems the quantity that increases over time is information, measured in 'bits'. Consequently we say that states of progressive self-organization correlate with the negative of entropy in energy-processing systems, and information content in information-processing ones.

Focus on the strategic level of the whole system is extraordinarily fertile. Bronowski can outline the processes of evolution in their most general form in these terms, and account for the local reversal of entropy in the self-organizing systems. the local reversal of entropy in self-organizing systems.

> 'The Second Law describes the statistics of a system around equilibrium whose configurations are all equal, and it makes the obvious remark that chance can only make such a system fluctuate around its average. There are no stable states in such a system, and there is therefore no stratum that can establish itself; the system stays around its average only by a principle of indifference, because numerically the most configurations are bunched around the average.
> But if there are hidden relations in the system on the way to equilibrium which cause some configurations to be stable, the statistics are changed. The preferred configurations may be unimaginably rare; nevertheless, they present another level around which the system can bunch, and there is now a counter-current or tug-of-war within the

system between this level and the average. Since the average has no inherent stability, the preferred stable configuration will capture members of the system often enough to change the distribution; and, in the end, the system will be established at this level as a new average. In this way, local systems of a fair size can climb up from one level of stability to the next, even though the configuration at the higher level is rare. When the higher level becomes the new average, the climb is repeated to the next higher level of stability; and so on up the ladder of strata.

So, contrary to what is usually said, the Second Law of Thermodynamics does not fix an arrow in time by its statistics alone. Some empirical condition must be added to it before it can describe time (or anything else) in the real world, where our view is finite.

When there are hidden strata of stability, one above the other, as there are in our universe, it follows that the direction of time is given by the evolutionary process that climbs them one by one . . . . What evolution does is to give the arrow of time a barb which stops it from running backward; and once it has this barb, the chance play of errors will take it forward of itself.' [12]

The general model of system we choose for consideration can be restated as follows. We take a whole system which is sufficiently complex and large to pass through a series of intermediary states on its way to equilibrium. Allow that some of the intermediary states have more stability than others, i.e. can be maintained as quasi-stationary states for a relatively extended period of time. Cut the system in two, and call one part 'open system' and the rest 'environment'. You will find that the open system organizes itself through a series of equilibrium states to states where it is able to resist disturbance from its environment. As the whole system goes to equilibrium, its open system component becomes fully adapted to its environment.

## INTERPRETATION OF THE MODEL FOR SCIENCE

We conceive of the observable and inferable universe as 'environment' and of the knowledge systems and values of scientific communities as 'open systems'. We call the former 'nature' and the latter 'science' for short. If we allow the whole system (nature + science) to progress toward equilibrium, we find that science becomes progressively more resistant to disturbance from nature. The 'ideal' or 'perfect' science would be fully adapted to nature, i.e. it could explain and predict all empirical inputs.

Next we allow that science is endowed with subsidiary equilibria, represented by organizations of constructs ('theories') which are relatively impervious to disturbance from nature. The strata of equilibria are not uniquely determined by resistance to disturbance by nature but are co-determined by the ideals of science held by the investigators. Thus inputs from nature impact on a state of science which is governed by internal constraints. The match or mis-match of the empirical input with the internally constrained existing theory results either in the confirmation of the theory, or its disconfirmation. In the latter event science organizes itself to the next state of possible equilibrium, given by a kind of theory which can absorb the disturbing empirical input and still correspond to the ideals of science of the investigators.

$$\begin{array}{ccc} \text{empirical input} \longrightarrow & \text{existing theory} \longrightarrow & \text{maintained or new} \\ \downarrow & \uparrow & \text{state of equilibrium} \\ & \text{ideals of science} & \end{array}$$

The 'ideals of science' which specify the 'equilibrium states of science' consonantly with the theory's compatibility with nature can be defined in reference to invariant values possessed by the scientific community. Two basic values are chosen here as determinant: *empirical adequacy* ($A$), and *integrative generality* ($G$). Empirical adequacy is a measure of the number of facts accounted for by the science, and the precision, detail, and predictive power whereby it provides its account. It corresponds roughly to Popper's concept of a theory's verisimilitude, without drawing on his concept of truth. It also corresponds to Kuhn's notion of puzzle-solving ability when the number of puzzles and the precision of their solution is taken into account rather than the elegance, consistency, or generality of the conceptual tools whereby the solutions are proposed. Integrative generality ($G$) is a measure of the internal consistency, elegance and 'neatness' of the explanatory framework. It is determinable in reference to the number of separate assumptions made in a theory concerning its subject matter. Generality increases proportionately to the range of application of the basic existential assumptions and hypotheses. The smaller the number of such hypotheses in relation to a constant number of facts explained, the higher the generality of the theory. A balance between the two factors, ($E$), represents a state of theory where the optimum precision is reached with regard to the largest number of facts by deduction from the smallest number of existential assumptions. Two scientific theories, $t_1$ and $t_2$ can be compared in regard to the degree to which they satisfy $(A/G)^E$ by determining the number of facts taken into account, the precision of the accounting, and the economy whereby it is produced. A scientific theory can be compared to an extra-scientific one by determining that the scientific theory, $t$, satisfies the criteria of balanced adequacy and generality whereas the extra-scientific theory, $t'$, does not. The latter may, for example, account for all the facts with a degree of empirical adequacy comparable to $t$, but does so by means of a multiplicity of *ad hoc* assumptions, some of which may be redundant and others mutually incompatible. We are then dealing with some practical application of a set of rules, such as one finds in surveying, some forms of engineering, practical politics, and even organized crime.[13] We call these instances of 'praxiology'. It may also be that $t'$ is internally consistent, elegant, and economical, satisfies the criterion of integrative generality, but fails to account for the facts with precision and in detail, or leaves some facts unaccounted for. Such theories do not stand up to the severest tests one can design for them, or simply offer no grounds for testing in some respect. Examples of such theories include metaphysical theories of human nature, philosophical cosmologies, vague but perhaps persuasive forms of explanation in the social and behavioral sciences, and similar systems of thought. Collectively we denote them as comprising the field of 'metaphysics'.

Theories $t_1$ and $t_2$ are both within science proper, yet they may turn out to be mutually incompatible, i.e. explain the same facts by deduction from non-interconvertible axioms. Science is said to reject $t_1$ and opt for $t_2$ if the scientific community perceives $t_1$ as violating the balanced adequacy/generality ratio whereas $t_2$ is perceived as satisfying it. The subjective factor is accounted for by introducing the concept of a *threshold* of equilibrium, dependent on the degree of openmindedness of the scientific community with regard to their accepted theories. The more critically a scientific community examines its theories, the smaller the threshold of its perceived equilibrium. Since the prevalence of criticism is also a function of the availability of alternatives to the existing theories, the threshold in question likewise correlates with the level of innovation current in a discipline.

Acceptance of a theory $t_1$ as valid signifies that $(A/G)^E$ functions homeostatically. Experiment and observation provide generally corroborative evidence for the theory, and the latter is becoming progressively established in the process. This phase is typical of early periods following theory innovation, when a powerful theory has become available for exploration and seems to offer unlimited application to the problems that beset the field. Under such conditions the perceived threshold of equilibrium is comparatively high, as minor disconfirmations are dismissed or explained away. Science in this phase is comparatively 'unreactive' and performs negative-feedback operations typical of morpho*stasis*. Hereby it ensures the transmission of tradition and permits the piecemeal exploration of a conceptual scheme which gives the field its esoteric character and consistent search for detail. The damping mechanisms of normal science have upper thresholds, however, beyond which disconfirming evidence is perceived as such, and the theory itself, and not only its application, is questioned. When this phase is initiated, morphostatic activity gives way to the processes of morpho*genesis*: the field reorganizes itself to deal with the accruing problems. When reorganization is achieved, we get a theory $t_2$ which is perceived as lying within the threshold of $(A/G)^E$: a new equilibrium state has been achieved. Whereas in normal science $(A/G)^E$ functions homeostatically, in crisis the same set of criteria function to *amplify* deviation between the anomalous theory $t_1$ and some new (to be discovered) non-anomalous theory $t_2$. The latter is the basis for a new phase of negative-feedback normal-science activity in the next phase of the field's development.

(We need not conceive of the deviation reducing and deviation amplifying phases as temporally distinct and mutually exclusive. Rather, these are characteristics of trends within a given science which coexist at all times, but of which the one or the other gains prominence. due to the proportion of scientists engaging in them, the amount of attention paid to them, and so on.)

In this interpretation we conceive of science as an open system with "hidden strata of stability" (Bronowski). The strata are introduced by the presence of internal constraints in the form of invariant ideals of science. Empirical inputs to these represent perturbations which make science settle into the equilibrium position most consistent with the input. (See Waddington's allegorical illustration: "A puppy going to sleep on a stony beach — a 'joggle-fit', the puppy wriggles some stones out of the way, and curves himself in between those too heavy to shift — that is the operational method of science (and of the evolution of biological systems)").[14] It is not the case, however, that science in its history exploits all possible strata of stability. To do so, observational anomalies would immediately have to result in adjustment of theory to optimum fit. Scientific development, while not entirely continuous, would not exhibit the revolutionary shifts which characterize its real history. Additional discontinuities are introduced by two principal factors:

(i) The insensitivity (unreactivity) of normal research to anomalies;
(ii) The chance factor which leads to the discovery of some of a possibly large number of new theories or subsidiary concepts which satisfy the dominant ideals of science.

If thresholds of reactivity in normal science were eliminated, and scientists would systematically scan all possible constructs capable of satisfying the internal constraints (ideals) of their science in view of the observed facts, the development of science would appear almost continuous: it would progress by small shifts rather than striking quantum leaps. However, such progression would call for a magnitide of search-capacity on the one hand, and a degree of openness to innovation on the other, which exceed the real potentials of scientific communities. Hence such communities will discover some, but not all, strata of stability, and they will hold on to the attained states until an arbitrarily high threshold is crossed and crisis sets in.

Science's amplification of developmental discontinuities reflects the difference between a system with limited resources and one with inifinite capabilities. Only the latter could climb the strata of stability one by one. The former will hit on some strata to the exclusion of others, and will remain at that level until disequilibrium overcomes resistance, and anomalous findings give the impetus to search for a new stratum. The dynamics of this process applies to the evolution of complex open systems in the biological realm as well, but the closer connection of selection and innovation (mutation and environment) in science introduces more determinacy into the process than we find in the relatively disjoined causal dynamics of biological evolution. The total elimination of 'noise' factors could only be achieved by a system with infinite resources: such a system would immediately settle into the optimum state of equilibrium upon any disturbance from its environment. Science settles into such states with a good deal of indeterminacy, yet with less random noise factors than biological species. These three types of systems form a graded continuum in regard to degrees of determinacy: the system with inifinite capacities is fully determinate; the system of science is considerably less so, and the system of biological populations manifests the largest element of indeterminacy.

## FORMALIZATION OF THE MODEL

We subdivide 'input from nature' into corroborative and anomalous inputs (evidence for or against theory): $f_i$ or $f_j$. We define an organization of constructs that falls within the range of $(A/G)^E$ as an equilibrium state of science: $E$. The level of such states with respect to the set of all possible scientific theories of the empirical world that satisfy $(A/G)^E$ is given by $L_n$. Hence any given acceptable scientific theory, measured against all theories which have been accepted, will be or could be accepted, is defined by a state of equilibrium of science of a given level: $E_{Ln}$.

Now we endow the controls which define $E$, i.e. $(A/G)^E$, with a range of tolerance. Ideally, $(A/G)^E$ is single valued, representing just one organization of constructs that constitutes an equilibrium, given the kinds of facts taken into account in the field. But such 'ultrareactivity' in science would fail to offer the measure of stability required to develop theories even when they are beset by difficulties (Feyerabend's "principle of tenacity"). Hence the controls which determine what organization of constructs are perceived as valid theories must have thresholds of error tolerance. This threshold is determined by the mutual relationship of two principal factors: $r$, the factor of resistance to theory-innovation due to textbook indoctrination with a reigning paradigm (resulting in a failure to perceive anomalous data; its interpretation by *ad hoc* auxiliary hypotheses; or its suppression as a temporarily insoluble problem), and $g$, the genius for *Einfall* through which theory innovations are suggested and alternatives to the reigning paradigm become available. Actual thresholds of tolerance are a function of these two factors. Since without some theory to give meaning to data and direct attention in observation and theory formulation there is no science, science always functions within the context of some conceptual framework and will always manifest some degree of attachment to it. The limiting cases are the following. Let $r$ attain some absolute value — it then prevents $g$ from manifesting itself, and we have $r_\infty, g_0$. Conversely let $g$ reach some maximum value; it then offers viable alternatives to every attempt at saving the existing framework in the face of anomaly, and we have $r_0, g_\infty$. Between these extremes, the two factors are inversely related, $r/g$. The actual range of tolerance of $(A/G)^E$ is thus $r/g = h$. Within this range, nature reinforces equilibrated theory on its existing level of organization, $E_{Ln} \circlearrowleft$ . Beyond this range, nature violates the equilibrium of existing theory and produces an impetus for evolving toward theory on any of the successive levels of potential equilibrium: $E_{Ln+n}$.

Self-reinforcing (normal science) processes can now be described as

$$f_i \to (A/G)^E \lim h = (E_{Ln} \circlearrowleft ) \tag{1}$$

whereas deviation-amplifying (extraordinary science) processes are described as

$$f_j \to (A/G)^E \lim h = (E_{Ln} \to E_{Ln+n}) \tag{2}$$

Since whether any $f$ is $f_i$ or $f_j$ is a function of $h$ (an empirical datum *within* the threshold of tolerance is actually or potentially corroborative, and beyond it anomalous), we can rewrite Eqs. (1) and (2) as

$$f \leqslant h \rightarrow (A/G)^{E \text{ lim } h} = (E_{L_n} \rightleftarrows) \qquad (3)$$

and

$$f \geqslant h \rightarrow (A/G)^{E \text{ lim } h} = (E_{L_n} \rightarrow E_{L_{n+n}}) \qquad (4)$$

The dynamics of theory reinforcement and theory deviation can be more accurately represented in information flow charts. We first represent the negative feedback process of theory reinforcement (Figure 1).

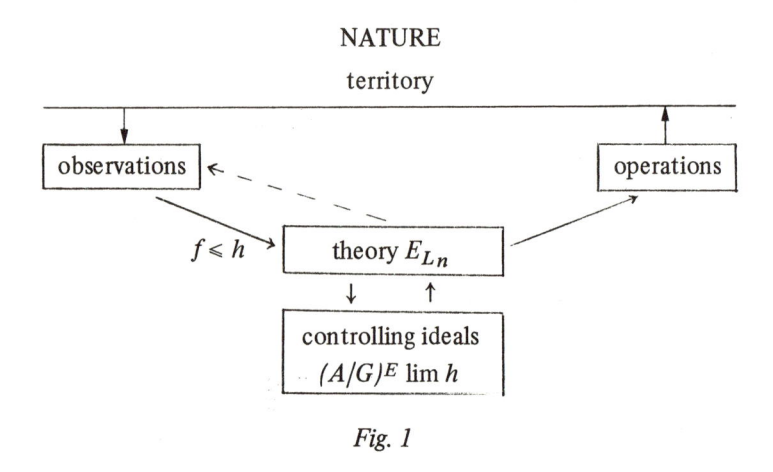

NATURE

territory

| observations | ← - - - - | | operations |

$f \leqslant h \rightarrow$ theory $E_{L_n}$

↓  ↑

controlling ideals
$(A/G)^E \text{ lim } h$

*Fig. 1*

The chart can be paraphrased as follows. The territory of an empirical science is some selected aspect (or slice) of 'nature', i.e. of the totality of observables. Of this territory certain observations are made, and these observations are checked against accepted theory. If observations match the predictions flowing from the theory, the territory is seen as the realm of entities described in the theories (or, more exactly, it is seen that the theoretical entities are instantiated in specific transformations). In Figure 1 we assume this eventuality. Consequently the value of the observations will be generally corroborative: it will fall below the threshold of tolerance of disturbance for the theory. An exact match between predictions and observations (or nature and theory) is an idealization: under concrete conditions there will always be some deviation. These can be dealt with within the limits of the theory in several ways. If the deviation is due to the intrinsic uncertainty of measurement, the theory's predictions will include a probability distribution of measured values, or predict a single value with a normal error curve. If the deviation goes beyond the thus permitted values, but remains below the tolerance threshold of the controlling ideals of science (as seen through the eyes of the given scientific

community), it
(i) may not be acknowledged, i.e. branded as irrelevant or simply ignored as observers concentrate on the more normal elements of their data;
(ii) may be put aside as a problem to be solved when more sophisticated techniques are available for attacking it; or
(iii) may be brought into line by articulating a further aspect of the theory.

In the case of (i) and (ii), there is a feedback from the controlling ideals through the existing theory to the observations, effecting a modification of the observational field [cf. reversed arrow to observations in Figure 1]. If (iii) occurs, existing theory is corrected as a function of the controlling ideals, and its consequences are tested by operations on the territory. If the consequent observations match theory within the predicted range, theory articulation has been successful. In all the above cases, however, theory matches nature sufficiently to satisfy the actual ideals of the scientific community; hence the circuit of testing and repeated matching of observation to theory constitutes a negative feedback process whereby existing theory gains reinforcement. An established state of equilibrium is maintained.

We now pass to the extraordinary situation where observations exceed the tolerance threshold of the controlling ideals and theory is disequilibrated: it has to be replaced rather than articulated. Figure 2 is the information-flow diagram of these events. Here observations fail to match predictions based on existing theory

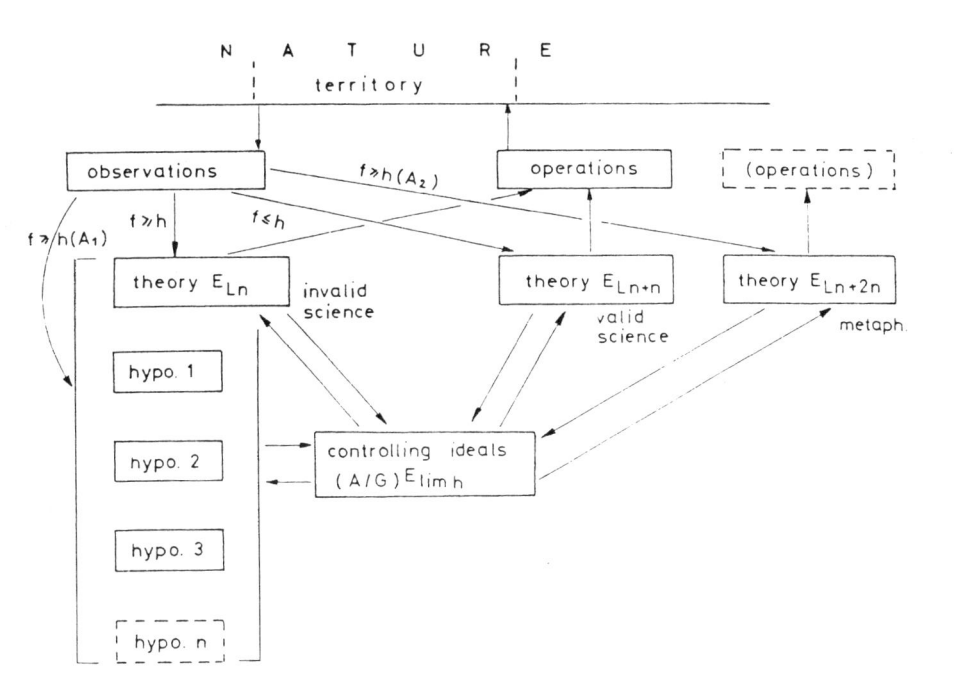

*Fig. 2*

(on level $L_n$), with the deviation transcending the threshold of tolerance of the controlling ideals of the community. Consequently the value of the observations for theory $E_{L_n}$ will be $f \geqslant h$. In actual fact this means that the observations in question can no longer be seen in terms of the entities with which theory populates the territory; anomalies are recognized and demand to be dealt with. Theory $E_{L_n}$ fails to satisfy $(A/G)^E$ for the scientific community, and a replacement theory is being sought. The controls now bias the process toward selection of a certain type of theory. The alternatives are likewise represented in the chart. Alternative (1): additions of auxiliary hypotheses to 'save the phenomena' (i.e. keep $f$ within the threshold $h$). Such attempts will be unsuccessful when they encounter the tolerance threshold beyond which $A/G$ becomes unacceptably high. The phenomena are now accounted for, but the internal consistency and unity of theory is fragmented (its integrative generality is excessively low compared with its empirical adequacy). Alternative (2): a theory of great sweep of generality, accounting for all observations without exception but using untestable assumptions to do so. $A/G$ is now unacceptably low (we are in the realm of metaphysics rather than science). Thus the observations, though accounted for, still exceed the tolerance range of the scientific ideals ($h$).

There remains a specific kind of theory which satisfies the controlling ideals of science in view of the actual mapping of the field's territory. This kind of theory may still form a class with numerous members, of which any one can furnish the content of the replacement theory. The class itself constitutes the 'stratum of stability' or 'equilibrium' which demarcates science from praxiology as well as from metaphysics. When such a theory is hit upon, and when it proves itself in testing, it becomes the new paradigmatic theory of the given field of science. Theory $E_{L_{n+n}}$ in Figure 2 will then function as theory $E_{L_n}$ in Figure 1 and another phase of negative feedback reinforcing research gets under way.

Because science (according to this model) is a complex open system possessing multiple equilibria (or hidden strata of stability) in virtue of the internal controls which specify, for any given relationship to nature, a set of 'preferred' states (= organizations of constructs=theories), the arrow of time in scientific development is given a barb which stops it from running backward (Bronowski). Since a level of empirical adequacy, once reached, cannot be significantly decreased without violating the controls, nor can the already attained level of generality be lowered, the replacement theory can only represent a higher level organization of the construct systems of science: it can not be $E_{L_{n-n}}$, only $E_{L_{n+n}}$. Consequently, the dynamics of theory choice, articulation, and replacement gives a direction of time in reference to the developmental process whereby science climbs its hidden strata of stability with greater or smaller leaps, spaced at longer or shorter intervals. Chance enters in the varying rate of discovery of anomalies; in the $(r/g) = h$ (anomaly tolerance) factor in given scientific communities, and in the timing and level of the *Einfall* which constitutes the next leap in the progression. Beyond chance, however, there is the lawful regularity that *in the course of time science maximizes both its empirical adequacy and its integrative generality within a mutually balanced ratio.*

This takes the accepted theories of science from some initial level $E_{Ln}$ to an asymptotically approached ultimate level $E_{Ln+\Omega}$. The latter is signified by the unavailability of observations of value $f \geqslant h$, a condition which signifies the attainment of the 'perfect' theory.

The progression from level to level can be represented, isomorphically with quantized processes of self-organization in complex open systems in general, as

$$E_{Ln} \to E_{Ln+n} = \psi < 0 = \frac{d\,info}{dt} > 0 \qquad (5)$$

Within limits of specificity, the overall dynamics of the development of science is isomorphic with the dynamics of other complex open systems, e.g. biological populations. Inasmuch as the variables in science are both less complex and more determinate than in biological systems, models of scientific evolution should prove to be easier to construct, and when constructed be more accurately predictive, than models of biological evolution. The development of such models merits therefore systematic follow-through, both because of the intrinsic interest of mapping a process of change with precision, and by reason of the extrinsic values attaching to a rational science policy which, equipped with a predictive model of scientific development, could control the rate of progress in different domains of research and experiment through informed fiscal and administrative measures.

## REFERENCES

1. Kedrov, B., History of science and principles of its research, *XIIIth Int. Congr. Hist. Sci.*, Moscow (1971).
2. Holton, G., On the duality and growth of physical science, *Am. Scient.*, V41 (1953).
3. Popper, K., *The Logic of Scientific Discovery*, Basic Books, London, p. 108 (1959).
4. Kuhn, T. S., *The Structure of Scientific Revolutions*, University of Chicago Press, Chicaco, 2nd ed., p. 145 (1970).
5. Ibid., postscript.
6. Toulmin, S., Does the distinction between normal and revolutionary science hold water? in *Criticism and the Growth of Knowledge*, Eds. I. Lakatos and A. Musgrave, Cambridge University Press, Cambridge, p. 46 (1970).
7. Monod, J., *Chance and Necessity*, Knopf, New York (1971), reviewed by Th. Dobzhansky in *Science*, V175 (4017), pp. 49-50.
8. Feyerabend, P., Consolations for the specialist, in *Criticism and the Growth of Knowledge*, op. cit., pp. 203f.
9. For general overviews, see Bertalanffy, L. von, *General System Theory*, George Braziller, New York (1968); and *Modern Systems Research for the Behavioral Scientist*, W. Buckley, ed., Aldine, Chicago (1968).
10. Cf. Ross Ashby, W., Principles of the self-organizing system, in *Modern Systems Research for the Behavioral Scientist*, op. cit., pp. 108-122.

11. Ibid., p. 116.
12. Bronowski, J., New concepts in the evolution of complexity: stratified stability and unbounded plans, *Zygon*, 5, pp. 33-34 (1970).
13. Cf. Feyerabend, p. 200 (1970).
14. Waddington, C. H., Paradigm for an evolutionary process, in *Towards a theoretical Biology*, C. H. Waddington, ed., Aldine, Chicago, V2, p. 120 (in italics) (1969).

# 8

## SYSTEMS AND STRUCTURES – TOWARD BIO-SOCIAL ANTHROPOLOGY*

One of the significant insights of contemporary science is the realization that nature does not come in isolated patches. The behavior of one set of phenomena is conditioned, directly or mediately, by the behavior of others, however different they may be. Another insight of current science is the postulational nature of scientific theory. Compare Newton's *hypotheses non fingo* with Einstein's statement that the "axiomatic basis of theoretical physics cannot be abstracted from experience but must be freely invented." From the scientist's creatively postulated axiomatic propositions testable hypotheses can be derived, preserving science's empiricism but giving it a new and freer context. Facing evidence concerning the interconnectedness of phenomena, and liberated from the straight jacket of classical empiricism, contemporary science struggles to overcome its historically acquired speciality barriers. Extreme compartmentalization, with special languages and special spheres of investigation, can neither do justice to the manifest systemic orders of nature, nor be justified by the methods and philosophy of contemporary science. In answer to the challenge of systematic explanation of interconnected phenomena, a whole series of 'hybrid' disciplines have sprung up: biophysics, biochemistry, astrophysics, etc. Most of the new disciplines connect neighboring discplines within the natural sciences themselves. Some, e.g. social anthropology and social psychology, connect a social science with one that is on the borderline of the natural sciences (i.e. anthropology, psychology). No 'hybrid' discipline has as yet emerged which would interconnect, in a rigorous theoretical framework, a natural and a social science. (Social Darwinism has attempted to do so, but its inadequacy prompted most investigators to abandon it (cf. below).) Thus even if the compartmental schisms between the particular natural sciences are closing up, a gulf still remains between the natural and the social sciences.

The problems raised by the hypothesis that there are no basic, categorical gaps between natural and social sciences, are indeed formidable. They are entailed

---
*Reprinted from *Theory and Decision* 2 (1971), 174-192.

by holding that natural and social phenomena are not basically different. Thus either the natural world would have to be looked upon as exhibiting properties hitherto associated with the realm of human society and history, or history and society would need to be conceived as a kind or species of natural phenomenon. The manifest differences between events in nature and in society were, at least until recently, so striking for the casual observer that suggestions for their unification could be readily branded reductionist (if society was thought of as a natural phenomenon) or vitalist (in the inverse event). But there have been methodological and conceptual developments in the sciences in the last two decades which permit bridging the gap between nature and society without either reducing the one to the other, or infusing it with characteristics foreign to itself. The most important are the concepts and methods of *systems theory* in America, and *structuralism* on the Continent. These are sophisticated theoretical frameworks which do not pretend to describe observable phenomena and penetrate their essence. Rather, they build models of certain perspectival features of phenomena and hold up the models for investigation and comparison. They seek the unity of science, and by implication of nature, in the isomorphism, or structural analogies, of the models themselves. "Unity of science," Bertalanffy says, "is to be sought in the uniformity of conceptual constructs or models applicable to diverse fields of phenomena and science, which hints at a unity of the 'world' (i.e. the total of observables) in its structure."[1] Thus if it would appear that models built in the natural and the social sciences are in some key respects uniform or isomorphic, we could hold that "they signify a unity of the observed universe and hence of science."[2] The implicit categorial schism of natural and social science could be bridged, not by a metaphysical *fiat*, but by the demonstration that rigorous theoretical models with isomorphic properties can be built of certain areas and features of the natural, as well as of the societal world. Philosophical conclusions of more speculative sorts could then be based upon a foundation more solid than individual insight and inspiration.

The purpose of this study is to show that isomorphies and uniformities of remarkable varieties can be exhibited between the theoretical models of systems biology on the one hand, and structural anthropology on the other. The one deals with an undoubtedly *natural* phenomenon — the biological organism — within the conceptual framework and method of general system theory, and the other treats an equally clearly *societal* phenomenon — networks of relations between human beings — through the method and concepts of structuralism. If the isomorphic features of these two contemporary theoretical models have not received due attention in the current literature, this may be ascribed to the mutual isolation of the principal investigators. Few American system theorists show explicit awareness of concurrent work done by structuralists, and few structuralists know much about research in systems theory. One could help to rectify this situation by defining some of the manifold parallelisms between these schools. We shall proceed by outlining what appear to be the basic postulates of each school, and then sketching the main features of their theoretical models. Some generalized conclusions can then be drawn concerning the uniformities of the models and their significance for bridging the persistent gap between natural and social sciences.

## BASIC POSTULATES OF GENERAL SYSTEM THEORY[3]

One of the main problems of natural and social science today is building models to map features of *organized complexity*. Concepts like those of organization, non-summative wholeness, control, self-regulation, equi-finality, self-organization (etc.) are not a part of classical physics; yet they are present in the biological, behavioral and social sciences. Classical physics deals essentially with two-variable interaction; organized complexity demands, however, treatment in terms of multiple variables constituting interacting systems. The behavior of the variables turns out to be different in isolation from that what it is within the system of variables; the latter is not a simple sum of all its variables but a constitutive whole which is irreducible to its elements. Wholes of this kind range from atoms (which are not the simple sum of their constituent particles and fields but dynamic-structural wholes irreducible to the properties manifested by the parts in isolation), through biological organisms (likewise different from the sum of the isolated properties of their component molecules, cells and organs) to the social 'epiorganisms' which define groups of biological organisms, including human beings, in ecological, sociological, economical and political organizations. If organized complexity in these diverse realms of investigation is the empirical datum, then it seems legitimate to request a theory which deals with organized complexity as such, i.e. with non-summative wholes manifesting certain properties of self-regulation, multi-variable interaction, self-organization (e.g. growth and differentiation), and others. "In this way we come to postulate a new discipline, called General System Theory. Its subject matter is the formulation and derivation of those principles which are valid for 'systems' in general." (Bertalanffy)[4]

Principles of systems in general can be stated mathematically, in formulating families of differential equations defining the parameters characterizing given spatial, temporal or spatio-temporal structures. Non-mathematical yet quantitative models can also be built of systems in general, using information-flow graphs, decision and game-theory models, etc. Artificial systems, such as Ashby's *homeostat* can likewise be constructed which exhibit the properties of systems in being self-regulative, and even self-organizing (e.g. 'learning machines'). It appears that a multiplicity of conceptual approaches is capable of describing a variety of systems, independently of the material substance, types of linkages, and natural, artificial, or even psychological origin of the latter. Throughout this diversity one can glimpse general uniformities or invariances which appear in various transformations, due partly to the empirical diversity of the phenomena and partly to the conceptual diversity of the theoretical schemes. Thus, if one can show that the schemes are isomorphic in regard to the basic underlying invariances, then these invariances (or uniformities) can be held to 'signify a unity of the observed universe and hence of science'. Their presence does not mean that all areas of reality are reduced to a single level, e.g. that of a biological or sociological organized complex, but that the various levels of reality, ranging from science as consisting in the search for, and the eventual discovery of, always more embracing invariances, e.g. those which render laws space and time invariant.[8] Invariances have definite limits of application, ranging from such trivial and narrow invariances as that incorporated in the working of an ordinary clock, which is invariant with respect to a limited passage of time but not to changes of humidity, magnetism or blows by a hammer, to the universal range of the Einsteinian interval which remains invariant with respect to space and time displacements anywhere in the cosmos.

A structure is defined by the set of transformations which is reducible to an invariance. As a square is invariant with respect to rotation in space at 90° and multiples of 90°, so a social structure is invariant to certain transformations, such as reversal of kinship systems, totems, forms of communications, etc. The invariances constitute the fixed parameters of the structure which reappear in various transformations. Thus to postulate a structure is to postulate its invariant characteristics or, which is the same thing, the range of the permissible transformations in the relations of its parts.

Structures exist as such as long as the relations of their parts do not exceed the range of the permissible operations (i.e. those defined by an invariant law or principle). Thus enduring structures must possess self-regulating mechanisms for ensuring that their characteristic invariances are respected. Such control presupposes a degree of closure in the structure. While closure is a necessary condition of all self-regulating systems, it does not signify that a given structure cannot enter into a larger structure as a sub-structure.[9] In fact, systems of self-regulating structure may exist, the parts of which likewise constitute self-regulating systems (hierarchies). The laws of self-regulation are the laws of the totality of the structure. Self-regulation is merely that aspect of the operations performed by a given structure which entails the conservation of the general relationships which underlie all specific operations. Thus self-regulation means the correction or prevention of errors, i.e. of the transgression of the limits of transformation imposed by the established invariances. A so-called 'perfect' self-regulating system prevents errors in the sense that in such a system no error can be produced. But such systems exist only in the field of axiomatics. Structural models of empirical relationships cannot *prevent* errors but can at best *correct* for them, if and when they occur. Such systems operate in time and the principle of self-regulation is usually that of *feedback*. That is, errors are corrected by a temporal modification of operations obtained in function of reducing the differential between the desired and the actual states of the system. It is a system of feedback which corrects for errors within empirical structures, by feeding back some of the output to control the input, and not a purely axiomatic mathematical principle, such as inversion or reciprocity.

## BIOLOGICAL SYSTEMS [SYSTEMS THEORY MODEL]

Von Bertalanffy defines biological organisms as 'open systems in a steady state'.[10] They maintain themselves in their environments by means of establishing a 'dynamic equilibrium' (*not* in a thermodynamic sense) between their own 'fantastically improbable' (thermodynamically disequilibrated) states and the surrounding medium. Organisms constitute systems, that is, functioning wholes constituted by the relationship of their parts, and since these systems continually exchange materials, information and energies with the environment, organisms constitute *open* systems. Their condition of subsistence is a state of dynamic balance between themselves and their environment; organisms attain it by compensating for degeneration by regeneration through the 'import of negentropy' (Schrödinger). Failing the constant balancing of their highly unstable structural components by the requisite materials, energies, and the necessary information, organisms soon deteriorate (die): the functional coordination of their parts ceases to constitute an integrated whole.

The organism consists in a structural form imposed upon a continuous stream of substances which represents its 'input' and 'output'. The organism receives such substances from its environment, imposes its own structural properties on them, and, after a varying amount of time, surrenders them to the environment. (Even the most permanent organic substances, such as the genomes of DNA, are interchanged with fresh substances in the organism's lifetime.) The condition of self-maintenance by an organism is the imposition of such structural form on the inflowing substances which represents the dynamic equilibrium of the total structure in its environment. Thus the organism incorporates invariant steady-state norms (the values of which may vary, however, in function of time), of which the various possible states of dynamic equilibrium constitute the permissible range of transformations. The series of permissible transformations may be characterized as constituting a chemical flux, fluctuating around the steady state (or *quasi-stationary* state) norms. The chemical flux is controlled by the set of reactions taking place within the organism's boundaries. These, being semi-permeable, allow some out of a large number of translational processes to take place and thus act catalytically. Within them the organism functions selectively, setting up and preserving rate-constants. A stationary pattern is specified by the total kinetic situation, the pattern being regulated in accordance with quasi-stationary state values. These values are independent of the initial quantitites of any organic component. According to Kacser, disturbances are 'buffered out' by the self-regulatory situation, with the organism ending up with the same composition regardless of their occurrence.[11]

These are necessary regulatory mechanisms which enable the cells and the molecular components of the body to adjust to disturbances from a changing environment. The mechanism of adjustment, whereby the invariant organic norms are respected despite changing relations within the environment, is negative feedback. Herein lies the secret of self-maintenance of organisms: fantastically improbable structures dynamically maintaining themselves in their environments. Feedback stabilization guided by inherent norms is already manifested by the virus, which, as one biologist puts it, is 'lifelike in its actions only when it is coupling events in the manner that is typical of feedback circuits."[12] Cells, bacteria, and of course all higher organic forms manifest, and essentially depend on, feedback stabilization in their organic functioning.

In the case of a complex biological structure, such as the human, negative feedback control is manifested in a wide variety of processes. The most evident of these come under the heading of *homeostasis*. The examples of homeostatic processes are legion. Since many of them are well known, it should suffice to remark that they are all designed to maintain the quasi-stationary state norms of the organism. These norms include blood pressure, oxygen content of blood, water content, the supply of protein, sugar, fat, and many other constancies within what Claude Bernard called the *'milieu interieur'*. In addition to the standard cases of homeostasis, special homeostatic processes may also be distinguished. These include the phenomena of healing and regeneration, the general adaptation syndrome and even reproduction. (The latter may be so viewed since it maintains the norms typical of the human species over different generations; it is but a complex mode of regeneration, namely a 'rejuvenation' through a large-scale exchange of old for new substances.) In fact, Sinnott insists that the whole process of biological organization, involving not only physiology but also the growth and development of the entire organism, may be called a complex case of homeostasis.[13] It occurs as long as the organism lives, and is a characteristic property of the functional whole it constitutes. Removal of the homeostatic control spells death; the disassociation of the parts and disintegration of the living system.

Negative feedback control, exemplified in the manifold processes of a living organism, is what maintains the organism in the face of the entropic disorganizing tendencies of its physical environment. As Wiener said, "while the universe as a whole, if indeed there is a whole universe, tends to run down, there are local enclaves whose direction seems opposed to that of the universe at large and in which there is a limited and temporary tendency for organization to increase. Life finds its home in some of these enclaves."[14] And, very significantly, he added, "It is with this point of view at its core that the new science of Cybernetics began its development."[15] The biological organism, in the systems theoretical view, can be understood as a cybernetical control system which processes information obtained from its environment for its own purposes of organization (life, said Schrödinger, feeds on negentropy.) Living systems are environmentally transacting open systems which 'control' or 'hold back' entropy (Wiener) and maintain their ordered, non-summative structures by means of error-reducing negative feedback.

## SOCIAL STRUCTURES [STRUCTURALIST MODEL]

In the currently dominant view, advanced by Lévi-Strauss, social structures are theoretical models which do not belong in the realm of observable facts.

The fundamental principle is that the concept of social structures does not refer to empirical reality but to the models constructed of it. Thus appears the difference between two concepts so close that they were often confused. I mean those of *social structure* and of *social relations*. Social relations are the raw material employed in the construction of models which explicate the *social structure* itself.[16]

Thus social structures theoretically explicate social relations, and differ from them as 'theory' differs from 'nature' in any science whatsoever. Lévi-Strauss states that such models must satisfy four conditions.

In the first place, a structure offers the character of a system. It consists of elements such that the modification of any among them entails a modification of all others. In the second place, all models belong to a group of transformations of which each corresponds to a model of the same family, thus that the ensemble of these transformations constitutes a group of models. Thirdly, the property here indicated permits the prediction of the way in which the model will react in the event of the modification of one of its elements. Finally, the model must be so constructed that its functioning could account for all the observed facts.[17]

The difference between 'accounting for all the observed facts' by means of the functioning of a theoretical model, and a description of the observed facts themselves through empirical observation, renders Lévi-Strauss' structural system-model applicable both to overt and to covert social phenomena. Whereas the description of observed facts is limited to the actually observable social relations, theoretical model-building can furnish accounts of phenomena lying below the empirical surface. In fact, the construction of models of social structure is facilitated by the absence of a consciousness of the structure in the minds of the relating individuals: "the clearer the apparent structure, the more difficult does it become to grasp the fundamental structure, owing to the conscious and deformed models which intervene as obstacles between the observer and his object."[18] In sum, Lévi-Strauss clearly distinguishes between models ('social structures') and empirical data ('social relations') and brings the field of social anthropology into the sphere of the model-building theoretical sciences.

How closely Lévi-Strauss' structural anthropology emulates such natural sciences as contemporary mathematical physics and biology becomes evident when we consider his emphasis on models which belong to a group of transformations of which each corresponds to a model of the same family. Similarly to physics, which builds models for types of systems of which specific models are transformations of the group (e.g. a model of the hydrogen atom is a transformation of the group of models which is postulated in atomic physics), so Lévi-Strauss constructs theoretical models of types of social relations thus that the ensemble of the transformations constitutes a group of models. He is thus able to speak of social structures e.g. of the Australian tribes, and to distinguish in these structures transformations which correspond, for example, to the Arabanna, Aranda, Kaitish or Warramunga systems.[19] The group of transformations is presented as a theoretical edifice which may, in time, even be transferred to punched cards: "with the help of a computer their [the Australian tribes'] entire techno-economic, social and religious structures can be shown to be a vast group of transformations."[20]

Insistence on theoretical structures, abstracted from concrete observables in much the same way as such constructs as fields, photons and taxa are abstracted through the postulational methods of theoretical sciences, aligns Lévi-Strauss' structuralism with the theories of the contemporary natural sciences. The updating of a formerly descriptive and mainly qualitative discipline to the level of a postulational theoretical science seems to introduce a serious schism between Lévi-Strauss' structural anthropology and the theories of such eminent anthropologists as Malinowski and Radcliffe-Brown. Lévi-Strauss accuses the latter of adopting a mistaken empiricism, seeing the origin and model of kinship ties in biological ties and considering the integrated social structure as an empirical observable. But this is not so. Radcliffe-Brown conceives of social anthropology as "the theoretical natural science of human society, that is, the investigation of social phenomena by methods essentially similar to those used in the physical and biological sciences."[21] He agrees that the subject matter of social anthropology is, in the most fundamental sense, the study of social structure. However, social structures are held by him to be just as real as individual organisms and the many sub-structures (living cells, complex molecules, interstitial fluids, etc.) which compose them. Radcliffe-Brown asserts that 'direct observation' reveals to us that human beings are connected by a complex network of social relations, and this he denotes by the term 'social structure'. He regards interpersonal social relations as well as the differentiation of individuals and of classes by their social role as part of the social structure. He sums up his position in saying, "In the study of social structure the concrete reality with which we are concerned is the set of actually existing relations, at a given moment of time, which link together certain human beings. It is on this that we can make direct observations."[22] From this one may infer that he can make direct observations on social structure. Yet this conclusion (which justifies Lévi-Strauss' criticism) follows only if we interpret the 'theoretical science of human society' which uses 'methods essentially similar to those used in the physical and biological sciences' as a *descriptive*, rather than as a *theoretical* science. It is evident, however, that the natural sciences, which Radcliffe-Brown admits are theoretical, are by no means merely descriptive. It may be argued, then, that if social anthropology is a theoretical natural science, then it is not descriptive, and if it is descriptive, then it is not a theoretical natural science. If the contemporary investigator is asked to decide the issue, he would have to hold that, if not as yet in fact, then plainly in intention, social anthropology is a theoretical natural science and hence not descriptive. Lest this poses difficulties for the remarkable accomplishments of the Radcliffe-Brown school, one merely has to make the semantic change of substituting '*form* of social structure' as used by Radcliffe-Brown, in place of his use of 'social structure'. His 'form of social structure' is in fact a theoretical model similar to Lévi-Strauss' 'social structure' as well as to the theoretical models of the natural sciences. This conclusion emerges if we consider that Radcliffe-Brown emphasizes that what we need for scientific purposes is not a description of the observed, particular social relations between given individuals, but an "account of the form of the structure" by which these relations are united. Individual relations are transient and changing; the form of the structure which unites them remains constant. In the latter we may see a theoretical model built by the scientist for purposes of rendering his observables intelligible. Radcliffe-Brown calls attention to the "important distinction, between structure as an actually existing concrete reality, to be directly observed, and structural form, as what the field-worker describes..."[24] Had he said in reference to 'structural form', "what the field worker *postulates*", 'structural form' would have been disclosed as a theoretical model such as Lévi-Strauss' 'social structure'. But Radcliffe-Brown said 'describes' and this may testify to nothing more than a disregard of the postulational nature of contemporary natural scientific theories. It is thus entirely possible that what divides his important school from Lévi-Strauss' is not an intentionally rigid empiricism but an unsophistication in regard to contemporary scientific method.

Contemporary social anthropology may be viewed as attempting to do what the natural sciences are doing: to build formal models for the explanation of its own region of 'nature'. These models, called (forms of) social structures, refer to a group, where 'group' is defined as a set of social phenomena chosen for study, rather than as a group of socially related individuals. The chosen groups can be integrated within a common framework of space and time. Similarly to the space and time of physics, 'social' space and time are distinct from subjective or common sense space and time. They have, as Lévi-Strauss tells us, no other properties than those of the social phenomena under study. Thus time, for example, may be reversible or nonreversible, according to the 'strategic value' of the concept; and both space and time may be 'micro' or 'macro' depending on the properties of the constructed structural model. The models deal with discontinuities within the field of social phenomena and, regardless of whether these discontinuities are small, such as an isolate, or large, as a culture, the models reduce their properties to postulated invariances. The group is disclosed by discontinuities, marking off its boundaries. Here the character and rate of interpersonal relations change. Within the boundaries, the relations are facilitated by a high level of 'communication' — resembling in this context the 'reactions' of the biochemist. Communication embraces kinship relations (the 'communication of women'), the economy (the 'communication of goods and services') and language (the 'communication of messages'). In consequence a 'super-science' is called for, synthesizing social anthropology, economics and linguistics in a science of communication.[25] Such science will dislose a social structure defined by discontinuities of types of interrelations at its boundaries and, within them, obeying invariant laws of defined range of transformation. The structure will have non-summative properties.

Models of this kind can be abstracted from the phenomena in reference to which they were constructed and can be explored in relation to different species of data. As Lévi-Strauss points out,

Structuralist researches would hardly offer anything of interest if the structures would not be translatable into models of which the formal properties can be compared independently of the elements composing them. The structuralist's task is to identify and isolate the levels of reality which possess a strategic value from his standpoint, in other words, which can be represented as models, whatever their nature ... our researches have but one goal, and that is to construct models of which the formal properties are, from the viewpoint of comparison and explanation, reducible to the properties of other models, themselves relevant to different strategic levels. Thus can we hope to overcome the barriers between neighboring disciplines and promote between them a real collaboration.[26]

Lévi-Strauss holds that the main interest of social anthropology lies in the construction of models which can be explored for isomorphisms with models in different areas of investigation, and Radcliffe-Brown emphasizes the analogies between the forms of social structures and the structural forms of biological phenomena. Insistence on the *sui generis* specificity of societal phenomena has been all but abandoned in social anthropology's current striving to achieve the status of a model-building natural science.

## THE SIGNIFICANCE OF ISOMORPHY IN THE BIOLOGICAL AND ANTHROPOLOGICAL MODELS

Social theorists have long speculated on the nature of human society. Some have thought that it is an association entered into by free agents for mutual aid and benefit (e.g. the social contract theories of Rousseau and Locke); others saw in it a natural resultant of essentially social beings (e.g. Aristotle and Marx). The present perspective justifies neither the one nor the other viewpoint, while not contradicting either. We need not engage in metaphysical speculation concerning the ultimate essence of society; we can merely note the remarkable isomorphies between cogent models of individual human beings *qua* complex species of biological organism, and social structures, as forms of relationships entered into by human beings. Both models constitute non-summative wholes; both exhibit self-regulation; both control entropy through negative feedback; both can be interpreted as systems of communication between their elements. It is evident that the models refer to different orders of complexity in phenomena and that their sphere of application is related through ties of domination and subordination. Biologically individual human beings compose societies, but the jointly constituted social systems impose constraints on the individuals and control their behavior. The case is precisely analogous to that obtaining in other spheres of organized complexity: for example, electrons and nucleons jointly compose atoms but the whole atom imposes constraints on their individual behavior. Likewise with molecules composing cells, cells composing organisms and organisms composing ecosystems. Each of these types of phenomena is a 'Janus faced entity' (Koestler), a *whole* when facing downward and a *part* when facing upward. Each has its own qualitative properties, lost when reduced to the parts in isolation. Thus we encounter an inclusive hierarchy in 'morphic' (as contrasted with 'entropic') nature (Whyte[27]), of which the units or 'modules' are hierarchically related and endowed with specific qualitative properties. But these hierarchically related modules exhibit significant unitary traits when we compare the theoretical models built of them in the contemporary sciences.

Two such models were chosen here for explicit consideration, the general system model of biological organisms and the structuralist model of social systems. If the dictum 'uniformity of conceptual constructs signifies the unity of the observables' is valid, the uniformity of the basic constructs of the GST model of organisms and the structuralist model of social structures suggests a unity of the individual human being as a system, and the social network of relations as a structure. Each of these entities is Janus faced, i.e. a whole in relation to its parts and a part in relation to a superordinate whole, and each disposes over qualitatively distinct manifest properties. But they can be jointly analyzed in terms of certain invariant theoretical constructs, the most important of which include non-summativity, self-regulation, control of entropy through feedback, and systematic communication between all components. Both can, in other words, be conceptualized as self-maintaining and self-evolving open systems, forming hierarchical links in the chain of negentropic nature.

Physical laws are inadequate by themselves to account for organized complexity on the biological level.[28] Biological laws may be likewise inadequate to account for organized complexity on the sociological level. But social anthropology need no more be reduced to biology than biology to physics. Irreducibility does not mean a break in the uniformity of organized nature, for it does not suggest contradiction. Biological organisms do not violate the laws of physics even if they are not adequately explainable in terms of them. And social systems do not violate the laws of biology although they, too, cannot be explained in purely biological terms. Thus we must reject both reductionism and categorial pluralism. The indicated philosophical position is what Bunge calls integrated pluralism.[29] It is a position which allows for the diversity of phenomena but, at the same time, searches for their underlying unity. In disclosing such unity it does not reduce differences to identities. Conceptual isomorphies in theoretical models do not suggest that the models refer to identical phenomena. The very notions 'theoretical model' and 'isomorphy' guard against these fallacies. Models may be abstracted from the frameworks of their original reference and compared, and if found ismorphic, only the fundamental consistency and unity of nature need be affirmed in the corresponding respects, and not its undifferentiated identity. The latter would disregard the possibility that the models may apply to phenomena on different levels of organization and complexity, i.e. that the unity in question may be *hierarchic*, rather than linear. The fallacy of Social Darwinism is precisely to confuse empirical observables with theoretical models and to mistake certain uniformities among the former for identities (e.g. in the concept of society as an 'individual [organism] writ large'). Isomorphies appear in conceptual schemes, not directly 'in nature', and they require to be integrated within a superordinate conceptual scheme, for example, a hierarchy of integrative levels. Failing this, crass reductionism results. As Taylor points out,

> To suppose that the higher level can be reduced to the lower is to commit the error of reductionism. On the basis of this principle, Social Darwinism is demonstrably fallacious. Even as the structure and organization of organisms are more complex than inorganic phenomena, so in turn human societies make use of the inorganic and organic levels of organization as a physical foundation while, in addition, functioning at a new and still more complex level of organization and integration. Consequently, to describe a human society as an 'organism' is to reduce its stage of organization to a lower level and, concomitantly, to lose those very qualities of structure, self-regulation and self-direction unique to its own plane.[30]

Instead of disregarding the emergence of properties at higher levels of organization (well exemplified by such principles as Pauli's exclusion principle, which applies only to the 'emergent' exclusion-property of two or more electrons in relation to nuclei; the principles of pressure, temperature and entropy, applying to aggregates of molecules in a gas rather than to single molecules in themselves; and by the principle of homeostasis, applying to integrated groups of cells forming an organism and not to the individual cells themselves), we may find unity and consistency in nature through the isomorphy of models applicable to phenomena on *different* levels of organization. 'Bio-social anthropology' could observe a distinction between the levels of the biological organism and the social system. It could demonstrate that, given the hierarchical relation of the levels, high-level uniformities are exhibited, suggesting that nature is in no sense deviant in producing complex ordered systems of which the elements are not atoms, molecules and cells, but multiatomic, multimolecular and multicellular structures: individual human beings. The *natural* and the *social* need not be categorically disjunctive, nor must one be reduced, or inflated, to the other. Both could be aspects of organized complexity ordered into a multidimensional hierarchic sequence, in which the biological and the sociological represent distinct but isomorphic integrative levels.

## REFERENCES

1. Ludwig v. Bertalanffy, 'General System Theory as Integrating Factor in Contemporary Science and in Philosophy', *Proceedings of the XIVth International Congress of Philosophy*, Vol. II, Vienna, 1968, p. 339.
2. *Ibid.*
3. I am indebted to Dr. v. Bertalanffy for suggesting the principal features of the theory he founded for presentation in this paper. I remain solely responsible, of course, for any errors which may appear in the presentation.
4. L. v. Bertalanffy, 'General System Theory', *Main Currents in Modern Thought*, Vol. 11, No. 4 (1955), reprinted in *General System Theory*, Chapter 2, New York, 1968.

5. A treatment of various cognitive and cultural phenomena in terms of isomorphic feedback-controlled information-flows is proposed in Ervin Laszlo, *System, Structure and Experience: Toward a Scientific Theory of Mind*, New York, 1969.
6. Jean Piaget, *Le Strucuturalisme*, Paris, 1968.
7. *Ibid.*
8. Cf. Henry Margenau, 'Esthetics and Relativity' in *Open Vistas*, New Haven, 1961.
9. Piaget, *op. cit.*
10. Cf. *Problems of Life*, New York, 1949; and numerous other writings.
11. Cf. *Biological Organization at the Cellular and Supercellular Level*, R. J. C. Harris, ed., London and New York, 1963.
12. Robert Thornton, 'Integrative Principles of Biology', *Integrative Principles of Modern Thought*, Henry Margenau, ed., New York, 1970.
13. Edmund W. Sinnott, *The Biology of the Spirit*, New York, 1955, and *The Bridge of Life*, New York, 1966.
14. Norbert Wiener, *The Human Use of Human Beings*, New York, 1950, Preface.
15. *Ibid.*
16. Claude Lévi-Strauss, *Anthropologie Structurale*, Paris, 1958, p. 305. My translation: the wording of the English edition (New York, 1963), while more elegant stylistically, obscures the meaning of the quoted passages.
17. *Ibid.*, p. 306.
18. *Ibid.*, pp. 308-9.
19. Lévi-Strauss, *The Savage Mind*, Chicago and London, 1966, Chapter Three.
20. *Ibid.*
21. A. R. Radcliffe-Brown, *Structure and Function in Primitive Society*, London, 1952, p. 189.
23. *Ibid.*, p. 192.
24. *Ibid.*
25. *Anthropologie Structurale, op. cit.*, p. 329.
26. *Ibid.*, pp. 311, 313.
27. Lancelot Law Whyte, 'Organic Structural Hierarchies', *Unity Through Diversity: Essays in Honor of L. v. Bertalanffy*, New York, 1971.
28. Among those who again emphasized this classical tenet we find Michael Polanyi ('Life's Irreducible Structure', *Science*, 160, pp. 1308-12), and Barry Commoner ('Is Biology a Molecular Science?', *The Anatomy of Knowledge*, M. Grene, ed., Amherst, Mass., 1969).
29. Mario Bunge, 'Metaphysics, Epistemology and Methodology of Levels', *Hierarchical Structures*, L. L. Whyte, A. G. Wilson and D. Wilson, eds., New York, 1969.
30. Alastair M. Taylor, 'Integrative Principles of Human Society', *Integrative Principles of Modern Thought, op. cit.*

# 9

# THE REDUCTION OF WHORFIAN RELATIVITY THROUGH A GENERAL SYSTEM LANGUAGE*

This study will address the issue posed by Whorf as follows: "Every language is a vast pattern-system, different from others, in which are culturally ordained the forms and categories by which the personality not only communicates, but also analyses nature, notices or neglects types of relationships and phenomena, channels his reasoning, and builds the home of his consciousness". (B. Whorf, "Language, Mind and Reality", in Carroll, ed. *Language, Thought and Reality*. Cambridge, 1962, p. 252).

We shall take 'language' to include both natural and scientific languages, possibly coexisting within the same culture. We shall not address the question of the origin of these languages but consider only their synchronous relations. We shall also not speak to the problem of coexistence of these languages on the level of entire societies or cultures, but speak merely to their presence within the cognitive maps of individuals, and groups of analogously cognizing individuals.

Hence this study will address the problem of epistemological relativism induced by different but coexisting natural and scientific languages within individuals and tight epistemic communicates, in a synchronic analysis. More specifically, we shall examine (i) the fragmentation of the world picture of average individuals and communities of such individuals through the use of the natural language typical of contemporary Western cultures; (ii) the fragmentation of the reconstructed world picture of individuals and communities using Western scientific languages without integration among them; and (iii) the potentials of a general system language to reunite the contemporary Western world picture in a meta-scientific reconstruction.

---

*Reprinted from *Communication and Cognition*, Vol. 6, No. 1 (1973).

## THE FRAGMENTATION OF THE COMMON-SENSE WORLD PICTURE

The evolution of common sense logic and ordinary language presents each user with a framework for viewing the empirical world. This framework is functional for the purpose of handling information in the context of interpersonal behavior, but is not necessarily true to the nature of the empirical world.

The world picture shaped by experience in the framework of ordinary language contains terms for objects and events which are assumed to have counterparts in the world, existing independently of being named and experienced. For example, the term 'tree' is assumed to refer to trees which are empirical realities beyond the confines of language and cognition. However, the range of objects and events assumed to have such reference is narrower than the range of existential terms in the languages of the arts, sciences and religions. For many persons in contemporary Western societies, the empirical world consists primarily of the persons with whom the language user is in personal contact, and of the class of persons he assumes to exist elsewhere in the world. Secondarily, independent existence is assumed with regard to the things which form the background of interpersonal relationships. These are animals, plants, and the inanimate natural objects and artifacts of the environment. But the microcomponents which constitute persons, as well as animate and inanimate things, are usually conceived as abstractions, populating the minds of theoretical scientists, with little if any reality apart from their theories and formulas. The social and ecological entities formed by the interactions of many living things appear likewise abstract and pale in comparison with the concreteness of the everyday world. In the context of everyday common sense, ordinary language confers reality on the persons and things which one can touch and which have a noticeable influence on one's purposes and projects.

Because of their subject-predicate structure, Indo-European languages confer substantially on the reified things of everyday life. Predicates refer to real, material things and persons, clothed with the predicated properties. Greenness refers to the substance of grass; tallness, handsomeness and similar predicates to the substance that makes up persons — the flesh and bone. In order to account for mental attributes and traits of character, the logic of common sense Western languages posits a "mental substance" — a mind or personality of which one can say that it is good or bad, likeable or detestable. Consequently common sense combined with the structure of ordinary language structures a world picture for Western man which has in its sharpest focus oneself and those around one; in lesser focus the animate and inanimate things of the immediate environment, and then fades toward abstraction as one goes down the scale to micro-phenomena and up to macroentities. The reified entities appear as substances clothed with qualities — physical as well as (in the case of persons) mental.

Such a world is relatively narrow; it is implicitly dualist; and it is anthropocentric. It is the world of childhood when the elements of fantasy are dispelled and one is left with 'stark reality'.

The sciences as well as the arts, and religion, expand this anthropocentric bubble built by common-sense logic and ordinary language. The language of art (if indeed it uses a language) expands the bubble through imagination. The language of religion expands it through faith. Science expands it through a suspension of common sense and ordinary language, and a reliance on its own method of hypothesis formulation and validation. Already life in a complex social community expands the bubble by bringing into the sphere of immediate concern various multiperson entities and man-machine systems. Businesses and corporations emerge into the realm of reality; one speaks of them as entities subsisting independently of the persons forming them. Legal and political doctrines reinforce this conceptualization by endowing formally constituted multiperson entities with rights and responsibilities. Group-identification has provided a particularly sharp focus for multiperson entitation. At the dawn of civilization tribes and clans, later communities, city-states, small and large states, and presently even bloc alliances among states, provide a vehicle for reifying entities beyond the level of persons. In a complex and interdependent world, the bubble of common sense and its language expands upwards, as persons fit themselves through specialized training and role functions to enduring social, economic and political systems. The subject-predicate structure of our languages conditions our perception of these entities and masks the fact that we cannot commonsensically assume that they have a substance of their own. Hence we can speak confidently, if inconsistently, of teams, corporations, social, political and cultural organizations, and entire nation-states, being good or bad, efficient, or malicious, or aggressive. If questioned, common sense would dictate that we clarify our language and point out that we mean the character of the individuals making up the predicated entities. But in fact we do not mean the individuals, for individuals can be transient whereas the character of the entities may be relatively invariant. Thus the character of multiperson entities 'inheres' in some unperceived substance, much as psychological characters inhere in minds and personalities. The logic of common sense and the structure of ordinary language forces such conceptualizations on those who would use them indiscriminately.

## THE FRAGMENTATION OF THE SCIENTIFIC WORLD PICTURE

The Whorf-Sapir hypothesis can be extended to the logic and language of the sciences. Scientists tend to perceive the world in terms relevant to their scientific specialities. Since different specialities use different concepts and modes of structuring their empirical data, scientists in different disciplines tend to have differing organizations of empirical reality.

The differences occasioned by adherence to specific scientific theories take the form of partial qualifications of the everyday world picture. No scientific theory meshes fully with common sense and ordinary language. Bertrand Russell pointed to contradictions between the assumptions of common sense and the theoretical postulates of contemporary physics.

What Russell said of physics can also be said of other natural and social sciences. Inasmuch as they go beyond the description and classification of observations and attempt an explanation of their data, they make use of theoretical frameworks of which the axioms as well as the rules of deduction are constructed in reference to the methods and criteria of the sciences, not of common sense. Thus theoretical sciences do not hesitate to postulate unobserved entities provided thereby consistency can be introduced into the explanation of observations, as well as parsimony, elegance, extensibility to other phenomena, predictive power, and so on. The consequence is that the processes of reification become autonomous in science; and the reified world of the scientist differs from the common sense world. Insofar as a scientist does not fully divorce his professional and his private spheres of cognition but demands some degree of consistency between them, he will begin to qualify his everyday logic and language in the light of his theories.

The modification is likely to vary with the kind of specialty embraced by the scientist. The almost monolithic unity of modern science, induced by the paradigmatic role of Newtonian physics, was shattered with the advent of relativity. Physics as the paradigm to be emulated was increasingly questioned by the life sciences when it became apparent that the equations of quantum mechanics are incapable to provide an explanation of living phenomena. Also, the social sciences came into their own, and the sweeping reductionism, expressed in the last century in Fechner's concept of a "psycho-biological physics" as the perfect science, came to be replaced by relatively independent theories, building conceptual universes as best suited to account for the phenomena of their particular concern.

Although contemporary science is pluralistic, it is nevertheless different from the logic of common sense and ordinary language. It rejects the subject-predicate structure of ordinary Indo-European languages as a mode of conceptualizing reality. *What* a thing is, independently of its attributes, cannot be answered in science; nor does it make sense to explain observations as attributes, since they would then resemble the grin of the Cheshire cat. Instead, science conceptualizes by building models of the structure and function of diverse entities and of their interactions. These models answer questions concerning how the entitites are organized and how they function when conditions are specified. They are incommensurate with the entities reified in ordinary discourse as having qualities inhering in substances.

Scientists tend to modify their everyday construction of the world in accordance with the language they use *qua* scientists. A nuclear physicist is likely to modify his common-sense world picture to accommodate the existence of elementary particles as the constituents of all observed things. Introspectionist psychologists will expand the mind-concept of common sense to a rich internal structure consisting of drives, tensions, emotions, fixations, and similar structural elements, whereas psychologists of the classical behaviorist school will look on human beings as complex reactive systems. Life scientists recognize unicellular organisms, genes, and species as furnitures of reality, and the ecologists among them tend to affirm the reality of ecosystems. Social scientists recognize the entities on the level of their investigation: microsociologists and social psychologists entitate groups and other primary units of social, economic and political interaction, and macrosociologists and international relations theorists may reify nation-states, supranational blocs, transnational organizations and universal actors, such as the United Nations. Since scientists participate in the everyday world and use ordinary language, their specialities condition their everyday world outlook but do not totally replace them with the perspective of their discipline. Scientists structure their perceived world to include persons, other animate things and the observed inanimate things in their milieu, but also include in their world picture the principal units of their professional investigations. For natural scientists other than astronomers and ecologists, these units tend to lie below the order of magnitude of the sense perceived world: for astronomers, social scientists and ecologists, above the perceived magnitudes. Their respective world pictures are extended in these directions beyond the confines imposed by common sense logic and the structure of everyday language.

## THE REUNIFICATION OF SCIENTIFIC WORLD PICTURES THROUGH GENERAL SYSTEM THEORY

The great cultures of the past have not fragmented the world picture but conserved some element of consistency in the way they structured experience for their members. Classical Hellenic culture, for example, saw man as part of the plan of creation, of the evolution of the cosmos from chaos to order, and regarded human institutions as partaking in the universal scheme. There were gods, men, animals and other living things, as well as inanimate nature, but these were all products of a creative demiurge or of the crystallization of order through the separation and conflict of opposites. Classical Oriental thought likewise distinguished various levels of reality but did not isolate or oppose them. Man was to fit himself into nature and seek union with the cosmos through illumination. Also the Middle Ages produced a more harmonious and unified world picture by ascribing the reason for the existence of all things to God. Man alone had a divine soul, but the whole world was God's creation and man was to seek his salvation by fitting himself into the temporal order without arrogance or aggression. The rise of modern science with its technological spin-offs, and the contemporaneous rise of a protestant ethic of hard work for the good of man equated with the glory of God, splintered the harmony of the Medieval world and placed man above nature as its master. It gave free reign to the development of science, only to find that the mechanistic world view of Newtonian physics, and the transcendental spiritual outlook of classical religion, provoked a fission which philosophers, even of the stature of Hume and Kant, were unable to mend. The result was the separation of a common sense perceptual world based on sole reliance on ordinary language; the worlds of the specialized sciences; and the distinct worlds of the arts and religions. There are currents taking shape today which seek to overcome the multiple splintering of the empirical world picture through the creation of an internally consistent general meta-language to give structure to perception. One of the most powerful elements in these currents is general system theory.

General system theory adopts natural science's emphasis on structure and function, but extends it to all sciences and, through systems philosophy, to the humanities as well. The result is a new structuring of the empirical evidence, into levels of organization. Two general level-structures are distinguished. One level includes the entities of physics and astronomy: space-time field, elementary particles, atoms, cosmic dust and interstellar matter in micro aggregations (meteorites, etc.), stellar objects of all kinds, satellitic systems, star-families, stellar clusters, galaxies, galaxy clusters, and the metagalaxy as the totality of astronomical objects. The other level comprises a level structure evolving on the surface of the earth and assumed to be paralleled in some respects on other suitable planetary surfaces. This structure can be conceptualized as starting with some varieties of stable atoms, molecular sysystems, crystals, macromolecular compounds, cells, multicellular organisms in species-specific populations, and inter-specific ecosystems. It includes man and the social and political world system (see Fig. 1).

Abstracting here from the astronomical hierarchy of stars and galaxies, we can introduce order into our knowledge of the terrestrial scheme of things by observing that some general system laws hold true on all levels of its organization. All modules can be conceptualized as structures maintaining themselves amidst change and adapting to the patterns of change by regulating whatever exchanges they have with their environment. Thus the theory of open dynamic systems will apply, and with it the concepts recently developed in cybernetics, information theory and related fields. Recurrent factors can be observed, applying to the microhierarchy as a whole. (1) The higher we penetrate on the scale of organization, the more openness we find in the modules. Stable atoms are closed unless disturbed by radiation exceeding their bonding forces. By contrast multicellular organisms and their ecosystems are continuously open and depend on their environmental transactions for their persistence. (2) The lower level modules are strongly bonded (e.g. nuclear and electronic forces bond the structure of atoms) whereas the higher modules make use of progressively weaker bonding forces (organisms have chemical bonds, populations and ecosystems bonds are based on niche structure and symbiotic behavior coded by genes, and social systems bonds use acquired and retransmitted values, mores, laws and so on). (3) The higher modules depend on self-regulation for their persistence rather than the force of the bonds. Theirs is not a structural form of stability, but a cybernetic form of ultrastability: the capacity to respond to the environment, and cope with it through adaptive changes in the systems themselves. (4) As we ascend the scale we find that the abundance of the modules decreases: there are more atoms than molecules, more molecules than cells, and so on. Indeed, the level structure forms a branching Chinese-box hierarchy, with many lower-level modules inside every higher level module (e.g. many molecules constitute cells, many cells multicellular organisms, and many organisms populations and ecosystems). But the decreased quantitative abundance of the systems is balanced by an increased variety of species and a correlated diversity in their manifest structural and

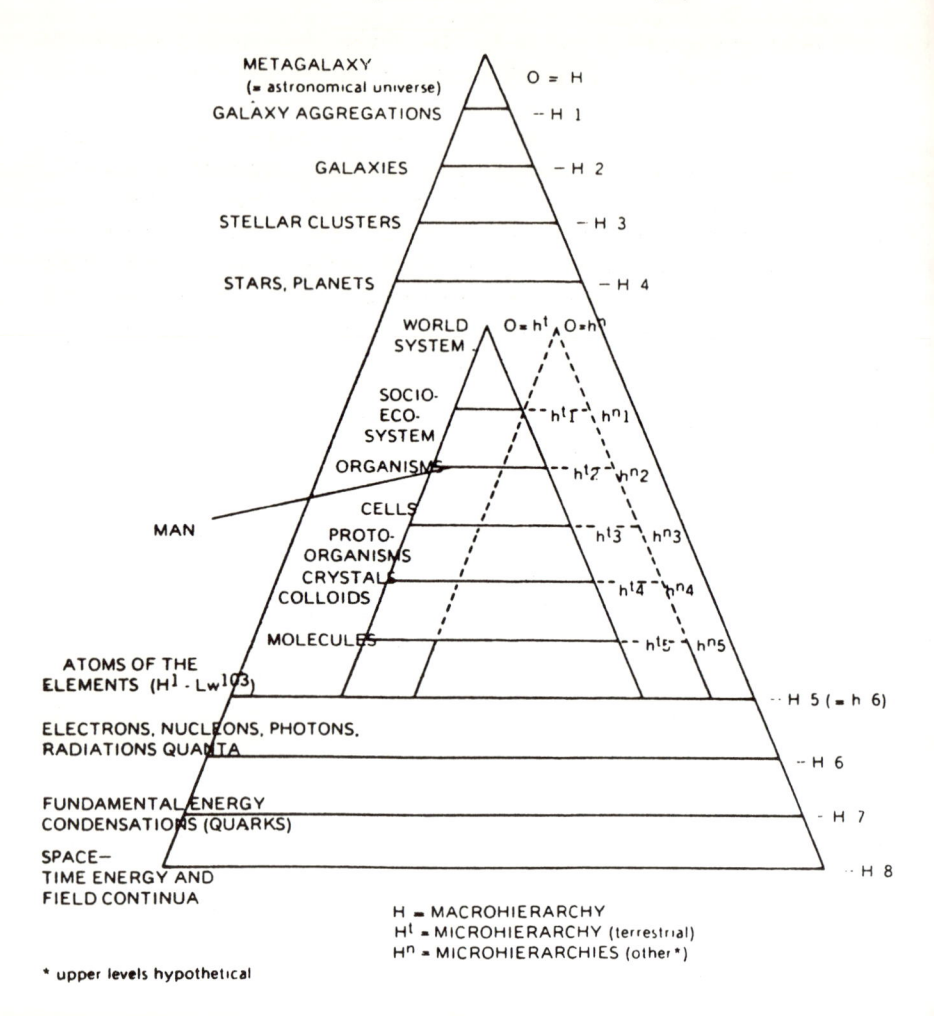

*Fig. 1*

functional features (there are but eighty-two stable forms of atoms, but many thousands of molecules, untold millions of organic species [the roughly one billion species assumed to have existed on earth — of which 99% are now extinct — are but a fraction of all the species which could arise by combinations of genetic codons based on nucleic acids], and the variety of possible ecological and social forms is probably beyond human imagination).

Some species of systems have highly sophisticated self-regulative functions: these emerged by mutation and natural selection in evolution. In such species we find an enhanced capacity to adapt organism and environment by manipulating the latter to the needs of the former. Cooperative patterns can develop among members of local populations, selecting for a flexible mode of intercommunication.

These patterns of communication can facilitate the development of consciousness, the imaginative recreation of perceived objects and events, and reflections on ultimate purposes. In sum, culture may evolve out of a reliance on a high level of self-regulation in a population of organisms. Therewith we may witness the emergence of justice, morality, beauty, knowledge, and so on. These phenomena are not strangers in the natural world, but may be accounted for in the context of the evolution of a particular species of complex open systems. The living and the nonliving, as well as the individual and the cultural, are united through the general system conceptions of persistence and development. These provide a 'vertical' linkage among the sciences specializing on diverse levels. A statement of the specialized languages of the sciences and the humanities in the general meta-language of systems can bring about a reunification of the world pictures fragmented by adherence to different theoretical paradigms. Hereby the effect of Whorfian relativity within contemporary Western culture can be mitigated, and better conditions provided for communication and understanding among scientists and humanists.

## CURRENT EFFECTS OF THE REDUCTION OF WHORFIAN RELATIVITY THROUGH A GENERAL LANGUAGE OF SYSTEMS

The reunification of the perceived worlds of contemporary scholars through the adoption of a general language of systems already bears some remarkable fruits.

It should be noted, first of all, that the person who masters the general system paradigm can readily adapt to different sciences: he can translate their theoretical languages into his own systems metalanguage and offer new insights by relating one theoretical language to another. The writer had occasion to work with biologists in the past, and is currently engaged on a research project with specialists in international relations theory. He experienced little difficulty in moving back and forth among these fields, and communicating with specialized workers. Moreover insights gained in one field have repeatedly proved to have value when applied to others, when the application concerned a systems model which could be specified to simulate behavior on different levels of observation.

Secondly we should note that interdisciplinary communication occurs these days at a high level of competence through the meetings organized by the Society for General Systems Research. The Society has members coming from a wide variety of disciplines, including biophysics, international relations, computer sciences, history, philosophy and linguistics. At the meetings of the Society the membership gathers to exchange information and comment on each other's work. The level of communication at these meetings (some of which were organized by the writer) is as high or higher than at comparable meetings within the boundaries of a single discipline. It is not that the biologist acquires an instant knowledge of economics or the computer expert a knowledge of international relations. Rather, the language of the analysis frames a set of concepts that are familiar to all, and make possible the assessment of phenomena on fields different from one's own narrow domain. The participants share a language which restructures their world pictures along isomorphic lines.

The level of communication at these meetings may be contrasted with that typical of interdisciplinary meetings. The writer participated in several such meetings as well, of which one recent experience stands out particularly clearly. The meeting was called to discuss the nature and goals of human purpose from various perspectives — biological, cultural, epistemological, social, and theological. The distinguished participants included two physicists, three biologists, a neurophysiologist, an anthropologist, a sociologist, two philosophers, and two theologians. Most participants have been acquainted with one another from previous contacts, and all have read each others' published works. The *entente* was excellent and cordiality high. But the sessions, which lasted for six days in an idyllic secluded spot of the New York Catskills Mountains, bogged down through mutual incomprehension. The physicists failed to see what the theologians were driving at; the three biologists, of whom one was a specialist on termites, another on genetics and the third on population dynamics and evolution, disagreed among themselves; few conceded that the philosophers had any real competence to speak on the subject, and no one understood the dualist ideas put forward by the neurophysiologist. It so happened that three of those present — a theologian, a biologist and a philosopher — shared the general language of systems. They had no difficulty in communicating, but were unable to convince the others of the cogency of their viewpoint. (That something of value might still come out of this meeting is possible: all participants agreed to exchange papers and revise them in accordance with feedback from the rest. Given the close personal *entente* among the group, there are powerful motivations to bridge professional differences).

Our final example will be a meeting bringing together systems theorists who differed not only in disciplinary, but also in cultural-ideological background. The occasion was the XIIIth World Congress of the History of Science in Moscow where a section was devoted to the history and concepts of general system theory. Present at the sessions were a large number of Russians, an almost equally large number of Americans, and a few Europeans. Papers were given in Russian, English, French and German. A condensed summary was provided of Russian papers in English, and of the rest in Russian. Despite obvious linguistic difficulties of comprehension, the comments were incisive and the discussion live. Moreover the sessions were prolonged into informal discussion groups and dinner-table exchanges, with a level of communication as high as that of any disciplinary meeting in one country. Friendships were formed between Soviet philosophers and American mathematical psychologists, American sociologists and Soviet historians of science, etc. which would not have been likely to form in the absence of the general language of systems, even among members of any one nation. Apart from an unspoken agreement not to raise specifically ideological questions, there were no areas in the respective world pictures which would have been too differently structured to permit real dialogue. Contacts established at that meeting issued in a number of publications of Soviet researchers in America, and of Americans in the Soviet Union, Poland, and other Eastern-bloc countries.

The above examples were offered to illustrate the thesis of this study: that the effects of Whorfian relativity include the fragmentation of the world picture among scientists and humanists belonging to different specialities, and that such fragmentation can be reduced through the use of a general meta-language of systems which assigns reality to hierarchic sequences of dynamic open systems from atoms to global socio-cultural systems, and thus effects a vertical unification of the disciplines without reducing one to another. The general system theorist perceives the world as constituted of systems within systems, in complex hierarchical structures with multiple feedback paths, and can select for detailed attention systems and relationships on different levels without distorting his general framework and isolating himself from investigators interested in other levels and relationships. The consistency introduced into the ordering of our empirical knowledge through the use of this meta-language merits further study and refinement.

# 10

## CYBERNETICS OF MUSICAL ACTIVITY*

Problems of music aesthetics occupied the minds of thinkers through the ages: Plato and Aristotle wrote on them (and disagreed), and with the rise of the new era in music in the eighteenth century, theories and opinions have multiplied. Published writings range from critical studies, largely presupposing their aesthetic premises, to inquiries in depth into the psychology of the creative and appreciative processes. If there is little agreement as to the nature of music and its meaning for man, it is because present studies are predominantly based on personal introspection, and the generalization of the findings to music (or musicians) as such. More rigor would, of course, be desirable. Yet it could only be achieved if we could penetrate the highly complex mental and neural phenomena that takes place in the mind of persons when they compose, perform, and listen to music. Meaning is not a property of sounds, but of persons perceiving the sounds. Yet psychology can offer us merely qualitative models of aesthetic processes: quantitatively it has not penetrated beyond the understanding of basic sensory perceptions and their correlated sensations. Neurophysiology, while progressing with giant strides, is still at a loss to understand higher cognitive events, and problems of artistic appreciation and creativity appear to elude it completely. Under these circumstances it may be well to follow the lead of such cyberneticians and systems theorists as Ashby,[2,3] von Bertalanffy,[4,5] MacKay,[23,24] Boulding,[6] and Deutsch,[9] and attempt to construct a simplified model of musical processes which would have the basic properties observed of the real thing. If such cybernetic or systems models can be proposed for phenomena as complex as a cell, an organism, an ecology, the economy, certain aspects of the human brain, and even international relations, perhaps a similarly simplified but isomorphic model can be outlined for the processes of musical creativity, performance, and appreciation. This is the objective of the present study.

There is something intrinsically displeasing about cybernetic concepts for persons accustomed to high-flown aesthetic prose in the description of musical

---
*Reprinted from The *Journal of Aesthetics and Art Criticism*, XXXI/3, Spring 1973.

events. Yet we must keep in mind that the cybernetic scheme does not pretend to describe such events and processes, only to outline their logic — the underlying *logos* that, as Heraclitus believed, regulates the flux and flow of manifest phenomena. Thus our scheme is proposed as a skeleton only, to be clothed with the living flesh and blood of qualitatively rich musical experience. Its merit can lie in offering a basis for understanding the structure of these phenomena in reference to clearly defined concepts. Moreover, such a theory, if successful, can link up the apparently *sui generis* nature of musical experience with creative, interpretive, and appreciative processes in other realms of human endeavor.[13,15,18] Thus it is at least worthy of a good try.

## THE BASIC CONCEPTS

There are few points of agreement concerning the nature of musical enjoyment and meaning among critics and aestheticians, but one of these few concerns the affective response elicited by music. That music creates feeling, and is itself a kind of embodiment of feeling in sound, is seldom contested. The evidence on this score is overwhelming and has received the attention of virtually all composers, performers, and critics, from C. Ph. E. Bach, through Liszt to Stravinsky. The interpretation of this factor varies with each writer, and so does its valuation. (Plato argued that art's effect is to "water the passions" and make men emotional and irrational, whereas Aristotle held that the emotive effect of art is to purge emotionality and make men more rational.) Philosophers of art see the emotional factor in music as expression (Croce, Carritt[7], Collingwood[8], etc.) or as symbol (Cassirer, Langer[10], and others). Attempts to grasp this element in reference to the pattern of sounds in a given musical work use mathematics in reference to phenomenology (Ansermet[1]) and modern information theory in relation to a psychological theory of emotion (Meyer[25]). In the general cybernetical model we propose here, no specific interpretation will be championed at the expense of any other. We simply note that feeling is a key factor in the aesthetic enjoyment of music, and that when such enjoyment or experience obtains, the feelings of the subject match with the perceptional qualities of the work experienced. Since the match in question contains two terms or variables (the feelings of the subject, and the qualities of the perceived music), it is determined by the *coincidence* of these terms. We can examine the conditions leading to such coincidence in reference to both factors, to wit: (i) the perceptual properties of music, and (ii) the emotive properties of persons.

(i) The expressivity of music finds its roots in the perception of the emotive suggestiveness or connotation of musical sounds. Individual musical sounds are distinguished in reference to three principal variables: timbre, pitch, and loudness. Each can be given an explanation in terms of the physical properties of the waves constituting the sounds; but our concern is only with the suggestiveness of the sounds in reference to emotive factors. Thus, timbre is said to determine the quality of the perceived sound. The sound of a violin has a different quality than that of an

English horn, even if both instruments play the same note at the same level of loudness. The difference is determined by the timbre, and it is often described in terms of tone color, brightness, texture, or density. Pitch, on the other hand, is a factor which differentiates sounds on a given scale, regardless of the instrument or voice producing them. Pitch is closely correlated wih the basic frequency of the sound wave and is perceived in reference to the notions "high" and "low". Significantly, these notions connote not merely spatial positions, relevant to the location of the given sounds on the scale, but also states of mind. In fact, low sounds tend to have a soft or rumbling effect, while high ones tend to sharpness and excitation as perceived. Finally, loudness is the factor which strongly conditions the emotive intensity of the effect of sounds. Dramatic build-ups usually involve a *crescendo*, with the climax stated in *fortissimo*. Loud sounds tend to connote either triumphant feelings or hardness; soft ones intimacy or depression.

But, musical enjoyment is not just the enjoyment of the emotive qualities of individual musical sounds. Musical enjoyment arises, rather, in the context of variously combined sounds. Music can be "expressive" of feelings because the many emotively perceived sounds coalesce into wholes strongly appealing to ways of feeling. Yet the problem of devising an "emotive language of music" appears insoluble. Although we may point to the known effects of intervals, rhythms, harmonies, and the combination of these, it remains impossible to give definite descriptions of musical passages in terms of the feelings they connote, and seem to express, for hearers. The difficulty lies in the relational qualification of each musical component in its particular musical context. Each component lends its proper "feel" to the larger whole in which it is heard and is in turn determined by the "feel" of that whole — ultimately by the full musical composition.[10] Thus the same combination of sounds may take on entirely different emotive meanings in different works and, conversely, different works, consisting of an analogously structured sequence of sounds, may yet have closely related emotive meanings, even if they have no single sound in common.

(ii) The emotive properties of persons are determined by their genetic and socio-cultural endowments and environment. Persons possess different degrees of sensitivity to feeling, different degrees of awareness of their own feelings, and various degrees of training in, and habit of listening to, music. Each individual brings to his musical experience his entire "aesthetic set" defined by the specific level of his sensitivity to, and appreciation of, musical works of given styles. This set is not static, but is constantly molded by the experience of the person. Both extramusical and musical experience influence it. For example, events which elicit an upsurge of feeling in extramusical experience (such as love relationships, bereavement, friendship, etc.) increase the person's sensitivity to feeling in musical sounds. And repeated exposure to new styles in music can alter his appreciation of them, both positively (in 'getting to like', e.g. Bartok) or negatively ('getting tired' of, e.g. romanticism). One may observe, in general, that the necessary conditions of musical enjoyment include (i) some degree of sensitivity to feeling in whatever form, (ii) some degree of sensitivity to feeling as expressed or embodied in musical sounds, and (iii) some degree of familiarity with and appreciation of the given musical style.[19] These factors form levels, based on (i) and progressing toward (iii). Only if (iii) — and hence also (i) and (ii) — are given does musical enjoyment occur. In that case there is a *match* (correspondence or coincidence) between the established (but changeable) modes of feeling of the subject and the emotive connotation of the music.

The coincidence of ways of feeling and connotations of musical sounds can be conceptualized in terms of form and content, syntax and semantics, or invariance and transformations. We shall use the latter; it has the most neutral, and hence for our purposes most desirable quality. Under *invariance* we understand the commonality underlying change within a set. *Transformations* refer to the in-themselves different members of the set which exhibit the commonality in some relevant respect. In this case we speak of 'modes of feeling' as invariances, and 'specific apprehensions corresponding to the modes' as the transformations. For example, I now have an invariant mode of feeling *sadness* of a certain kind — rather tranquil, contemplative, almost sweet. This represents an invariance in my feelings which can occur in various transformations. Some of these transformations are elicited by the perceptions of Chopin Nocturnes.

'Invariance under transformation' applies to all realms of cognition.[15] Mathematicians point out that the triad group, for example, can be represented in many different ways: as all the possible cyclic permutations on three letters; as the rotations of a labeled triangle, or as a set of algebraic matrices. But all these representations have one thing in common: they are all triad groups. That is the invariance which underlies all transformations. Similarly, musicologists recognize that a major triad can be constituted by different notes (C E G, F A C, etc.) and that there is no single set of notes which specifically constitutes a major triad as such. The relationship of the notes transcends their specific individuality. *Triadness* is what all the different musical sounds in that relation have in common, regardless of their particular pitch, timbre, or intensity.

The use of invariance under transformation in this study applies to the emotive connotation of musical sounds. Each composition is unique, and if it was perceived in its uniqueness only, each first audition would be a difficult puzzle for the listener. That different musical works can be understood even on first hearing is due to the invariance of their structure in reference to other works. Such invariance extends to the emotive connotation of the sounds. For example, anyone who has some sensitivity for feeling in general, sensitivity for musical feeling in particular and for classical music specifically, is likely to enjoy the final hymn of joy in Beethoven's Ninth Symphony on first hearing. It coincides with his ways of feeling joy in general, joy in music in particular, and joy in Beethoven specifically. Yet we can acknowledge that Beethoven's Ninth provides us with a unique emotional experience. Until we have first heard that Symphony, we have most likely never encountered the particular kind of joy it inspires in us. Yet we can understand that work; and the feeling itself, while new, is not unfamiliar. There is no paradox involved: the answer is that we relate the feelings elicited by the work to our established modes of feeling in virtue of their common properties: their invariance. The Ninth gives us a new transformation of the invariance represented by our ways of feeling joy.

The foregoing considerations derive additional importance because we can construct a cybernetic model of musical experience in reference to such concepts. The 'way of feeling' here discussed, although nebulous, can now be called an 'aesthetic construct' (analogously to the sense in which, for example, an atom is called a 'scientific construct' in the philosophy of science[13]). Musical works match or mismatch our aesthetic constructs to various extents. If they match them, we are inspired with a familiar yet fresh feeling, and musical enjoyment obtains. If a mismatch occurs, we only perceive sounds without aesthetic meaning or significance. Now, musical works exist in our environment in the form of variously structured sounds (in a physicalist interpretation, as sound waves of different frequencies and intensities, produced by vocal chords or instruments). They can only match or mismatch our ways of feeling (aesthetic constructs) if they are 'transduced' by the ear and nervous system into 'heard' sound with all the richness of immediate experience. Hence, if we select a symbol for any given musical work as it exists 'objectively' in our environment (let us say $E$), then we must connect this symbol with another ($P$) representing our perception of the sounds in all their qualitative richness, before we can make a connection to our aesthetic construct ($C$). If the musical work, as heard, matches our aesthetic construct, we shall insert a double shafted arrow between $P$ and $C$ in our graphs; if it mismatches it, we shall use a single shafted arrow.

So far we have a basic blueprint for grasping the communication of music to the subject; not, however, for showing how the subject can produce, interpret, or otherwise manipulate the music. Obviously, we need to complete the sequence of events by allowing that the musician (or listener) has some means of restructuring the sequence of sounds reaching his ears. Hence we insert a term for creative activity ($R$) into our scheme; this term connects our aesthetic constructs to the musical sounds objectively given in our environment. We may conceive of $R$ as the neuromotor activity acivated by purposive motivations set up in our mind (brain), due to the musical experience itself. Such activity can take the form of putting on or taking off a record, repeating a passage with different emphasis, simply setting forth the ongoing sequence of sounds, or changing it altogether. In general, and in the absence of extraneous factors, we may assume that $R$ will tend to correct the sequence of music reaching our ears as a function of assuring a more exact match with our aesthetic constructs. In other words, creative activity is deployed to increase our musical enjoyment.

We now have a complete cybernetical circuit, with the requisite closure and a flexible yet effective control element. $C$ (our aesthetic construct) controls the pattern of events flowing in the circuit by maximizing the match with $P$ (the sounds as heard). This is accomplished by directing $R$ (creative behavioral activity) to structure $E$ (the sounds as existing in the environment) to our liking. Figure 1 represents this model in the simplest terms.

This cybernetic circuit finds empirical interpretation in elucidating the logic of events in the musical experience of three types of persons (all of whom

```
            musical works
        (sequence of sounds in
            environment)
                E
              ╱   ╲
             ╱     ╲
emotively  P╱       ╲R   creative
connotative ╲match  ╱    activity
perception of╲     ╱
sounds        ╲   ╱
               ╲ ╱
                C
        aesthetic constructs
      (ways and sensitivities of
           feeling in music)
```

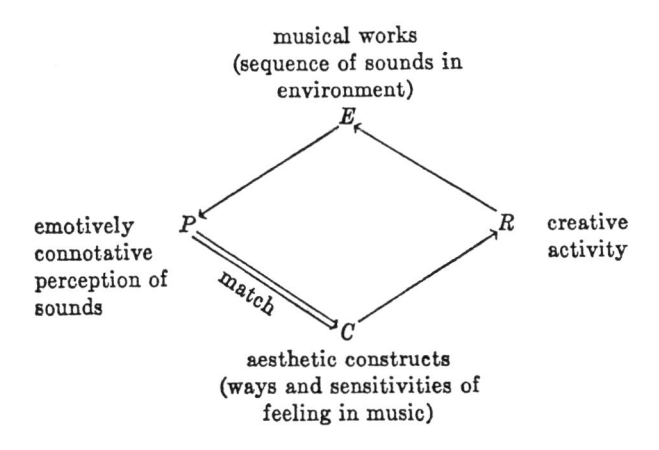

*Fig. 1*

are assumed to have evolved aesthetic constructs): composer, performer, and listener. Each of these types of persons can be analyzed in reference to three types of musical activity: creativity, learning, and communication.

## Creativity in Music

### The Composer

The process of composition is guided by the composer's aesthetic construct ($C$) which he attempts to match with musical sounds. At one point in his experience, the composer envisages ways of feeling which are as yet unexpressed in existing musical compositions: he proceeds to express (or symbolize) them in sound. He tries out various combinations of sounds in directed, creative activity ($R$), having as his goal a match between his aesthetic construct ($C$) and heard sound ($P$). To this end he structures sounds in his environing world ($E$). (Instead of the latter he may substitute the imaginative envisagement of the sound — in that event, i.e., if the composer is composing in his head, the terms $E$ and $P$ exist only in imagination.)

The process of composition can be a conscious and deliberate one, in which case it consists of a purposive searching out of the patterns of sound which match (express, symbolize, embody) the composer's aesthetic construct; or it can be a more complex creative process, where the sounds heard (or imagined) suggest further aesthetic constructs, or refine the one already envisaged by the composer. Here 'creativity' refers to the development of new aesthetic constructs. In another sense (which we shall prefer since it agrees more closely with habitual usage) 'creativity' refers to the process of composing itself, i.e., to the matching of sounds to one's ways and sensitivities of musical feeling. In the latter sense all composition is creative, and the 'pure' evolution of aesthetic constructs (without aid of feedback from the act of composing) is referred to the general patterns of experience and response of the composer. Such experience and response make him a genius (if he is one); his acts of composition make him specifically a composer.

The written score is the record of the composer's creative activity. It is the public embodiment of the aesthetic constructs developed in his mind. The written score, of course, is but a blueprint for creating musical sounds in specific patterns. And musical sounds derive their aesthetic importance in being perceived with felt emotion. Hence, if we denote the score with $E'$, we get the following chain of events connecting the composer's creativity to his, or his public's enjoyment of the fruit of his labors: $E'$ (score) $\rightarrow E$ (sound produced in accordance with score) $\rightarrow P$ (sound perceived by appreciator) $\rightarrow C$ (aesthetic construct of appreciator). The success of the endeavor as a form of communication (if composer and appreciator are different persons) depends on the matching of $P$ with $C$, which presupposes, in general, some similarity between the composer's and the appreciator's aesthetic constructs. These problems will be dealt with in more detail below. We note here that $E'$ (the score) can be eliminated as a phase in the process if the composer performs the work directly. In that event, $E$, i.e., the sound objectively existing in the environment, can be 'observed' by all persons within range of hearing.

$E'$ need not, of course, be a written score: it can also be a transcription in another medium. Recordings of music performed by the composer can function in this capacity or, even more directly, electronic music created by the composer himself on magnetic tape. Such media have the advantage of transcribing the composer's intentions faithfully (provided his transcription skillfully expresses his intentions), but have the disadvantage of eliminating the additional degrees of creativity of a live performer. This we discuss next.

*The Performer*

The creativity of the musical performer is limited by the rigorous task of having to reproduce the musical work created by the composer. Notwithstanding this limitation, the work of the performer is not a purely mechanical or historical one. He can infuse the performed works with his own feelings and hope thereby to reproduce to some extent the intentions of the composer. Regardless of whether or not such reproduction does indeed take place, the basic objective of performers is to match the sounds of musical works to their own ways and sensitivities of feeling. To this end they can first of all select, from among all works written for their instrument or voice and available to them, those which best express what they themselves wish to express. Second, they can interpret the selected works. Within the limitations intrinsic to the style of given works, they can creatively manipulate them to suit their own aesthetic constructs. Whereas performing Bach in the style of Tchaikovsky is no longer within the limits of interpretation, but appears as an arbitrary modification of the specific style of the piece, playing Bach with precisely those shadings of tempo, dynamics, and emphasis which express the essence of the work for the performer is a genuine case of artistic interpretation. It is what distinguishes a mechanical reproduction of sounds from the score from a truly valid musical performance. The latter means restructuring the sequence of sounds ($E$) as a function of rendering one's musical sensations ($P$) concordant with his musical tastes ($C$). Producing this match defines the range of the performer's creative activity ($R$).

*The Listener*

The listener neither composes nor performs music, and in consequence his creative manipulation of sounds is restricted to (i) the selection and (ii) the imaginative adaptation, of live or transcribed musical performances. Selecting performances is facilitated by the electronic reproduction of sound which, through recordings and radio, puts at each listener's disposal works by a multitude of composers performed by a great variety of interpreters. The creativity of the listener involves a choice of both work and interpreter. These choices enable the listener to apprehend those complexes of musical sound which satisfy his own aesthetic constructs — his ways of musically expressible feeling. Second, the listener imaginatively adapts the music he hears to his musical tastes: he hears the music in reference to his aesthetic constructs. Hearing, as seeing, is a gestalt phenomenon where we reduce stimuli to our established norms and standards. In the case of music, this reduction occurs to aesthetic constructs, i.e. to invariant types and sequences of feeling, to which the heard sounds are assimilated in virtue of their joint emotive connotation. Thus you and I do not hear the same thing even when we listen to the same performance: you assimilate the perceived sounds to your ways of feeling music, and I to mine.

Gestalt psychologists demonstrate to us that we do not see what is there: we see our own gestalts clothed in the sensory stimulants we select and imaginatively modify in the field of vision. Hearing is likewise a gestalt phenomenon, and musical hearing doubly so. Here we hear in large part what we think we hear (or want to hear), since we assimilate heard sounds to our expectations and conceptions of the music. This confers a large degree of creative freedom to the listener — a spontaneous, non-deliberate freedom — to adapt imaginatively the music he hears to his own tastes by hearing it in accordance with his own musical constructs.

**Learning in Music**

Creativity in music involves the structuring of patterns of sounds to match the musician's ways and sensitivities of feeling. It is a cybernetic control process coded by the established musical constructs of the musician, and resulting (if successful) in a sequence of emotively perceived sound that satisfies the requirements of its creator. However, we must concede that these requirements are not always and necessarily preestablished, but may manifest growth and development themselves. Hence we come across a different phase of a cybernetic control process, one namely that consists of the self-organization of the control element itself. The analogues to such circuits in the realm of artificial systems are the "learning-machines". As Wiener,[29] MacKay,[23,24] and Ashby[2,5] (among others) have shown, such systems represent simplified, but functionally isomorphic models of learning processes in human beings. Even the austere heights of musical composition, interpretation, and appreciation may be, if not scaled then at least mapped, in reference to cybernetic concepts.

We can represent the process of learning in simplest terms by using two graphs: a 'before' and 'after' snapshot of the flow of information in the learning process. The 'before' graph shows a mismatch between the heard music and the aesthetic constructs of the musician, and motivates exploratory searchings leading toward a better match through the discovery of new aesthetic constructs (i.e. new ways of understanding the music in question). We denote the mismatching aesthetic construct $C_1$, and the newly discovered ("learned") aesthetic construct $C_2$ (Figure 2).

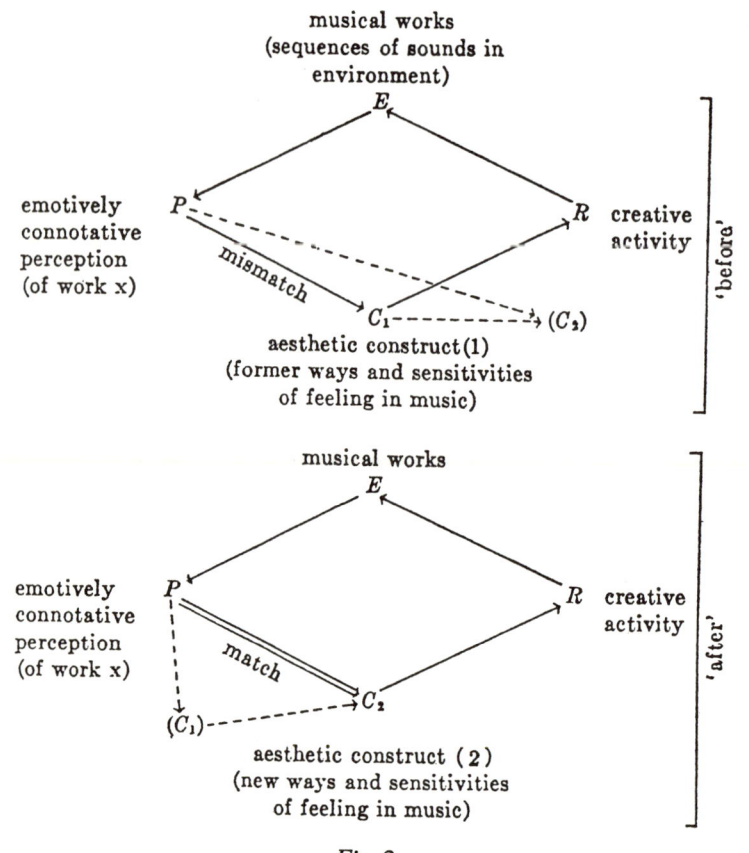

*Fig. 2*

We shall not enter into the problem of how $C_2$ is derived from $C_1$. It is sufficient for our purposes to note that all learning is held to be a form of creative response to challenges in the experience of the subject, and that learning in music need not be an exception.[13] Similarly to the learning that takes place when we are faced with a puzzling configuration of lines and planes in our visual experience, and try out various gestalts until we hit upon one that 'organizes' or 'codes' the pattern satisfactorily for our requirements of intelligibility, in music exposure to new and puzzling sequences of sounds (rhythms, harmonies, and melodies) triggers an exploratory process which leads to the reexamination of one's existing aesthetic constructs and evolves, if necessary, new constructs, i.e., new ways of listening to and understanding the given piece of music.

*The Composer*

To distinguish between creativity and learning we have to keep in mind that creativity occurs when one's aesthetic constructs outstrip one's musical experience; and learning occurs if the inverse is the case: when one's musical experience outstrips one's aesthetic constructs. Composers, by definition, belong by and large to the class of creative people. Their activity is triggered by the evolution of their own musical ideas in relation to the kind of music prevalent in their times. Hence, they are motivated to compose, i.e., to create the music which matches their requirements. However, this does not mean that musical learning would be irrelevant to composers. Much of their own creativity could have been triggered by exposure to works by other innovative composers — the mutual inspiration of the members of the avant garde. Composers, too, may be faced with music they are initially at a loss to understand. They, however, unlike less creative musicians, not only learn to evolve the kind of aesthetic constructs which lend meaning and significance to the music, but also go on to evolve constructs of their own, which go beyond the music of others, and call for creativity of their own. The learning of composers is comparable to the learning of the exceptionally bright pupil who not only assimilates what his teacher tells him, but also contributes to the field of knowledge himself. Insofar as composers learn, however, they learn through the sequence of processes characterizing most learning processes: problem, hypothesis, test, and confirmation. The problem is posed by the mismatch of music actually heard with the established aesthetic insights of the musician; the hypothesis is a creative envisagement of alternate ways of understanding the music. The test comes when the composer 'plays around' with his own musical ideas in reference to the given passage of music; and confirmation is had when he has satisfied himself that his new understanding is indeed adequate to the music in question. But insofar as he is a composer, he does not stop there, but goes on to devise aesthetic insights which have no actual counterparts in existing music. This, then, extends the composer's learning process into his process of creativity.

## The Performer

Performers may or may not be already familiar with pieces they are called upon to interpret. If the new piece is in a style known to the performer, it represents an invariance under transformation and poses no problems of understanding. (Anyone familiar with one Haydn concerto finds any other classical concerto easy to grasp.) But works in unfamiliar styles make demands on the performer's learning capacities. Not only must the notes of such works be learned, but the musical content must be understood as well. Here we encounter the element of problem calling for a hypothesis in the form of an envisaged meaning attributed to the music. The performer imaginatively or actually tests his hypothesis by going through the new interpretation of the piece in his mind, or trying it out on an instrument (or singing it). If the mismatch of the sounds with his aesthetic sensitivities is now replaced by a match, the new and matching construct is confirmed. It is used in subsequent interpretations as the insight which controls the work's performance. It is then a relatively simple matter to extend the new construct to other pieces in the same style, since these manifest but novel transformations of the stylistic invariance coded in the newly discovered sensitivities of the performer. Thus by means of learning, performers extend and enlarge their repertory of understood and meaningful music, from the simple pieces they started out with as beginners to the full range of compositions in their chosen instrument or musical medium.

## The Listener

In principle, each listener is free to choose to listen to music with which he is familiar and which is intrinsically satisfying to him. In practice, however, various pressures — cultural, social, educational, etc. — combine to expose the listener to new styles that, on first hearing, appear puzzling and meaningless. On such occasions a motivation presents itself for 'trying to understand' the music, and the process of musical learning is initiated. It may or may not be successful. If it is, the listener will begin to appreciate and enjoy music that was hitherto unfamiliar and puzzling to him. If the process is unsuccessful, the listener is likely to turn away from the style in disgust, branding it meaningless or even 'crazy'. The difference between evolving the aesthetic constructs which 'decode' the music in the new style, and failing to evolve them, is the difference between discovering how the music expresses (symbolizes, embodies) human feelings, and hearing only a jumble of sounds without rhyme or reason.

The testing of the hypotheses by listeners is restricted when compared to the testing by composers and performers. Listeners cannot change the music itself to suit their envisaged interpretations of it; they can merely select alternative performances of it, in buying recordings and attending concerts. Hence the learning process of the general public tends to be considerably slower than that of composers and performers, creating the 'cultural lag' omnipresent in all innovating art media.

## Communication in Music

*Communication Between Composer and Performer*

The physical outcome of the creative activity of the composer is a certain structure of sound produced by vocal chords or instruments (lately also by electronic means). The sounds themselves, being ephemeral phenomena, require to be coded by some means of transcription. The traditional coding of musical sounds is the musical notation, constituting the score of a given piece. This represents a blueprint for the production of certain kinds of sounds in certain combinations. It is the usual vehicle of communication between composer and performer.

Notwithstanding romantic notions to the contrary, performers do not penetrate the musical ideas of composers by some direct empathy or insight. They use the score (or the composer's comments or recordings, if any) and attempt to match the prescribed sounds with their own ways of feeling. If the sounds appear to express just what they have felt themselves, it is natural for interpreters to assume that they have found the right interpretation – and that it is the one intended by the composer. But whether performers precisely recreate the composer's intentions is immaterial (it is the 'intentional fallacy'): what matters is that they match sounds to their own genuine feelings. If so, they 'bring the score to life', to their *own* life, which is the only kind they can lend to it. Thus, communication in music involves the matching of aesthetic constructs and heard sounds, using the objective sound-patterns prescribed by the composer. Since it is unwarranted to assume that two people can ever feel exactly the same thing, or the same way, we may conclude that there cannot be 'perfect' communication of aesthetic constructs between composers and performers. But since such communication is precluded, and since the meaning of music is an act of communicating with sound, rather than with musicians, this need not disturb us. Communication takes place sufficiently for all aesthetic purposes if the performer, upon interpreting the score and creatively matching the prescribed sounds to his own ways of feeling, finds that the music expresses (symbolizes, embodies) his own feelings. Then we can reasonably assume that the patterns of sound which served him in this capacity also served the composer and that, in fact, the sounds themselves are the record of the composer's genuine artistic creativity.

*Communication Between Performer and Listener*

The scheme of communication between performer and listener is analogous to that between composer and performer, except for the nature of the transcription of the sounds, if any. Whereas the standard mode of objectively coding the patterns of sound created by the composer is the score, any objective coding of a performance in terms of symbols proves to be unfeasible. It was highly fashionable, some forty to fifty years ago, for great interpreters to edit scores and make detailed notes on the interpretation — including the dynamics, tempo, and even the position, fingering, or use of pedal for the given work. Such super-edited scores proved to be either confusing to others or conducive to a rather mechanical interpretation, due to the rigorous attention required to follow the detailed instructions. By and large, attempts to preserve interpretations through symbolic notation have been given up. They have been made superfluous by the advent of popularly priced and widely distributed recordings. Here — whether by the grooves of records or the distribution of electric potentials on magnetic tapes — sounds are non-symbolically transcribed. These (electronic or mechanical) transcriptions can be reconverted into patterns of sound similar to those produced by the recording artist. Hence, if we are to use the graph depicting the cybernetics of communication between composer and performer for understanding the analogous cybernetics of communication between performer and listener, we must mark $E'$ "recording — mechanical or electronic transcription". For the rest, the graph (of Figure 3) remains unchanged. The paradigmatic case of communication between performer and listener remains, of course,

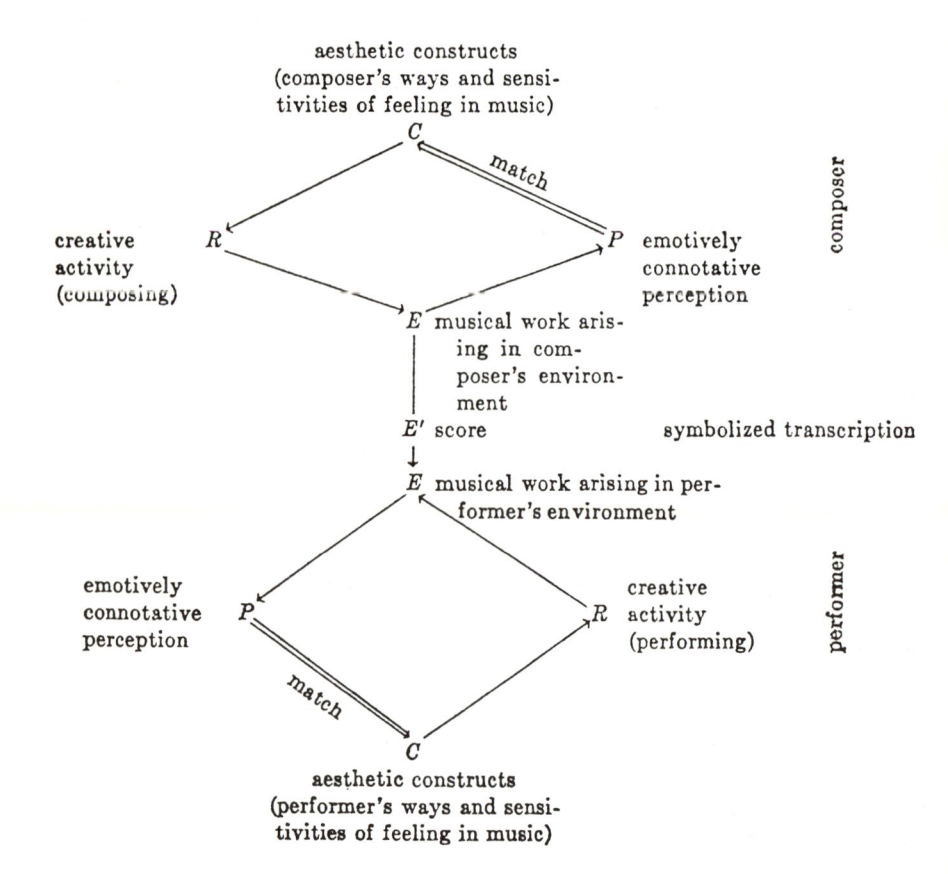

*Fig. 3*

```
                    aesthetic constructs
                    (performer's ways and sensi-
                    tivities of feeling in music)
                           C
                                match
creative        R                       P  emotively
activity                                   connotative
(performing)                               perception
                           E   musical work in shared environ-
                               ment

emotively       P                       R  creative activ-
connotative                                ity (listening
perception         match    C              [selecting, en-
                                           visaging])
                    aesthetic constructs
                    (listener's ways and sensitiv-
                    ities of feeling in music)
```

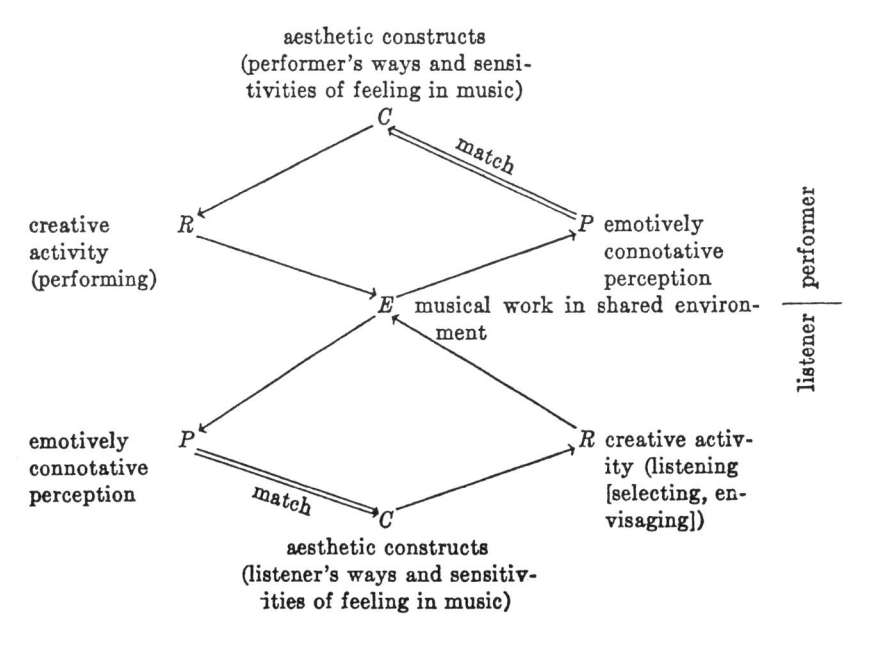

*Fig. 4*

the live performance. Here there is no $E'$ — the environment of objective sound wave propagations is shared by performer and listener. (Figure 4.)

The unique advantage offered by live performances is the possibility of communication by means of more than one channel (sense organ). Whereas sound remains the single most important component, the overall experience of a concert performance is often a vital accessory. The general air of expectancy, subdued excitement, festiveness, shared pleasure, and so on, contribute the backdrop against which the sounds produced by performers for their public stand out in sharp relief. And in most cases the visual elements of a performance contribute to the acoustic elements — this is especially true for conductors who, through gestures, communicate their aesthetic constructs to the members of the orchestra and supply their gestures, as so many helpful pointers, to the audience as well. But even where gestures are not used instrumentally in the performance of music, the spontaneous, unreflected behavior of performers tends to contribute to the enjoyment of their performance by giving further clues as to their interpretation of the music. Rhythmic body movements, facial expressions, while not beautiful or enjoyable in themselves (as they are in the case of mimes and dancers) are indices of the musical ideas of performers and thus help the public to approach the heard sounds in a similar spirit. Consequently it is not accidental that live concert performances tend to offer more intense musical enjoyment than most recordings.[11]

Communication between performer and listener, whether direct or transcribed, rests on the assimilation of the heard sensation of music to one's own ways of feeling. It is predicated upon finding the relationship of 'invariance under transformation' by each individual. The invariance is given by his own ways and sensitivities of feeling in music, and its transformation is provided by the particular (and unique) musical work he hears. For example, a feeling of grief and tragedy, coupled with courage and humility, is an emotive invariant which is variously matched by great funeral marches, from Beethoven up and down. Each performer must solve the problem of matching the sounds prescribed by the composer to the way he can feel grief, (etc.) and, producing the best match he is capable of, must offer his interpretations to his public on the assumption that they too have at their command an invariance in feeling which can be matched with the interpreted piece. In each case the match involves a communication, first of all, with the perceived sounds and then, through the sounds, with those producing the sounds. Since the understanding of music (or of any art) is less precisely definable than the understanding of discursive terms (such as 'cat' or 'sleep'), we can only guess, and never be quite certain, that our own way of perceiving the music is truly that of the performer (and the composer). Yet if we take the intentional fallacy to be truly a fallacy (as it appears in the light of the present considerations), then *bona fide* musical enjoyment can obtain regardless of whether the musical ideas of the communicators are exactly reproduced. Hence communication in music means communication *with* music, and not *through* music with *musicians*. This may be disturbing to those (like Tolstoy) who look upon music as a means of communicating with one another, but presents no difficulties for all (like Croce, Carritt, Collingwood, and others) who look upon music — and all art — as a self-centered activity having no other end than one's own aesthetic satisfaction.

## CONCLUSIONS

In this study we attempted to clarify some problems, which have attracted the attention of musicians and aestheticians of music in all ages, by recourse to concepts recently developed in the sciences of cybernetics and systems theory. Such concepts are neutral, that is, they are applicable to living, non-living, psychological, and social phenomena alike.[5] They merely fix for our attention certain relationships between factors and processes which may, in themselves, be entirely dissimilar.

The premises upon which this study is based include the thesis that musical enjoyment and appreciation obtains when the heard music coincides with the hearer's aesthetic sensibilities. This general thesis is further specified to show that these sensitivities are ways of feeling which may be matched by different patterns of sound. Thus the feelings themselves represent an invariance which reappears in diverse transformations within the experience of music.

We further suggest that the various processes of music (composing, interpreting and listening; creatively, adaptively, and communicatively) have as their goal the optimization of the match between subjective feelings and perceived music. With these tenets we construct a simple cybernetic circuit which maps processes of goal-seeking behavior in the various forms of musical activity. *Creativity* occurs when musical sensitivities run ahead of existing music and prompt the restructuring of musical sounds; *learning* obtains when existing patterns of music exceed the range of musical sensitivities and call for new efforts at understanding; and *communication* is the process of matching, from a commonly perceivable objective form, a pattern of heard sounds to the respective musical sensitivities of the communicators.

These simple graphs for cybernetic circuits may assist in avoiding *ad hoc* hypotheses in the explanation of facets of musical experience and activity, and in exhibiting the general isomorphy of purposive and valuative behavior in music with similar behavior in other areas of human experience.

## REFERENCES

1. Ansermet, Ernest, *Les fondaments de musique dans la conscience humaine.* Neuchatel, 1961.
2. Ashby, W. Ross, *Design for a Brain.* New York, 1960.
3. Ashby, W. Ross, Principles of the self-organizing system, in *Principles of Self-Organization*, Foerster and Zopf, eds., New York, 1962.
4. Bertalanffy, Ludwig von, *General System Theory.* New York, 1968.
5. Bertalanffy, Ludwig von, *Robots, Men, and Minds.* New York, 1967.
6. Boulding, Kenneth, General systems theory — the skeleton of science, in *Management Science*, 1956.
7. Carritt, E. F. *What Is Beauty?* Oxford, 1932.
8. Collingwood, R. G., *The Principles of Art.* Oxford, 1938.
9. Deutsch, Karl W., Some notes on research on the role of models in the natural and social sciences, *Synthese* 7, 506-33.
10. Langer, S. K., *Philosophy in a New Key* (esp. Chap. 8). Cambridge, Mass., 1942.
11. Laszlo, Ervin, The aesthetics of live musical performance, *The British Journal of Aesthetics*, 7, 1967.
12. Laszlo, Ervin, "Feeling, Feedback and Invariance", paper read before the American Society for Aesthetics, University of Texas, October 1968.
13. Laszlo, Ervin, *System, Structure and Experience: Toward a Scientific Theory of Mind. op. cit.*
14. Laszlo, Ervin, *Introduction to Systems Philosophy: Toward a New Paradigm of Contemporary Thought. op. cit.*
15. Laszlo, Ervin, Multilevel feedback theory of mind, in *Communication: General Semantics Perspectives*, L. Thayer, ed., New York, 1969.
16. Laszlo, Ervin, Cognition, communication and value. in *Communication: The Ethical Issues*, L. Thayer, ed., New York and London, 1973.
17. Laszlo, Ervin, Human dignity and the promise of technology, in *Human Dignity: This Century and the Next*, R. Gotesky and E. Laszlo, eds., New York and London, 1971. (Reprinted in chapter 13 of this volume.)
18. Laszlo, Ervin, The unity of the arts and sciences, in *Main Currents in Modern Thought*, Vol. 25, 1968.
19. Laszlo, Ervin, Fostering musical talent, *The Journal of Aesthetic Education*, Vol. 1, 1969.
20. Laszlo, Ervin, Artist-public-artist: communication in the concert hall, *Agora* 1, 1969.

21. Laszlo, Ervin, Affect and expression in music, *The Journal of Aesthetics and Art Criticism* 27, Winter 1968.
22. Laszlo, Ervin, The case for systems philosophy, *Metaphilosophy*, Spring 1972.
23. MacKay, Donald M., Mindlike behavior in artefacts, *British Journal of Philosophy of Science*, 1951.
24. MacKay, Donald M., Towards an information-flow model of human behavior, *British Journal of Psychology*, 1956.
25. Meyer, Leonard B., *Emotion and Meaning in Music*. Chicago, 1957.
26. Pepper, Stephen C., Autobiography of an aesthetics, *The Journal of Aesthetics and Art Criticism* 28, Spring 1970.
27. Pepper, Stephen C., Review of Ervin Laszlo's "System, Structure and Experience", *Zygon* 6, 1971.
28. Thayer, Lee, Communication – sine qua non of the behavioral sciences, *Vistas in Science*, H. Arm, ed., Albuquerque, 1968.
29. Wiener, N., *Cybernetics*, 2nd edition. Cambridge, Mass. and New York, 1961.

# 11

## GENERAL SYSTEM THEORY AND THE COMING CONCEPTUAL SYNTHESIS*

### THE NEED FOR CONCEPTUAL SYNTHESIS

Every age produced a synthesis of its most trusted items of knowledge. The synthesis has been more or less explicit, far-ranging and logical; and it has had various success in satisfying the cognitive needs and practical problems of its age. But there has never been an age of human cilivization without some degree of integration in its fields of knowledge, and the use of the integrated system in the guidance of its practical affairs.

Ours is perhaps the most diversified, least integrated, and most diffusely applied body of knowledge mankind has yet produced. It is also the most exact one on specific, fragmented areas, and the most operationalizable. That it produced the greatest disorder in the terrestrial household of man is little wonder. It is likewise obvious that unless we integrate and focus our knowledge the disorder will grow into disaster.

Without a synthesis of the items of knowledge held valid in a society, no individual or collective long-term purposes can be identified and rationally pursued. The more precise the knowledge system, the sharper the dynamics of the human processes oriented toward identified goals and conscious purposes. In the past, the synthesis of knowledge was based on items accepted on faith, and handed down in the culture's traditions. Even such syntheses faced concrete tasks in the orientation of action, since bodies of knowledge which gave consistently false directions were soon phased out in the process of natural selection acting on the biological bases of culture systems: the misdirected population was assimilated in more viable cultures, or faced extinction. This is not to say that every viable synthesis produced universal satisfaction; merely that it offered sufficiently tested orientations to enable the population subscribing to it to survive. A group of conscious beings will not rely on instincts alone any more than on blind habit and unreflected tradition. Every

---
*Reprinted from *Kybernetes*, 1974, Vol. 3, pp. 3-9.

major decision is justified in terms of a knowledge scheme, but every knowledge scheme is tentative and open to reexamination. Ineffective knowledge schemes are either replaced, or the population suffers for their continued beliefs. Viable cilivizations constantly modify their syntheses to keep them functional. Thus a long sequence of conceptual syntheses unfolds in history, each scheme holding sway for a time, to be succeeded by more updated and efficient modes of thought and views of the world. In the ancient Western world great writings, committed to paper and copied by learned scholars, served as pivotal points of the synthesis of knowledge. There was the Jewish Bible; the epics of Homer and the *Theogeny* of Hesiod; the works of Aristotle, and the *encyclopaedias* of Varro and Pliny. In the Middle Ages these syntheses of classical knowledge were elaborated by Christendom and Islam. The former produced Augustine's *City of God*, Justinian's *Corpus Juris Civilis*, the *Etymologies* of Isidore, and the *Summae* of Thomas Aquinas. Islam produced the Koran and such works as Al-Farabi's *Book of Traditions*, Avicenna's *Book of Recovery*, and Ibn Khaldun's *Universal History*.

Oriental civilizations produced their own syntheses of knowledge, and their own great texts stating particular formulations. In ancient India, the major syntheses were stated in the *Vedas*, the *Upanishads*, the *Puranas*, the *Bhagavad Gita*, and the works of six major schools of Hindu philosophy. In China the great expressions of synthesized knowledge were the Confucian canon, the systematic historical records of Ssu-ma Ch'ien and his successors, and encyclopaedias such as the *T'ai-ping yü-lan* of Wu Shu and Li Fang.

With the rise of modern science, the Western synthesis took on a mixed character. The ideal of pure inductive knowledge became incompatible with the acceptance of great metaphysical syntheses handed down from past ages. Bacon's *Novum Organum*, the works of Descartes and Leibniz, the 'natural philosophy' propounded in the language of mathematics by Galileo and Newton, produced a fundamental rift in the knowledge systems of our forefathers. Religious systems were separated from scientific systems, and our conceptual synthesis was split into a 'natural' and a 'moral' philosophy.

Attempts at producing inclusive world views were made by system-building philosophers, such as Spinosa, Hegel, Spencer. The project was also taken up by the French Encylopedists, who hoped to produce a synthesis by cataloguing the items of concurrent knowledge. A large segment of civilization came under the spell of the conceptual synthesis produced by Hegel, Marx and Lenin, but most Western societies learned to live with a world view fundamentally split into scientific and religious-moral components. Oriental civilizations came increasingly in contact with the Western world through faster and broader channels of communication, trade and transportation, and partly surrendered, partly shifted their own integrated conceptual systems to accommodate the new influences.

Presently all boundaries between cultures are rapidly disintegrating. It is no longer possible to simultaneously uphold several incompatible conceptual syntheses valid for different people at different places. Our bodies of knowledge are as interdependent as our patterns of life. There is only one science for East and

West, and though there are many religions and belief systems, they are becoming insignificant in terms of their influence on the operative knowledge of the age.

We are headed toward a new civilization and, as all previous smaller-scale civilizations, it too, will produce a conceptual synthesis. This synthesis can also be more or less explicit, far-ranging and logical, and it can have more or less success in satisfying concrete needs for guidance in the processes of human affairs. We cannot see into the future and predict what the nature and success of the synthesis of the coming world order will be like. But we can say that *if* the coming world order will be a viable one, its conceptual synthesis will be explicit, far-ranging, scientifically based, and pregnant with normative guidelines for practical behavior.

Conceptual syntheses perform at least five basic functions in the guidance of human affairs. They are the mystical, the cosmological, the sociological, the pedagogical or psychological, and the editorial functions.[1] The mystical function inspires in man a sense of mystery and profound meaning related to the existence of the universe and of himself in it. The cosmological function forms images of the universe in accord with local knowledge and experience, enabling men to describe and identify the structure of the universe and the forces of nature. The sociological function validates, supports and enforces the local social order, representing it as in accord with the nature of the universe, or as the natural or right form of social organization. The pedagogical or psychological function guides individuals through the stages of life, teaching ways of understanding themselves and others, and presenting desirable responses to life's challenges and trials. Finally, the editorial function of conceptual syntheses is to define some aspects of reality as important and credible and hence to be attended to, and other aspects as worthy only to be ignored or repressed.

The five functions of integral world views, or synthetic images, strongly condition the viability of present-day societies and cultures. Today, many of the classic functions of syntheses have atrophied or lie ignored and neglected. Mythology is currently relegated to the status of mere superstition; and contemporary individuals suffer from a profound lack of meaning in life, as both clinical reports and contemporary literature testify. Religions, the traditional agents of this function, suffer from a credibility gap and become increasingly concerned with community mental health and social justice. Science now performs the cosmological function, but does so in an atomistic, ultra-specialized manner which, together with the mathematical disciplinary jargon in which research reports are couched, prevents the thrust of scientific knowledge from penetrating the fabric of society. Bureaucrats and civil servants, who make no claim to understand or even to seek a larger picture of reality, carry out the sociological function of administering and enforcing local social orders. The pedagogical or educational function of guiding individuals through the stages of life has been relegated to secular institutions of mental health and psychotherapy, traditions having faltered and then completely failed in advanced industrial societies. The editorial function is now administered by technocrats, public relations experts, and the funding agencies which steer the processes of large-scale research and development. All of these functions, in so far as they are performed, originate from separate groups with fragmented and often mutually incompatible world views. Aside from a few countries, which are actively engaged in fighting for their existence, or carrying out revolutions to catch up with their peers (e.g. Israel, Iran, Poland, China), contemporary societies suffer from a lack of meaning and guidance, due to the atrophy and fragmentation of their conceptual synthesis. Alcoholism, drug-addiction, suicide and divorce rates, crime and corruption, are sharply on the rise; a sense of purpose, a vital image of the future, and meaningful individual and societal goals are lacking. Yet humanity needs a sense of purpose, a vital image of the future, and meaningful individual and societal goals now more than ever before in history. There has never been a period in history when there was so much need for purposively guided transformation, and so little room for error, than today. The industrial state complex creates progressively more problems and consistently reduces the error-threshold of its viable transformation. Times are past when a conceptual synthesis could fail to perform on all counts, or dictate partially counterfunctional patterns of behavior. With the advent of the contemporary community of interdependent, in part highly technological societies, insufficient and incorrect guidance and motivation results in major breakdowns and the suffering of millions of people. This is why the coming conceptual synthesis will have to operate on all levels, and why its main inspiration will have to be based on the sciences.

By calling for a 'scientific' synthesis we need not mean a universal worship of science and the view that all our knowledge is either derived from the sciences or is plainly nonsensical. That the inspiration of our conceptual synthesis must be based on science does not mean that it must be limited to the scope of contemporary validated scientific theories. It must extend, on the contrary, to all the functions which conceptual syntheses have traditionally performed. But inasmuch as it suggests guidelines for concrete action, it must respect the reduced error-tolerance of the contemporary situation; hence it must base itself on the empirically tested knowledge accumulated in the sciences. Science is a body of knowledge which is hallmarked by the fact that it is constantly tested against experience (as well as, to some extent, against rival theories) under controlled conditions. This fact recommends science as the mainspring of our conceptual synthesis in view of our reduced degrees of freedom in effecting the needed societal-cultural transformations. This same fact does not mean that we can afford to restrict our synthesis to science, for pure science makes a poor religion, an inadequate basis for morality, for existential meaning, and for individual and collective purpose. Our conceptual synthesis will have to be scientific at its core, but move beyond the concurrent reach of the sciences in satisfying our demands for coherence in the more esoteric regions of human experience. Binding the scientific and the spiritual domains, the new knowledge must remain coherent and self-consistent, replacing the incoherence, and the tacit as well as overt contradictions traversing our existing scientific, religious and moral systems of ideas.

The new conceptual synthesis cannot content itself with remaining a plaything of the mind, cherished and cultivated in isolated ivory towers of learning and culture.

Ivory tower philosophy and 'pure' science may continue to be pursued by a small number of researchers for the intrinsic value of gaining knowledge for the sake of knowledge, but the bulk of the conceptual synthesis will have to be moved by concerned investigators into the worldly arena of practical application. There, its task will be to suggest the norms by which the new civilization of man can be purposefully guided, and also the detailed processes whereby such guidance can be effected. Fragmented knowledge, even if deriving directly from the sciences, is incapable of fulfilling this task. It treats the many systematically interdependent factors of human existence as the separate domains of disciplinary territories, each jealously guarded by specialists well endowed with the instincts of cognitive territoriality. The human future can only be assured by a synthesis based on science but integrating the relevant pieces of scientific knowledge with one another, and thus integrating scientific knowledge with those insights that have been won without benefit of scientific method but which have nevertheless proven to be meaningful in themselves, and valuable in guiding the imagination and focusing the thrust of individual and social motivation.

## THE PROMISE OF GENERAL SYSTEM THEORY

General system theory arose in the last few decades specifically as a response to the contemporary need to counterbalance fragmentation and duplication in scientific research, induced by ultraspecialized modes of inquiry. As other innovative frameworks of thought, it passed through phases of ridicule and neglect. It has benefited, however, from the parallel emergence and rise to eminence of cybernetics and information theory, and their widespread applications to originally quite unsuspected fields. Presently the rise of this theory is aided by societal pressures on science, calling for the development of theories capable of interdisciplinary application. General system theory grew out of organismic biology, and has soon branched into most of the life and behavioral sciences. Its recent applications include the areas of social work, mental health, the policy sciences, and the humanities.[2] Its extension to the new field of studies rallying around the concept of 'world order research' is a logical next step.

The specific contribution of general system theory derives from its de-emphasis of traditional concepts of matter, substance, idea or spirit, and its explicit orientation toward grasping phenomena in terms of *organization*. 'Organization' can be loosely defined as structure (in space) and function (in time). Structure and function are not rigorously separable, however. That which is structure is the record of past functions and the source of present ones. Function in turn is the behavior of structure and the pathway leading to the formation of new structures. The relativity of the concepts derives from the dominance of the concept of organization. Not what a thing is, what it is made of, or for what purpose it exists, defines it, but how it is organized. Its organization specifies the internal relations of the events which constitute it, and the external relations of the constituted entity and other entities in its environment.

The simplest conceptualization of an entity defined by its organizational invariance is *system*. A system in this definition is a collection of parts conserving some identifiable set of (internal) relations, with the summed relations (i.e. the system itself) conserving some identifiable set of (external) relations to other entities (systems).

The definition tightens considerably when we consider that if any set of events conserves identifiable sets of internal relations, it must be endowed with the characteristics of pattern-maintenance, i.e., it must be capable of at least temporarily withstanding the statistical outcome of disorganization predicted by the second law of thermodynamics. There must be organizing forces or relations present which permit the conservation of structure (and function). Any system not possessing such characteristics conserves an identifiable set of internal relations only if externally constrained (e.g., the molecules of a gas kept at constant pressure and temperature). Otherwise the relations tend to degrade until a state of thermodynamical equilibrium is reached. Any system which does not degrade its organization to thermodynamical equilibrium in virtue of the balance of its internal relations with its external relations is a *natural system*. It may be contrasted with sets of events of which the internal relations are artificially constrained to remain invariant: *technical systems*.

The noteworthy fact is that with the exception of human artifacts, almost all the things we can identify as 'the furniture of the earth' are natural systems, or parts of natural systems, or aggregates formed by natural systems. Stable atoms are natural systems, and so are molecules, cells, multicellular organisms, and ecologies. Communities, states, complex human sociocultural systems, and indeed the global system itself, form natural (rather than technical) systems.[3] This is important, for certain general propositions are true of natural systems, regardless of their size, origin, and complexity, which may not be true of technical systems. These propositions are true in virtue of the fact that in a universe governed by uniform laws certain sets of relationships are required to conserve and enhance order over time. Much can be understood of the system's basic 'nature' by assessing its behavior in reference to the imperatives of natural system dynamics.

The promise of general system theory consists in (1) discerning natural systems in diverse areas of investigation, i.e. identifying those real entities which can be analyzed in terms of general system laws, (2) providing an inventory of natural systems from atoms to ecologies and possibly to social systems and the world system, (3) formulating the general principles accounting for the evolution of systems on multiple hierarchic levels, crossing the boundaries of the inorganic-organic, the organic-multiorganic, and their many subdivisions, and (4) referring chosen problems of philosophic-scientific-humanistic interest to the systems analysis of the relevant phenomena, carried out in the contex of the integrated scheme of hierarchically organized natural systems.

Thus if *world order* is (4) the chosen problem of philosophic-scientific-humanistic interest, the task of general system theory is (1) to inquire whether the world system can be identified as a natural system, (2) if yes, to analyze the world system in the context of the repertory of natural systems, taking into account (3) general principles of organic-sociocultural evolution. This method can relate the description of observed phenomena to the dynamics of viable natural systems by determining whether the structures and functions observed of the phenomena correspond to the preconditions of persistence and development of natural systems. In the area of multihuman systems, the investigation can yield norms of conduct, values and lifestyles, as well as norms of social, economic, cultural and political organization.

## REFERENCES

1. Cf. "Changing Images of Man", *Discussion Draft of a Study by the Center for the Study of Social Policy, Stanford Research Institute* (June 1973) (in mimeographed form).
2. See, for example, G. Klir (ed.), *Trends in General Systems Theory*, John Wiley, New York, 1972; E. Laszlo (ed.), *The Relevance of General Systems Theory*, George Braziller, New York, 1972; the journals *Behavioral Science* and *Kybernetes*, and the *Yearbooks* of the Society for General Systems Research (since 1956).
3. Ervin Laszlo, *Introduction to Systems Philosophy. op. cit.*

PART TWO

**WORLD ORDER STUDIES – IN A SYSTEMS PERSPECTIVE**

# 12

## THE PURPOSE OF MANKIND

The title of this essay suggests that its topic is nonsenical. First, purpose cannot be associated with anything other than a conscious human being. Second, mankind as such does not exist, only individual men. These objections make an essay on the purpose of mankind a study of an impossible characteristic of a nonexistent entity.

We hold, however, and offer to demonstrate, that these objections are unsound. 'Purpose' can be operationally defined as a property of a class of entities which may, but need not, be endowed with consciousness. And 'mankind' can be shown to be an entirely reasonable conceptualization of a network of relationships binding the members of the earth's human population. 'Purpose' can be legitimately attributed to 'mankind', and there is evidence of various sorts that mankind does indeed manifest a purpose. Such purpose may well be a *sine qua non* of the long-term future of human life and culture on this planet.

### PURPOSE

The dictionary defines purpose as "1. something one intends to get or do; intention; aim. 2. resolution; determination. 3. the object for which something exists or is done; end in view" (*Webster's Dictionary of the American Language*, 1964). The first of these definitions is the one intended in this essay, the second one is too narrow to be of use here, and the third serves primarily as a contrast to our intended definition. In fact, "the object for which something exists or is done; end in view" is the traditional definition of purpose which immediately springs to the

---
*Reprinted from *Zygon*, vol. 8, nos. 3-4 (September-December 1973).

mind of classical theologians and philosophers. In this definition purpose can be associated only with things or persons created or undertaken for the sake of something. Thus, the purpose of tragedy is, according to Aristotle, to evoke pity and fear, and that of a walk to move the bowels. Theologians speak of the purpose of mankind as the attainment of divine grace or salvation. Speculative historians saw in the unfolding of cultural history the realization of a purpose, divine or secular. Persons and even nations perceive their own existence as having a purpose when they can answer the question, What are we here for? The difficulty of purpose in the sense of a final-cause teleology is that it applies only to purposively created things. Purpose, however, also informs the act of creation. Such act can be described, without mysticism and vagueness, as active behavior directed toward the attainment of a goal. This is basically definition 1, "something one intends to get or do; intention; aim."

We shall use purpose in the sense in which it informs goal-directed active behavior, rather than associate it with that with which such behavior endows its products. Thus, unless we believe that people are created for a purpose, we cannot speak of human purpose, or the purpose of mankind, in the sense of definition 3. However, if we acknowledge that people, and possibly mankind, manifest active goal-directed behavior, we can associate purpose with them in the sense of definition 1.

The operational definition of purpose in the sense of definition 1 was given by Rosenblueth, Wiener, and Bigelow in a paper published in 1943.[1] They defined purpose in the context of behavior: purposive is behavior that is directed to the attainment of a goal. 'Behavior' in turn is defined as "any change of an entity with respect to its surroundings". The kind of behavior involved in purposive behavior is one in which the entity is the source of the output energy involved in a given action. The entity may store energy supplied by a remote or relative immediate input, but the input of energy to the entity does not direct the energy output. Hence, the behavior is 'active': it is energy stored within and directed by the entity. This introduces a useful distinction between the behavior of entities such as stones (which, when thrown, largely convert all the energy applied to them in their immediate behavior output) and entities such as birds (which store the energy needed for their flight by means of biochemical gradients activated and directed by their nervous system).

Since 'active behavior' is that where the energy is controlled by an entity and 'purposeful (active) behavior' is that which is directed to the attainment of a goal, 'purpose' is defined as the goal, aim, or intention underlying behavior. Consquently, conscious awareness of a goal may, but need not, be involved in purposive behavior. We know from our own experience that human beings are mostly (though not always) conscious of the goals which their behavior is directed to attain. We also know that torpedoes with target-seeking mechanisms have no such goal consciousness. And we can argue about whether at least some species of animals are, or are not, conscious of some of their goals. The consciousness factors becomes immaterial for the definition of purpose. All entities that (1) store energies which are used in the energizing of specific actions, and (2) direct such actions toward the attainment of some specific goal, qualify for purposive behavior. The presence of conscious awareness of the goal by the entity itself makes the process of attaining it more reliable, but this awareness is not essential for the activity by which the entity is striving for the goal.

Wiener *et al.* further distinguish several levels of purposeful behavior, in reference to the use of feedback and extrapolation by the entity. In such behaviors the human brain provides an accomplished instrument, but not an irreplaceable one. Less evolved nervous systems, as well as computers, can carry out the processing of information needed to read out feedback signals and extrapolate from them to guide the ongoing activity.

The above-outlined operational definition of 'purpose' establishes that purpose, in the sense of the operational version of definition 1, can be attributed to entities other than conscious human beings. We shall now show that it can be attributed to mankind.

## MANKIND

Is there an entity called 'mankind'? Common sense suggests that there are only individual human beings. Thus, mankind no more exists than does, for example, the class of green chairs. On the other hand, anthropologists tend to speak of cultures which exist as entitites over and above individual human beings (the 'World 3' described by Eccles is an instance of such postulation[2]), and social scientists find no difficulty in speaking of human institutions, nation-states, political systems, etc., as entities in their own right. And some scientists actually do speak today of mankind itself as (in the words of Glenn T. Seaborg) "a global civilization — man and nations not only coexisting with each other and nature but essentially living and acting as an organic whole."[3]

Now, the existence of diverse viewpoints on a subject does not necessarily mean that one is right and all the others must be false. Phenomena do not appear to our eye in pristine purity to be projected onto a blank slate inside our brain, to be described without interpretive additions. Instead, the phenomenal world is given to us in the form of various patterns of radiation, some of which fall into wavelengths which can interact with our principal sense receptors, the eye and the ear. Here the radiations are translated into complex patterns of nerve impulses, which enter into a vast system of structured activity in our central nervous system. The interaction of the impulses conducted from the receptors with this pattern of autonomous activity provides the data for the interpretive centers of our brain for analysis. The left cortical hemisphere is capable of carrying out processes on levels which enter into the consciousness of the subject himself. Our knowledge of the external world, as well as of our own body, is our conscious readout of these complex interactive-interpretive processes. It is anything but the simple recording of an objectively given 'sense datum'.

It is entirely possible to become consciously aware of the presumably same object in several different ways. Consider, for example, the famous drawing from the textbooks of Gestalt psychology (Fig. 1).

*Fig. 1*

It is possible to see the sketch as depicting a fashionable young woman, as well as an old 'Parisienne'. In fact, with a little practice one can learn to produce the 'Gestalt switch': see it now as the young woman, now as the old. Of course, 'realistically' we would say that it is neither a young nor an old woman, but merely some lines formed by printer's ink on white paper. Consider now, if it is possible to switch gestalts in the case of simple sense objects in front of our eyes, how possible it must be to switch gestalts in the case of abstract models we make up in our heads! Almost all of our scientific knowledge of the external world consists of such abstract models. And, whereas with a shared background knowledge of printer's ink and paper we can agree what it is that we 'really' see in the picture, it is extremely difficult to agree what the 'real' objects of our scientific models are, since we have no background knowledge of them at all. All we have are our scientific models, plus some commonsense assumptions that science seems flatly to contradict.[4] (The paper under our hands seems relatively solid and inert, but physics claims that it is made up of the 'heat dance' of millions of molecules, each consisting of many atoms representing complex integration of multidimensional force fields.)

In the history of the empirical sciences, many different models of the world have been built in people's heads, and many — probably most — of them were believed to be not just possible models, but the genuine article itself. Classical science, especially since Galileo and Newton, represented the universe as the lawful concourse of material particles (mass points), which in combination gave rise to the multiplicity of observed phenomena. Mind was a puzzle in this mechanistic material universe and prompted philosophers such as Kant to postulate separate worlds or realms for it. With the advent of relativity theory, the backdrop of empty space and of time as "equitably flowing through all eternity" fell away, the meaning of absolute simultaneity of separate events was rejected, and the equivalence of energy with mass (when mass is multiplied by the square of the velocity of light *in vacuo*) postulated. Later, all units of material events were found to be quantized, and still later the essential indeterminacy of a single quantum of mass energy was established. It is presently believed that the smallest discernible units of mass energy do not exist in single states, like more reasonably behaving macroobjects, but in a superposition of several states, out of which an observation-interaction selects one.[5] One may well ask what meaning the concept 'matter' still possesses in the light of these developments. It is not surprising that the physical sciences have largely eliminated it as the basic category of their discourse.

Currently, scientists concentrate on structure and function, rather than matter or substance. They construct the empirical world in terms of invariances of organization — recurrent patterns of events in space and time. It is now thought that all empirical cognition proceeds by the discrimination of such recurrent patterns. The infant recognizes a red ball when he has succeeded in constructing a model of it in his head in terms of invariant characteristics of shape, color, and behavior,[6] and the scientist recognizes the species 'cat' when he encounters the invariance associated with its specific genotype and phenotype in observation.

Persons, whether scientists or not, tend to view those aspects of their experience as elements of the real world which they have most explicitly modeled in their head. Thus, for most physicists atoms have reality, whereas for some psychologists (of the introspectionist schools), minds do. Life scientists recognize unicellular and multicellular organisms as well as genes as furniture of reality, and the ecologists among them tend to affirm the reality of ecosystems, constituted of sets of interrelating organisms. Social scientists usually have little difficulty in 'entitating' multiperson organizations, such as institutions and states. (These can crisscross. For example, where an economist sees the Common Market and perceives a unit, the political scientist sees separate governments and multiplicity.)

All scientists are people, and thus none can ignore his own reality. It is logical, therefore, that physicists and biologists recognize each other's constructs as elements in the real world. But it is also understandable that they do not reify the organizational invariances which represent real entities for social scientists. In the world picture of natural scientists, social and cultural (and sometimes even ecologic) systems are just so many partly ordered—partly disordered relationships of physical and biological entities. Social scientists, on the other hand, cannot very well ignore the social and ecological systems that they investigate in their professional life, and thus for them the terrestrial world is made up of more levels of organized entities than for the majority of the natural scientists.

The above excursion into the epistemology of science was understaken to show that it is not inconsistent for natural scientists to deny the existence of an entity called 'mankind' and for social scientists dealing with globe-straddling processes to affirm it. Each person reifies those orders in phenomena with which he is most directly involved. Thus, genes may be an abstraction for the man on the street, but they are real for the biologist. Quantized particles in states of superposition may be abstractions for everyone other than physicists. And mankind may be an abstraction for all people who are not directly concerned with the mapping of global processes involving all of the earth's human population.

## THE PURPOSE OF MANKIND

The conclusion of our epistemological excursion is that it is not intrinsically unreasonable to conceive of mankind as an entity, a thing in its own right, endowed with an organizational invariance and its correlated observable and theoretically reconstructable properties. As a matter of fact, properties associated with mankind as a whole are not likely to be discerned if mankind is taken merely as an aggregate of individual human beings, or even of individual nations, societies, or cultures. Thus, the question whether mankind has a purpose or not can only be decided if we heuristically understand mankind as an entity in itself, and inquire whether there is evidence suggesting that it possesses goals which its active behavior seeks to realize. The hypothesis to be evaluated is this: Is there a purpose of mankind (and not merely purposes of human beings and sociocultural systems)? The commonsense mind boggles at this possibility. So does the mind of the scientist who does not conceptualize mankind as an entity in its own right. But for anyone for whom the concept of an entity called 'mankind' has empirical significance, the hypothesis is intrinsically reasonable. It remains to be tested against the pertinent evidence.

The evidence for the purpose of mankind comes under two categories. One is axiomatic, the other empirical.

Axiomatically, we say that mankind has a purpose in the sense of a goal if mankind is a dynamic open system possessing cybernetic mechanisms that tend to reduce deviations from its norm. We know that dynamic open systems maintain themselves in stationary states far from thermodynamical equilibrium by a negative (and sometimes positive) feedback process described by Emerson as 'dynamic homeostasis'.[7] The behavior of such systems is active: they possess stored energies which are deployed by their cybernetic mechanisms in activating specific responses to their environment in ways to maintain their norms as a system. These responses are, therefore, goal oriented. Their purpose is offsetting, by means of negentropy imported from the environment, the entropy produced in the system.[8] (If the system's structure codes information calling for a time-dependent change of state, the concept of purpose refers to the maintenance of the chreod, or developmental pathway, normal for the system.[9]) Thus, an entity has purpose if it is a cybernetically controlled dynamic open system. This much is true axiomatically. Among dynamic open systems are biological organisms and species from amoebae to men. Do entities formed by interdependencies of biological organisms likewise qualify?

There are two principal varieties of suprabiological organization on earth. One is the ecosystem, the other the human sociocultural system. Ecologists conceive of ecosystems as dynamic open systems. They identify ecosystems as the integration of the communities of living organisms and their total nonliving environment in a geographical region of the earth at a particular point in time. The basic units are the individual living organisms. They form the nodal points of a network whose strands are formed by their interactions. The network is enmeshed in, and integrated with, the environmental matrix. The whole entity is then identified as the ecosystem.

Ecosystems can be identified at different levels, ranging from a small system, such as the ecosystem of a pond, to the ecosystem of the biosphere, including its human population. At each level pattern-maintaining and pattern-evolving characteristics have been identified. At a given season of the year the average number of individuals per unit area is similar to that of previous years in most species, despite some variations in weather conditions, in factors causing mortality, and others that tend to increase or decrease the numbers. Explosions in populations (locust outbreaks, marine algal blooms, deer irruptions, etc.) are exceptional phenomena associated with major perturbations of the ecosystem, and normally they are regulated through a number of distinct processes. Ecologists point out that these self-adjustments of the population emerge from the field dynamics of the system.[10] In this regard it is legitimate to conceptualize ecosystems as dynamic open systems, receiving energy from the sun, recycling it in various ways among their many trophic levels, fixing some of it in biomass, and radiating off some proportion into space in the form of heat.

A somewhat analogous conceptualization applies to human sociocultural systems as well. Here the basic entities are individual human beings, and the hierarchical structure is formed by their interactions in primary groups, such as the nuclear family, and the incorporation of these groups in organizations progressively more complex and embracing political, legal, economic, and social spheres. The approach to social science through systems conceptualization has been demonstrably fruitful in the work of such social scientists as Parsons, Buckley, Cadwallader, and Easton.[11] Systems analysis has been applied to various social subsystems, from the military to the economic and political. Such work presupposes that human sociocultural systems be thought of as dynamic open systems, receiving information from their environment, processing the information through a complex structural network, and responding to their environment. In the feedback process pattern-maintaining and pattern-evolving trends become manifest. These serve to sustain given sociocultural systems within their environment and permit them to map change within their internal structure. In these adaptive and normative functions, sociocultural systems exhibit purposes, in a fashion analogous to ecosystems (and to cybernetically regulated dynamic open systems in general).

The manifold goal-directed activities associated with sociocultural systems represent integrations or coordinations of individual human purposes. Katz speaks of them as Purpose (with a capital P). Human purpose is a general characteristic of man, while Purpose is its expression in maintaining the particular society of man.[12]

So far, we have adduced evidence to the effect that multispecies and multiorganic systems, such as ecosystems and human sociocultural systems, can be legitimately conceptualized as self-maintaining open systems. Thus, by means of the axiomatic proposition that self-maintaining open systems possess purpose (in a generalized dynamic-analogue sense), we can say that ecosystems and sociocultural systems possess purpose. The question is whether mankind as a whole is a self-maintaining open system, or merely the aggregate of partially ordered individual nation-states.

Social scientists, until recently, perceived nation-states as the sovereign actors on the international scene. The legitimacy of this conceptualization has been increasingly questioned lately, for example by Alastair Taylor and Richard Falk. A field or systems theory of international relations has also been under development. It is not possible at this point to argue with cogency either for or against a systems concept of mankind. We may note that such conceptualization is not unreasonable. If sociocultural systems of national scope can be conceived as self-maintaining open systems, so can the entity formed by the relationship of all existing sociocultural systems. This entity is mankind.

Instead of pursuing the argument axiomatically, let us consider the empirical evidence. Does mankind as such, and not only particular men and particular sociocultural systems, manifest a purpose?

In the first place, *sapiens* as a biological species is as much of a self-regulative open system as any other species. But many question that this would make human social systems collectively self-regulatory. In order to consider this question, it is necessary to distinguish among purposes on the individual, the sociocultural, and the mankind levels. I shall denote individual human purpose "purpose$_1$", the sociocultural expression of purposes (that is, Katz's *Purpose*) "purpose$_2$", and purpose associated with mankind as a whole "purpose$_3$". We can now consider evidence relevant to purpose$_3$.[13]

If we take some recent models of the world system, such as that produced by Forrester and Meadows et al.,[14] our first impression is that there is no purpose associated with mankind as a whole. These models are premised on the assumption that rates of growth in the world system can only be controlled by external pressures, such as famines, overcrowding, depletion of natural resources, overpollution, etc. Thus mankind is not a self-regulative dynamic open system. On the contrary, the human population is a source of constant disturbance in the global ecosystem which, at least in the absence of man, is a self-regulative (i.e., purposive) open system itself.

But one of the oft-voiced criticisms of these models of the world ecosystem is that they do not map or specify human values and purposes. Individual and sociocultural values and goals are not variables in the models, although Forrester himself stresses that such values do enter into the dynamics of the world system.[15]

Hence, the lack of discernible purpose$_3$ in these world-system models is not evidence that it does not exist in reality. It only shows that it is not readily integrated in a computerizable model.

There is important evidence for the existence of purpose$_3$ before our eyes. We need merely a good conceptual model to perceive it. If we look for statements by individuals, we are likely to get purpose$_1$. If we focus our attention on statements of national goals or social ideals, we get purpose$_2$. Few people speak in the name of mankind, and there may not be any good way that we could get an explicit statements of purpose$_3$ by a person or group of persons. But purpose$_3$, similar to purpose on any level, need not be stated but can be read out from active behavior. Thus, to find evidence for purpose$_3$, we must look to the behavior of existing social systems within existing international frameworks. The most evolved of these is the United Nations and its many specialized programs and agencies. Here the primary actors are nation-states, and their collective behavior gives rise to behavior on the international (that is, mankind) level. Some facts concerning international behavior within the United Nations organizations are therefore of direct relevance to purpose$_3$.

The crystallization of collective behavior relevant to purpose$_3$ within the United Nations is most noteworthy in relation to the environmental crisis. As U Thant pointed out, man is becoming increasingly aware of the urgent need to act to preserve the planet. He is becoming increasingly sensitive to the overriding reality that his one and only habitat is threatened, not by the forces of nature, but by his own negligence and greed.[16] Such purposes$_1$ jointly constitute purposes$_2$ as public opinion provides input into national governments. On the level of purposes$_2$ we now get statements from national leaders that are indicative of this. Edmund Muskie said that he took the view in the United States Senate that no measure can be regarded as a national good if there is a serious danger that it would run counter to the human good.[17] Party Secretary Leonid Brezhnev said that the Soviet Union is prepared to participate together with the other states concerned in settling problems such as the conservation of the environment, communications, prevention and eradication of the most dangerous and widespread diseases, and the exploration and development of outer space and the world ocean. His country is also prepared to participate in collective international schemes for the protection of nature and the rational use of natural resources.[18] Similar views are expressed by representatives of the governments of most of the world's developed nations. There is thus a crystallization of awareness of mankind problems in relation to the environment. This prepares the ground for concerted action, which could result in behavior that could be read out as purpose$_3$.

The first such action came with the Stockholm Conference on the Human Environment. The U.N. Secretary-General said that, for the first time in history, the nations of the world joined together to act on a variety of problems that affect the existence of all living things. It shows, he added, that the world community recognizes that environmental problems are the concern of all men, that they are international problems that must be dealt with through concerted action by all nations.[19]

The crystallization of awareness may prepare the ground for action, but action can follow only when national priorities (purposes$_2$) are coordinated with mankind priorities (purpose$_3$). This is a slow process, and overly optimistic expectations were quickly extinguished in Stockholm. However, it is a fact that a number of international agencies are now in operation which work on mankind problems and evince purpose$_3$. The Inter-Governmental Maritime Consultative Organization has prepared a convention aimed at preventing pollution of the seas by oil. The Food and Agriculture Organization has numerous programs in soil conservation, water development and management, and conservation of marine mildlife, as well as forest resources. The World Health Organization is active in identifying, measuring, and evaluating air and water pollution. The World Meteorological Organization is establishing a global network to measure pollution in the atmosphere. Other agencies of the United Nations, such as the United Nations Development Program, the International Civil Aviation Organization, the International Labor Organization, and the International Atomic Energy Agency, have become involved with international environmental problems. The United Nations Educational, Scientific, and Cultural Organization has undertaken a program, called "Man and Biosphere", aimed at developing a scientific basis for the rational use and conservation of the biosphere's resources and the improvement of the relationship between mankind as a whole and the environment. These are definite manifestations of purpose$_3$.

Environmental issues have elicited purpose$_3$ soonest and in the most explicit form. Global tensions in the area of military aggression have also provoked some activities that can be read as crystallizations of purpose$_3$. Here we may note the virtual collapse of earlier "power paradigms", that is, of the conceptualization of the world arena of nations as dominated by polarized superpowers with their attendant allies and satellites. Indications that in place of this paradigm we are now getting something like a mankind-system thinking include the deescalation of the cold war, the reduction of the armament race (SALT talks), the new contacts and limited economic cooperation among the United States, China, and the USSR, the ending of armed conflict in Vietnam, and multilateral efforts on the part of the great powers to settle the Middle East crisis. Purpose$_3$ is implicit in these events, read as components in more long-term trends to convert a polarized arena of international relations between sovereign states into a coordinated system of international order achieved by national governments who perceive that, as Muskie says, no measure can be regarded as a national good if it runs counter to the human good.

The emergence of purpose$_3$ is also implied in the shift of consciouness underlying today's expressions of purposes$_1$. Many individuals now speak of purposes and goals associated with mankind as a whole (they sometimes even appear to speak in the name of mankind). For example, *Cooperator*, the quarterly journal of the International Cooperation Council, is devoted to "fostering the emergence of a new universal man and civilization", and it editorializes that "man must increasingly learn to develop a consciousness of mankind and life as a whole and see himself as part of that totality" (vol. 4, no. 3). John Platt said that "the World Survival Movement will become self-conscious, integrated, and trans-national" (personal communication).

The overall shift in the consciousness of youth today, which Reich calls "Consciousness III", is a good general index of the preparation of the ground, in purposes$_1$, for a global purpose$_3$. The chauvinistic narrowness and competitiveness of earlier forms of mentality ("Consciousness I") and even the managerial transformation of it ("Consciousness II") block the emergence of an integrated purpose on the level of mankind by drawing hard and fast boundaries between 'we' and 'they'. Inasmuch as youth, not only in America, but in many parts of the world, does not think in these dichotomic terms, but identifies itself with people wherever they may live and whoever they may be, it is readying the ground for the emergence of particular sociocultural purposes$_2$, which lend themselves to coordination in mankind's higher-level purpose$_3$.

There are more areas of international cooperation, motivated by a perception of the entity formed by all men and all nations, than can be listed here. They include cooperation among scientists, humanists, artists, and many others. Some of these areas are fostered by such U.N. bodies as UNITAR (the U.N. Institute for Training and Research) and the UNU (the U.N. University). These developments can be read as the crystallization of a purpose associated with mankind as a whole. Yet they can also be read as purposes$_2$ associated with individual nation-states, or even as purposes$_1$ exhibited by individual human beings. The divergences in reading the evidence are due to the different world pictures of the investigators. And the differences in world pictures are determined, in the last analysis, by our individual concerns and competences. Hence, we are not suggesting that perceiving mankind as such is necessarily more 'true' than seeing only nation-states, or even just individual human beings in various (social, economic, cultural) relationships. We merely submit that if one is concerned with the survival of the human species and the development of its culture and civilization, the conceptualization of mankind becomes as important as the conceptualization of the gene is to the evolutionary biologist. It is only by conceptualizing mankind as an entity that we can assess empirical evidence relevant to its purpose, and it is only by gathering and evaluating such evidence that we can work for those national and international processes which contribute to the timely emergence of whatever purpose mankind may possess.

After these somewhat lengthy discussions the reader may well ask: granted that purpose is operationally defined as active goal-seeking behavior, and that mankind is a justifiable conceptualization, and even that we admit evidence to the effect that mankind does possess purpose, *what is this purpose?* The answer is simple. Mankind's purpose is the self-regulation of human life and civilization in accordance with the objective requirements of its existence. Such self-regulation is likely to be too little for those who see a lofty purpose underlying the unfolding of human history, and too much for those who see mankind as no more than a rather random aggregate of human beings and institutions. But if mankind possesses purpose in a sufficiently effective form to get us into the twenty-first century without major catastrophes, it will be enough. The fossil record is littered with species that possessed purpose in a less effective form.

## REFERENCES

1. Arturo Rosenblueth, Norbert Wiener, and Julian Bigelow, "Behavior, Purpose, and Teleology", *Philosophy of Science* 10 (1943): 18-24.
2. Cf. J. C. Eccles, "Cultural Evolution versus Biological Evolution", *Zygon*, vol. 8, nos. 3-4 (1973).
3. *Christian Science Monitor*, May 9, 1970, p. 14.
4. Bertrand Russell, *An Inquiry into Meaning and Truth* (Baltimore: Penguin Books, 1962), p. 13.
5. Cf. Richard Schlegel, "Quantum Physics and Human Purpose", *Zygon*, vol. 8, nos. 3-4 (1973).
6. Cf. Ralph Wendell Burhoe, "The Concepts of God and Soul in a Scientific View of Human Purpose", *Zygon*, vol. 8, nos. 3-4 (1973).
7. Cf. Alfred E. Emerson, "Some Biological Antecedents of Human Purpose", *Zygon*, vol. 8, nos. 3-4 (1973).
8. See Erwin Schrödinger, *What Is Life?* (New York: Doubleday & Co., 1956). Originally published in 1944 in Cambridge, England, by the Cambridge University Press.
9. Cf. C. H. Waddington, "The Theory of Evolution Today", in *Beyond Reductionism*, ed. Arthur Koestler and J. R. Smythies (New York: Macmillan Co., 1969), p. 366.
10. Helmut K. Buechler, "The Ecosystem Level of Organization", in *Hierarchically Organized Systems in Theory and Practice*, ed. Paul A. Weiss (New York: Hafner Publishing Co., 1971), p. 50.
11. Cf. Talcott Parsons, *Structure and Process in Modern Societies* (Glencoe, Ill.: Free Press, 1960); Talcott Parsons and Edward A. Shils, eds., *Toward a General Theory of Action* (Cambridge, Mass.: Harvard University Press, 1951); Walter Buckley, *Sociology and Modern Systems Theory* (Englewood Cliffs, N.J.: Prentice-Hall, Inc., 1967); Karl W. Deutsch, *The Nerves of Government* (London: Free Press of Glencoe, 1963); Mervin Cadwallader, "The Cybernetic Analysis of Change in Complex Social Organizations", *American Journal of Sociology* 65 (1959: 154-157); David Easton, *A Systems Analysis of Political Life* (New York: John Wiley & Sons, Inc., 1965).
12. Cf. Solomon Katz, "Evolutionary Perspectives on Purpose and Man", *Zygon*, vol. 8, nos. 3-4 (1973).
13. We shall note that it is not sufficient to say that purpose$_2$ is simply the sum of purpose$_1$ and purpose$_3$ is the sum of purpose$_2$ — thus making purpose$_3$ the integral sum of purpose$_1$. This is the reductionist assumption which, in this case, would have to proceed to attribute individual human purpose (purpose$_1$) to the goal-directed behavior of bodily organs (purpose$_0$) and these to the similarly goal-seeking behavior of the constituent cells (purpose$_{-1}$). Consequently any purpose we may perceive in connection with mankind would be no more than the total sum of goal-seeking behavior coded in individual human body cells. With this assumption we would be utterly incapable of discussing human and social purposes of any kind. Instead, we may assume that the *collective product* of purpose in entities on lower levels crystallizes as purpose on the higher levels.
14. Jay W. Forrester, *World Dynamics* (Cambridge, Mass.: Wright-Allen Press, 1971); Donella H. Meadows et al., *The Limits to Growth: A Report for the Club of Rome's Project on the Predicament of Mankind* (New York: Universe Books, 1972).
15. Jay W. Forrester, "Churches at the Transition between Growth and World Equilibrium", *Zygon* 7 (1972): 145-167.
16. U Thant, Keynote Speech, International Organization and the Human Environment Conference, Rensselaerville, New York, May 1971.

17. Edmund Muskie, Keynote Speech, International Organization and the Human Environment Conference, Rensselaerville, New York, May 1971.

18. Quoted by Konstantin Ananichev at the International Organization and the Human Environment Conference, Rensselaerville, New York, May 1971.

19. U Thant (n. 16 above).

# 13

## HUMAN DIGNITY AND THE PROMISE OF TECHNOLOGY*

To produce a meaningful study on the topic of human dignity and technology is by no means a simple task. It presupposes that the meanings of 'dignity' and 'technology' are clearly understood. But whereas the meaning of 'dignity' is by no means clear, that of 'technology' is highly controversial. A simple argument to the effect that technology does, or does not, contribute to human dignity is certain to miscarry. It could be understood in almost diametrically opposite terms. In view of the difficulties, two different approaches can be adopted. One can either survey the hitherto offered definitions of 'dignity' and assessments of 'technology', or he can offer his own, carefully elucidating his meaning. Since the former approach calls for an entire book,[1] in this study we shall adopt the latter. We shall argue that technology can, but at present does not, contribute essentially to human dignity and will offer thoughts on how this situation may be rectified. First, however, we shall be concerned to define these terms in order to avoid a misreading of the argument.

An irreverent younger generation tends to use 'dignity' pejoratively, as something claimed by snobbish members of the establishment. This use shall not be our own, since we shall be endeavoring to assess 'dignity' in a positive sense. Current dictionaries offer little help, defining 'dignity' in terms of other words, such as 'excellence', 'status' and 'esteem'; which also require definition. For purposes of a study such as this, it is evident that 'dignity' must mean a positive attribute of human beings. Further, 'human dignity' must not constitute an analytical proposition. If the concept 'human' includes the concept 'dignity', all human beings possess dignity, and it becomes pointless to assess the relevance of technology to it. Rather, we shall define 'dignity' so, that technology could, but need not, be 'dignity-making'. That is, human dignity could be dependent on the contribution of technology to the quality of human existence. Since 'dignity' will carry a positive connotation, if

*Reprinted from *Human Dignity – This Century and the Next*, ed. R. Gotesky and E. Laszlo, Gordon and Breach, New York, 1970.

technology is found 'dignity-making' it will be predicated 'good', and in the opposite case it will be held 'bad'. More specifically, the problem is to state, (i) what are the 'dignity-making' factors of human life, and (ii) what is the relevance of technology to these factors.

## DIGNITY AND TECHNOLOGY: CONCEPTS AND DEFINITIONS

Concerning (i), we suggest the concepts 'being' and 'well-being'. Biological existence (being) together with biocultural satisfactions (well-being) constitutes the dignity of human life. It defines an existence in which wants and wishes are satisfied through the presence of the appropriate objects and events. The dignity-making role of technology will be viewed in this study in the optic of its capacity to match the demands of human beings by providing the corresponding objects and events in their environment. This optic accords with current theories in biology, psychology and anthropology, and may be concisely stated in terms of the concepts developed in modern system research.

Both 'being' and 'well-being' can be viewed as states brought about by the matching of intrinsic norms or codes of the organism in the environment. These are normative organism-environment transactional states, representing specific input-output patterns. That the 'being' of a human being represents such states is directly acknowledged by biology, in recognizing that man, as all organisms, is an open system in a steady state, maintaining itself by a series of normative interactions with his environment. (For example, the organism's normal water content, blood pressure, temperature, etc., are homeostatically maintained by the feedback-control of input and output in reference to the organic needs.) But it is not generally recognized that cultural needs may also be satisfied by controlled environmental transactions based on intrinsic norms. Our thesis is that both the biological being, and the cultural well-being of the individual represent normative organism-environment transactional states, in which the individual's needs and demands are matched by the appropriate environmental states and events.

The classical *S-R* scheme of behaviorism can be restated in information theoretical and cybernetical terms as a control circuit involving the input and output of 'information' (in the wide sense of the term in which it applies to substances and energies, as well as perceptions and meanings) in reference to normative 'codes'. The inadequacy of the classical *S-R* scheme has become evident in recent years, when it was observed that organisms never act as reflex-mechanisms, however conditioned, but always interject a controlling factor — Tolman's and Hull's 'intervening variable' — between stimulus and response. The presence of this variable is what differentiates a self-regulating living organism from a rigidly pre-programmed machine. In a machine a given input always produces the same output — pushing a key on the typewriter always produces the same imprint on the paper. In contrast to this, living organisms respond to their stimuli in reference to their own needs, and tend to produce that output which optimizes their chances of achieving their goals. Thus, it appears that the *S-R* pattern is coupled by an intervening variable or 'code' (*C*), and the action of the code is such that it selects certain states in the environment and avoids others. The effectiveness of the code resides in modifying the input by means of the output. The code can add to the input through a properly correlated output, or it can reduce it. In cybernetical terms, a 'feedback loop' obtains which can be positive or negative. The feedback loop consists of an information-flow between four components, the input (*S*), the output (*R*), the intervening variable or code (*C*), and the relevant state of the environment (*E*) (it is the latter which, when 'sensed', gives the signals of the input). The code couples input and output so that the output brings about states of the environment which bring about the desired kind of input ('goal'). One may represent this feedback loop as follows:

STATE OF ENVIRONMENT

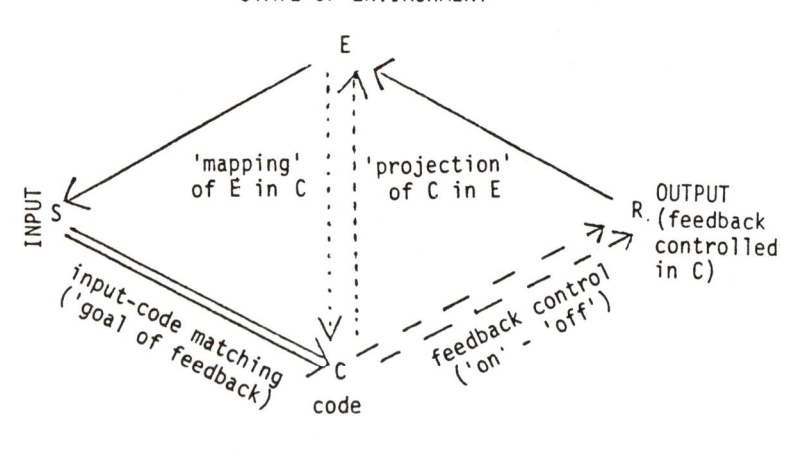

```
                              E
                         'mapping'    'projection'
                         of E in C    of C in E           OUTPUT
              INPUT  S                               R.   (feedback
                         input-code matching              controlled
                         ('goal of feedback')             in C)
                                       C   feedback control
                                      code    ('on' - 'off')
```

('intervening variable')

*Fig. 1*

The outcome of the operation of such a feedback loop is the correlation of its codes with states of the environment. We may say that the system 'maps' the environmental states in its codes and that it 'projects' its codes in the environment. In either case it brings about an input-code matching which functions as the 'goal' of the feedback. Thus the system's 'preferred state' is that wherein its intrinsic codes (or norms) are matched by the states of its environment.

The various properties of such systems have been considered by this writer elsewhere.[2] Here he can concentrate on the one question basic to the present study: can technology bring about states of environment which, when sensed, match the intrinsic codes of a human being? The question is not limited to his 'being' but encompasses also his 'well-being'. That is, we shall assume that the 'codes' of the human being are not merely homeostatic norms, but also cognitive and aesthetic standards.[3] Each of these 'codes' must find an environmental state as a counterpart if the individual is to be satisfied in its regard.

The assumption that cultural satisfactions, and therewith the intrinsic excellence and status of human life, depends on states of the environment may meet with criticism. Traditionally, 'spiritual' goods were sharply distinguished from 'material' goods and only the latter were allowed to be dependent on factual conditions in the surroundings. It is true, however, that every type of satisfaction is closely correlated with the states of the individual's environment, when these states are not assessed in terms only of the relevant biological survival needs but are also allowed to function as sources of satisfaction of cognitive and aesthetic requirements.

First of all, there is no categorical line to be drawn between genetically programmed homeostatic self-regulation and purposive behavior. Bergson remarked that, when at the end of its growth within the egg the young chick breaks the shell by a peck of its beak, it performs a purposive behavioral act which represents the culmination of its embryonic processes of growth. This idea can be carried further, according to Sinnott, by saying that such behavioral activities as the building of a bird's nest is simply a continuation, in the form of an instinct, of the processes of development.[4] Secondly, there is also no categorical dividing line between instinct-guided non-cognitive, and conscious goal-seeking (cognitive) behavior. The same basic motivation may underlie both kinds of behavior and this motivation can be stated as the 'need' of the organism to achieve certain transactional states in view of an existing imbalance in relation to its environment.

Experiments show that there are established norms of organism-environment relations which must be respected if the organism is to function properly. A reduction in the quantity or quality of stimulation, for example, produces strongly motivated activity in animals and, if prolonged, can lead to serious malfunctioning in their nervous system. Recent sensory deprivation experiments on human subjects show the disastrous effects of transgressing the input norms. Sometimes within a matter of hours, a reduced sensory input occasions hallucinations, impairs thinking ability and can lead to the breakdown of the entire nervous system.[5]

The experimental data suggest that the maintenance of a correspondence between the organic norms of an individual and his interactive relations with the environment is a basic precondition of his normal existence. The preservation of such transactional norms may well provide the motivation of behavior — cognitive as well as non-cognitive — and define the 'need' of the individual.

Now, the word 'need' defined in terms such as the above refers to basic biological functions, e.g., those which homeostatically maintain the organism in its environment. If one speaks of 'being' as the product of need-satisfactions, he is no doubt justified in doing so. But if one would suggest that well-being is also a product of need-satisfactions, and include under the term the 'dignity-making' properties of a satisfactory human life, he could be accused of biologically minded behavioristic reductionism. We do suggest that satisfactions motivated by need constitute a life worthy of esteem and possessing excellence (hence having 'dignity'), but do not mean to restrict the term 'need' to basic biological goals. Such need is the motivation of but one species of behavior, directed toward a goal which, when attained, assures for a time the existence of the organism. This, however, does not exhaust the concept of 'need'. Tolman defines 'need' as "a readiness or tendency to persist toward and to perform a consummatory response relative to a certain more or less arbitrarily chosen 'standard' goal object or situation and to avoid or go away from other objects or situations".[6] In this definition need can also state a cultural requirement, such as the satisfaction of the scientist's curiosity and the artist's desire for self-expression. If we pursue this interpretation, we get a generalized organism-environment balance definition of need which transcends survival needs and takes in cognitive and aesthetic 'transactions' as well. Following Cameron, we can further define need as "a condition of unstable or disturbed equilibrium in an organism's behavior, [which] ... may arise directly from a change in the organism's relationship with its environment ...".[7] Cameron cites as examples a drop in temperature and such metabolic resultants as hunger and thirst. But he also mentions symbolic behavior — talking, reading and thinking. Here we can extend the physiological need-concept to the cultural need (or requirement) concept. For example, we may have a cultural requirement to understand, which motivates a behavior pattern which is just as 'real' and goal-directed as that motivated by thirst. In each case an organism-environment imbalance is to be rectified through the resulting behavior. For example, a state of thirst represents the partial dehydration of the organism, and it motivates 'water-seeking' activity which, if successful, issues in the 'consummatory act' of drinking. Thereby the imbalance is rectified, the motivation temporarily reduced, and the proper organism-environment relationship reestablished. Such behavioral goal-seeking acts extend into the cultural sphere. This writer is in the habit of noting on a slip of paper his most urgent commitments as to research and writing. He also reserves a special shelf for the books and articles he most definitely wants to read. When the slips reach a certain number, and the shelf becomes loaded with books and reprints beyond a given point, a strong motivation is set up to leave off whatever other concerns he may have and pursue these goals. When the slips are one by one discarded, and the shelf gradually empties, the motivation wanes and a feeling of balance prevails.

The above 'feeling of balance' is not merely a subjective sensation but has its roots in a dynamic organism-environment equilibrium which includes not only biological, but also cultural factors. A 'cultural equilibrium' is one wherein cognitive and aesthetic goals are attained and satisfactions obtained. A disequilibrium sets up a motivation toward goals which are to be attained. Whereas the biological goals are genetically programmed transaction norms, the cultural norms are empirically acquired ('learned') inherently flexible variables, interconnecting the input and output of information. Whereas I cannot choose not to be thirsty when my body's water content drops below the normal level, I can discipline myself not to be motivated toward the attainment of a given cultural norm — such as an obligation to process information by reading, thinking and writing. But as long as the cultural motivation persists, it is just as real as the biological one. Its satisfaction contributes to my 'well-being', in contrast to the contribution of biological goals to my 'being'.

In either case the satisfaction of the need brings about a quiescence pattern which connotes the dynamic equilibrium of the organism with its environment. The reductionist flavor of this assertion vanishes when we remember that dynamic equilibrium is defined not merely by the genetic codes of the organism, but also by its acquired cultural norms. A culturally satisfied individual is in dynamic equilibrium with its environment whereas a culturally frustrated one is not.

In the context of cultural satisfactions 'environment' is not a rigid concept, as it is in biological satisfactions, but functions merely as a statistically probabilistic one. Whereas the environment must provide a source of potable liquids if my thirst is to be quenched, it need not, in every case, provide the appropriate cognitive or aesthetic object if my thirst for knowledge, or that for artistic expression and comprehension, is to be satisfied. These latter needs may also be satisfied in the imagination. It is possible to write transcendental poetry in a bare room and to postulate the laws of motion in one's own study. The 'inspiration' of the poet, musician or painter may derive from his own artistic imagination, and the scientist may rely on his rational faculties to come to grips with the nature of reality. The actual 'control objects' may be eliminated in both cases. But they cannot be entirely missing, for the very development of the imaginative and rationative faculties depends on their presence in the individual's growth and development. The behavioral sciences discovered the vital role of the environment not only in supporting life, but in making it healthy and satisfying. The environment is held to be overwhelmingly responsible for human life becoming capable and happy, or else frustrated and confounded. Psychologists find that some eighty percent of these effects have been wrought upon the individual by his environment by the time he reaches the age of four, and ninety-eight percent by the time he is thirteen. Thus the environment does play a decisive role both in the being and in the cultural well-being of the individual, even if the cultural factors are flexible and are temporarily eliminable (especially in maturity). To paraphrase Lincoln, although some of the people may substitute imaginary things and events in place of real environmental ones all of the time (at least after they reach maturity), and all of the people are very likely to do so some of the time, all of the people cannot make do without a both biologically and culturally satisfying environment all of the time. Cultural needs must, in the long run, have their appropriate counterparts in the environment. The well-being of the individual depends, in a very real sense, on the state of his milieu.

## TECHNOLOGY: 'CAN'

Let us assume that, accepting the foregoing considerations, 'need' is a generic term covering both biological and cultural requirements, and that its satisfaction presupposes the presence of the appropriate environmental objects, if not every time, then at least in a significant number of instances. What, then, is the role and potential of technology in helping man to achieve his biological and cultural satisfactions?[8]

One can speak to this problem by analyzing the above outlined basic feedback-loop in reference to the simple and familiar room thermostat. In that device the 'input' corresponds to the state of the temperature-sensing coil, which is modified according to the temperature of the air in the room. The coil bends or expands according to the actual air temperature, thus conducting this 'information' to the thermostatic system. The 'output' of the system is the furnace, which the system activates and deactivates in reference to its input. But the thermostat turns the furnace on or off not directly on the basis of the sensed air temperature, but on the basis of the correspondence of the air temperature to its setting. That is, a given input (state of the coil) turns on the furnace only if the setting of the control unit calls for it; at another (lower) setting, the furnace will not be activated. Here is our 'intervening variable' defining the programmed 'need' of the thermostat for a given range of air temperature. This 'need' is satisfied through the proper activation of the furnace — by turning it on when the actual air temperature is below the setting, and turning it off when it is above it. The thermostat 'satisfies its need' by bringing about an environmental condition (room air-temperature) which represents a counterpart to its setting (or code). The case is essentially similar in human motivated behavior: we strive for the environmental states corresponding to our incorporated 'codes' in function of bringing about those organism-environmental transactional states which 'satisfy' us. These transactional states range from basic biological processes, such as drinking to satisfy one's thirst, to higher 'cultural' ones, such as observation and experimentation to satisfy his 'thirst for knowledge'.

We can see that the role of technology in these instances is analogous to the role of the furnace in the case of the thermostat. It is to actively manipulate the environment to bring about the need-satisfying (and motivation-reducing) conditions, conducing to satisfaction by matching the input to the 'setting' (or 'codes') of the system. But, whereas the thermostat is set by an external agency, the human being's codes are self-programmed, and are brought about by a combination of genetically inherited and empirically acquired factors. Also, whereas the thermostat has a 'rigid personality', reacting to its input always in the same manner (as long as its setting is not changed by external agency), the human being possesses a 'flexible personality', adjusting his codes to conditions in the environment. This is the cybernetical meaning of the concept 'adaptation'. Man's adaptation-limits are defined by the biological survival range of the human organism on the one hand, and by the various, and more vaguely known, limits of cultural satisfactions on the other.

We now have the problem in focus. The 'dignity-making' capacity of technology depends on its ability to bring about environmental states which correspond to the individual's biological and cultural codes. These are normative, motivation-reducing transactional states. But just how efficiently can the 'furnace' of the 'human thermostat' function in matching man's self-regulated 'settings' in the environment?

On the plane of biological 'being', technology can function remarkably efficiently. To judge from the multiplication of our species on this globe, basic survival needs are being increasingly met by such technological achievements as more secure and hygienic housing, balanced diet, protection from other forms of life, and the many techniques of rearing the young and caring for the old. The evident counterinstances to these postulates cannot be ascribed to inherent failings of technology. Starvation, poverty, crime and war may be side-effects of technological conditions and may even make use of technological tools, but technology does not dictate such effects and use. Technology is capable of providing food and shelter for any and every human being (at least at the present time), and if some are deprived of its benefits, it is not the fault of technology, but of its application.

On the higher levels of cultural needs and motivated behavior, the 'human furnace' is called upon to function in a cognitive as well as an aesthetic capacity. Cognitively, it is deployed to structure the environment in a manner satisfying our 'rational codes', stated as the rules and principles of common sense and the laws and principles of science. Technology produces bicycles which are driven on the principle of the lever and aeroplanes which fly on the principle of least resistance. The life of contemporary man is populated with technological devices which serve not only his biological needs but satisfy at the same time his cognitive requirement of rationally understanding nature. That nature is so understandable is never questioned by the technology-habituated person. If he turns on the light switch and the light fails to go on, he suspects not that the principles of electricity have failed, but that the connection is broken. If a plane crashes it never occurs to the distinguished team of investigators to suspect that at the time of the accident the laws of nature may not have held. Technology affirms our implicit trust in the consistency and law-like rationality of our surroundings, satisfying thereby a cognitive urge to understand, and not merely to enjoy, our environment. In some persons such understanding remains implicit, and in others it is fully satisfied in the immediate technological surroundings. An average woman driver will be content to know that her car behaves in a knowable and regular manner, and that her mechanic knows enough of it to fix it if it goes wrong. The mechanic may be content to understand some mechanical principles of energy transfer in the engine and transmission of the car and leave the understanding of the laws and principles of automotive design to the engineers of Detroit. The latter in turn may be content to explore the understanding of their field without inquiring into the principles of molecular recombination, which underlie combustion, and of thermodynamics, which form the basis of the car's energy transformations. But observations and experiments are available to the scientist, whose urge to understand is not satisfied by ready-made technological devices. We thus encounter the pure scientist at the far end of the continuum that starts with the trusting housewife who operates shifts and buttons, in her car as well as in her home, in the comforting belief that their proper functioning is guaranteed by the rationally comprehensible nature of things. For each level of cognition there are corresponding contributions of technology, exhibiting and affirming the principles. These range from bicycles to atom-smashing devices, and from eyeglasses to radio-telescopes.

People today tend to ask of their world for more things than the satisfaction of their rationality, and hence the role of technology, in bringing about the appropriate environmental conditions, does not cease with the production of devices which exhibit the law-abidingness of nature. The aesthetic needs of cultural man cannot be disregarded, and these too, represent 'settings' or codes which must be matched through the presence of corresponding environmental states and events. If, for example, I wish to behold the workings of human destiny, inscrutable, often surprising but ultimately just, I look to the works of poets and dramatists, and not to that of engineers. Art, similarly to engineering and science, is a motivated activity, leading to the actualization in the environment of objects and events which satisfy one's innate desires. This assumption is independent of the specific theory of art one may wish to espouse. (Difficulties for it would be created only by the extreme Crocean view, which regards the work of art as complete in the mind, and the physical object as a mere artifact. But as soon as one allows that the physical work of art has value, the present views are vindicated.) The creation of symphonies, ballets, paintings, plays, pleasing buildings and gardens, and the many things and events which add up to an 'aesthetic environment' are, one and all, manipulations of the environment which either already make use of technology, or could benefit from such use. In an extended interpretation one may even say that every such activity benefits from technology, since the painter's brush and canvas, as well as the musician's pen and notepaper, are technological products. But beyond such trivial technological benefits, we have the reproduction of paintings and the recording of music as more remarkable varieties of technological contribution. At the far end of the spectrum we have computer-drawn pictures and computer-composed music, with merely an initial idea or design supplied by the programmer. There is no need to enter here into the relative merits of machine-contributions to artistic processes. It is sufficient to note that in all fields of artistic and aesthetic endeavor a physical 'control object' is likely to result which is instrumental in procuring and communicating aesthetic enjoyment. If this much is admitted (and even Croce would admit the role of the control object in communicating the aesthetic experience), then it follows that technology, insofar as it facilitates the creation of such objects, contributes to the satisfaction of the aesthetic needs of man. In this sense art-technology becomes an aesthetically motivated activity, analogously to the cognitively motivated products of engineering.

In neither case is technological endeavor directly motivated by these goals. Monetary status, and a host of other motivations may supervene in individual cases. But, whether people realize it or not, technology contributes to the cognitive undertaking exemplified in science as well as to the aesthetic efforts expressed in art. Its contribution in each case consists in facilitating the production of environmental states and objects which correspond to the intrinsic requirements of the person. The mind acts as the 'setting' for the desired 'temperature' which activates the technological 'furnace' in function of bringing about the corresponding environmental conditions. This function of technology may be concisely represented in this composite figure:

```
                    STATES OF ENVIRONMENT
                       ("room temperature")
  SENSING            E
  ("heat-                            responding
  sensitive          ∧               ("furnace")
  coil")            ┊ resulting
                    ┊ correlation:
    S               ┊ 'projection'
                    ┊ of C in E           R
       input-code match:        goal-seeking
        "goal" (satisfaction)  feed back-control
                         C
                   NEUROLOGICAL CODES
                   ("thermostat setting")
```

*Fig. 2*

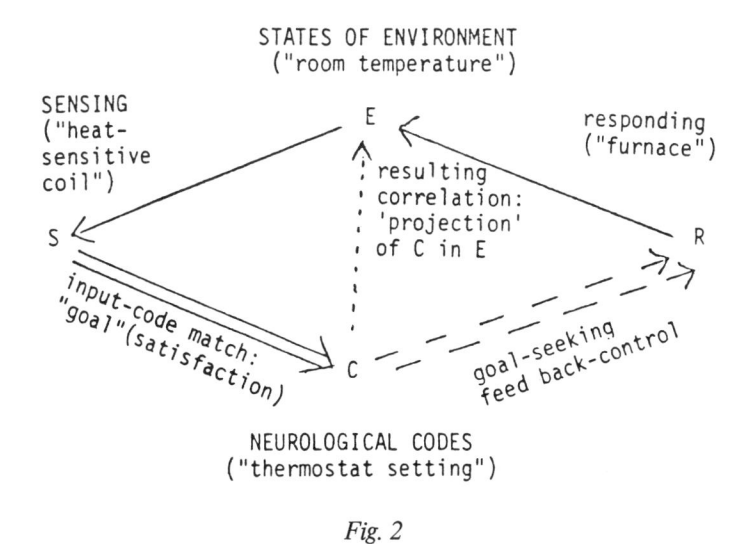

'Human dignity' resides in the sum of the satisfactions of the human being: in the sum of the matchings of innate norms with the corresponding environmental states. Thus human dignity signifies the being (biological need–environment matchings) as well as the well-being (cultural requirement–environment matchings) of the person. An existence in which intrinsic requirements are matched with extrinsic conditions possesses excellence and is worthy of esteem. One would be perplexed by any interpretation of dignity which does not refer to such matchings of the biological and cultural demands of the person and the actual conditions of his life. And one would be equally perplexed by an interpretation of technology which does not allow that it is intrinsically capable of projecting biocultural codes into environmental states.

## TECHNOLOGY: 'IS NOT'

The above picture of technology suggests unconditional approbation. In concentrating on what technology *can* do, it considers only the positive side of the coin. Unfortunately, however, that coin also has a negative side. If it is true that technology is capable of bringing about the environmental states and events which correspond to man's intrinsic demands, it is also true that it is equally capable of bringing about conditions which frustrate human ends. Technology can be dignity-making, but it is not necessarily that. And in fact it is often the opposite: an instrument of inhumanity.

Perhaps the strongest critique of technology in recent years was offered by Lewis Mumford. He complains that modern technology disregards the human factor and instead of serving humane purposes, automates even the human being. The creators of technology, from Francis Bacon onward, have dreamed of an automated economy under which, as Aristotle said, the shuttle would weave by itself, the lyre would play by itself, and the loaves of bread would spring out of the oven untouched by human hand.[9] But now we are beginning to discover that the 'scientific ideology' which underlies technology cannot be attached to valid human ends. This ideology excludes the very words *human, history, value, purpose,* and *end* as extraneous and undesirable, being irrelevant to quantitative measurement and prediction. Consequently, in order to enjoy the goods of our present scientific technology, we must "strictly conform to the dominant system, faithfully consuming all that it produces, meekly accepting its quantitative scale of values, never once demanding more essential human goods, above all a more meaningful human life . . .".[10] Hence, Mumford continues, "Humanly speaking, the proper name for automation is organized impotence; and the archetypal hero of our time is no other than Eichmann, the correct functionary, the perfect bureaucrat, proud to the end that he never allowed a moral scruple or a human sentiment to keep him from carrying out the orders that came from above."[11]

The contrast between the previously sketched potentials of technology, and its actual accomplishments as assessed by Mumford, is exceedingly sharp. On the one hand technology can contribute to achieving true human ends, biological as well as rational and aesthetical, and on the other it tends to frustrate such ends, by disregarding their very existence. And this is not all. Technology, if it can create a most viable environment for human beings, can also create a definitely unviable one. Whereas humanists complain of the evident inhumanity of our present technology, scientists worry about its threats to human life altogether. Norbert Wiener, the father of much of our contemporary technology, said, "There is a real possibility that changes in our environment have exceeded our capacity to adapt. The real dangers at the present time — the danger of thermonuclear war, the computing-machine sort of danger, the population-explosion danger, the danger of the improvement of medicine (to the extent that we shall very soon have to face not letting people live as part of the policy of letting them live) — all of these dangers make one wonder whether we have not changed the environment beyond our capacity to adjust to it, and whether we may not be biologically on the way out. We may not be, but this is not at all clear . . .".[12]

Wiener suggests that there is a real possibility that we may gradually program ourselves out of existence through technology. While biological survival needs can be satisfied with the aid of technology, they can also be frustrated through it. Thermonuclear war can render the globe uninhabitable for centuries. In that catastrophic event no biological needs can be satisfied — the environment is unable to produce the states and conditions necessary for our very existence. The 'computing machine sort of danger' consists in programming machines to bring about results without due regard for the costs. As Wiener says, a machine is terribly literal minded. It will give you what you ask for, not what you should have asked for, nor necessarily what you want. Thus there is a danger that, being short-sighted in what you ask for, you get something which in the long run you do not want. The examples are many: we ask for products of comfort and build plants to produce them: the result is the discomfort of an industrial area. We build factories to produce fishing gear and their waste products pollute the streams; we build cars to get to the country and they pollute the air when we get there. The population-explosion danger is equally acute. Recent computations show that fifty couples, reproducing themselves at the rate of a 1% population growth per year, will issue in three billion individuals in a matter of five thousand years. The present population of the world is four and a half billion individuals, and the rate of population growth is considerably above that of 1% in most countries. Where will we be *fifty* years hence — not to mention five thousand? Space does not expand with need, and chances of colonizing some other suitable planet are so slim as to be negligible. (And even if we did succeed in exporting half our population into outer space, we would have as many people as we have today in just 37 years!) Lemmings commit mass suicide when their population density exceeds a critical threshold; will thermo-nuclear war be our means of reducing — if not completely eliminating — our populations? Technology brought about this dilemma, by reducing infant mortality and extending individual life expectancy. Thereby it upset an ecological balance which maintained the human population relatively constant over a hundred-thousand year history. Here we encounter Wiener's "danger of the improvement of medicine" as well. Ecological balance normally reduces the optimum life-expectancy of individuals to the rate which is compatible with the coexistence of all species within the community. When for some reason the individuals of one species are favored, the balance is upset and ultimately even the favored species is disadvantaged. When coyotes were killed off by Arizona ranchers, deer multiplied to such population size that many of them starved. Today modern medicine kills off the natural 'predators' of our species — the bacteria — and may bring about a human population exceeding the available food supply. This is already the case in some parts of the world and, when the synthetic food-supplies and the new food resources — such as those of the oceans — are exhausted, it may be the case everywhere. We can adapt to a wide variety of conditions, but we do encounter definite limitations. We cannot adapt to a life without a minimum of nourishment, and we also cannot adapt to a life beyond a given (and as yet not quite clearly known) population density. We do know that 'individual distance' is a definite biological requirement in animal species (sparrows observe it in sitting on telephone wires and rats and other animals refuse to reproduce, or eat, or fail to care for their offspring, when their distances are violated in artificially contained populations), and the high rates of suicide, divorce, drug addiction, alcoholism and neurosis in cramped urban areas may give us a clue as to the maximum density that human beings can adapt to.

The sum of technological comforts, beneficial as they may be in the immediate experience of individuals, yet harbors another danger, to be appended to Wiener's list. It is the danger, to paraphrase a once popular TV commercial, of 'the spoiler'. Human beings adapt to the existing ways and means of satisfying their needs. Thereby genetic strains which introduced superfluous characteristics are gradually eliminated. It is no longer necesssary for men to grasp objects with their feet, and the anatomy of the foot adjusts to its present function of walking. It is no longer necessary to have keen eyesight since eye-glasses are readily available, and hence future generations will increasingly rely on them. Futuristic stories refer to men with large heads and hardly any legs, called upon to think and push buttons but not to walk. There is a real basis for such changes, in mutation and natural selection. Organically defective mutants are preserved by medical technology and the defective strains are handed down from generation to generation. Instead of being weeded out, the defective strains become technologically standardized. Whereas it was a serious defect not to be able to climb trees eighty thousand years ago, or to be shortsighted, or obese, these things no longer connote serious defects. Technology modifies the environment and thereby reshuffles our notions of 'fit' and 'defective' characteristics. The new values are valid as long as the technology which brought them about remains active. To be myopic is not defective as long as optical lenses are available to correct vision. But if technology would fail us, most of us would change from 'fit' to 'defective'. We are, in other words, growing dependent on the technological environment. We are getting 'spoiled'. If today we still live in a partly natural, partly artificial environment, and if compelled most of us would still be able to lead the life of a Robinson Crusoe, far from technology, tomorrow we may be creating a predominantly artificial environment for ourselves, from which there may be no sudden return to nature. If the technology of that future environment would fail, we would not have the time to produce the new genetic variants which would again enable us to live in a natural climate. Technology may be a one-way street. If it does not exceed the limits of our biological adaptability, we can live with it, and may even live with it very well, but the more we rely on it the more dependent we become upon it.

### TECHNOLOGY: 'OUGHT'

Now that we have looked at both sides of the coin, let us try to see how the positive side could be realized and the negative side eliminated and avoided. Technology can contribute to the satisfaction of human needs and purposes, but it often frustrates them. Technology can assure our existence on this planet, but in fact it endangers it. There is a gap here between *is* and *can* which demands an *ought*, regardless of whether it is permitted by the logic of moral discourse or not. We *ought* to make technology subserve human ends since it can, but it fails to do so. The task is ours, and so is the blame. An IBM advertisement points out that men should think; machines should work. Machines do in fact work, but men have been poor at the task of thinking. To make a machine work toward the attainment of a short-sighted want, rather than a valid biocultural need, is poor thinking. The outcome cannot be charged to the machine's account. The failure occurs at the human level, in ignoring the difference between an immediate want and a true need. It is the failure of producing a balanced 'ideology' which, as Mumford says, would be "capable of uniting physical processes and organic functions with human purposes, the cosmos without the microcosmos within, the outer with the inner world . . .".[13] Human needs must be restored to the center of our schemes of thought if mechanization is to be brought back into the service of human existence. Man must take upon himself, once more, the wide range of capabilities and potentialities he surrendered when he developed the machine.[14] This calls for integral and balanced knowledge; for a science of human needs, biological, social and cultural. One could point out on behalf of our species that this is an immensely large order. This may do as an excuse, but not, however, as a solution. For if the unregulated machine-age runs away with a series of pernicious environmental changes, there may soon be but a few to care about the excuses and perhaps no one to utter them.

The inhuman machine-age is a miscarriage of science. Science is capable of producing a technology which can bring about human satisfactions of the most diverse kinds. The inhumanity of present technology is the result of a one-sided concentration on short-term wants rather than on basic long-term needs. At present we live in an age of machines and robots, in a world insensitive to the human needs for intuitive understanding and emotional harmony and relevance. Such a world is no more a necessary result of technology than the worlds of the electric guitar player and televised soul-singer. On the whole, the present world is inhumanly automated and disdainful of aesthetic needs. But the same technology which produced this world could also be instrumental in bringing about a supremely human, aesthetically relevant world. Technology can produce, reproduce, and disseminate works of art as well as machines, and can contribute to our determination of nature's rationality as much as to its aesthetic relevance. If we have two cultures, it is because technology is such an efficient instrument. It brings to you canned foods and microscopes, as well as videotaped soul-singers, with almost equal facility.

But technology is literal minded. It gives you what you ask for, and not necessarily what you need. Hence we must know what we need before we can ask technology to bring it to us. The needs of individuals are often obscured by their wants. And their wants, unlike their needs, may be incompatible. If you ask a scientist, an engineer or a politician what he wants, you will get an answer that is radically different from the one you get from an artist, a revolutionary and a hippy. The two-culture gap extends into the generation gap and presents contrary aspects of the same problem. We all need satisfactions — both biological and cultural. We need a life of intrinsic excellence and meaning — a life of dignity. But our wants conflict. Cultural wants may conflict with biological needs, and one's cultural wants may conflict with another's. It is not enough to ask technology to satisfy one or another of these wants, and to satisfy one combination of them without regard to others. Technology will do so, but the result may be catastrophic. You may ask it for the conditions under which you can have as many children as you wish. If you are a normal couple, technology will enable you to have a child every year for a decade or so, and if your contemporaries do the same, you shall be unable to feed your children. But you can also ask technology to provide the contraceptive devices so that having a modest number of offsprings will not interfere with sexual satisfaction. You can ask technology for thermonuclear warheads and intercontinental missiles to assure international dominance, but you must also realize that if you are called upon to use them, your flag may fly over a lifeless planet. You can ask for a well-regulated, machine ordered society, of flawless hygiene and minimum pain. You and your contemporaries could create any and all of these worlds through the purposive use of technology. But will you, and all others (also having a right to being and well-being) find enduring satisfactions in it? The answer is *no*. To ask for any one of these alternatives is to ask for what you *want*, rather than what you *need*. It is to ask for a fulfilment of your wishes regardless of the consequences, either for yourself or for others. This is how technology has been used, by and large, until now. If it continues to be so used, the result may well be that we shall modify our environment beyond the limits of our biological adaptability, and that in our quest for fulfilling one type of cultural demand we hopelessly frustrate others.

We must know what to ask for, and then we must ask for what we – biocultural human beings – really need. Our dignity resides in our being and well-being. Modern technology can fulfil almost any reasonable demand made upon it in these respects. But it does not care if, by so doing, it frustrates other demands. The technological 'furnace' has a complex task in matching our 'thermostatic control settings' by relevant modifications of the environment. An entire series of mutually independent furnaces can be activated, all of which eventually converge upon the conditions in our own 'room'. If we want the temperature which is the precondition of our being as well as of our well-being, we must know how each of these furnaces affects it. And, more importantly still, we must know our own norms: what temperatures we really require. Without such knowledge we endanger our well-being and, in the long run, even our being.

## DIGNITY THROUGH TECHNOLOGY: APPLICATION PRINCIPLES

Let us suppose for the moment that our individual biocultural norms are adequately known. (This is a theoretical assumption, not an assessment of our actual state of knowledge.) The question arises then as to the conceptual framework which could direct the techniques of bringing about the need-satisfying environmental states and events. These techniques repose on the very same conceptual foundations as contemporary technology itself.

In the first section of this study a basic feedback loop was outlined in reference to the patterns of activity of living organisms (Figure 1). This scheme rests on the view that input and output are coupled by a code (or 'intervening variable') which is goal-seeking by means of negative feedback, activating the system's responses in view of bringing about states of the environment which correspond to the norm represented by the code. Such correspondence is known in cybernetical literature as 'goal-matching', and the pertinent information as 'match-signal'. The function of the codes is to produce an output which brings about a match-signal (just as the thermostat's function, in activating the furnace, is to bring about the air temperature which, when sensed by the coil, corresponds to its setting). In human affairs the furnace is represented by technology: it is the modern means for manipulating the environment in view of goal-matching. Its purpose is to bring about an environment which affords counterparts to the biological and cultural codes of individuals. A considered technological 'environment-structuring' would be goal-pursuing in the same manner as an individual is, and, in the optimum event, in which not just the immediate and sometimes deceptive *wants*, but the true *needs* of individuals are known (as hypothesized here for the sake of argument) it would be dignity-making for the human community. That is, it would optimize the chances that members of that community could find biological as well as cultural satisfactions in the technologically modified environment. The striking fact about the appropriate conceptual framework of such structuring is that it is identical with that which fathered contemporary technology. To illustrate this point let us consider first a modern approach to social theory, and then contrast it with the approach to artificial servomechanisms.

Buckley argues that the mechanical equilibrium model and the organismic homeostasis models of society, which were at the basis of most of the modern sociological theories, have outlived their usefulness.[15] He suggests that a much truer model of society is evolving out of the modern systems perspective, based on general system theory, cybernetics, and information as well as communications theory. Buckley's models of society is the 'complex adaptive system'. One need not agree with it in every detail to see that it is useful as an example of the kind of systems-thinking which is on the rise in the field of sociology. 'Complex adaptive systems' are open as well as negentropic systems. They are open both internally and externally, since the system may bring about changes in the relations of its own components, i.e., it can adaptively regulate its structure. Internal and external interchanges occur through information-flow channels, making up feedback loops which make possible self-regulation not only in view of maintaining the system's existing structure, but also giving it self-direction (or self-organization), such that the system's structure is changed and elaborated in function of its viability. The properties of such a system (which apply to systems on the biological, psychological as well as the sociocultural levels) are listed as follows. "(1) some degree of 'plasticity' and 'irritability' vis-à-vis its environment such that it carries on a constant interchange with environmental events, acting on and reacting to it; (2) some source or mechanism for variety, to act as a potential pool of adaptive variability to meet the problem of mapping new or more detailed variety and constraints in a changeable environment; (3) a set of selective criteria or mechanisms against which the 'variety pool' may be sifted into those variations in the organization or system that more closely map the environment and those that do not; and (4) an arrangement for preserving and/or propagating these 'successful' mappings."[16] Consequently the system adapts to its environment by restructuring itself if necessary. We agree with this model as far as it goes, but wish to add that biological, psychological and sociocultural systems, if relatively complex and evolved, not only adapt to their environments, but also actively adapt the environment to themselves: they modify their surroundings. Thus they not only 'learn' to map the features of the environment in their codes, but also bring about those environmental features which correspond to their existing codes (they project their codes in their environment). Such systems are both self-organizing (adaptive) and self-stabilizing (manipulative).[17] The latter capability becomes clear when we contrast Buckley's systems-description of a society with the cybernetics of a servomechanism.

A modern anti-aircraft gun is a good example of such a mechanism. It is equipped with radar and computing devices which enable it to 'sense' a flying object interacting with its beam and to 'interpret' it as an airplane. The interpretation brings about the self-regulation of the gun's position to aim at the flying object, aiming not at its sensed position but at its predicted position at the time when the missile reaches it. If all operations are free of error, the gun shoots down the airplane. Here we have an example of an environment-manipulating feedback system which does not change its existing structure (is not 'adaptive' in Buckley's sense) but brings its environment in correspondence with its codes. *Adaptive* systems are goal-matching by mapping the relevant aspects of the changeable environment in their codes, and *manipulative* systems are goal-matching by projecting their codes in the relevant aspects of the environment (modifying their environment in accordance with their codes). Whereas Buckley's adaptive system treats the factor of environment-change as an *independent* variable (he speaks of a 'changeable environment' which does not appear to be under the system's control), the servomechanism takes the environmental change-factors relevant to its codes as *dependent* variables, and channels their determination through the feedback controlled activity of the system.

Now, while there is some question as to whether or not servomechanisms can be truly adaptive and not merely manipulative systems (Wiener's 'learning machines', for example, suggests that they can be),[18] it is clear that psychological and sociocultural systems are both adaptive, and efficiently manipulative systems. Many thinkers (e.g., Whitehead in *The Function of Reason*) saw the purposive, manipulative activity of organisms as a typical characteristic of higher forms of life; and few social theorists and anthropologists would fail to recognize the great capacity of sociocultural systems to purposively modify their environments in accordance with their intrinsic goals and requirements. Opinions diverge as to whether such environment-modification is guided by conscious wants and wishes, or by often unrecognized sociodynamic factors. Yet it is evident that sociocultural systems can modify their environments — whether consciously directed or not — both positively and negatively. One may decrease the freedom of men and frustrate their needs by prisons, big city slums, aesthetic bareness and anarchy, or one may provide a milieu which is ordered, harmonious and satisfying. The most striking affirmation of the possibility of positive and conscious environment-modification this writer has come across was proposed by Buckminster Fuller: "Comprehensive physical and economic success for humanity may now be accomplished in one-fourth of a century. Now and henceforth it is not only normal for man to be a physical and economic success but to be so without endangering the success of any others and without interfering with the degree of freedom of others."[19] Fuller states that "the discovered principles governing the inter-transformative structuring of universe permit the individual to reform the environment in such manner as to provide ultimately higher advantage for men, and in such a manner as to regenerate in other individuals the drive to further transform the environment to even higher advantage to all."[20] His concept of a science of environment-modification is 'Design Science'. Whether or not one shares Fuller's optimistic assessment of the potentials of this science, it is important to note its characteristics: these are clearly evident in his recommendations for its Curriculum. According to him, Design Science involves a study of, (1) Synergetics (defined as "unique behaviors of whole systems unpredicted by any behaviors of their component functions taken separately"), (2) General Systems Theory, (3) Theory of Games (v. Neumann), (4) Chemistry and Physics, (5) Topology, Projective Geometry, (6) Cybernetics, (7) Communications, (8) Meteorology, (9) Geology, (10) Biology, (11) Sciences of Energy, (12) Political Geography, (13) Ergonomics, and (14) Production Engineering. The heavy emphasis in the list on systems-theory and related disciplines (Synergetics, GST, Theory of Games, Cybernetics, Communications) leaves little doubt about Fuller's agreement with the general principle proposed in this study, to wit, that the theoretical foundations which gave birth to modern technology are also those which can guide its purposive application. Modern technology creates relatively complex manipulative negative-feedback controlled systems (servomechanisms), and human socio-cultural systems likewise appear to be systems of this sort — with the additional property of self-organizing adaptability. But technology is not concerned with adaptation to existing conditions but with the forming and reforming of conditions. It is a manipulative tool rather than an instrument of docile adaptation. Thus, if we recognize the manipulative capability of modern technological societies, we come to the insight that human societies are adaptive as well as manipulative complex systems. Figure 1 gives the basic information-flow chart of such systems and Figure 2 emphasizes their manipulative capacity.

The manipulative capacity of societies resides in the projection of the codes or norms of the system in its environment, through feedback-controlled capacity of the systems, whereby the states and events which match the intrinsic 'preferred states' of human beings can be efficiently brought about in their environment. Whereas birds 'project their codes' in building nests and beavers in building dams, men build cities and reform the entire landscape. Their added projective capability is due to the tools they use, and the modern variant of the human tool is technology — ultimately the automated computerized servomechanism. The use of such tools in environment engineering — the Design Science outlined by Fuller — is essentially analogous to nest-building by birds and the destruction of enemy planes by radar-tracking anti-aircraft guns. In regard to their manipulative capacities, cybernetical machines outclass human beings and human societies (it is in regard to flexible adaptive capabilities that they are more deficient). The goal of negative-feedback controlled environment-manipulation is the harmonization of the environment with the norms of the system. Such norms are the 'settings' of the thermostat, the programming of the computerized device, the physiological standards of the subhuman organism, and the biocultural (neuro-physiological and cognitive-aesthetic) 'codes' of the human being. Goal-seeking in the above sense describes human motivation and lends meaning to the generalized concept of 'need'.

Thus, the application of systems theory is not restricted to the particular machines and instruments which act on the environment and modify it in accordance with human biocultural need, but extends both to the individual exhibiting the need and to the society in and through which the needs are satisfiable. Nevertheless, sociocultural systems, as well as electronic servomechanical ones, must be programmed on the basis of a knowledge of the factors which can bring about their goal-matchings, i.e., which harmonize their intrinsic codes with the relevant extrinsic events. Human societies have muddled along so far relatively successfully, because the environmental changes they effected did not exceed the range of their members' adaptive potentials. Individual adaptations and genetic variability could compensate for the often pernicious changes in the environment, the outcome of impulses based on immediate want rather than the fruit of insight into need. But now that modern technology intensifies our capacity to change our environment, such muddling becomes dangerous. We could find ourselves in an environment which exceeds our biological capacity to adapt. Moreover the lack of purposive environment-engineering almost certainly frustrates more cultural needs than need be, by favoring a random selection of needs (those which harmonize with the wants of the power elite) at the expense of the general cultural need-distribution. Hence an insight into human biocultural need is called for, and this insight must 'program' the 'complex adaptive and manipulative system' which much of contemporary social theory is beginning to recognize our societies to be.

The conceptual framework of contemporary technology is peculiarly applicable to natural and social phenomena at the most diverse levels of organization and complexity. Modern technological thinking is in harmony with the nature of reality, as we are beginning to assess it. Let us not forget, however, that the natural systems we recognize on the diverse fields of investigation are self-programming systems, operating on the basis of norms and codes which evolved gradually in time, without purposive guidance by conscious agency. The artificial systems of technology, on the other hand, are consciously programmed pre-set systems. Herein lies their danger — but also their great potential benefit. They can be programmed to achieve consciously entertained goals. Technical systems do not think — they work. They have to be told what to do. We have remarkable knowledge how to build such systems; what we lack is the knowledge how to program them in our best interests.

The most urgent task facing man today is to acquire such knowledge. It is to recognize the nature and repertory of human biocultural needs, and to employ the remarkable instrumentalities of modern technology to engineer the environment accordingly. If man is a natural self-organizing and self-stabilizing system in an inclusive hierarchy of biological and sociocultural systems, he has the advantage over all other systems in being the only one capable of knowing his own codes. The advantage of self-reflective rationality can be exploited if the relevance to human need of the various hierarchical systems which surround us is recognized, and these systems are purposively manipulated to provide the greatest number of us with the optimum conditions of existence. This is the potential of technology on the positive side. On the negative side its potential amounts to prompt and thorough mass-destruction, amounting to the suicide of our species. The choice is clear: we can continue to muddle along, using technology to realize immediate wants, and hope that in the process we shall not exceed the range of our adaptability or press the lethal button; or we can start structuring our environment with regard to the repertory of actual biocultural needs. To effect a real choice good intentions are not enough: we need a dependable science of man, as a conscious sociocultural biosystem. Could there be a more challenging, as well as a more noble task than to evolve such a science?

## DIGNITY THROUGH TECHNOLOGY: GUIDANCE PRINCIPLES

In concluding this brief study, the best that we can do is to sketch out the universal points of reference which a concentrated and responsible study of human biocultural need may take.

The conceptual foundations are given by the norms of the human organism-environment equilibrium. Need arises when the equilibrium norms are violated; then, the appropriate behavioral responses are motivated toward regaining it. Just what constitutes a state of dynamic equilibrium for us is determined by our 'codes'. On the non-cognitive biological level, the codes are genetically preprogrammed and relatively inflexible. Behavior motivated by them is best exemplified by ant societies, where complex behavioral acts are carried out on the basis of pre-programmed codes. In our species such codes motivate homeostatic processes, regulating body temperature, water content, blood pressure, and all the immensely complex factors which together add up to the constancy of what Claude Bernard called the *milieu interieur*. Certain basic 'drives' penetrate into the active behavioral scheme and motivate the biological behavior patterns the goals of which are food, drink, rest and reproduction. The environmental states which satisfy these genetically coded behavior patterns are universal. Thus the absence of potable liquids represents a state of disequilibrium for all human beings, who have a universal need to replenish their water supplies. Similarly with air, food, shelter, mate, and the other basic requirements of existence. But in the case of *cultural* needs, just which environmental states represent equilibrium and which disequilibrium, and whether a given state is the one or the other, depends on *individual* factors. A saying, present in most languages in one form or another, holds that "one man's meat is another man's poison". This is evidently untrue if taken literally (in which case it refers to biological needs which designate meat as satisfaction and poison as a threat to all men), but it is just as evidently true if taken metaphorically— as it is intended. A hippie may shudder at the very thought of leading a life which connotes the essence of satisfaction to a retired cavalry officer and, of course, *vice versa*. The ideal life of an artist may appear to be one filled with emotive gibberish to a logician, and the precisely regulated schedule of a statesman can appear inhuman to the poet.

The metaphorical "meat of one man, poison of another" applies to entire culture groups as well. East and West, American and Indian, Israeli and Arab, represent so many different syndromes of cultural needs. Yet underlying the differences, basic commonalities emerge. All men demand of their environments that it should satisfy their existential needs: there must be environmental counterparts to all our biological codes. Further, although imaginary 'control-objects' may provide satisfaction in some cases, civilized men tend to demand that their environments actually include factors which exhibit the reliable rationality of nature, and factors which render the surroundings aesthetically satisfying. The particular environmental state or event which conduces to such satisfactions may vary from individual to individual and from culture to culture. But their common denominator will be cognitive rationality on the one hand and aesthetic meaning on the other.

If in the foregoing analyses we gave the impression that the various biocultural codes of the organism are purely individual properties, then we must hasten to rectify the position. Contemporary Marxists often refer to the human mind as a social organ, following Marx's assertion (in his *Theses on Feuerbach*) that the human essence is no individual abstraction, but the ensemble of the social relations.[22] While a kind of metaphysical 'socialization' of the human mind (or nervous system) is arbitrary, there is evidence to the effect that biocultural codes are socially evolved. After pointing out that at birth the infant develops needs which only the environment can satisfy, and that such needs could, at least theoretically, be satisfied by some automatic machinery, taking care of each lack as it arose, Cameron tells us that in practice "the satisfaction or removal of infant need always requires the help of older persons, and it is through the reactions of these other human beings to him that an infant becomes socialized ... as biosocial maturity progresses, every individual develops new needs and new satisfactions on the basis of new activities and new relationships".[23] And later he says that "we continually meet with situations in which such obviously learned needs as those for human company, for prestige and for esteem actually crowd out hunger, thirst and sex need".[24] The entire sphere of motivated human behavior is influenced by social factors, and at times social needs may even dominate the biological need-patterns. In Gestalt Psychology needs are regarded as 'vectors', corresponding to the relation of the individual to his environmental objects. Referring to the social variety of 'bipolar organizations', Kohler admits that the particular physiological conditions which determine their organismic sides are not known. "For instance, after being alone for long periods, most persons will feel a strong 'drive' toward social contact, even with strangers. In some respects this vector operates in a way which is quite similar to the need for food, drink, or a mate. Could it be that prolonged lack of social contact, and as a consequence, of sufficiently interesting 'objects' establishes a particular condition in the nervous system, and that, in a general way, this state is comparable to lack of food, water, and so forth?"[25] Although at present no definite answer to this question is forthcoming, the reality of 'social drives' or 'social needs' is quite evident. It conditions the manner in which biological and cultural satisfactions are striven for. In virtue of it society is not merely a class-name of an arbitrary collection of independent individuals, confined by extraneous circumstances to a given geographic area, but stands for an interactive set of people whose functional modes of assuring their being and well-being interpenetrate. It is impossible to view science and art, and the various human endeavors which share in the rationality exhibited by the former and in the intuitive comprehension manifested by the latter, without considering them as 'interthinking' social institutions, transcending individual goal-strivings. One need not hypothesize a concrete universal such as an 'objective spirit', or side with Social Darwinism in regarding society as a vast organism, to appreciate the social character of human existence. The social factors are built into the very goals which individuals pursue from their birth onwards, and penetrate both their biological and cultural patterns of being and well-being. Kluckhohn affirms that "The main outlines of hierarchical preferences have only exceptionally been created out of the stuff of unique biological heredity and peculiar life experience. They are usually cultural products in the main; and from the life-ways that constitute the designs for living of his community, or tribe, or nation, or socio-economic class, or civilization, the ordinary individual derives most of his basic conceptual orientations."[26] The pattern of interactive behavior in a social group is not necessarily reflected in the conscious purposes of its members. It is entirely possible that the fundamental structure of social relations be unrecognized by the relating individuals, and a conscious 'model' may even obscure the real social structure.[27] In Kluckhohn's words, "Every good way of life, then, is a structure: not a haphazard collection of physically possible and functionally effective patterns of belief and action, but an interdependent system whose influence is greater rather than less because the fundamental premises and categories are seldom brought into the realm of explicit discussion."[28]

Emphasizing another aspect of sociocultural conditioning, Handy points out that "The individual cannot be separated sharply from his social context and that context frequently is the most important single factor in determining what needs are satisfied and how they are satisfied. Obviously some people are better than others in surviving and prospering under adverse social circumstances, but even such favored individuals are extremely limited by the circumstances in which their behavior occurs."[29] Anthropologists of the structuralist school emphasize that invariant social relations define the social intercourse of transient individuals, permitting the theorist to set up structural models of societies, despite the constant interchange of its individual members.[30] Since the invariant relationships, into which individuals enter for varying periods of time, define the manner in which they satisfy their many needs, utmost consideration must be given to society's existing social structure. Individual patterns of goal-seeking behavior accord with the patterns of social relations, and goals are attained in and through the existing structures. Therefore, if we are to evolve a science of man as a biocultural need-motivated adaptive-manipulative system, we must take the actual social structure into consideration. If machines are to work toward enabling us to achieve satisfactions, we must think not only in terms of the individual's goals of survival, reproduction, rational cognition and aesthetic enjoyment, but also in terms of the sets of relationships which define how any of the environmental counterparts of these norms are utilizable by the individual.

Technology can only serve human biocultural need within the framework of the existing social structures. This is not to say that technology could not also be made to change the existing social structure, insofar as it is in need of revision. It is only to suggest that individual biocultural goals must be seen to be attainable within the social structures, and that these structures can only be reformed, and not ignored. Reformation — whether by evolution or revolution — is justified if the existing structure is incapable of fulfilling the biocultural demands of the individuals in a satisfactory manner, and if a realistically envisaged reformation of the structure could optimize its functional capacity. But for this we must know both the individual biocultural goals and the social patterns of interdependence within which they are pursued. If such knowledge is at hand, technology can be purposively and effectively applied. Its instruments are many and their effectiveness is great. 'Environment-structuring' could bring about satisfactions for most, if not all people. Technology could be made to structure the environment, in recognition of biocultural needs and social systems, to put at each man's disposal the environmental states and events which match his particular syndrome of requirements. Thereby individual satisfactions could be optimized in providing the conditions for the dynamic (biological and cultural) equilibrium of persons with and in their environments.

The new 'ideology' we now need is but a new answer to the time-honored injunction 'know thyself'. Today it becomes the imperative 'know your norms (or codes)'. These define under what conditions man can live and obtain satisfaction. We need an up-to-date science of man, as a being who is part of his environment, and capable of adapting to it as well as actively modifying it. His modifications must respect the limits of his adaptability, and structure his environment to optimize the chances of satisfaction for all men. On a more basic economical level he has already achieved such structuring. The modern supermarket is a good example. Its virtues are known best by contrast. Americans living in relatively underdeveloped countries, conscious of its convenience through the contrast of the local facilities to the official 'PX stores', wistfully refer to America as the 'land of the giant PX'. If the concept can be extended to non-material goods as well, the denomination is a flattering one. Perhaps our modern technological environment should be structured as a giant biocultural PX. In it, biological conditions of life would be offered to all. And cultural satisfactions would be available in a variety of offerings which could match, within the existing social structures, the diversity of individual tastes. Overpopulation and war would signify the collapse of this PX, and a unilaterally structured environment, whether 'machine-like' or 'flower-like', its poor management. The master-plan for such a structured environment would have to be drawn up by the technicians of the new knowledge. These would replace Plato's philosopher-kings, if not as philosophers turned engineers, then as engineers turned philosophers.

## REFERENCES

1. See the difficulties discussed by Professor Spiegelberg in his article in Part I of *Human Dignity – This Century and the Next*, ed. R. Gotesky and E. Laszlo, (Gordon and Breach, New York, 1970).
2. Ervin Laszlo, "Multi-Level Feedback Theory of Mind" in Lee Thayer, ed., *Communication: General Semantics Perspectives* (New York; Spartan Books, 1970), and *System Structure and Experience: Toward a Scientific Theory of Mind*, present series, Vol. I (New York, 1969).
3. A detailed definition of these standards is given in *System, Structure, and Experience, op. cit.*
4. Edmund W. Sinnott, *The Biology of the Spirit* (New York: The Viking Press, 1955), Chapter III.
5. Cf., for example, Solomon, P. (ed.), *Sensory Deprivation* (Cambridge: Harvard, 1961).
6. Edward C. Tolman, "A Psychological Model", in Parsons and Shils, eds., *Toward a General Theory of Action* (Cambridge: Harvard, 1951), p. 335.
7. Norman Cameron, *The Psychology of Behavior Disorders* (Boston: Houghton, 1947), p. 105.
8. Here, as throughout this paper, I understand under 'technology' the hardware and software of applied science as they condition human need and satisfaction. No doubt, other definitions of technology are possible but, as I pointed out at the beginning of this paper, I do not attempt a survey of all hitherto offered definitions, but offer my own, carefully stating its meaning. (I should add that my definition accords with that of Watson and includes as a subspecies ['social factors', cf. pp. 130-132] the 'social technology' discussed by Peterson. Cf. their articles, below.)
9. Lewis Mumford, "The Automation of Knowledge", *Vital Speeches of the Day*, 30, pp. 441-446.
10. *Ibid.*
11. *Ibid.*
12. Norbert Wiener, "The Monkey's Paw", Martin Greenberger, ed., *Management and the Computer of the Future* (Cambridge: MIT Press, 1962).
13. Mumford, *op. cit.*
14. *Ibid.*
15. Walter Buckley, "Society as a Complex Adaptive System" in Buckley, ed., *Modern Systems Research for the Behavioral Scientist* (Chicago: Aldine, 1968), pp. 450-513.
16. *Ibid.*, p. 491.
17. Cf. E. Laszlo, *System, Structure and Experience, op. cit.*
18. Cf. "The Monkey's Paw", *op. cit.*
19. Buckminster Fuller, "Letter to Doxiadis" in *Main Currents in Modern Thought*, Vol. 25, No. 4 (March-April, 1969), p. 96.

20. *Ibid.*, p. 91.
21. *Ibid.*, p. 95.
22. Cf. Ervin Laszlo, "Marxism-Leninism vs. Neurophysiology", *Studies in Soviet Thought*, XI, 2 (1969).
23. Cameron, *op. cit.*, p. 104.
24. *Ibid*, p. 126.
25. Wolfgang Kohler, *Gestalt Psychology* (New York: Liveright, 1947), Chapter IX.
26. Clyde K. Kluckhohn, "The Special Character of Integration in an Individual Culture", in *The Nature of Concepts: Their Interrelation and Role in Social Culture* (Stillwater, Okla., 1950), p. 80.
27. Cf. Claude Levi-Strauss, *Structural Anthropology* (New York: Basic Books, 1963), Chapter XV.
28. Kluckhohn, *op. cit.*, p. 81.
29. Rollo Handy, *Value Theory and the Behavioral Sciences* (Springfield, Illinois: Charles C. Thomas, 1969), p. 163.
30. Cf. Levi-Strauss, *op. cit.*; also Radcliffe-Brown, "On Social Structure", *Journal of the Royal Anthropological Institute*, LXX (1940).
31. A. N. Whitehead, *The Function of Reason* (Boston: Beacon Hill, 1929), p. 4.

# 14

## CHILDREN AND THE FUTURE OF HUMANITY*

The present generation of adults may well prove incapable of coping with the changes and problems that beset our troubled times. It will take a new generation, a healthy and an open one, to evolve the patterns of life, the values, the relationships, and the institutions suitable for managing the world's problems and mastering the tides of change. It is our responsibility, however, to bring forth a healthy and creative new generation, by lengthening our time frames and adjusting our priorities, and putting children directly in the centre of our plans and policies of development.

### COPING WITH CHANGE THROUGH THE GENERATIONS

Change is part of the texture of human life and social development. Although not a continuous phenomenon (mankind's history is replete with long periods of stability and the seemingly endless repetition of cyclical patterns), when it occurred, it was usually precipitated by new relations between man and nature and man and man, and it always called for prolonged adjustments in values and lifeways. These were seldom smooth, and they usually called for several generations to accomplish.

The first truly great leap in history – the 'neolithic revolution' – took centuries to accomplish, for many generations came and went before the nomadic hunting and food-gathering tribes turned into settled villagers. As this revolution spread, more people came to be supported by the available lands, and more of them could devote their time and energies to specialized tasks other than the raising of crops and the caring for animals.

Cities came into being, and established trade routes criss-crossed the inhabited world. The taboos and mores of primitive agrarian and pastoral societies – gods and

---
*Reprinted from UNICEF News, 102/1979/4.

goddesses and rites of fertility and of the earth — came slowly to be replaced by new values, new symbols and new religions. The classical empires of Greece, Rome, and Constantinople arose, conquered, and ultimately fell. The tenor of existence varied from the opulence of emperors, the discipline of legionnaires, to the misery and hardship of slaves. But even as Europe lapsed into the medieval age, time as yet stood almost still in many of the non-European civilizations, where it was measured only by the reign of ruling houses and dynasties.

Then — unforeseen and unheralded — the modern age burst upon mankind in seventeenth century Europe. The laws of the earth and of the heavens were united by Newton, after having been removed from the sphere of the unknowable and the supernatural by Galileo and Copernicus. Modern man found that he could control more and more of his milieu, and believed that nothing could ultimately escape his influence. Ancient handicrafts were joined with precise measurements and abstract calculations. Science, whereby — as Bacon proclaimed — man can "wrest the secrets of nature for his own benefit", gave birth to modern technology.

An entire age of adaptation and reorganization followed. First in Europe, then over much of the Northern hemisphere, modern technical civilization emerged in diverse yet seemingly inexorably evolving forms. Science and technology were divorced from religious beliefs; the secular state from the Church. The change from the feudal and rural to the industrial and urban pattern of life was more profound and more rapid than anything mankind had previously experienced, its 'side-effects' — the misery of farmers and the creation of the urban proletariat — bore witness to the severe social lags and stresses that accompany rapid and profound transformation.

The social and political systems created in the process of the first industrial revolution are those in which we still live today. They are those that spread to the four corners of the earth, to peoples and civilizations that did not experience the intervening phases but which were conquered first by industrial civilization's military might, and later remained captive of its economic power.

## OUR AGE OF MALADAPTATION AND CHALLENGE

Today a new, and even more profound and rapid 'revolution' is upon us. It is a revolution of globe-encircling trade, resource extraction and flow, of food production, and of material and energy consumption. It is fed by the myriad new technologies, and by the quasi-unsatiable appetites of modern technological-industrial societies. It weaves all people and societies into an ever-tightening web of interdependence. It exploits, and theatens to deplete and despoil, our life-supporting ecosystems and their mineral resources. And its economy is still dominated by those nation states that were the most adept at using science and technology for their own benefit, reinforcing patterns of economic, if no longer political, colonization.

This is where we stand today. We are in a world we no longer master. We made ourselves globally, although asymmetrically, interdependent. We still trust nothing and no one but our own nations and our own organizations. We still operate with the frontiersman mentality that makes might — whether economic or military — equal to right. We still hold that only the sky is the limit to our growth and to our demands. Thus we drive ourselves towards greater and greater economic inequities, social disparities, and political abuses of power. We defend our technology-given advantages by force of arms if necessary, and do not hesitate to use military power as a threat. In fact, we have saddled ourselves with a malfunctioning international economic system, and a precariously balanced and totally unaffordable arms race. We possess neither justice nor security, only fears and wants.

## OUR BEST HOPE — THE CHILDREN

Can humanity achieve a sustainable social, economic, and political order? Can we learn to master the technological genie that leaped from science's lamp of Aladdin? Can we evolve the values, the relations, and the institutions of a globally interdependent yet just and productive society? Can we learn to live together — all four and soon six billion of us — without destroying each other?

Serious doubts persist if we look only to the present adult generation for an answer. The roots of nationalism, competitiveness, material possessiveness, and of the cults of power and privilege, are strong. Our people are thrown upon each other in a complex world system, yet they act with the mentality of warring tribes. Truly, we may not be able to change in time.

But the answer could be very different if we look to the children of this world. They could, if given a chance, cope with the problems of the present great transition, and steer humanity toward the peace and safety of a sustainable and equitable world order.

But how can we be sure that we are not pinning false hopes on the capability of our children? Very simply: because the modern age of materialism, nationalism, and egoism is not part of the genetic programme of our species. These values and behaviors are only part of our 'cultural programme', in other words, of our nurture, not of our nature.

We must remember that:
— no healthy, normal child is born with a built-in loyalty and identification for only one nation and one flag, and a built-in suspicion and animosity toward the rest;
— no child is born with a need for fast cars and the diverse consumer goods and luxuries produced by our Western technological civilization;
— no child is born with a higher regard for a thing than for a person, or with an inexorable desire to own and possess material goods;
— no healthy child is born with a disregard for nature and for things living; and
— no child is born with a prejudice against his fellows on the basis of color, race, or sex.

On the contrary, all normal children are endowed with capacities for all kinds of loyalties and group identifications, for an appreciation of all living things, for sharing and for fellowship, and for empathy with nature.

Man is not evil by nature; he merely appears to become so when his nurture lags behind the requirements of his times. All human beings have the potential for thinking, feeling, and acting justly as well as unjustly, for loving as well as for hating, for sharing as well as for exploiting. The children of this world could become the architects of a new and equitable society as readily as they could become the embittered and frustrated defenders of the old order. If we refrain from purposively and stubbornly enculturing them into our own shortsighted materialistic civilization, we could help them to develop the sensitivity and openness needed to perceive and to adapt to the many clues of the coming age — clues to which we ourselves have already become blind and deaf.

Culture is continuous, however, even if it is capable of change. There can be no radical break between one generation and the next; we can no more present our children with a *tabula rasa* than with the values and behaviors of an age yet to come. But we can see to it that our children preserve and evolve their natural egalitarianism, their sense of fellowship and solidarity, their empathy with nature, and their sense of justice. We can take care not to program them for hate, for unbridled competition, for the love of material possessions, and for the social structure that associates status with wealth and power. We can give our children the chance to be partners in the building of a society that knows how to harmonize the local and the global, the immediate and the long term, and the material and the spiritual.

We can and must take care that the children of this world grow up strong, healthy, and in possession of all their faculties. We can and must exercise restraint in presenting them our own views, values, and convictions as though they were the gospel truth and the paradigms of rationality. We can and must enable them to experience all aspects of life, and to share their experience with children of other cultures and societies.

The self-transcendence of human civilization, previously the labor of centuries, must now be accomplished within the span of a generation. It is our duty as well as our privilege to ensure that this miracle of our species can occur yet once again. accomplished within the span of a generation. Let this year of celebration of the child remind us that it is our duty as well as our privilege to ensure that this miracle of our species can occur yet once again.

# 15

## NEW CONDITIONS AND OBSOLETE PERCEPTIONS*

It is a remarkable fact that there is hardly a government today that would not profess to favor disarmament, and yet the world keeps arming itself at a madly accelerating rate. There is hardly any expert who would contest that we already have more weapons than are needed for any conceivable peacekeeping function, and that a strategic balance at lower levels of armament is possible and desirable, yet spending on arms and the military continues to increase. It appears that we all want one thing but do something else. Yet this is not Alice in Wonderland but presumably the real world. Perhaps we failed to pay attention to the underlying reasons for the arms race. The vital but neglected aspects of disarmament include the whole issue of values and perceptions.

Is it possible that contemporary humanity at large, and especially the majority of national governments, suffer from what anthropologists call a 'culture lag'? This is a lag in values, beliefs, perceptions and conceptions compared with the evolution of objective societal conditions. It occurs whenever the tempo of change is faster in the economic, social or political domain than in the culture, or when lack of information and education, or strong vested interests prevent some classes or groups of people from perceiving changed conditions. This was the case in every major societal transformation in history, from the neolithic to the industrial revolution. And it is occurring today, in the process of industrialization of developing countries, and in the process of 'post-industrialization' of some developed ones. The masses of the people, who have too little information on the new conditions, and the dominant elites, whose interests are vested in the previous order, fail to grasp the new context and fight the tides of change with increasingly obsolete values and behaviors. Such a culture-lag affects all aspects of contemporary society, on both national and international levels. It affects especially the

---

*Reprinted from *Disarmament: The Human Factor*, ed. E. Laszlo and D. F. Keys, Pergamon Press, Oxford, 1981.

process of disarmament, by preserving outmoded conceptions and policies of national and world security.

The culture-lag always involves two poles: an objective pole constituted by economic and social conditions which exist regardless of whether or not they are perceived, and a subjective pole, represented by the values and perceptions of people. Today, the objective conditions of society include these factors:

- the systemic interdependence of states, economies, social processes and cultures;
- overdevelopment of military establishments compared with other sectors of society, and overspending on arms and military R and D compared with spending on humanly beneficial sectors such as health, social services, infrastructure, etc.;
- overexploitation of some non-renewable natural resources, such as fossil fuels and industrially important metals and minerals;
- progressive impoverishment and despoilation of the environment, including loss of productive top soils, reduction of rain forests, desertification, and the various forms of urban and industrial pollution;
- overpopulation in certain rural regions compared with the availability of local food potentials, and overpopulation of certain urban regions with respect to the availability of housing, employment and the basic social services;
- major and still growing income and production gaps between as well as within countries, making for the emergence of 'dual economies' both inter- and intra-nationally;
- the progressive disappearance of established cultures and means of self-identification of peoples in the face of the 'coca-colonization' of the world by high-powered advertising and profit-motivated private interests;
- instabilities in the international economic and financial system, leading to the progressive loss of foreign exchange of the poorer countries, to world-wide inflation and unemployment, and to unused industrial capacities in some developed countries;
- major disparities in the scientific-technical potential of countries, and its further aggravation through the phenomenon of the brain-drain.

If we went into further detail, the list could be extended almost *ad infinitum*. But these key concepts suffice to highlight the new but poorly structured global systems conditions of humanity. They were not a major factor in world affairs two decades ago, and some emerged into prominence only in the last few years.

Contrasting with these new conditions, there are a number of still influential perceptions which have become obsolete. These include the following:

- the 'survival of the fittest' theory: each man is for himself, and the strongest and most resourceful prosper while the weak go down;
- the 'self-regulation' concept of the economy: there is an invisible hand that harmonizes individual and public interest so that everyone can look out for

himself in the happy knowledge that this will automatically benefit others in his society;
- the 'trickle-down' theory: wealth inevitably penetrates from the richer to the poorer strata of society so that the best way to help the poor is for the rich to get still richer;
- the 'efficiency cult': maximum productivity for each person, each machine, and each organization is the ultimate goal and achievement;
- the 'technological imperative': if something *can* be produced, it *must* be produced even if demand has to be created for it;
- the 'economic man' image: people are purely economic actors: producers and consumers of goods and services, and their behavior can be computed in terms of these activities;
- 'consumerism': happiness is epitomized by having the greatest variety of consumer goods at the disposal of a mass public with adequate buying power;
- the 'profit motive' concept of human nature: what people want is profit and wealth, everything else is but superficial window-dressing;
- and finally, the 'man, Lord of nature' image: humanity has proved itself smarter than all the rest of nature and has an indisputable right to bend nature to his own will and benefit.

These perceptions are mostly economic and social in nature. They are closely allied, however, with political perceptions such as these:
- the 'survival of the fittest' theory of the state (Social Darwinism): each state is for itself, and the strongest state triumphs by conquering and annexing the territories, peoples and resources it needs for its survival;
- the 'self-regulation' concept of international relations: there is a balance of power toward which international power configurations tend; this means that each state must attempt to maximize its own power since its opponents will do the same, thus keeping the balance;
- the 'trickle-down' theory of international wealth and development: the best chances of emerging from poverty for the less developed countries lie in a strong and wealthy group of developed countries, who will spread wealth and the benefits of development to the rest;
- 'Westernism': all people, inasmuch as they managed to overcome their spiritual backwardness, want the things that modern Westerners want regardless what customs their forefathers observed and where they go to pray on their holy days;
- 'chauvinism': 'my country, right or wrong' — people are not to reason and question the actions of their country but give it their undivided loyalty, even to the extent of dying for it if necessary;
- the 'sovereign state' concept: all countries are sovereign and independent

nation-states, accountable only to their own people and no one else;

— and finally, the 'life-boat ethic': *we*, at least, have the duty to survive no matter who else may perish, for we must hand down the great accomplishments of humanity to future generations.

The thrust of the above perceptions is this: all people and societies want wealth and power, all are out for themselves, and those that manage to get a good piece of the pie are the winners. Ergo: our primary duty is to ourselves. On the happy assumption of an invisible hand, of the trickle-down effect, of the balance of power doctrine, and of the life-boat ethic, fulfilling our duty to ourselves also benefits others. At least, there is no need to feel very guilty about being selfish.

But the conditions under which perceptions such as these were viable no longer exist. Local confrontations can flare into regional conflagrations and eventually into a global cataclysm. Measures that ensure short-term economic benefits — such as protectionism, price-maximizing cartels, competitiveness on all fronts, tied aid measures, political power-backed deals, etc. — aggravate existing disparities and feed tensions, threatening a breakdown of the existing system of economic relationships. Mindless exploitation of nature and natural resources leads to unviable environments and premature shortages. Concentrations of wealth and power trigger countervailing movements to which even the wealthiest and most powerful are not immune.

In the expanding and relatively pristine world environment of the recent past, high degrees of independence and much abuse of natural resources could be tolerated. Each could act to maximize its own interest; the negative consequences were relatively well absorbed while the positive spin-offs produced a self-righteous glow of being a benefactor of the weak, the poor, and the backward. Conflicts arising from perceived or real injustices could be contained, and usually even the loser could recover, or move on. These times are now definitely over. But have beliefs to the contrary lost their hold?

As long as the kind of perceptions enumerated here remain influential, nations will not disarm. The arms race will not slacken. Military R and D will continue. Funds will not be released from armaments toward development. Protectionism, price-wars, and all forms of economic pressures and unfair practices will persist. The poor will get poorer although the rich will not get richer for long. Injustice and inequity will dominate. And it will be only a matter of time before the arsenals of mass destruction are put to their awful use.

Disarmament cannot occur in an insecure world; it is hopeless to pursue serious efforts toward it as long as the perceptions which lead to world insecurity are neglected. Disarmament is not purely or even primarily a military matter. First and foremost it is a matter of perceptions and goals. It is as useless to ask a contemporary government to disarm itself as it was to ask a frontiersman in the California goldrush to do so. Governments perceive themselves as acting in a highly predatory international environment, only marginally if at all regulated by law and justice. And, as long as they thus perceive themselves, their perceptions will be justified.

How to break the vicious cycle of self-fulfilling prophecies? It is very likely that a major breakthrough would require the more or less simultaneous emergence of new perceptions in the majority of the world's governments. At the present time their culture-lag is due partly to the disproportionate influence of the military-technical establishment compared with independent scientists and intellectuals, and partly to the still low level of education and information of the general public. The powerful military and business elites reinforce obsolete perceptions, and the general population fails to counteract their influence. It is not surprising that the majority of governments operate on obsolete assumptions in their assessment of the basic issues of national and world security.

Perhaps governments would do well to listen to those groups in their societies which are both well informed, and have no vested interest in the status quo. If they did so, they could soon come to see what independent scientists and other intellectuals the world over are seeing with frightening force and clarity: that to maintain arms and delivery systems that can wipe the adversary off the face of the earth, and to spend over 600 billion dollars a year in further adding to and perfecting these capabilities is not only totally unnecessary, but sheer madness.

If the culture-lag could be eliminated, or just reduced in a significant way, the problems of disarmament, which now appear so formidable, would become tractable. Expert studies show that almost all aspects of disarmament have politically, economically and socially sound solutions, and the host of studies currently under way will no doubt add further to this storehouse of relevant information. The intractability of the problems lies not in their intrinsic nature, but in the perceptions of the decision-makers. What is lacking is the political will. And it is precisely this element that could be added to negotiations on disarmament if the obsolete perceptions still dominating national thinking on the issues would give way to a more objective and informed assessment of the contemporary world situation. At least the following basic perceptions would need to gain influence:

— the 'symbiosis' theory of human relationships: humanity is not exempt from nature's rule that he who survives is not the most aggressive, but the most symbiotic and adaptive with respect to others and the environment;

— the 'altruism is pragmatic' insight: in an interdependent situation all long-term destinies coincide. One humanity, one destiny; we either hang together or we hang separately;

— the 'unity in diversity' thesis: people and societies are and can be different, culturally, economically and politically, yet can respect one another and strive to maintain harmonious and mutually beneficial relations among themselves;

— and finally, the 'multi-level loyalty' concept: it is not any less moral and possible for individuals and groups to profess loyalty to the world community as a whole than it is to profess loyalty to their family, business, institution, community, culture or religion. National and supranational loyalties do not conflict, but reinforce one another.

Insights such as these derive directly from a systems approach to contemporary human, national and world order issues. If they would become more widespread, real progress could be achieved in the efforts to create a new international economic system, to meet basic human needs, and to eliminate economic and political injustices. And, at the same time, disarmament would become a real possibility. The updating of the international community's software is a necessary condition of reducing its military hardware. We should no longer neglect this unsuspected pay-off of modern systems science and philosophy.

# 16

## GLOBAL GOALS AND THE CRISIS OF POLITICAL WILL*

Everybody talks about the weather, said Mark Twain, but nobody does anything about it. Something similar could be said about the problems facing mankind. Many, though by no means all, people talk about the major world problems, and merely a handful attempt to do anything about them. But unlike the weather, global problems would yield to human intervention. They are not the work of fate but of men, and they need not await disposition by Providence but can respond to human agency. But for the time being at least, the will to cope with them is lacking. This is not merely an accidental manifestation of some temporary quirk of sociopolitical reality. It goes deeper: it may be the defining, and indeed the determining, characteristic of our age.

The world has changed; this much we know, and to assert it is a platitude. But it is seldom realized that the change is fundamental and in all likelihood not reversible. We live in a qualitatively different world from that of our grandfathers or even fathers. Our numbers have doubled; our energy consumption gobbles up the known nonrenewable reserves; practically all readily habitable lands are settled and all cheaply cultivable lands worked; our technologies can build on all parts of the globe and destroy any part of it; flows of communication and trade connect all settlements; the natural environment is exposed to severe stress and is being selectively despoiled; and tens of millions are crowding into dehumanized urban jungles. Mankind is beginning to feel the limits of the planet but is as yet unprepared to face them. As material-technological growth encounters limits and slackens, expansive processes are bound to turn inward, and not overall progress but relative distribution will be the key issue. Mankind is beginning to feel the ills of unjust distribution in a finite world but is unprepared to cope with this challenge, too.

The present age is qualitatively new in being, perhaps for the first time in history, global in reach. The human factor has become planetized; hardly anything or process on the surface of the globe can any longer escape it. Human beings can

---

*Reprinted from *Journal of International Affairs*, Vol. 31, No. 2, 1977.

escape least the effects of their collective activities. Garrett Hardin said that we can no longer do just one thing; we must now add that we can no longer do just one thing *locally*. All we do has multiple effects and consequences, and these radiate with greater or smaller magnitude across the network of human activities. They ultimately feed back to us, the doers. In this increasingly globalized, increasingly self-enclosed and interdependent world, altriusm has become pragmatic. For we can not harm others without harming ourselves as well.

These are new realities, but reality is not the determining factor of human response: *perceived* reality is. Eventually, reality will be perceived as constraint, and possibly as catastrophe. But as long as man persists in the acrobacy of reading the handwriting on the wall only when his back is up against it, a new reality can pass for the old: business is as usual. This, of course, is not quite the case, but even if concern is mounting, positive behavioral change is scarce: changes tend to be confined to *verbal* behavior.

But the trends and processes continue, and it is only a matter of time before the new reality intrudes into perception in some unpleasant form. As many as 2.2 billion people will be added to the human population by the end of the century; the known reserves of fossil fuels other than coal will be all but depleted; dozens of nations will be armed with nuclear weapons; stagflation in the industrialized world and deprivation in the developing will produce unprecedented alienation and misery; and the environment may become locally unviable and generally more severe. By the year 2000 the new reality will be hammered home: mankind will find itself on a plundered and overcrowded planet. The reactions will not be difficult to predict. The relatively well-off will create enclaves to protect their remaining privileges, and the less privileged will fight for a greater share of the diminishing pie of benefits. The rich-poor confrontation will be played out nationally and internationally. In the former it will constitute a class struggle of unprecedented scope and possibly of violence. In the latter it will bring to its logical conclusion what is already known as the North-South confrontation. Since potent and portable arms are being constantly perfected, no enclave of privilege will be impenetrable — but none will be without powerful defenses. The new reality will have arrived in the eyes of the least perceptive. It will not be a welcome reality.

Trend is not destiny, however, and a process underlying a trend may have more than one continuation. The new age is not likely to be reversible to the old, but its unfolding can be open to multiple possibilities. The range is wide, for it parallels human social and technological potency. The eventual outcome will be situated somewhere within this range, determined by human foresight and wisdom — or the lack of them. *The issue deciding the fate of our species is not the finitude of the planet, and not even the number of humans inhabiting it. It is the will of the present and the next generation; and the wisdom from which it springs.*

There are no 'problems' in nature, only in and for human conscious activity. And there are no problems for humans unless there are also solutions. The expansion of the universe, or the speed of light in vacuo are not problems: they are facts, to the best of our knowledge. But hunger, illiteracy, overcrowding, alienation, injustice, and despoilation are problems: they are related to human activity — and they have solutions. The solutions are necessarily commensurate with the problems. One cannot solve a global problem by local action any more than one can create a system of social justice by punishing one man or rewarding another. Global problems have global solutions, although global solutions have widely distributed local effects. To redress local imbalances through isolated local action when they are outcomes of global processes is like treating the local symptom of an illness instead of the organic cause. The relief will be temporary, and it may worsen the condition of the patient. But mankind is not accustomed to dealing with global problems and hence it deals with them as the man who searches for his key not where he lost it but where the light is. People look for local solutions not because the problems are local, but because that is what they are accustomed to do. The results are surprising only to those who have selectively blocked out the globality of human affairs from their vision, that is, to the vast majority of mankind. It is not without reason that our age is said to be the age of surprises.

But what is a global solution? Nobody can 'act globally', and few can act regionally or even nationally. Fortunately, global action does not hinge on the power of some selected individuals. If it is true that we cannot do just one thing locally, then it is true that human actions interpenetrate whatever they are and wherever they are performed. A global action is therefore a conscious coordination of local actions for their global (and hence distributed local) outcomes. Coordinated actions could turn the course of present and future history: they could cope with the global problems of our globally extended and interdependent age. Coordination, harmonization, mutual adaptation: these are basic imperatives of the biological and social worlds. They have become imperative for mankind as a whole, and not only its nation-states, sub-national, multinational, and transnational communities and organizations ... for global problems are problems *for* nation-states, communities, provinces, transnational enterprises, and multinational regions, although they are not national, community, corporate, and organizational problems. The distinction is not trivial, for it defines the reason why national, community, corporate, and organizational solutions will not work. But this insight has not yet dawned on the majority of the decision-makers. Contemporary decision-making occurs under the assumption of a zero-sum multi-player game theory. Each plays for his own advantage, and the gain of one is the loss of some of the others. The number and multiplicity of players — economic, political, social — creates fantastic degrees of uncertainty. Our age is properly called the age of uncertainty as well.

But our age need not be one of surprises and uncertainty. Mankind could achieve reasonable control over its own destiny if it recognized the reality which it unwittingly created, identified its problems, and mounted a concerted effort to solve them. Although mankind could well do so, it is not likely that it will. The reason for this pessimistic outlook is the gap between the policy requirements of the new age — the goals and objectives of coping with global problems — and the level of political will and motivation in human societies.

## GLOBAL PROBLEMS AND GOALS

Global goals and objectives must be defined in relation to global problems and their possible solutions. A global problem is a problem precisely because it disappoints, depresses, or kills human beings, doing so globally, not by necessity but through mismanagement or lack of attention to the pertinent factors. Better management and more attention to pertinent factors could alleviate, and eventually remove such problems. This would not transform earthly society into paradise, for other problems would remain, and not all global problems would be fully solved at any one time. But the sword of Damocles would be removed from over the head of mankind: the human world would become relatively peaceful, adequately nourished, properly supplied with basic energy and material resources, endowed with a viable environment, and not overly imbalanced and unjust. Sources of conflict would remain plentiful, there would be room for competition and for success as well as failure, and diversity would not be flattened. The basis for a viable society would, however, be achieved. Since society is rapidly becoming globalized, the achievement in question must be correspondingly global. It is a fresh challenge awaiting the members of our society. They will not be likely to respond to it, however, unless they perceive that they are members of a *global* society, confronting global problems.

The list of global problems ranges from one to infinity. It can always be said that every problematic event or outcome is part of a complex macroproblem or *problematique*, and that the number of mankind's problems reduces to unity. And every problematic event or outcome can also be analyzed to subsidiary aspects practically *ad infinitum*, with each new analysis yielding another 'global problem'. But such sophistries aside, a reasonable and finite list of problems can be identified as global. These have as defining characteristic global scope, and unresponsiveness to anything but globally coordinated action. They occur in the areas of *security, food, energy* and *resources*, and balanced *socio-economic development*.

Insecurity is an entirely man-made problem.[1] On the surface it is a problem of armaments, but on second look it becomes one of distrust: the generating source of arms. The governments of nation-states function in this age of globality as pseudo-autonomous actors. They consider the entities they govern as sovereign. Such sovereign entities have eternal interests but not eternal friends. Alliances are to serve national interests; all moves are to render the nation more secure, powerful, and prosperous. Noble aims, but sadly behind the times. For today, no individual nation can be secure, powerful, and prosperous if others are insecure, powerless, and poor. The politics of the rich nation-states are the precursors of the defensive power-politics of the future's enclaves of privilege, and the politics of the poor nation-states are the precursors of the future's underprivileged desperados. Both operate with the logic of inter-national and inter-regional zero-sum games. Both bolster their immediate national security at the cost of deteriorating their common world security. Whether to protect privilege, or to assure access to it, capital and manpower are poured into arms of aggression and destruction. It is naive to ask that unequal partners who consider themselves sovereign should renounce, or even limit, their arms. They need their arms, in the light of their own perceptions.

Insecurity is a global problem: it is created by the behavior of all peoples, and it can only be resolved by the coordinated change of all national behaviors. A rich nation would risk the loss of its wealth and possibly even its territory, were it to surrender its arms unilaterally (*vide* Japan which first thought to rely on U.N. collective peacekeeping following its World War II defeat, then effectively relied on the U.S. Pacific military presence, and is now contemplating a rapid build-up of national arms to assure its defenses); and poor nations would individually expose themselves to their predatory neighbors and collectively give up one of the means of pressuring the rich world to yield up some of its privileges. Neither rich nor poor nations will beat their swords into ploughshares alone; they may as well beat them into shovels to dig their own grave.

Insecurity proves to be an intractable problem when approached with the logic of the 'modern' (i.e., the mid-twentieth century) epoch. In the post-modern age there is no real security in the absence of world security, and there can be no world security unless and until nation-states cease treating themselves and each other as independent and sovereign. If and when the logic changes, the outlines of the new age are perceived and the commonality of interests is recognized, the goals and objectives of world security can be realized: scrapping of all nuclear weapons, halting of plutonium production and export, limitation of conventional arms manufacture and trade to levels needed to cope with local disputes, and institution of a collective peacekeeping machinery with adequate capabilities of arbitration and enforcement.

Hunger is another global problem.[2] About one billion people are permanently hungry today, and their numbers will grow with the increase of population among the world's poor. But this problem, too, is man-made, not only in the sense that it is human beings who produce human beings but inasmuch as adequate food could be made available even to a growing population. World food production has outstripped population growth since the end of World War II, and could continue to keep pace with it well into the 21st century — at which time population size may stabilize. But the yield of world food production does not reach all of the world's peoples. Its distribution is skewed in favor of the rich. Grain is fed to cattle to produce expensive beef; it is fed to pets; and it is wasted. The U.S. is actually consuming more grain than India even if Americans eat but one-tenth of the grain eaten by Indians. In India, however, as in many other poor countries, inefficient storage and distribution leads to the waste of almost forty percent of the stocks. World poverty combines with high fertility among the poor to further widen the gap between the overfed citizens of the industrial economies and the starving denizens of Third World hamlets and urban slums. Current grain production, if evenly distributed, would be enough to feed the entire world population (the world produce of 1,400 million tons could provide 300 kilo per person the world over, well over the 200 kilo minimum), but it is wasted through indulgence by the rich and inefficiency by the poor. Even the growth of world food production over coming decades would be sufficient if its benefits were equitably distributed: world population grows at a rate of about

1.8 percent while food production is still growing by about three percent. Such global figures ignore the fact, however, that the areas of the world which grow the fastest in population are also the most undernourished, hence grow fastest in demand. When these regional disparities are taken into account, the inadequacy of the world food distribution system is underscored. For demand in the developing world as a whole grows by 3.6 percent, while indigenous food production grows by only 2.6 percent. Since it is unreasonable to expect that indigenous production can catch up with demand, the solution must lie in better world distribution.

Coping with the world food problem likewise calls for the global coordination of behaviors and policies. It is not enough that the rich should evolve an altruistic restraint in food consumption and transform their dietary habits: if the international economic system is not restructured, production would soon drop to meet lowered demand. It is also not enough to revamp the international market system for food: if the rich keep abusing the production patterns and the poor keep wasting their meagre share through inefficiency and underdevelopment, hunger will persist. And it is not enough that poor nations become more efficient in distributing and storing foodstuffs, they also need access to the most appropriate of the new food technologies, they need a better system of land ownership, they need more and cheaper energies and fertilizer, and they need a world food bank for emergency supplies. But all these things together, in a globally coordinated attack on hunger and undernourishment, would suffice. Coordinated action does not mean that all do the same thing — each must do his own, but within the syndrome of the required tasks. If we would create a genuine food *system*, the world hunger problem could be licked, and mankind could confront the other challenges awaiting it without the debilitating effects of under-nourishment and starvation.

That energy is a global problem needs no special emphasis. Since the 1972/3 oil crisis, which hit all nations rich and poor alike, the fact that the world energy system is truly a world system has become apparent. But the oil-crises of the past were but polite dress rehearsals compared with the crisis that would come if supplies are cut due to the depletion of the known reserves and the world's economies have no alternative energy source at hand. At current increases in the rate of consumption, known oil and natural gas reserves would be seriously depleted within the next thirty years. (This period could be somewhat stretched by the development of secondary extraction technologies and the discovery of further large oil and gas deposits.) Coal would last for a few hundred years, but its extraction on the required large scale would pose serious health and environmental problems — and its use would call for more water than is likely to be available. Even by the more optimistic estimates, mankind will need a renewable energy source, or one that is in large supply, by the beginning of the next century. The lead times between research and development, and development and national and international application, are long. Light water nuclear technology is developed but it uses scarce and expensive uranium ($U^{235}$) and it involves the highly toxic and explosive plutonium ($P^{239}$) as byproduct. Heavy-water reactors could stretch the uranium supply by using the more abundant $U^{238}$ and breeders could produce fissionable material on a practically infinite basis. But if the somewhat safer fusion technology does not pan out in time and the world is forced into the nuclear fission option, it will have to be prepared to face the possibility of a widespread misuse of the technologies. Such misuse includes thermonuclear warfare spreading to, or being triggered by, any of dozens of nuclear nations, and generalized nuclear terrorism. It is questionable whether mankind is mature enough to handle thousands of tons of plutonium (of which ten pounds suffice to create a device that can destroy most of Manhattan) without mishaps, organized aggression, and maverick terrorism.

There are, however, energy sources that are abundant, almost universally accessible, and that could become economic as well.[3] These are all based on the constant flow of energy from the sun. Some technologies convert sunlight directly into electric power, others use it to heat water or another working fluid and use that for heating, cooling, or to drive turbines. Still others exploit the temperature differential between the warm surface layers of tropical seas and the cooler deep layers, while ingenious devices make use of sunlight to pump water into irrigation ditches, and cook meals on methane generated by human and animal wastes. Even the force of the tides can be harnessed in certain coastal regions, exploiting the energy of lunar gravitation. The technological know-how required to make use of renewable energy sources already exists; it is economic cost, coupled with the power of vested interests in fossil and fission technologies, that obstructs application. Economic cost in itself is not a permanent obstacle. The cost of solar power could be dropped to levels below the cost of nuclear fission power by the late 1980s — provided mass production can begin (this is especially crucial for solar cells and concentrators, which are currently still hand-fashioned in response to a miniscule and unreliable market). Mass production of the new energy devices will not start, however, unless the market grows or their production is subsidized. Based on the free market forces a vicious circle locks renewable energy technologies out of the world energy system. If the energy future of mankind is entrusted to the operation of free market forces, economic rationality will dictate using fission reactors to substitute for depleting oil and gas sources well before fusion technologies and renewable energy sources become economically competitive. And the world will then be almost irreversibly committed to enter the nuclear age — the dream of science fiction writers of the sixties, and possibly the nightmare of energy producers and consumers alike in the eighties and nineties.

To bring to all people and societies energies that are safe, abundant, environmentally clean, and economical, globally coordinated action would be required. The rich nations, with highly evolved research and development facilities, would need to devote the lion's share of their energy development budgets to the most promising of the solar and nuclear fusion technologies; international investment and financial institutions, such as the World Bank and the International Monetary Fund, as well as their regional counterparts (especially in the well-endowed banks and Funds of the Arab world) would need to catalyze mass markets in the developing countries where more energy is desperately needed; countries with large, highly insolated and otherwise unused surfaces, i.e. those with deserts, would need to invest in large-scale solar farms and hydrogen conversion facilities for exporting the converted energies; and multinationals in the energy technology field would have to concentrate their best engineers and planners on the task of mass producing safe, simple and low-cost devices suitable for use in capital-poor and labor-intensive markets. A global systems approach could evolve the technologies to suit the exigencies of the users with respect to investment, operating and maintenance costs, skill levels, and end-use needs.

An effort of this kind would start producing tangible benefits in the developing world first, where intermediate technology solutions are the most needed. Its real pay-off would come later, however, in by-passing the nuclear fission alternative before private investors and national governments make an irreversible commitment to it. The pay-off would consist in the creation of a world energy system that is safe, adequate to meet demand, environmentally clean, and affordable by poor nations as well. This would lead to a broad geographic distribution of the bases of the industrial system and would contribute to the reduction of the development and income gap. It would thus make for a more equitable and less violence-prone world — evidently in the interest of all people. But while these benefits would come after a few decades, they already demand certain economic sacrifices. As long as the logic of national prosperity in the short-term prevails, energy goals such as these will be dismissed as idealist or utopian.

The availability of safe and abundant energy would go a long way toward solving the resource problem as well. Many resources can be recycled and many more can be extracted from secondary sources — if enough energy is available. A decentralized world industrial system, coupled with a more equitable (and hence radically new) international economic order could place sufficient material resources — metals as well as minerals — at the command of mankind to last for centuries of intense industrial production.

The current international economic system presents another global problem. To build a more equitable world with a fairer distribution of basic resources, technologies and material benefits, the asymmetrical relationship between the industrialized and the developing countries must be rectified. The major goals elaborated in the United Nations, in the historic Sixth and Seventh Special Sessions devoted to the New International Economic Order, and to Development and International Economic Co-operation respectively, must find appropriate forms of implementation. The economic and technical infrastructure of developing countries must be built up to enable them to become progressively self-reliant, and this calls for far-sighted collaborative policies both among the developing countries themselves, and between the developed and the developing nations. The problems must be tackled not only on the international, but also on the regional level. Waste, generated by over-consumption and artificial obsolescence in the rich nations and by inefficiency and under-development in the poor, must be cut.[4] For example, it is estimated that North America now uses five times as much energy as all of Asia — and per capita energy consumption is about twenty-four times higher. Indeed, the U.S. alone wastes about as much fossil fuel as is *used* by the poorer two-thirds of the world population. Economic systems are geared to maximize turnover, with the result that high-grade materials are rapidly converted into low-grade junk, depleting reserves and despoiling the environment. A new mode of economic accounting is needed, one which associated benefits with the actual use of energies and materials, rather than with their turnover. This means a social and environmental accounting, rather than a short-term economic one. Short-term economic rationality on a finite and crowded planet is a sure recipe for long-term social (and eventually also economic) disaster.

Again, we must note that these global problems call for global solutions through coordinate action in view of the attainment of long-term benefits. And again, we must question whether the will exists in today's world to implement such solutions.

## THE GOALS AND PREOCCUPATIONS OF TODAY'S PEOPLES

Let us assess, then, the dominant goals and objectives of the world's nations and organizations, in view of the objective requirements of a viable global society.

The people of the United States are not accustomed to formulating explicit and long-term goals for themselves and their nation.[5] They tend to believe that the least planning produces the best results, as free competition regulated by the mechanisms of the existing market forces spreads benefits to all. This was indeed the case in a period of rapid growth spurred by the availability of large quantities of cheap energies and resources and vast new markets. But the logic of an interdependent world with grave inequalities and increasingly scarce and expensive resources demands a different set of mechanisms, a global vision and long time horizons. The need for these is recognized by a few scientists, planners and administrators but their implementation is constrained by the established ethos and the established institutions. While opinion polls indicate that the people themselves are increasingly aware of the problems and would go some way toward supporting the required policies, even the White House's efforts are frustrated by a lack of organized public support. President Carter's summons to an age of sacrifice in energy conservation was toned down only a month after it was pronounced, and efforts to stop the breeder reactor are now abandoned. Well-endowed and powerful industrial-military lobbies dominate the nascent strands of awareness and concern. Rather than debating and setting goals of long-term international benefit, the nation as a whole is in the grip of fear lest sacrifices are attendant upon reforms.

Canada, with its smaller population and medium-power status, could shift its sights more rapidly and efficiently. It is led by a government well aware of the global situation and bent on making it known to the people. But notwithstanding Premier Trudeau's persistent and sometimes heroic efforts (which earned him little more than criticism and a weakened political base), the traditional growth-orientation still prevails. Radical intellectual currents are afoot, however, and the last word in the debate has not been spoken.

The countries of Western Europe have a relatively prolonged history of attempted cooperation, individually with each other and jointly with the developing world, through the institutions of the European Community.[6] They are faced with major inequalities in levels of economic development among themselves, and varying degrees of dependence on world markets. In the throes of crises — such as the oil crisis of 1972—73 — they tend to turn to the 'tested methods' of promoting their own national advantages. At the same time the majority of the European people are becoming slowly convinced that certain policy objectives (among them the protection of the environment, applications of science and technology, political balance, and security) are better handled jointly on the Community level than individually by national governments. The governments of the European nation-states nevertheless conserve the power of final decision on all issues; the direct election of a European Parliament in the beginning of the eighties was the first significant move toward European supra-nationalism. The business and financial interests of the wealthier nations are worried about too much integration, while the leaders of the poorer states are pressing for it, expecting economic benefits. On the domestic front a wide array of political ideologies is in evidence, ranging from conservative Christian parties to social democrats and Euro-Communists. The Scandinavian experiment with socialism is noteworthy for its attempt to place the management of the economy on a collective basis, institute high level of services, and the world's highest personal income taxes. Euro-Communists in Italy, France, and Spain profess advanced views on running the economy for collective benefit and engaging in broadscale projects of international cooperation, but their mettle is yet to be tested in positions of national governance. Despite the new currents of thinking and the occasional experiments with innovative policies, the vast majority of Europeans is more preoccupied with debating politics and ideology than occupied in translating them into practice. As debates rage, and public security erodes in many lands together with the prospects of prosperity, individuals continue to produce and consume in the time-honored Western manner.

Australia, a geographically distant part of the developed world, is likewise oriented toward economic growth.[7] Its people are becoming more conscious of their interdependence with other peoples, not only with the Organization of Economic Cooperation and Development and the Commonwealth countries, but also the masses of nearby Asia. But a mounting sense of malaise is yet to spark decisive behavioral change. The more open search of the Labor government for goals of an egalitarian and internationally aware society soon led to a reversal of its electoral support when economic recession threatened.

Japan is at a cross-roads: the economic miracle has petered out, but the domination of Japanese technological expertise, wielded by the enormous and paternalistic Japan-based multinationals, is undiminished.[8] Material expectations have been largely fulfilled, and the people are divided on the question of whether it is better to revitalize the economy as a first priority, or to move toward a more egalitarian, more participatory, and more welfare-oriented society, incorporating (to the extent possible) some of the traditional Japanese values.

The Communist world is no less heterogenous than the industrialized free-market countries. Its major division is between the Soviet and Eastern European countries, vis-à-vis China and the smaller Asian Communist states. The Soviets disclaim responsibility for the ills of both over- and under-development. They are intent in catching up and overtaking the free-market countries in economic growth and industrialization, with special attention to some selected fields of high technology such as space and arms. They also desire to gain influence among Third World countries, thus backing international cooperative ventures of a strategic nature. Soviet internationalism is further prompted by the recognition that the key applications of science and technology for industrial development cannot be fully mastered by them without exchanges with the industrialized countries of the free world. Yet these applications are badly needed to contain the rising aspirations of the masses within the proper socialist mold. Thus attention is now selectively turning toward 'cooperation with countries of different social and economic structures', as it is also turning from emphasis on quantitative growth (expressed for example by production quotas) to qualitative factors such as product quality, work ethic, and productivity.[9] The sights of the Soviet and Eastern European masses are firmly set, however, on enlarging their own sphere of material benefits, with more than a shade of consumerism and Western-type self-centeredness.

China, as far as it can be ascertained, is struggling to maintain its emphasis on balanced and self-sufficient development, confronted as it is with new alternatives for Western-style economic growth and the creation of power and wealth elites.[10] The remarkable achievements of the past were predicated on rapid advances relative to colonialism, underdevelopment, and dictatorship, and the charisma of Mao Tse-tung. China is not likely to remain as modest and as self-concerned in the future as it has been after 1948. In the past, aside from its insistence on nuclear arms, it has championed goals and objectives highly appropriate for developing countries in view of global exigencies. But not only is China's own path in question, uncertainty also pervades the exportability of its developmental model. What has been feasible for China, given its austere and disciplined cultural heritage and its independence from the West, may not be possible for the masses of Latin America, Africa, and the rest of Asia.

Latin America had a major love-affair with Western-style industrialization and economic growth, pursuing the elusive vision of duplicating such economic miracles as those of Western Germany and Japan. Economic miracles did not come off, however, except partially in Brazil, and the level of frustration is high.[11] It is expressed in the clashes of extremist groups, and by the authoritarian regimes of generals and military juntas. For the present, the upper one percent of the population controls about thirty percent of the wealth, while some sixty-nine percent of the people control merely about twenty percent. The continent is one of contrasts: those between sprawling urban concatenations and small hamlets, between the superaffluent urban elites and marginal village and slum people, between flashy modernism and unrelieved traditional backwardness, between skyscrapers and favelas, and modern hospitals and magical witch doctoring. Some forty percent of the people are still engaged in relatively primitive forms of agriculture, and for them, and for the shantytowns ringing the big cities, the economic miracle is only a dream. But the dream is clear and persistent, and leaves little room for concern with longer-term and broader issues. World security, the problems of environment, the application of appropriate technologies, and other matters of this kind are raised in the circles of Latin American intellectuals, but few among the people and the governments take them seriously. Industrialization, urbanization, the incorporation of the marginal populations in the economy, and the growth of national wealth and power dominate policy-making. Coping with the more abtruse issues is said to be the responsibility of the superpowers and their developed allies, who have created the problems to begin with.

Africa south of the Sahara is a continent still wrought by ethnic struggles and the fight for freedom from all vestiges of colonialism. The new leaders of the independent African states have concentrated on creating some sense of national unity and integrity in their countries, whose borders were arbitrarily drawn by the colonizing powers. But the methods which proved successful in assuring independence seldom panned out when it came to containing ethnic disunities and creating democratic political structures. Well-meaning attempts have failed for lack of support, and military governments often took their place. It is only now that a few countries, mainly in Western Africa, experiment with the implementation of multi-party democracies.

But the sights of African leaders have shifted again.[12] After independence they moved from goals of national unity to those of economic growth through the diversification of agriculture and the creation of an industrial base. Now they move to embrace, in addition to these, the aims of a better distribution of the (as yet meager) benefits of development, overcoming the urban-rural gap, revitalizing the indigenous cultures, and improving the educational systems (mainly in view of alphabetization and basic skill training). Development is still the key word, but it has come to mean not only economic development in terms of national averages, but also qualitative socio-economic development in reference to gaps and injustices. These shifts have yet to penetrate from rhetoric in the formulation of national development plans to the level of implemented policies. Internecine struggles among ethnic and power groups, between countries opting for different (Western or socialist) modes of organization, and between the elites and the intellectuals confuse the picture and obstruct efficient policy formulation.

The overwhelming majority of Africans themselves — some eighty to ninety percent — live a marginal and largely traditional existence. Their imagination has been captured, however, by the miracles of life in the cities and centers of the rich world, and the revolution of rising expectations shows no signs of slackening. It moves the more adventurous and the more desperate among the rural masses to leave their roots and search for a better life in the cities. For the most part they, as their counterparts in the rest of the developing world, end up on the outskirts of the cities leading a life that is even more miserable, if that is possible, than the one they left behind.

The countries of the Middle East are rocked by the impact of money.[13] A traditionally austere and ascetic people, they found that many of them are sitting on top of undreamt-of wealth: the black gold of oil. The havoc wrought by the sudden introduction of prodigious wealth is new in Middle East history, but the aftermath is still very much a part of its present and is likely to be part of its future as well. A few of the Arab countries, with populations totaling not more than three percent of the region, earn up to fifty percent of the oil revenue. The larger oil-producing states, such as Algeria, Iran and Iraq, have large populations and need immense capital to modernize their infrastructure. The countries less fortunate with respect to oil, such as Egypt and Sudan, struggle on the edge of bankruptcy. Large military expenditures syphon off important sums from development budgets. Balance of payment deficits grow, while basic industries struggle with outmoded equipment and the rural sector continues to practice subsistence farming. The region as a whole is in the grip of a desperate attempt to modernize and become economically competitive with the advanced nations before the oil income runs out. Policies that spur overall economic growth dominate all other objectives, although social welfare, health care, and education have become important concerns in recent years. But they remain a luxury which only a few small and rich countries, such as the Gulf states, can afford to implement.

India is permanently occupied with coping, in a varyingly democratic manner, with the immense problems posed by a population that is already over seven-hundred million and will in all probability grow to one billion by the turn of the century — and one that is, and will probably remain, exceedingly poor. Average per capita income is not much over the equivalent of eighty U.S. dollars, while total unemployment (not even counting hidden unemployment and underemployment) is of the order of ten percent of the total population. Increasing the efficiency and productivity of the agricultural sector, moderating the gap between city and countryside, coping with high fertility and high mortality, dropping the seventy percent rate of illiteracy, and putting to use the relatively evolved scientific-technological expertise of educated Indians — these are the main preoccupations of the leadership.[14] Their efforts range from orientation toward a Nehru-type socialism on the Soviet mold to Ghandian *sarvodaya* nonviolent egalitarianism, with occasional excursions into autocratism on the one hand and utopian idealism on the other (the pendulum is now swinging toward the former). Sincere affirmations of commitment to world solidarity, to the plight of all developing peoples, and to the cause of peace are somewhat marred by the impotence imposed by poverty, and the development — notwithstanding cost — of nuclear capabilities.

The nations of Southeast Asia, except for the few communist states, are unanimous in wishing to spur rapid Western-style economic development. Although the risks connected with imported models of development are recognized — and something of the unique character of each nation does color the actual form of development — most leaders feel that pollution, alienation, urban violence, and the other side-effects of Western-type development are problems that will not become serious until well after the benefits of development have emerged.[15] Economic growth is seen as a way of achieving national, and if necessary regional, self-sufficiency, since the Southeast Asian countries do not have much trust in each other but even less in the developed world. But here too, as almost everywhere in the developing regions, national unity hangs on the thin thread of inherited frontiers, and is eroded by criss-crossing racial and religious traditions. Hence the implementation of unitary national policies is greatly hindered by internal dissention, and it is further aggravated by the Westernization of the urban elites who, in the eyes of the more traditional highland peoples, represent but another form of colonialism. Other than the wish to preserve their ethnic identities, the broad masses of Southeast Asia show little concern with national, regional and world issues beyond the pale of their immediate welfare. The growing urban populations, however, throw themselves with abandon into such widely varied pursuits as the ideals of communism on the one hand, and the accumulation of personal wealth on the other.

Thus the goals and objectives of contemporary peoples are by no means uniform but have nevertheless a singular consistency: they all center either on the preservation, or on the acquisition, of material goods and comforts. While this should be no surprise to connoisseurs of human nature, the spread of the aspirations to almost five billion humans, and the frustrations they occasion in view of inherited and still worsening inequalities, constitute a threat to the future that is not fully recognized. Materialistic aspirations make for short-term and self-centered horizons, which seldom equate the human good with the personally desirable. Paradise lost may inspire nostalgia, but a paradise practically attained and now threatened, and a paradise once almost in reach but always further receding (while shamelessly enjoyed by others) inspire only frustration and breed violence.

National and regional goals are, of course, interfaced with transnational and international objectives and processes. Giant transnational corporations span the globe and bring some indubitable benefits of modern technology — and some doubtful benefits of the technologic-economic rationality — to hitherto undeveloped traditional peoples. In their search for corporate growth and profit, which entails hitting upon the most efficient methods of production and marketing, MNCs seek out the most favorable national business environments, wherever these may be.[16] Sometimes they also seek to make some environment more favorable, and to protect others from social and political threats, and go as far as to bribe officials, purposively condition consumer patterns, and engage in covert activities. But several multinationals also show a rising awareness of the strategic importance of corporate social responsibility and contemplate long-term planning in recognition of national developmental priorities.

International organizations have grown exponentially in number since 1945, but this numerical growth has not been paralleled by the growth of their authority. The United Nations, set up in October 1945, had originally fifty-one members while today its membership is 157, with only a few states (North and South Korea, Taiwan, Namibia, Switzerland, and a few remaining islands and colonies) outside its fold. The International Court of Justice has been revived, and the International Labour Organisation is supplemented by other agencies beginning with the United

Nations Educational, Scientific and Cultural Organizaton and continuing with the creation of further bodies, usually in the wake of the World Conferences (e.g. UNEP after Stockholm, and the World Food Council after Rome). This impressive array of international organizations holds meetings and conferences; names commissions and committees which hold their own meetings; it passes and defeats resolutions; it joins in or abstains from declarations — and it produces a few legally binding and even fewer internationally enforceable covenants and decisions. Its range of goals matches in brilliance the names of its councils, institutes, agencies, commissions, and committees. Security, disarmament and peacekeeping were the U.N.'s original goals, joined in subsequent years by high-priority objectives in the field of refugee care, children, human rights, economic development through international cooperation and assistance, energy development and regulation, food and agricultural productivity, health and education, population, environment, and international law.[17] The U.N.'s attention is presently taken up by the debates on the Global Round of Negotiations, the key project of the bloc of nonaligned nations. Regional security problems produce heated debates, and the occasional interposition of U.N. troops — mainly through the good offices of the Secretary-General — are important interim measures, but they do not add up to lasting and effective peacekeeping. There are Special Sessions devoted to disarmament, periodic debates on economic cooperation, and committees on the uses of outer space, the quality of water, and renewable energies — among many others.

The list of U.N. and U.N.-related accomplishments is long and may be read in full on brochures put out by the Department of Public Information in valiant attempts to bolster sagging public support for the organization. But the list is pale in comparison with the urgency of the global problems confronting the international community. The fault lies mainly with the political will of the member states (even if the organization itself is not free of guilt in engaging in the orchestration of hairsplitting games of committee politicking and giving in to the all-too-human weaknesses of personal and departmental rivalries). The U.N. is both an organization of member-states serving their sovereign national interests (as defined by the national leaders) and an organization dedicated to the welfare and development of all mankind. These mandates coexist but uneasily, and with a great predominance of the former over the latter.

This birds-eye view of the political will of mankind in relation to global problems and their solutions does not present an encouraging picture. People are intent on their immediate material benefits, leaders play games of power and wealth, while the clouds of doom gather overhead. Only a few realize that they can be dispelled, and that the sun may shine behind them more warmly and brilliantly than at any time within human memory. These few are almost powerless, confronted with the massive inertia of traditional institutions and obsolete values. Mankind is in the throes of the greatest and most rapid transformation in species history, but lets it proceed unrecognized and unmanaged. The challenge of our age is that the transformation is as much fraught with grave dangers as it is liberally endowed with positive potentials, and that a positive outcome requires conscious planning and concerted execution: systems thinking not only in theory, but in international practice.

## REFERENCES

All references are to Ervin Laszlo, et al., *Goals for Mankind* (GFM), *A Report to the Club of Rome on the New Horizons of Global Community* (New York: Dutton, 1977); Laszlo and Bierman, eds., *Goals in a Global Community* (GGC I), *Original Background Papers for Goals for Mankind*, Vol. I. Studies on the Conceptual Foundations (New York and Oxford, Pergamon Press, 1977); and *Idem*, Vol. II (GGC II), The International Goals Studies (New York and Oxford, Pergamon Press, 1977).

1. For details see GFM Chapter 12.
2. See GFM Chapter 13.
3. See GFM Chapter 14 and GGC I Chapter 6.
4. See GFM Chapter 15 and GGC I Chapter 3.
5. GFM Chapter 1 and GGC II Chapter 5.
6. GFM Chapter 2 and GGC II Chapter 3.
7. GFM Chapter 8 and GGC II Chapter 1.
8. GFM Chapter 4, GGC II Chapter 4.
9. GFM Chapter 3 and GGC II Chapters 9 through 12.
10. GFM Chapter 4 and GCC II Chapter 8.
11. GFM Chapter 5 and GGC II Chapter 18 through 20.
12. GFM Chapter 6 and GGC II Chapters 13, 15, 16 and 17.
13. GFM Chapter 6 and GGC II Chapter 14.
14. GFM Chapter 7 and GGC II Chapters 21 through 23.
15. GFM Chapter 7 and GGC II Chapter 24.
16. GFM Chapter 10.
17. GFM Chapter 9 and GGC II Chapter 25.

# 17

## EDUCATING WORLD LEADERS FOR THE COMING AGE*

The world today is badly in need of true leadership. It needs people with vision, as well as pragmatism; with broad general purview as well as scrupulous attention to detail. Unless a new generation of people with such caliber emerges within the next ten to twenty years, the world community will not be able to provide constructive responses to the many problems that it confronts.

### THE WAYS OF EDUCATION IN THE PRESENT AGE

In order to assure proper education for the next generation, and optimize the chances that leaders of the proper quality emerge among them, the ways of contemporary education need to be reformed. The lag between the tempo of world developments and our capacity to cope with them must be overcome. The distance between local, national and global events must be reduced. Only by providing education relevant to today's global and interdependent world can international education promote the cause of world peace.

A suggestion will be advanced in this study concerning a feasible method of accomplishing this. First, however, we should have a closer look at the problem; provide a more thorough diagnosis of the difficulties to be surmounted.

When our children go to school, they learn what an older generation hands down to them. This was well and good when the older generation mastered the problems of human life and society and was up to date on developments. When change is faster than the thinking of the adult generation, to hand down knowledge created by that generation to a new one is dangerous and unsound. Our children may learn to think like their elders and will be twice as outmoded in their milieu as adults are today in theirs. Somehow, society must find a way to bring the most

---

*Reprinted from *Lux Mundi*, International Association of University Presidents, Seoul.

up to date kind of knowledge to its young generation, and equip them to think for themselves in creating their own patterns of thought and action.

This means more than simply assuring that recent textbooks are used and that educators have degrees from respected institutions. The lag of formal education compared with our changing times is not merely in the substance of particular disciplines. It also involves the way in which subjects are taught in the school curriculum, and the way they are taught by individual teachers in the classroom.

Knowledge is still highly compartmentalized, although advocacy of interdisciplinary thinking and teaching has become fashionable. Almost from his or her first exposure to formal education, a child is taught about physical nature in one class, living nature in another, social concerns in a third, and about the humanities in a fourth. That they could be interconnected is seldom emphasized; that to understand one we need to understand the others is left mostly implicit. Textbooks are repositories of quasi-sacred wisdom, established 'facts' to be memorized, not just reflected upon and possibly questioned. Because of the time delays built into mastering a discipline, assembling received knowledge about it, writing a textbook, and then having it published and adopted, the quasi-sacred facts taught in our schools tend to be ten to twenty years old. They reflect not only partly transcended concepts and theories, but also outmoded forms of perceiving the world and reasoning about it. Such built-in time lags can be a handicap even in the relatively 'hard' natural sciences, and can become a major element of obsolescence in the softer social sciences and humanities.

The delays also affect the mind and personality of the teachers. Most teachers, especially in the middle and higher levels of education, are required to possess advanced degrees, and spend long years in schools and universities. They often enter their first teaching assignment after graduation, and remain all their lives within the hallowed walls of academia. They are exposed to similarly sequestered and sheltered colleagues, and to the books and studies written by them. They thus come to see the world through the spectacles created within this environment, rather than forming an idea of it through first hand experience and involvement.

Academics are astute people and are trained to analyze and observe. Yet in the present system their astuteness is often wasted, since they analyze and observe what other academics analyzed and observed before them, and that was often as not what still previous generations of academics analyzed and observed. In certain disciplines, such as philosophy for example, one has to go back fifty years or more before one comes across the first-hand sources of the theories now debated in the classroom. In social sciences the lag may involve a decade or two. As a result students are encultured into a worldview and an associated value system that perceives the physical universe as a giant and complex machine, the world of the living as a random process in which the strongest and most fit survive, and the world of society as a struggle of competing nations and, within nations, of competing interests, classes, or ethnic groups. Students meet with the exercise of power and the principle of action and reaction wherever they look: as force in physics, ability to outwit predators and reproduce in biology, and as economic and political power in social studies. If there is an implicit integration of the disparate strands of knowledge handed to the young generation by our schools it is an obsolete one: of the world as a machine, of life as a struggle for survival, and of society as dominated by the exercise of power among competing groups and institutions.

It is small wonder that students complain of the lack of relevance of their school education, and that performance indicators show a serious decline in learning. Those who do well in adult life may be precisely those who did not submit to the discipline of the current school system but maintained an interest in what went on in the world outside. Today's 'poor' students are likely to do well not only in such pragmatic fields as business and politics, but even in the intellectual disciplines where innovation calls for questioning established knowledge rather than accepting it as fact or dogma. To be a 'good' student and still maintain one's integrity and interest in new developments calls for a constant battle with the educational system: creating one's own curriculum, arguing against dominant views, and doing it in a manner acceptable to teachers and administrators. That this can be done is a tribute to the inherent flexibility of contemporary school systems, but that it needs to be done is a sad commentary on the obsolescence of their ideas and methods.

## EDUCATING FOR LEADERSHIP IN THE FUTURE

The above lags and problems of contemporary education raise the basic issue: how to educate the next generation so that it could produce the kind of leadership the world so desperately needs? We cannot leave this to the happy chance that the members of the next generation will somehow transform themselves and their worldviews and become relevant to the changing times. Society should make provisions already now, to expose its future leaders to the kind of experiences and environments which could inform their thinking and reshape their values. To educate our future leadership is especially important in the disciplines that deal with the problems and processes of contemporary societies. These problems and processes cross traditional disciplinary boundaries, involving high energy physics, ecology, demography, atmospheric sciences, chemistry, as well as the more directly concerned disciplines of economics, sociology and policy and management sciences. Students in such fields must have an intimate knowledge of what goes on in the world. Those aspiring to leadership positions should be required to undergo, not further former schooling, but a process of lifelong learning through direct participation in the affairs society conjoined with detached study and reflection.

We need to create a conceptual framework in which policy-makers can become interdisciplinary in basic knowledge and sensitive to the changing world around them. This will be, of necessity, a systems framework. In addition, our future leaders must have an opportunity to educate themselves through exposure to the world outside the walls of academia. This is not as difficult to achieve as it may seem. It may be enough to allow future policy-makers to tack back and forth between the academic and the outside policy-environment in an ordered manner. This would provide them with a lifelong learning experience that would benefit them as much as society. Approximately five phases in the ongoing education of the future leadership should be distinguished, and ways found by educational and public administrators to allow them to pursue the sequence.[1] The phases can be grouped roughly under the following headings.

### Phase One: The First Academic Environment (late teens – early twenties)

The lifelong development of the mind and personality of our future leaders should begin with a system-theory based curriculum encompassing the humanities, as well as the natural and social sciences. They must acquire a broad perspective embracing the history of culture and civilization, no less than the history of science and technology. The perspective must rest on a thorough familiarity with the main concepts and tenets of the contemporary systems sciences, with special regard for those branches whose applications influence the lives of people and the development of societies. It must also include a knowledge of alternative schools of thought, especially those that represent the principal social and ideological currents of our times.

Graduate studies should concentrate on familiarizing the future policy-makers with the major trends, problems and prospects of humanity, in the immediate as well as in the long-term future. Human needs and problems must provide a frame of reference for viewing the accomplishments of the major systems sciences. A comparison of needs with possibilities, and of problems with opportunities at present and in the future can provide the context for assessing human and social prospects in coming decades.

Systems studies are needed in order to maintain the globality and wholeness of vision. In an interdependent world, the further one looks ahead the more the effects of diverse and distant actions interpenetrate, creating a shared (though not identical) future for all. Just as the world can no longer be divided into autonomous nation-states, each pursuing its own destiny independently of the others, so the problems and opportunities of the coming age cannot be neatly classified into single academic fields for study by independent specialists.

### Phase Two: The First Practical Environment (mid twenties)

Prior to concluding their formal studies, prospective young leaders should spend a year in internship at a major planning or executing agency or organization. The host institution can be operating on the local, provincial, federal, regional, or on the international level, and it can be concerned with a single sector (such as energy or communication) or with a broad range of issues (such as development or foreign policy). In any case, it will offer a means of applying the young people's earlier experience in their academic environment. This will create a valuable insight into political constraints in the real world, and should trigger a healthy motivation to expand scope and concern, and place matters of social and policy interest in a global systems perspective.

The young policy-makers will receive much needed insight into the values and workings of public bodies; and they will be stimulated to outline and advocate ways and means for their better organization and functioning.

### Phase Three: The Second Academic Environment (late twenties – early thirties)

According to statistical studies of the time of life when great conceptual and scientific discoveries and innovations are performed, the period of greatest intellectual creativity is in the late twenties and early thirties. The leaders of the future should be given the opportunity to work out their ideas and conceptions from their mid-twenties onwards, by having access to all that the academic environment can offer. This means a constant contact with students, further constructive dialogues with colleagues, and access to a good library. The academic environment offers time to reflect and time to write, and our future leaders should be given ample opportunity to do both.

Phase three in the education of the future leadership is likely to culminate in the publication of several studies – articles, research notes, or books – stating the global and integrated systems approach adopted by the evolving mind of the young leaders concerning some problem or issue of social relevance.

### Phase Four: The Second Practical Environment (mid thirties – early fifties)

The future leadership should enter the maelstrom of the practical affairs of society armed with vision and knowledge, but ready to learn and to adapt, to modify and make practical their aims and goals, without sacrificing the integrity of their values and ideals. They should be afforded every opportunity to immerse themselves in the practical workings of a public or public-spirited institution, and forget about any special status associated with academia. The new leaders would have a real axe to grind – their own normative conceptions deriving from an evolved systemic vision – but past exposure to public policy bodies should prevent them from falling into utopianism or dogmatism. They should know by now what is feasible and what is not; what are 'green lights' and 'going through channels', and how to size up the ambitions and rivalries of various personalities and offices.

### Phase Five: The Third Academic Environment (mid fifties – retirement)

In their mid fifties, the leadership of the next age should return to the world of education to teach and disseminate their experience in society. They should turn their attention not only to curriculum design, academic structure and organization, student affairs, and the revision of old and the creation of new textbooks, but endeavor to come in contact with the broadest range of civic groups. They should give public lectures, publish, consult, and engage in a broad range of relevant civic activities.

Future policy-makers who follow such a life-long learning-decision-making experience would be crucial factors in reducing, and ultimately removing, the gap between the educational establishment and the outside world. Even more important, they would have a major role in catalyzing the self-renewal of society: they would bring together new and relevant concepts and theories with basic social and institutional issues. No society can hope to cope with the mushrooming problems of this time of change and transition unless its population has wholeness of vision and expertise in problem solving. And no society can hope to have such vision and expertise if it does not have leaders who unite in mind and personality a genuine science and philosophy of evolving systems with practical experience in the affairs of society.

# 18

## TOWARD AN EARLY WARNING SYSTEM AT THE UNITED NATIONS*

### INTRODUCTION

A worldwide debate on the possibility of 'outer limits' to growth and development on this planet is relatively new. It has been triggered in the wake of the controversy surrounding the first report to the Club of Rome by Donella and Dennis Meadows and associates, *The Limits to Growth*. Since then we have witnessed a proliferation of increasingly sophisticated world models, computerized for the most part: refinements of the original Forrester-Meadows Worlds 2 and 3; a Japanese World 6, a Latin American model (the so-called Bariloche study), the regionalized Mesarovic-Pestel model (also for the Club of Rome), and related efforts by private and public, national and international organizations (e.g., DEMATEL by the Batelle Institute, RIO [Reshaping the International Order] by Jan Tinbergen and associates for the Club of Rome; energy, environment and urban studies by the Institute for Applied Systems Analysis at Laxenburg, Austria, etc.). There are also several noteworthy efforts in this area underway at the United Nations: the 'outer limits' projects at UNEP, UNESCO's Man and Biosphere Program and others, currently in the planning stage.

This rise in awareness of 'limits' is not confined to any one problem area (energy, environment, resources, population, pollution, livability, ...) or to any one type of research organization. It represents the emergence of a consciousness of dangers and an associated research priority by intellectuals and research organizations. It is evident that if at least some of the limits are real — and there are limits other than the material-economic ones discussed in the early studies, including social, cultural, political limits, and limits to the rate of change in perceptions, ethics and desired goals, and scientific and technological innovations — we need all the knowledge we can get concerning them. Some organizations, such as the Club of Rome, are fully

*Reprinted from *Technological Forecasting and Social Change*, 8, 147-161 (1975).

dedicated to this task; others, such as IIASA, various national Academies of Science and major universities, now include it in their programs.

Early warnings must not only be issued, however, they must also be heeded. Nobody can foretell what source is likely to be perceived by different decision-makers as the most authoritative. In this respect the United Nations presently occupies an ambiguous position. It has lost prestige in the eyes of the U.S. due to current events connected with the Middle East and the behavior of delegates from the Third World in the General Assembly. On the other hand it still constitutes the only universal intergovernmental forum with direct channels to all but a few minor nation-states. As long as this is the case, a continuous flow of information on current and extrapolated future trends via U.N. channels remains a necessity. It may yet be ignored; it may always be ignored. Or it may secure the attention of some governments and eventually all. The alternatives are tied up with the future of the U.N. itself. Yet if the scenarios of the current world models are at all trustworthy, there is a definite need for a stronger, more effective U.N. We seem to have entered an age of interdependence and complexity. We are unlikely to succeed in coping with it otherwise than through cooperative action based on reliable advance information. Inasmuch as the power of national governments is still a major factor in world affairs (though no longer the *only* major factor), and as long as the only universal communication and information channel among nation-states is the U.N., the latter must evolve, and operate on a sustained basis, an expert early warning system.

This study presents an outline for the constitution of such a system, emphasizing the conceptual factors rather than the operational ones. In regard to the latter it should be noted that the system's final form will reflect not only conceptual desirabilities, but operational constraints specific to the U.N. These are, at this time, unpredictable. However, the desirability of such a project can and should already be raised, and its conceptual basis discussed.

## WHY WE NEED AN EARLY WARNING SYSTEM

Opinions diverge as to whether the world is on a collision course, headed for doomsday. But few if any impartial observers can deny that problems of global scope and staggering dimensions crop up in unforeseen and unprecedented numbers. We now know that we must count with a total human population that is not likely to level off below eight billion and could go as high as fifteen billion. We know that new technologies have to be evolved to feed, house and employ such a population and meet their basic needs for survival. We know that the arms race funnels funds much needed in the poorer sections of the Third World and the lower strata of all nations into armaments capable of destroying all contending parties and bringing about highly deleterious conditions for the rest of humanity. We know that the high-grade, easily accessible portions of mineral, ore and fossil fuel resources will be exhausted within a matter of decades. We know that the dumping of wastes poisons the oceans, fresh water, land and the atmosphere, that we need controlled emissions and recycling to head off ecodisasters. And we also know that to deal with these problems calls for unprecedented collaboration of individuals, groups and corporations within nations, and nations and transnational corporations on the world level.

It is less widely recognized that considerable time-delays are built into all policies attempting to deal with these issues; that action, if postponed, will have to be more drastic to be equally effective; that, in short, we need reliable advance information, giving early warning, when the options are still broad and the solutions not overly coercive.

(I) The developed nations are agglomerated in Europe, North America, Northern Asia (the USSR), the Japan islands, and Australia. The developing populations are spread over East and South Asia, Latin America, Africa and Oceania. The developed world as a whole is expected to grow at a rate of 49% from 1960 to the year 2000, whereas the projected growth rate for the less developed world is 150%.

Before the world population stabilizes, sometime in the late 21st century, the human masses of South Asia would swell to 4.1 billion, those of Africa to 2.1 billion, while the population of Europe and North America combined would not exceed 800 million. Sooner or later these trends will bring about a global population imbalance that precipitates famines, mass migrations and large scale deprivations. These could occur already within ten or twenty years. However, developing nations do not have that much time to institute population policies. If such a country has a 3% annual growth rate and wishes to level off its population at double its present size, it must reduce its average family size from over four children to just over two within the next ten years. If it waits twenty years before starting such a program, its population will quadruple before it can level off. Or, alternatively, it will be levelled off by major resource shortages, having both national and international repercussions.

(II) The developed world consumes a disproportionate percentage of the world's energy and natural resources and contributes the greatest share of its pollution. Unless the investment rate is equalled by the depreciation rate, the composition of the GNP is shifted from material products toward services, consumer goods are redesigned for longer life expectancy and technological equipment for prolonged usefulness, pollution rates are drastically cut, alternative energy sources are found, and the waste of irreplenishable raw materials is reduced through substitution or recycling, the nations of the developed world will find themselves in serious difficulties, perhaps already within a decade. These nations cannot afford to put off policies designed to cope with environmental and resource problems, since within a matter of years resource shortage and pollution levels can reach critical, and for practical purposes irreversible thresholds. Crises within the developed nations could produce a major deterioration of the global environment, mainly through the depletion and pollution of the oceans, changes in the composition of the atmosphere and attendant climate changes. National crises could also trigger violent conflict in the competition for scarce resources and hostilities connected with differentiated responses to the problems. An alliance of the thermonuclear powers could coerce the rest of the world into submission, but even such international totalitarianism would be prone to breakdown with the rise of famines, epidemics and discontent in the less developed world, and disagreements among the members of the nuclear alliance.

For developing and developed nations alike, there are not reasonable alternatives to coming to grips with the problems of the future in the immediate present.

However, decision-making in the contemporary world is still guided by relatively short-range and narrowly conceived perceptions of national interest. The governments of sovereign nation-states are not answerable to any supranational authority, and enter into trade and political partnerships for the sake of maximizing their own advantages. As Carrillo-Flores said, "I do not know of any country in the world that in defining its national policies does not put its national interests first".[1] The politics of sovereign governments determine the evolution of human life on this planet, and they respond to immediate national interests although they face long-range global problems.

Faced with the problems of the future and today's inadequate ways of handling them, one can envisage one of three methods of bringing about improvements: by the use of (1) force, (2) inducement, or (3) persuasion. In today's world there are no political entities possessing sufficient power and motivation to overcome the dangers of the future by coercing governments to adopt a more long-range global perspective. The only universal actor on the scene is the United Nations, but its effective force is insignificant compared with the power wielded by most national governments. There are no supranational entities that could offer effective inducement either, to prevail on governments to review national targets and policies. The only international body that has a mandate to improve the conditions of existence for all (or most) of mankind is the United Nations, and its lack of funds prevents it from offering realistic inducements of an economic nature to its member states. The inducements it could offer in the area of nonmaterial rewards, for example, through international acclamation or approbation, are similarly pale in comparison with concrete attainments of economical and political gain. The United Nations would have to grow considerably in wealth and stature before it could offer inducements to national governments that would have a realistic chance of being accepted.

There remains persuasion as the sole realistic option for handling the problems of the future. But persuasion by whom and through what means? The sole major actor on the international scene today whose interests coincide with that of mankind is the United Nations. What are the means at the U.N.'s disposal for persuading governments to act in the collective, long-term interest of men? It has neither the legal nor the moral authority to persuade by force of authority alone. Its persuasion must rely on the power of pertinent information concerning future threats to the national interests of the member states. If the U.N. is to become an effective force in averting the crises looming on the horizon in the next decades, it must demonstrate to member governments that their own national interests demand adaptive actions today, prior to the unfolding, or even the general awareness, of the crises. The best instrument the United Nations has at this time to bring about preventive modification in the structure of the world system is early warning. It must set up an effective information system, with data inputs from all major areas of the globe, and information output to all member governments and their public news media.

Recent evidence indicates that anticipatory information does have some effect in changing behavior patterns, and can directly or indirectly affect national policy making. Concern over issues with the environment has led to the epoch-making decision of dropping the SST project, reversing a trend of many decades which said, if we can make it, we need it — especially if it puts the United States first in some economic or technologic race with the rest of the developed world. Fertility in the U.S. has also dropped significantly, to about 2.1 children per family — just below replacement level when infant mortality and the number of unmarried persons are taken into account. At least part of the reason for the drop is a wide-spread recognition among young people of the dangers of overcrowding and consequent environmental deterioration. The oil crisis of 1972/3 has functioned as an early warning of later shortages produced not by political decision but by the exhaustion of sufficient quantities of oil reserves. Although the politically induced energy crisis is over, its enduring results include lower driving speeds and a plethora of smaller size cars with greater fuel economy and better emission control devices.

Early warning provided by the United Nations could become an effective force in world politics if it is factual, and not doused either with technological optimism or doomsday scares. The thrust of the information must be that there are well-defined ways in which we can conceptualize and model the human condition, using the concepts and theories of the systems sciences. In this way we can identify problems to deal with, and a limited set of cooperative policy options. If a member government wishes to avert the foreseen crisis, it must undertake adaptive policy changes well in advance, and seek the collaboration of other member nations. Inasmuch as crises face both developed and developing nations, the call for international collaboration will not be unilateral. The need for it is already evident when OPEC governments seek to overcome the economic effects of inflation in developed countries by indexing the price of oil — and thereby fueling the inflation mechanism in the consumer countries. Neither a simple OPEC price policy, nor a correspondingly unilateral economic sanction policy by the consumers can do anything but escalate the problem. Only negotiations in view of a clear appreciation of the multiple spin-offs of any decision can bring desirable results. The need for such negotiations, as well as the mutually desirable objectives that can be reached by them, must be elucidated through a competent and supranational early warning information system: yet another area where interdisciplinary systems approaches can bear significant fruit.

## CONCEPTUAL FOUNDATIONS OF THE EARLY WARNING SYSTEM

The main source of crises in the contemporary world is the attempt of national entities to satisfy their demands without regard for the simultaneous demands of all other entities in the global system. In a finite planet situation even technological breakthroughs have a finite capacity to expand limits. Many of the constraints are already felt: urban space, food supply, pollution absorption capacity, fossil fuels, easily accessed high-grade minerals and ores, thermal effects on climate, and so on. In the world system demands can be met only if they do not irrevocably conflict with basic human needs. We may define demand as economists do, in relation to an equilibrium with supply governed by price. Demands, then, would drive up prices beyond the reach of an always increasing percentage of the world's people for most commodities and many services. This will cut into needs. Needs may be defined as the quantity of products and services without which a minimum standard of life cannot be maintained. The early warning system must clearly use needs as its yardstick, and attempt to deflate or rechannel demand through pertinent information whenever it cuts into present or future fulfilments of need.

Needs must be estimated in terms of the resources (in the broad sense where they encompass all goods and services in the relevant categories) required to maintain a specified minimum standard of life. Needs can thus be calculated for nations by multiplying the per capita resource quantities with the present and forecast population. While this method abstracts from problems of allocation, it does conform to the charter of the United Nations in aggregating processes within nations rather than interfering with their domestic processes (see below). The computations can provide two sets of forecasts: the evolution of national needs, and the availability of the pertinent resources.[2]

### National needs

Needs reflect the minimum quantities of resources required per capita and per nation to maintain standards of life at or just above a specific minimum. Needs fall into two categories: those which are *universal* for all societies, and those which *vary* with culture and socio-economic level of development, as well as natural (geographic and climatic) factors. In each category, per capita needs times population = national needs.

| *Universal needs* | *Pertinent resources* |
|---|---|
| Food | Minimum normal caloric intake |
| Water | Minimum normal liquid intake |
| Space | Minimum living, working and recreational space |
| Environmental quality | Minimum water, air and land standards to operate life support systems |

| Variable needs | Pertinent resources |
|---|---|
| Energy | Minimum required to operate essential product and service technologies |
| Raw materials | Minimum required to operate essential product and service technologies |
| Working capital | Minimum required to provide employment and operate essential product and service technologies |
| Information | Minimum required to maintain communication technologies, literacy and job training levels and political and juridicial process |

The calculation of the variable needs must be based on a number of factors. These include the following:

(A) Natural factors

*Geographic-climatic conditions*: Temperate; Tropical; Arctic; Mountainous; Plain/habitable; Plain/jungle, desert, wasteland.

*Territory*: Superlarge (over 3 million square miles); Large (between ½ and 3 million square miles); Medium (between 100,000 and 5,000,000 square miles); Small (under 100,000 square miles).

*Natural resources*[3]: Rich; Medium; Low (agricultural, mineral, other).

(B) Economic factors

*Level of development*: Post-industrial (high income); Industrial (high income/medium income); Pre-industrial (medium income/poor); Traditional (poor).

*Rate of unemployment*: Under 5%; Between 5% and 10%; Between 10% and 20%. Over 20%.

(C) Demographic factors

*Population distribution*: Rural (low density); Rural (high density); Mixed rural/urban (low average density); Mixed rural/urban (high average density); Urban (medium density); Urban (high density).

*Migration patterns*: Rapid urbanization; Rapid decentralization; Rapid emigration; Rapid immigration; Low rates of change.

*Growth rates*: Over 5%; Between 3 and 5%; Under 3%; Stable; Negative.

(D) Ideo-political factors

*Societal structures*: Post-modern; Modern/industrial; Traditional/agricultural.

*Organizing principles*: Western democratic; Marxist socialist; Chinese socialist; Independent socialist (or Eurocommunist); Dictatorial/autocratic; Traditional/mythical.

The variables in each category may be computer matched and general classes of nations evolved based on natural, economic, demographic and ideo-political similarities. A standard variance of socio-technological needs may then be devised for each class. Such variance is not to be based on subjective evaluations but on the objective diversity of essential needs in differently organized and developed societies. A less developed nation requires relatively smaller quantitites of per capita energy, raw materials, working capital and information to assure the fulfillment of actual needs, although it may require more *increases* in these areas than some developed nations. Developed nations, while requiring larger relative quantitites of such resources, may find that they have excesses and wastes. Differences occasioned by non-economic factors, such as geographic-climate conditions, territorial size, population distribution, migration and growth patterns, societal structures and organizing principles, can also be determined.

**National resources**

The standard per capita needs of nations in each category, multiplied by their population size, equal the current levels of national need. National needs imply the availability of national resources to satisfy them. The relevant resources can be inventoried in reference to domestically available and importable quantities.

|  | *Domestic resources* | *Imported resources* |
|---|---|---|
| Food | Amounts and varieties of national produce | Amounts and varieties of food imports |
| Water | Territorial supplies | Rivers, lakes, springs and oceans partly under control of other nations or constituting international territory. |
| Space | Physical size of sovereign territory | — |
| Environmental quality | Average national water, air and land standards, discounting effects of foreign or international pollutants and sinks | Foreign or international pollutants and pollution sinks |
| Energy | Sources and forms available nationally (not counting potential future sources and forms) | Imported energy sources and forms |
| Raw materials | Reserves located on sovereign territory, including natural deposits and stockpiles of raw or recyclable previous imports | Raw material imports |

| | | |
|---|---|---|
| Working capital | savings, and investment in industry, agriculture and services | Foreign aid (outright aid, loans, bonds, etc.) |
| Information | Literacy and job training institutions, local public media | Foreign educational and training aid, foreign broadcasts and press |

By means of such inventories, resource availability can be measured against actual resource need, specific to each class of nation. The inventories disclose whether a matching of needs with resources does or does not occur. They further disclose whether, if it occurs, it does so on the basis of national supplies or relies on the cooperation of other nations. Since the inventories show resources excesses as well as deficits, they also indicate whether a positive trade balance is feasible by exchanging surpluses for needed supplies.

The simultaneous availability of similar inventories for other nations exhibits sources of potential exchange as well as of conflict. International negotiations can become more purposive and fruitful and the outcomes more humanistic than in the absence of such information.

Resources evolve over time, and so does need. The national situation is characterized by the ratio of resources to population: if growth occurs in population without matching growth in resources, standards of living go down. Apart from unequal allocation, if resources grow but population remains stable, standards of living go up. Since in the world as a whole population increases while resources become depleted, the broad statistical trend in nations will be toward lower living standards. Such trends can be balanced by (1) optimizing resources, and/or (2) regulating population growth. Options are available in regard to both for most governments. They must recognize, however, the need for such policies as well as the opportunities for them.

Since there are important time delays with respect to all major societal policies, especially if they involve arresting or reversing existing trends, governments must be able to anticipate resource optimizing and population regulation needs before they become acute. To this end charts must be prepared, which extrapolate existing trends into the future and enable policy makers to read off the consequences. Charts that use present patterns of resource and population development in a nation to project the future relation of human needs to resources we shall call *Resources/Needs Development Charts* (RND Charts).

RND Charts can be prepared on the basis of standard system dynamics principles.[4] Since their purpose is not to forecast the future, but to demonstrate the longterm consequences of current trends in each nation, they will be in the form of 'standard runs'. They *exclude* two kinds of modifications: (a) modifications due to future technological innovation (such as new energy sources, improved recycling techniques, alternative raw materials, more efficient emission control devices, etc.), and (b) modifications due to future value or policy changes (new national policies, changing popular consensus and its effects on decision making, new life-styles, consumer patterns, foreign relations postures, and so on).

The method of constructing the charts is as follows. We take the previously established standard per capita need for the type of nation modeled, and multiply it with the nation's population size. We get an estimate of the needed quantitites of food, water, space and environmental quality (the universal human needs) as well as of energy, raw materials, working capital and information (the socio-technologically variable needs). The time series projection of these quantities is determined uniquely by the nation's population growth rate: the more population, the larger the sum of needs, keeping per capita needs constant.

We now have a normal projection for resources based on needs. To this we match the graph for actual and projected resource availability. The eight resource types, suitably quantified, and separated into domestic and imported fractions, represent simultaneous variables in a dynamic system. Change in each variable entails change in all others. The interrelations of the variables are defined by questions, for example, in DYNAMO notation. The interrelation of all eight variables constitutes the system model. It serves as a computer program for purposes of calculation. The print-out is in the form of real time series graphs giving the simultaneous evolution of all variables under mutual influence. The graphs show the curves for the eight basic resources specified in the need graph, and demonstrate their ongoing relationship to needs within the nation.

The individual curves of the print-out can be analytically separated and mapped against the pertinent need curve. Thus we get eight special charts with three graphs each:

(1) A national need graph for the given resource, evolving over the charted time period as a function of population growth;

(2) A fractional national resource availability graph evolving as a function of the interrelations of the resource with the remaining seven resources and showing the domestically produced quantitites;

(3) A fractional national resource availability graph evolving as a function of the interrelations of the resource with the remaining seven resources and showing the imported quantities.

The eight special charts complete the set of RND charts for a given nation.

National RND charts are not forecasts of what *will* happen, but extrapolations of what *would* happen if current trends remain unchanged. Since they do not involve estimates as to possible and likely changes, they cannot be dismissed on charges of subjectivity. Rather than being forecasts of change, they serve as catalysts of change: they indicate long-range dangers as well as opportunities.

National RND Charts are to be complemented by a global RND Chart. The latter is constructed on analogous principles, but differs on the following points:

(a) Socio-technologically varied need standards are averaged;

(b) All resource quantitites are summed on the global level;

(c) All resources are indigenous to the system;

(d) The sum of the domestic resources of nations is less than the sum of global resources: the latter also includes international resources connected with the oceans and the atmosphere.

A set of eight resources/needs graphs constitutes the global RND Chart. It serves as general reference for the evaluation of national development targets. For example, if great resource abundance is mapped on the global chart, and resource scarcity with respect to the same variable appears on a national chart, other things being equal it is rational for policy-makers to attempt to increase import quotas for that resource. Where global scarcity is demonstrated, alternative measures are normally indicated for satisfying national needs, and so on. The use of the global chart presupposes familiarity not only with the general availability of resource quantities mapped against levels of need, but also with access to the available resources. In the latter regard socio-economic and political considerations enter as well.

## PRACTICAL APPLICATIONS

National RND charts will show great diversity among themselves. Four characteristic types of charts can be anticipated. These represent ideal-types for purposes of classification (individual variations are likely to occur in all cases). The basic ideal-types are as follows:

Type 1: *High resources/need ratio.* Either most resource quantitites remain above extrapolated need level, or some show sufficient excess to permit importation of needed resources. The nation faces no serious shortages in the forecast period.

Type 2: *Low resources/need ratio.* Either most resource quantitites remain below the extrapolated need level, or some show sufficient deficiency to preclude the importation of all needed resources. The nation faces serious shortages during the forecast period.

Type 3: *Increasing resources/need ratio.* Either most resource quantities move progressively above extrapolated need level, or some move high enough to permit importation of needed resources. The nation eliminates serious shortages during the forecast period.

Type 4: *Decreasing resources/need ratio.* Either most resource quantities move progressively below extrapolated need level, or some move low enough to preclude importation of all needed resources. The nation faces increasingly serious shortages during the forecast period.

R/N ratios are determined by the evolution over time of resources as well as of population size. Thus a nation of Type 3 may move into the high ratio area due to a combination of stable or decreasing population and stable or optimized resources, and one of Type 4 may move into the low ratio area due to stable resources and rising population; declining resources and stable population, or declining resources and rising population. For example, the USSR, Canada, and to a lesser extent the USA, are Type 1; the 35 nations listed as 'least developed' by the U.N. Type 2; the OPEC countries Type 3, and the majority of the world's medium size and resource nations (including those of Europe) Type 4. Empirical studies will produce positive classifications as well as individual details within the ideal-types.

A classification of national RND charts according to the four ideal-types will immediately disclose the main sources of prospective international conflict. Nations of Type 1 and 3 will tend to have conflicts with nations of Type 2 and 4. Those in the former category are either already well off or expect to become reasonably prosperous in the future. On the other hand, nations in the latter category are either poor or expect to face serious shortages in coming decades. As major powers are included in both categories (although they do not now belong to Types 2 and 3), conflicts may endanger global security.

In the absence of a global overview, national goal setting can be expected to follow short-range objectives. These involve safeguarding existing resources for nations of Type 1, and assuring the unfolding of expected resource maximization for those of Type 3. By contrast the priorities of nations of Types 2 and 4 center on changing the conditions which would normally lie in store for them. Thus whereas nations in one category are set on preserving or optimizing the *status quo*, those in the other are equally set on accomplishing basic changes.

Given these factors, global conflicts can be averted only through negotiation. All nations must be held responsible for averting catastrophe through assuring adequate conditions of life for the coming generations. However, since the present conditions of nations are greatly divergent, their expected behavior should likewise be differentiated. It should not involve the surrender of national ideals or rational projects of development, but remain commensurate with the common need to prevent major conflicts through the reduction of disparity-generated tensions in the contemporary multipolar world.

The globally responsible modification of national behavior patterns has as its objective a better balance in the areas of resources and needs in the international community. Nations with high resource/needs ratios have the responsibility to make their excess resources available to low resource/population nations. The latter in turn have the responsibility to reestablish a balanced ratio through reduction of population growth rates and the acquisition of resources. Apart from open negotiation with the position and responsibility of each participant known to all, international trade, the flow of information, environmental processes, and population trends may be locked into disastrous pathways. For example:

(i) Cartels may be formed by developing but resource-rich nations, driving up the prices of certain resources and creating squeezes in the countries needing them. (There are thirteen raw materials besides petroleum considered essential for industrial growth, including bauxite, manganese, nickel, tin, zinc and chromium. These, however, are concentrated in a few countries, mostly of a medium or low development level: Guinea, Jamaica, Australia and Surinam control 60% of the world's bauxite reserves; Chile, Peru, Zambia and Zaïre control 80% of the world's copper reserves; and Malaysia and Bolivia have 70% of the tin imported by industrial nations.)

(ii) Wealthy nations may outcompete medium-income nations for resources vital for national development; poor and very poor countries may end up with meager supplies obtained through political concessions and foreign aid, or suffer major famines and other forms of deprivation. Free market prices in international trade make it impossible that resources be allocated according to need; not only do the goods to to the highest bidder but production is geared to the latter's demand. Thus foodstuffs go to feed animals to produce high-priced meat, not to nourish underfed populations. Rising affluence shifts production patterns to satisfy the highest bidder and often reduces global resource potentials. (For example, it is less efficient to feed grain to raise cattle for meat than to eat it directly; it is also less efficient to refine crude oil into high-octane gasoline to power luxury automobiles than to use it to drive turbines and fuel heating plants.)

(iii) Developing nations may pursue developmental goals that are incommensurate with the evolution of their needs. National priorities may be associated with industrialization or rapid rise in GNP. Thereby a number of problems may be generated, the most important among which are excessive urbanization, creating large urban centers with high rates of unemployment and low levels of basic resources (food, housing, essential services); deteriorating environmental qualities (arable land buried under concrete or sprawling shanty-towns, polluted streams and rivers, degenerating health standards); sub-optimal use of agricultural lands (planting of cash crops such as cocoa or coffee in place of staple nutritional varieties); and social unrest due to changing and alienated patterns of life. Nations committed to such development may face serious internal crises that are likely to translate into external conflicts: resource importation then becomes critical and may have to be secured at all costs. Should resources fail to match needs, economic and ecologic catastrophes could occur, precipitating needless human suffering and syphoning off resources from neighboring areas as well as from other nations that have a stake in maintaining political standards and balance of power in the region.

(iv) Industrial nations, or those in process of industralization, may overtax their resource base as well as their environment. To maintain economic targets, or merely to keep the economy from collapsing, such nations may resort to force to obtain needed resources, and could contribute to the despoilation not only of the national, but of the international environment (i.e., the oceans and the air). Tensions of global proportion could thus be precipitated.

Each of these dangers can be averted through national policies which set goals and priorities in full cognizance of their long-term national as well as international consequences. To assure that such considerations enter into decision making, standards of international responsibility should be established. These should include (a) a mechanism to prevent the formation of cartels for short-term local economic or political gain; (b) price regulations concerning essential natural and human resources to prevent highest bidders from preempting the market and modifying its mode of production; (c) the flow of information and technology to control untenable rates of population growth; (d) a similar flow in regard to environmental safeguards; and (e) harmonious long-term developmental targets. In setting international standards, shared information concerning the relevant situation of all nations in the international community is *sine qua non*. RND charts prepared for each nation and disseminated to all governments can provide the required information.

## IMPLEMENTATION AT THE UNITED NATIONS

The early warning system is designed to avert international crisis and harmonize social and economic development through alerting governments to dangers as well as to opportunities connected with national targets and priorities. Carrying out such research and information tasks is within the mandate of the United Nations. Article 1 paragraph 3 of the Charter states that it is the purpose of the United Nations "to achieve international cooperation in solving international problems of an economic, social, cultural or humanitarian character...". Paragraph 4 adds that it is a purpose of the organization "to be a center for harmonizing the actions of nations in the attainment of these common ends". Article 55 in turn states explicitly, "With a view to the creation of conditions of stability and well-being which are necessary for peaceful and friendly relations among nations based on respect for the principle of equal rights and self-determination of peoples, the United Nations shall promote: (a) higher standards of living, full employment, and conditions of economic and social progress and development; (b) solutions of international economic, social, health, and related problems; and international cultural and educational co-operation; and (c) universal respect for, and observance of, human rights and fundamental freedoms for all without distinction as to race, sex, language, or religion."

Article 62 indicates that "The Economic and Social Council may make or initiate studies and reports with respect to international economic, social, cultural, educational, health, and related matters and may make recommendatons with respect to any such matters to the General Assembly, to the Members of the United Nations, and to the specialized agencies concerned." The General Assembly may in turn (Article 10) "discuss any questions or any matters within the scope of the present Charter or relating to the powers and functions of any organs provided in the present Charter...".

Should a United Nations early warning system identify the potential dangers and opportunities of international development, the Economic and Social Council could make recommendations for appropriate measures, to be determined by the General Assembly. Such recommendations could likewise be made by a specialized agency working on specific aspects of economic and social problems, such as WHO, FAO, UNESCO, etc. Indeed, the Pearson Commission submitted recommendations to the General Assembly, which the latter adopted in 1970, concerning the responsibility of developed nations in giving development aid. Such recommendations, involving pledges by the developed nations to offer specified minimum amounts and forms of development aid, are of the same general nature as standards for setting national priorities in view of the recognition of their consequences for international development. Because Article 2 paragraph 7 precludes that the United Nations intervene in matters which are essentially within the domestic jurisdiction of any state, national priority standards would have the character of non-mandatory guidelines. But if they are based on a two-thirds vote of the General Assembly (where a two-thirds majority is likely to include nations possessing resources vital to almost any powerful nation), the non-mandatory standards would nevertheless carry the force of collectively agreed upon sanctions.

The concrete tasks of carrying out the required early warning functions could be delegated to several U.N. specialized agencies, each working within its area of competence, or it could be assigned to a single agency. The latter alternative appears preferable from the viewpoint of assuring the required level of communication and cooperation among those charged with implementation. UNESCO (United Nations Educational, Scientific and Cultural Organization), UNITAR (United Nations Institute for Training and Research), and UNU (United Nations University) are among the organs suitable to implement the early warning system. The output of the system could be in the form of a periodic (e.g., annual) State of the World's Future Report, advising the Secretary General and the member governments of forecast dangers and the therewith connected policy imperatives. The Report could contain the following elements:

1. A preamble stating the need for, and the actual significance of, the State of the World's Future Report.
2. A global RND Chart, consisting of eight special Resources/Need graphs, depicting future conditions on the basis of trends occurring during the previous twelve months.
3. A full set of National RND Charts, consisting of eight special Resources/Need graphs for each of the almost 160 member states, depicting future conditions in each state on the basis of trends occurring during the previous twelve months.
4. Comments on the significance of the Charts for each general category of nation, alerting to dangers as well as to opportunities in the long-term global context.
5. An invitation to all governments, their representatives, and officers of the United Nations, to respond to the information contained in the Charts, by:
    i. Filling in, correcting and updating the data base;
    ii. Reviewing national policy in the light of the information provided;
    iii. Instituting procedures in the framework of the United Nations if international action is indicated in the light of the information.

Action by other United Nations bodies, including the General Assembly, is required in the event of the last named response. Other responses to the annual Reports call for direct U.N. action only in filling in, correcting and updating the

Report, and taking into account changing national policies in preparing subsequent Reports.

## CONCLUSIONS

In a period of impending difficulties, the rational mode of behavior is to assess one's basic requirements and inventory one's resources and abilities in relation to them. Families who face financial problems behave rationally when they estimate their basic needs and review their ability to meet them, setting their budget accordingly. Corporations facing market deterioration, production cost increases or social unrest likewise behave rationally when they assess their basic operating expenses, inventory their assets and set their policies accordingly. An analogous behavior is indicated for national governments. But first, the rapid and heady growth period of the last decades must be perceived as belonging to the past, and a clearer vision of the future must emerge. Nations have operated on the principle of demand, assessed in the non-zero-sum game context: demand spurs supply which in turn triggers more demand, with gains all around. Notwithstanding a continued non-zero-sum situation brought about by human ingenuity, the gains in further playing the growth game will be joined with significant losses both within a national situation and in the international community. The S-curve typical of growth processes takes its toll also in the area of national development and in the world community as a whole. It could be extended into a bell-shaped curve if imprudent policies fail to recognize the plateau and push growth beyond limits of feasibility.

A supranational early warning system is called for to bring about a clearer perception of the future prospects of nations by decision makers as well as by world public opinion. The salient feature of our future prospects is the flattening of the growth-curve and the danger of a bell-shaped curve. The salient feature of the required solution is international cooperation, indexed by human needs, rather than national demands. The reorientation of perceptions will in all likelihood be a slow process. It can be systematically furthered by the availability and broad dissemination of forecasts of trends relevant to basic human needs, i.e., the survival of vast human populations. The task of an early warning system is to spur decision makers to think in systems terms with a time horizon of a least one future generation.

## REFERENCES

1. Antonio Carrilio-Flores, Keynote Speech at the International Conference on The United Nations and the Population Problem. Rensselaerville, New York, May 1973.

2. Cf. Ervin Laszlo, The United Nations Commission on the Future, in *Energy: Today's Choices, Tomorrow's Opportunities* (Anton B. Schmalz, Ed.), World Future Society, Washington, 1974.
3. International agreements on the use of the oceans and the atmosphere will change the natural resources inventory of nations; further changes will be occasioned by discoveries of new reserves, and resources relevant to new technologies. For these reasons the resource factors of nations must be updated in shorter intervals than most other factors.
4. Cf. Jay Forrester, *Principles of Systems*, Wright-Allen Press, Boston, 1968.

# 19

## REGIONAL COMMUNITY-BUILDING AND INTER-REGIONAL AGREEMENTS: THE NEW IMPERATIVES OF PROGRESS AND DEVELOPMENT IN THE 1980s*

The start of the U.N. Third Development Decade contrasts sharply with that of the launching of the Second Decade in 1970. At that time there was confidence that overall progress in the world economy, coupled with suitable measures to insure that the developing countries can participate adequately in its benefits, would gradually close the gap between North and South and order the relations between powers big and small, rich and poor. Mainly economic processes and primarily quantitative indicators were designated to ensure that this happy state of affairs is achieved, or at least approached, by the end of the decade of the 1970s.

The quadrupling of oil prices by OPEC in the early years of the decade gave such hopes a political substance. Solidarity and cooperation among developing countries could reshape a major element in world economic relations; the domination of a handful of industrial powers and a few transnational corporations originating in them was successfully challenged.

The formulation of the Plan of Action at the Non-Aligned Summit in Algiers in 1973, and the adoption of the Programme of Action at the United Nations General Assembly a year later, brought the targets of a new international economic order fully into the realm of practical politics. The 1975 General Assembly Resolution on Development and International Cooperation gave the details of the new order, and it was passed by the Assembly on the basis of consensus. Thus, at mid-decade a political dimension to world economic progress was well established, and transformation of the system was inscribed alongside with growth as the hallmarks of progress.

In the second half of the decade serious problems appeared which overshadowed the mid-decade era of optimism. The non-oil exporting developing countries had difficulty keeping up with higher energy prices; the terms of trade continued to worsen for all developing countries as the price of manufactures rose

---

*Reprinted from *RCDC: Regional Cooperation Among Developing Countries*, E. Laszlo with J. Kurtzman and A. K. Bhattacharya, Pergamon Press, New York, 1981.

faster than that of commodities and semi-manufactured goods; and the share of developing countries in world trade as well as in world industrial production continued to decline, rather than rise to the agreed levels. More countries suffered food shortfalls and were obliged to import basic foodstuffs, and the import of basic necessities, together with the continued high level spending on armaments, worsened the balances of payment of the great majority of countries. Emergency stabilization measures were undertaken to qualify for IMF and similar World Bank group loans, with the result that the promised transformation of the international economic order was shortchanged in favor of its short-term stabilization.

By the end of the decade serious problems were experienced also by the industrialized countries, in the areas of employment, balance of payment, unused industrial capacity, loss of overseas markets, environmental deterioration and, above all, mounting inflation. Defensive measures were perceived as appropriate in a number of states, leading to retrenchment in development aid and assistance, protective barriers on trade, and hesitancy in the field of long-term overseas investment. Thus concurrently with the rapidly worsening situation of the non-oil exporting developing countries, the major industrial countries experienced difficulties which precluded their willingness to come to the rescue.

The overall situation became one of tension and increased competition, which could be exploited by some transnational corporate interests to reap windfall profits and generate political clout, but which benefited hardly any government or national economy. Stagnation or recession was combined with unemployment and inflation. The value of reserve currencies, held mostly in U.S. dollars, eroded and the debt burden became almost unmanageable for a growing number of countries, including some relatively advanced ones among them.

Thus the situation at the start of the Third Development Decade was radically different. A qualitative restructuring of the international economic order is still needed, since the present order continues to widen national and per capita gaps in all areas including income, production, trade, investment, R and D, education and employment. But the political context in which such restructuring could be effected has worsened. While the existing order does not work, especially for the non-resource rich developing countries, the fear that its revamping would produce additional disbenefits for the leading economic powers creates a stale-mate: those that have the will to restructure the system do not have the power to do so, while those that have the power lack the will for it.

The deadlock was clearly manifest in the 11th special session of the United Nations General Assembly on the world economy. A number of major issues, crucial to a new international economic order, had to be left unresolved, or found temporary patch-up formulations. These include reform of the international financial system, targets for official development assistance, and the insertion of energy as part of the new order. Even more significantly, the launching of the so-called global negotiations ran into the greatest difficulties. Not only are actual negotiations all but impossible to conclude with success; even negotiations about the holding of negotiations are prone to breakdown.

A mechanism for sustained negotiation on an entire package of issues vital to the economic future of all countries is desperately needed. Such a mechanism will no doubt be created, for without it tensions would soon reach crisis levels, and the plight of the least developed countries would assume catastrophic proportions. But what will the mechanism accomplish if the economic and political situation of the partners around the negotiating table remains as asymmetrical as it is today? One can bring the big powers to the negotiating table, but one may not be able to make them negotiate — to paraphrase a popular saying. Parallel with the creation of a negotiating forum, such as will be provided by the global round of negotiations, there must be concrete and speedy intiatives to balance the positions of the countries of North and South. This is to establish a functional structure in the international system.

The great economic powers of the North are either giant federated units such as the US or the USSR, or organized economic groups of states, such as OECD, the European Community, and the CMEA countries. These giant countries and groups of states do not merely form a common front in North-South negotiations; they also have concrete economic ties which range from a consistent exchange of information on vital areas, to the coordination of key policies, the setting of uniform standards and targets, and joint commercial and parliamentary structures. Common negotiating fronts can thus be backed by real economic power.

The countries of the South cannot match these large industrial and trade complexes under the present arrangements. While there are well over a dozen cooperative agreements and arrangements in effect, assuring South-South economic links, and although some are working effectively and are proving their worth every day, the common negotiating front of the countries, vested in the Group of 77, is not backed by the economic cooperation and integration levels of the North. In matters vital to national economic interests, the common front tends to give way to bilateral discussions in which particular countries expose themselves to unequal exchanges, overshadowed by large-scale economic interests. If a functional international structure is to be created, it is imperative that ECDC and TCDC (economic and technical cooperation among developing countries) be rapidly intensified.

Implementation of ECDC and TCDC involves all the countries of the Third World without exception. But this provision should not be confused with the fact that not all Third World countries can be involved in the same cooperation and integration packages at the same time. It is both economically and politically impossible to order over 120 countries occupying the great majority of the earth's habitable land mass and embracing over two-thirds of its population in a single economic cooperation scheme, however well conceived. A number of sub-regional and regional agreements, subsystems of the functional structure of the world system, are required to group countries along mutually complementary economic and geographic lines. At least a dozen major economic communities could be created in the Southern Hemisphere under the general aegis of ECDC and the new international economic system. Joined by inter-regional agreements of a preferential nature among themselves, such communities could evolve inter-regional ties with the already constituted economic complexes and communities of the North. If pursued with all due interest and will, the present asymmetries of the global economic system could be corrected to a significant extent by the end of the decade. Facing the five or six major powers and economic groupings of the industrialized First and Second Worlds, would be a dozen or so economically cooperative and integrated groups of the Third World. The structure of the world economy would become systemic and functional.

The benefits of such a better equilibrated world economic system would be distributed to all countries. The industrialized states would find that they can enter into long-term agreements with reliable partners commanding vast reserves of energy and other industrially needed natural resources, as well as vast labor forces and great potential markets. The developing countries would find that they have internal markets of sufficient size to produce economies of scale, and adequate joint financial, agricultural and technological capabilities to exploit such opportunities. Problems such as debt-renegotiation, code of conduct for transnationals, the insertion of energy into the new order, access to marine resources, commodity prices, and the stabilization of the terms of trade would prove easier to resolve in the systemic framework of an increasingly self-reliant economic grouping of states than through either bilateral negotiations among individual developing countries and one or two major industrial powers, or global negotiations where the positions of the South are not backed by coordinated and sustained economic arrangements.

The building of regional communities in the South, and inter-regional agreements among them as well as with the major economic powers and groupings of states in the North, are the new imperatives of progress and development in the 1980s, and the quickest and most efficient way to move toward a systemic order in the presently unbalanced world economy.

## SUMMARY OF THE SPECIFIC PROPOSALS OF THE CONFERENCE ON REGIONALISM AND THE NEW INTERNATIONAL ECONOMIC ORDER

Convinced of the truth of the above insight, and conscious of the need to take concrete measures to act on it in practice, the writer proposed and organized an international meeting at the United Nations (May 8–9, 1980) under the auspices of the U.N. Institute for Training and Research (UNITAR), the Center for the Economic and Social Studies of the Third World, and the Club of Rome.

The expert studies, speeches and discussions of the Conference considered numerous concepts, forms and modalities of cooperation among developing countries on the sub-regional and inter-regional level in an action-oriented perspective. The following is an illustrative rather than an exhaustive summary of the main proposals. They make up the Regional and Inter-Regional Strategy for Collective Self-Reliance in the fields of finance and development, industrial production, trade and marketing, agriculture and rural development, science and technology, resource, energy and environmental affairs, and social, cultural and educational policies.

Cooperation in the field of *finance and development* was proposed in view of the crushing burden of external debt and debt-service obligations on developing countries, in reference to the need to create joint financing facilities on a regional basis. Such facilities would have the task and the ability to:

(1) establish a body of principles to underlie the Facility's loan philosophy that would emphasize domestic production rather than export dependence; and

(2) disseminate a body of economic precepts and accounting principles, capable of analyzing Third World development in its technological, financial, demographic, ecological, social, and cultural dimensions.

Cooperation in the field of *industrial production* was proposed in view of the insufficient participation of developing countries in world industrial production, in reference to the need to establish joint regional centers for the promotion of industrialization on a regional basis. Such centers would have the task and ability to: task and ability to:

(1) formulate an investment code that offers preferential treatment for regional businesses by way of long-term loans, investment guarantees, and assured markers for the end products; and

(2) promote joint ventures among developing countries involving the supply of inputs and raw materials, location of industrial plants, and pooling of technical and managerial skills.

Cooperation in the field of *trade and marketing* was proposed in view of the insufficient expansion of the international and inter-regional trade of developing countries, in reference to the need to create joint centers for the promotion of trade and marketing activities on a regional basis. Such centers would have the task and the ability to:

(1) act as the central clearing-house for marketing intelligence on prices, surpluses, shortfalls, distribution outlets, and shipping conditions to promote intra-regional trade, and study the development plans of Third World countries and how they may be enmeshed with their exporting strategy and strengthening of their infrastructural facilities. The activities of the center could later be expanded to include downstream marketing operations in stocking, transport, finance, and related ancillary services.

Cooperation in the field of *agriculture and rural development* was proposed in view of the food import dependence and persisting rural underdevelopment of many developing countries, in reference to the need to create joint centers for the promotion of agriculture and rural development on a regional basis. Such centers would have the task and the ability to:

(1) develop a common agricultural policy, taking into account, as appropriate, price support systems, stockpiles and sales; and
(2) devise programmes to improve agriculture *inter alia* through such measures as appropriate fertilizer production, irrigation, prevention of soil erosion, storage, marketing, and creation of transport and distribution systems.

Cooperation in the field of *science and technology* was proposed in view of the continuing domination of this field by a handful of advanced industrialized countries and transnational corporations, in reference to the need to create joint centers for the promotion of indigenous science and technology capacities on a regional basis. Such centers would have the task and the ability to:

(1) promote regional and inter-regional cooperation in field testing, adaptation, joint industrial research, evaluation and extension of technologies;
(2) develop appropriate regional technological capabilities; and
(3) enhance regional capabilities to adequately transfer and control imported technologies.

Cooperation in the field of *resource, energy and environmental affairs* was proposed in view of the urgency to assure the development, appropriate use and protection of all natural resources, including raw materials, energy, and the environment, in reference to the need to create joint centers for resource, energy and environmental affairs on a regional basis. Such centers would have the task and the ability to:

(1) establish joint regional enterprises for the R & D, exploration, exploitation and preservation of endogenous land and ocean-based natural and energy resources;
(2) identify all existing and potential energy resources required to sustain regional development; and
(3) establish an energy clearing system at the regional level to promote and facilitate the inter-regional exchange of appropriate forms of energy.

Cooperation in the field of *social, cultural and educational policies* was proposed in view of the fact that international cultural relations can no longer be restricted to 'one-way' cooperation, and that current efforts to promote regional efforts in this area need to be further strengthened and complemented. Hence there is a need to create joint task forces for the coordination of social, cultural and educational policies on a regional level. Such task forces would have the task and the ability to:

(1) determine the development aspirations of indigenous populations and examine the impact of imported technologies and modes of economic and social organization on the cultures with a view to increasing socially equitable employment opportunities, reducing conflict and preserving the useful and appropriate elements of the cultural heritage of the nations and the region as a whole;

(2) review educational materials and curricula in regard to their appropriateness to impart required skills, provide useful knowledge, and sustain the basic values of human dignity, compassion and solidarity with a view to establishing a regional common market for knowledge; and

(3) coordinate the research, development and application of new educational materials and techniques with due regard for ethnic and national diversity, as well as for the commonality of problems and opportunities within the region.

# 20

## THE FUTURE OF RCDC
## (REGIONAL CO-OPERATION AMONG DEVELOPING COUNTRIES)

The future of RCDC will depend on a clear understanding of why it is needed, what obstacles block its realization, and what are its key objectives.

### THE NEED FOR RCDC

The world economy has become increasingly polarized since World War II between creditor and debtor nations, food-surplus and food-deficit countries, and high and low-productivity economies. Developing countries have run deepening trade deficits, which the non-oil producing countries among them have financed by foreign borrowing at rising interest rates. Increasing debt-servicing costs have led to growing balance-of-payment deficits, which require yet further borrowing, currency depreciation, and economic austerity. As a result, oil-importing developing countries are obliged to forego domestic investment and modernization in order to pay their foreign debts, and are required to use their scarce capital to increase their exports rather than to achieve domestic self-reliance and autonomy.

A solution to the worsening economic problems of the majority of developing countries would be to achieve significantly higher levels of collective self-reliance. For the majority of Third World countries, the foreign-debt burden and structural dependency for food, energy, and other essentials on a handful of industrial nations have grown so serious that virtually all their economic surplus is being diverted abroad rather than retained at home. This situation can be averted neither by nation-by-nation autarky in the creation of economic linkages, nor by adhering to the existing world economic disorder. The benefits conferred by the objectives of RCDC and the interregional strategy offer the best promise for enhancing Third World collective self-reliance and creating a balanced and equitable world economic system.

The solvency of developing nations is of vital interest also for the industrial powers. Their exports have been made increasingly on credit, and cessation of Third World borrowing would dry up industrial-nation export flows at a time when these nations themselves are suffering from stagflation. In addition, credit systems in North America and Western Europe are already strained by rising default rates, and defaults or outright debt repudiation by a large number of developing countries would threaten a serious break in the chain of international payments. An internationally beneficial goal of regional financing is to ensure credit to developing nations for productive loans rather than for unproductive borrowings which do not create their own means of repayment. Debts in areas where expectation of repayment is either unrealistic, or would oblige the borrowing countries to further reduce their investment and development rates, would need to be renegotiated, in the joint interest of both debtor and creditor nations. Regional financial institutions with a development-oriented (rather than austerity-oriented) philosophy are needed to enable developing countries to negotiate the rescheduling of their debts, and ensure access to future international loans for productive self-amortizing purposes.

Regional groupings of states could also enhance their position vis-à-vis transnational corporations. They would not be obliged to bid against each other to induce particular corporations to locate within their boundaries. A common regional front in negotiations would offer better chances of implementing the basic principle of international law, that affiliates of transnational corporations are corporate citizens of the host-country, subject to its domestic laws. Regional groups could establish guidelines for international investment to determine how economic gains resulting from such investments are to be allocated. They could also create and implement regionally appropriate guidelines for technology transfer and the repatriation of locally earned profits.

The financing of self-reliant agriculture and industry calls for both foreign-currency expenditure and domestic-currency investment. Developing countries need a more domestically oriented development model, reducing their reliance on loans that necessitate an export-oriented program for repayment. To fund self-reliance oriented development, regional banks for agriculture and industry are needed, to assess the foreign-exchange positions and debt-servicing capacity of the member countries, and articulate a self-reliant philosophy of regional development.

## THE OBSTACLES TO RCDC

A number of obstacles militate against the effective realization of RCDC in the current international environment. These include:

- *narrow and short-sighted forms of nationalism*, which can transform the legitimate claim for national independence into a request for national autarky, and can prove to be inimical to growth and development in conditions of systemic interdependence;

- *self-centered economic thinking* that gives rise to the irrational fear that assisting other countries and aiding in the creation of a more equitable international economic system will restrict national economic growth and development;

- *disparities in levels of development* that produce fears and suspicions in the less advanced countries or a region that the more advanced will overwhelm them with their more efficient production systems or greater resources (despite the experience of the currently functioning and successful economic communities which shows that the less developed countries can be compensated for short-term losses, and in the long term actually benefit more from regional cooperation than the wealthier and more advanced ones);

- *disparities in size and population* that give rise to the worry that the larger regional members will use their political power, or superior population size, to coerce the smaller into agreement (despite the possibility of establishing qualified voting procedures and other systems of checks and balances);

- *cultural chauvinism* that aggravates the above fears and makes ineffective the implementation of regional agreements (even though, if properly understood and taken into account, the diversity of culture can be a basis for complementary relationships, skills, and institutions);

- *dependency relationships* between developing countries and one or more industrial nations which, whether the legacy of colonialism or the result of more recent developments, produces a reluctance in developing countries to evolve alternative regional relationships for fear of jeopardizing their unwelcome but seemingly necessary North-South ties (notwithstanding the fact that regional integration could replace them with a wider ranging and more equitable set of international economic relationships).

A pragmatic orientation could cut across and mitigate such fears and blockages confronting RCDC objectives. A genuine systems approach is required, adaptable to divergent ideological, political, and constitutional realities, and allowing the simultaneous pursuit of several policies and programs in the relevant areas of economic cooperation. It must be task-oriented, building institutions only as needed to carry out specific tasks rather than to dominate and expropriate them; and enable different nations, cultures, and institutions to retain their identity while cooperating in the pursuit of specific tasks and objectives.

Overcoming the obstacles to RCDC requires an understanding of its potentials and benefits by leaders and citizens alike. The effective mobilization of public support constitutes a crucial factor. It calls for broader and more adequate flows of information concerning the current world economic situation, and the available alternatives. The general public must come to view regional cooperation as a process in which they as individuals as well as their countries will benefit, without loss of personal and national identity, and with enhanced collective self-reliance and standing in the world community.

## THE OBJECTIVES OF RCDC

Regional cooperation has a wide variety of goals and objectives ranging from trade relations in nonessentials to the creation of parallel social and legal institutions and policy coordination by a joint regional parliament. A logical sequence may consist of the following steps:

1. *Establishment of commercial trading patterns aiming at regional self-sufficiency.* Beginning with trade in superfluities, including specialized natural products, and extending to trade in food and other essentials.

2. *Development of a financial means of settling trade balances.* Beginning with reference to a common international standard (gold or a basket of convertible currencies), and extending to mutual credits and debits denominated in national currencies.

3. *Coordination of national investment programs to support regional self-reliance.* These may begin with programs to spur self-reliance in essentials, such as the European Coal and Steel Community (ECSC) in 1952, and the Common Agricultural Policy (CAP) in 1957.

4. *Establishment of a system of international subsidies and protective tariffs to finance economic modernization.* Again, the ECSC and CAP are leading examples.

5. *Fiscal coordination, to allocate the costs of national subsidies equitably.*

6. *Linkage of currency values, so that the costs of subsidies and tariffs are known and remain relatively stable.* The European "Snake" is an example, leading to closer forms of currency union such as the European Monetary System (EMS).

7. *Creation of a representative regional body to determine how regional costs and benefits are shared.* Again, the European Community (EC) provides a useful example: the European Parliament leaves existing national bodies intact; it advises governments in allocating the costs of national subsidies and currency support programs, and the benefits of how tax and tariff proceeds are spent.

8. *Technical coordination, to prevent given regions and classes from falling behind and thus suffering inequitable income and exchange rates.* This may involve regional education and extension services to upgrade the quality of labor, and capital subsidies to increase agricultural productivity as well as industrial productivity.

9. *Creation of parallel social and legal instititions, and free movement of labor,* issuing in an integrated labor force and a shared business environment.

In its proper historical perspective, the experience of the European Community may serve as a point of reference. Although the EC consists of nation-states historically defensive of their sovereign rights and independence, it has achieved a significant measure of regional cooperation and coordination. In its development, the role of a precursor body, such as the European Coal and Steel Community (ECSC), must not be lost sight of. Such bodies demonstrate their relevance by bringing advantages to their members in the short-term; they form a practical foundation for concluding more wide-ranging and enduring institutional arrangements later. Preparatory bodies analogous to the ECSC need to be established in various parts of the developing world to investigate problems and potentials of cooperation in such fields as trade, marketing, industrial production, raw materials and energy, food and agriculture; the transfer, control and creation of technology; and money and finance.

Even in its later and more evolved forms, RCDC need not impair or reduce the sovereignty of member governments in deciding on the use of their natural resources, labor forces, internal distribution of benefits, and models of development. Great diversity within a community formed by RCDC can exist as long as the agreed objectives are pursued through coordinated policy instruments. Not uniformity but complementarity can be the leading principle, as in all balanced forms of systemic interaction. Differences in natural resource endowments, capital accumulation, skills and technological capacities, and other geographic and human factors can form the basis on which to build schemes consolidating the comparative advantages and adopting mutually beneficial common fronts vis-a-vis economic and financial relationships with other regions.

On the interregional level, developing countries engaged in RCDC may give preferential treatment to other developing countries in similar RCDC schemes as well as in other sectoral, rather than regional, groupings. Interregional agreements between regional groups in Central and South America, West and East Africa, North Africa and the Middle East, and South and Southeast Asia, as well as between any such groups and the EC, or the OECD and CMEA countries as a whole, could be lasting, and bring significant benefits to all parties.

In view of progressing toward such interregional relationships, forward-looking developed countries could revise their traditional aid and assistance packages to help developing countries achieve their objectives in the area of South-South regional cooperation. Industrialized country policies would have a lasting multiplier effect if tuned to the needs of RCDC. For example, technical assistance programs could accelerate progress in devising and implementing schemes of regional cooperation by developing countries, and transfers of resources could bolster regional funds and pools to enable them to compensate the poorer members of a regional grouping for short-term losses due to their weaker agricultural and industrial production sectors and trade potentials.

The future of RCDC is closely linked with the future of the entire world economy. It is important, however, to keep the problem of building the world economic system in perspective. The major subsystems must be created before the whole system can become structurally balanced and functional. South—South ties, through new groupings formed by RCDC, are the logical basis upon which to construct broader interregional relationships to encompass all of the Third World, and to bring the latter into balanced and productive contact with the countries and regions of the industrialized North.

# 21

## TOWARD AN AGE OF HUMAN ECOLOGY

Beyond the chaos of today's transitional period, mankind can look forward to a more sustainable and equitable age, in which human ecology will play a key role. The concept of an ecology to which the human element is a conscious and purposive part, a positive contributing factor and not a negative destructive one, must be a leading principle in our efforts to reach the new age. We must begin to plan, and even before that, we must begin to reflect and debate, the coming age. Never before in history has mankind been confronted by the need to build a global civilization in conscious harmony with nature, and with purposive planning of the resources and the structures exploited or created by human communities.

The coming Age of Human Ecology can be foreseen in general outline. There are not many alternatives open for a species that will grow to eight to ten billion people, and that is intensely motivated by the need to assure at least a minimum quality of life for all its members. Certain definite principles of social and economic organization will have to prevail; certain types of ideals and values will have to predominate. There will have to be diversity, to assure adaptability and complementarity, as in natural ecologies, but the diversity will have to be harmonized.

The systemic features of the Age of Human Ecology which are imperative to know and observe are described in the following snapshot of a civilization that, if we do not destroy ourselves first, will come to flower in the 21st century.

### CITIZENSHIP

21st century communities will be voluntarily limited in size. Large urban agglomerations will be subdivided into autonomous zones, and smaller communities will not be allowed to grow beyond a certain size. Standards for maximum size will be defined by a combination of factors making up an integrated 'livability' index. It will include definitions of distance from home to work in terms of time travelled and means and convenience of transportation, distance from home to shopping, recreation and entertainment, and to nature preserves.

Size of population will be limited to a number that can fully benefit from existing employment opportunities, social and health services, schools and informal educational facilities, the arts and culture as well as recreational opportunities, and can adequately participate in community decision-making.

Decision-making will be participatory, with each adult citizen having an equal right to propose and discuss issues, and one vote. Communication technologies will be used to provide two-way channels of information between citizens and community administrations. Issues of concern will be the subject of referenda, following public debate. The context for all issues will be the relationship of the community and its wider environment. The environment will be understood to comprise both nature, and human political, social, economic and technical systems. Man-nature interactions will occupy the center of attention and concern on all levels from the community to the globe. No absolute boundaries of interest and interaction will be recognized. The community will be seen as part of its environing natural and human systems, which in turn are part of larger systems: continental ecologies and the biosphere on the one hand, and provinces, nations, continental regions and the world system on the other. The ultimate standard and frame of reference for community decisions affecting the interface between the community and the environment will be the effect such decisions will have on the biosphere and the world system, through successive causes and effects in the intervening systems. Interactions across system-boundaries will be sufficiently well understood to allow computer-assisted calculation of the effects. Thus issues of local concern will be tied sequentially into global concerns and processes.

Citizenship in the Age of Human Ecology will be world citizenship but without loss of personal identity or allegiance to family, community, nation and region. Each person will have multiple loyalties. Personal loyalties encompassing all spheres of private life will remain associated with the family. Civic allegiance will be with the community and its nation and region. A basic human solidarity will infuse attitudes and relations vis-à-vis people in other nations, regions and cultures as well. And a similarly basic sense of belongingness will infuse relations with nature and other living things, inspired by affinity and respect for the biosphere as a whole.

Since decision-making will coordinate policies and harmonize objectives between the various communities and their nations and regions, irreconcilable conflicts of interest will not occur. On the other hand, diversity among the communities and their social and natural environments will ensure that each citizen can have a well-defined identity, with a clear conception of his or her place and role in a particular community and culture.

## POLITICS

Politics in the Age of Human Ecology will embrace all levels of social and political organization from the grass roots to the global. But shared objectives will not impose uniformity. The specific objectives of particular societies will continue to exhibit a great variety of features. Liberal societies will continue to value civil liberties, equality of opportunity and freedom of initiative and enterprise above all others. They will adopt internal policies designed to optimize these elements in their society, but place it in the context of mutual benefit among the diverse social units. Socialistic societies will prize equity in income distribution and equal political rights and duties above all else. Deeply spiritual and religious societies will put the accent on interpersonal relations, contact with nature, and the freedom to adopt lifestyles consistent with people's values and beliefs.

Within the diversity of social objectives there will be basic elements held in common. Domestic policies will, in general, aim to encourage the enjoyment of work through work relations that promote human contact, and work conditions that are safe, sanitary and pleasing to the senses. Other policies will aim to preserve and enhance family life. With increasing average life expectancies and a lower average birth rate, families will extend across four or five generations. Community living structures that enable such cross-generationally extended families to keep together will be an important part of 21st century societies. They will be pillars of stability and continuity, and sources of personal identity.

The promotion of interpersonal relations will be a major element of domestic social policies. Work, commuting, leisure and cultural activities and travel can occur in a social setting where like-minded individuals pursue similar activities, and share the frustrations of problems and the joys of achievement. Non-material values will be consciously accented in all societies, regardless of their diversity. Values connected with personal dignity, honesty, family, civic role, creativity, intellectual inquiry and taste will have primacy over values conferred by conspicuous consumption, the accumulation of material possessions, and the concentration of personal wealth and power. Social policies will deliberately counteract tendencies to compute economic and social values in purely monetary terms, and to relate socio-economic status to level of spending. Waste in production and consumption will be heavily taxed in free enterprise oriented societies, and proscribed in others.

The perennial human quest for wealth and power will not disappear, but will be contained within bounds. Competitiveness will be channelled into the more highly valued spheres of social life and culture, rather than finding expression in the basic economic and political spheres. There will be lesser need for ostentation and proving oneself by accumulation of material possessions, and more to test one's worth against standards of humaneness, civic spirit, artistic creativity, intellectual depth, scientific acumen and political wisdom. Older people, with greater experience in such matters, will be correspondingly more valued. Given a simultaneous world-wide drop in both birth and death rates, societies will have several older generations. There will be vigorous people in their seventies and eighties, and possibly nineties, capable of assuming socially useful roles and probably eager to do so. Accommodating them will be possible through a greater emphasis on services and cultural production, compared with the production of basic necessities (which will be taken care of by a smaller and younger segment of the population). Work hours will be shorter, and leisure time activities more appreciated. People will be able to engage in hobbies and will diversify their interests. Education will be ongoing, and include opportunities to evolve socially useful skills, consistent with new tastes and preferences. Individuals will occupy several distinct occupational roles during their long active lifetime. Today's admiration for the specialist who knows much about a few things and little or nothing about the rest, will give way to an appreciation of more balanced personalities with multiple interests. Longer and more continuous learning environments, more free time, and a longer span of active life will enable people to combine expertise with general knowledge and diversified interests.

External policies will be guided by principles of mutually beneficial interaction, joined with respect for diversity and self-determination. Today's zero and negative sum games will be transformed into positive sum interactions. These will embrace all spheres in the intercourse of societies, from matters of security to those of population.

The resolution of global tensions, through higher levels of trust and the creation of a collective peace keeping machinery, will enable societies to reduce their military spending and channel more funds and natural as well as human resources to socially useful fields.

National and regional security will not suffer in consequence. Indeed, they will be enhanced: no society will risk being dominated by a better armed and more ruthless opponent or neighbor, and humanity as a whole will no longer face the specter of mass destruction.

The economic system will offer another field for positive sum interactions. No longer will the wealth and power of a few be won at the expense of the poverty and weakness of others. Economic advantages will accrue to all sides, as stable and equitable prices are achieved for basic commodities and raw materials, as industrial production becomes more equitably distributed, and the agricultural potential of all lands is more fully realized. Similar all-round benefits will accrue from the reform of today's unstable and inequitable monetary system and the system of international finance, trade, shipping and business. Benefits will include higher rates of agricultural and industrial production with less waste, fuller utilization of the labor force, better access to markets, and a greater sense of equity and satisfaction in a more prosperous world population.

Reductions in the birth rate and extensions of life expectancy will provide additional fields for positive sum interactions. Fewer children in one family or society need not be at the cost of more children in others. Stabilization of the human population in the late 21st century under ten billion will allow the satisfaction of all basic needs without the depletion of nonrenewable resources prior to the availability of substitutes, and without despoilation of the environment; A better transfer of more appropriate technologies, a world food and resource bank capable of providing emergency relief, collective regimes for the oceans, polar regions, the atmosphere and outer space — these and similar arrangements will bring benefits to the entire human community.

## ECONOMICS

Economics in the Age of Human Ecology will be as diverse as national and regional conditions, ideologies and cultures require. No single type of economic system will be prescribed as universally best and desirable for all societies.

The range of functional economic systems will not include all that has ever existed, or even all that exists currently in the 20th century. The range of economies will move within the bounds of mixed private and public systems. A total reliance on the free market with laissez-faire policies will not be possible due to the need to coordinate macro-economic processes on national, continental and world levels, and the consequent need for guidance — and occasional intervention — in economic processes. A fully centralized planning apparatus will also be counter-indicated, since collective decision-making on all levels from the communities upwards will introduce the necessary degree of self-management without the rigidity associated with large-scale central planning.

The precise mixture of the private vs. the public sector will not be determined by profitability, as in laissez-faire economies, or by prescriptive doctrines, as in communist countries, but by collective decision-making reflecting social priorities and cultural preferences.

Energy policy will be universal, but flexible enough to respond to variations in local needs. Fossil fuels will no longer be burned — the precious deposits of oil, gas and coal will be employed in medicines, chemicals, and other vital uses. Renewable energy sources, including sunlight, will supply the world's staple energy needs. They will be accessible to all communities, nations and regions, and they will be safe for the environment and for society, not being convertible into instruments of mass destruction. As a result of technological breakthroughs in the storage of energy, the intermittancy of solar radiation will not pose a major problem. Its universality will more than compensate for its diffuseness as well; a decentralized world energy system will prove to be more appropriate for self-reliant communities, provinces, nations and regions than today's centralization based on high-power technology and the geographic location of fossil fuel deposits.

Energy, food, commodity, and capital markets will be collectively planned and guided. Floor and ceiling prices will be in effect for all internationally traded goods. Buffer stocks will be maintained of the essential commodities at levels regulated by negotiated standards. Nonrenewable natural resources of vital interest to agricultural and industrial production will be jointly owned by nations within particular regional blocs. These resources will be their Common Regional Heritage, to be used with regard to the equitable benefit of all member nations, as well as of future generations. Universal standards of conservation will apply to such resources in all regions. These will include minimum standards for conservation in production and consumption, and for product durability, recycling, repair, replacement, and disposal.

The natural environment will also be part of the Common Regional Heritage. Uniform nature and wildlife conservation standards and minimum environmental quality norms will apply. These will be relaxed only in the case of exceptional hardship or temporary requirements connected with development.

Resources beyond national and regional jurisdiction will constitute the Common Heritage of Mankind. Permanent regimes for the oceans, the atmosphere, the polar regions, and for the resources of outer space will be administered by specialized agencies of the United Nations.

The regimes will specify safe and sustainable environmental quality standards for the earth's air and water envelopes and its polar zones in reference to natural balances, cycles and regenerative capacities. They will undertake measures to enforce compliance. The regimes will further control and supervise the exploitation of humanly or industrially useful resources, assuring equitable access by all nations and regions, and distributed benefits from their use.

## CULTURE

The culture of an age both reflects its dominant conditions and motivates their change and evolution. As contemporary culture reflects the searching, the clashes, the disharmonies and the occasional flashes of insight and glimpses of beauty of our era of transition, so culture in the Age of Human Ecology will reflect the complex yet ordered strands of interrelationships in human affairs, with their ever-changing variations, coalescence, renewal and transformation. There will be order, symmetry and harmony without monotony and static formalism. The key elements will be dynamic balance, the synthesis of new forms and patterns, and the discovery of the finer shades of human ecological and social experience.

There will not be a clear separation between 'high' (or 'classical') and 'popular' art. Participation in all dimensions of social life will bring people closer together; art and artists will not be outsiders. Art forms for all tastes and levels of sophistication will flourish, as people will search to express and behold the finer shadings of their experience through the work of persons of exceptional sensitivity and creativity. The art of today's subcultures will merge with the mainstream, as the arts find their proper place in the life of society.

The culture of the new age will not be a single monolithic culture spreading to all parts of the globe. It will be a new variation on a number of diverse cultures, each of which will maintain its own characteristics and identity. An enduring pattern of social, economic and cultural life will encourage the flowering of higher and higher cultural variations, overcoming and replacing the disorientation and alienation attendant on rapid and chaotic social and technological change. Symbolic values will be recovered; persons and institutions will not be made into objects, and the value of things will not be calculated uniquely in monetary terms. The Westernizing influence of the late 20th century will be replaced by a return to indigenous cultural roots and origins, in the search for symbols, beliefs and values which give acceptable and penetrating meaning to human existence.

Philosophy will regain its ancient role as the integrator of human knowledge. It will no longer be concerned with finding a respected niche for itself as another academic specialty, and will go beyond the crafts of linguistic and logical analysis in a systematic and sustained search for interconnection and synthesis. Its main conceptual bases will evolve from the 20th century roots of structuralism, cybernetics, systems philosophy and process metaphysics. Its crucial tasks will include the identification of the overarching paradigm of the natural, social and human sciences. This classically Greek task will take on new meaning, as the sciences themselves overcome their disciplinary biases and bring their particular aspects of physical and social reality within the focus of a shared framework. Philosophy will also clarify the ethics and the aesthetics of the many forms of human cooperation on the various levels, from the interpersonal to the global. And philosophers will no longer shun the responsibility of constructing theories of the patterns of history, of the evolution of the universe, and of the connections between them.

The evolution of the sciences will be guided by the values and methodological safeguards of scientists, and the motivating influences of society. The frantic search for new paradigms, typical of the human and social sciences of the late 20th century, will give way to a sustained and conscientious exploration of all reasonable alternatives. The mainstream of scientists will work within a conceptual framework that employs concepts of evolution, dynamic equilibrium, interrelation, system-formation and maintenance, replacing concepts of point events, units of action, and reduction to the smallest identifiable part. The evolution of diversity and the emerging strands of integration will be studied in great detail, on the basis of the empirical observation of the functions and structures of human societies. Models of integrated ecological and social systems will achieve considerable sophistication, and there will be new insights into the structures and processes of change and mutation in its myriad forms.

Religion will undergo a renaissance. It will return to its sources as a spiritual form of tieing and binding people together, as its name (*re-ligare*) implies. Concern with the here-and-now will not eclipse concern with realities beyond the pale of everyday experience. New developments in the arts, sciences and philosophy will make man more conscious of his small yet not insignificant role in the cosmic scheme of things.

Each new discovery, each new insight will also illuminate the vast reaches of remaining ignorance. Humility will replace arrogance in regard to what humanity can know empirically and do in practice. But man, never content with recognizing limits, will turn with new vigor and expectation to the spiritual sphere. In the setting of closer human contacts and a more intimate relation with nature, religious experiences will be more common. Organized religions, ceasing their preoccupation with fighting each other for the allegiance of a dwindling and sceptical brethren, will turn to understanding and giving form to religious and mystical experiences. Theologians will take up speculation where philosophers leave off, and seek the meaning of ultimate principles and purposes. Concious of limits yet eager to transcend them, humanity will seek to grasp all dimensions of the world in which it exists, the rational, the aesthetic, as well as the spiritual.

Artists, scientists, philosophers, and men of the spirit will not live lives apart, in studios, in laboratories and academies, and in secluded rectories. Their field of observation and activity will be the living and evolving reality around them. They will be integral parts of their communities, their nations, and their cultures as citizens, as observers, as well as guides and advisors.

Academics charged with research, and the dissemination and handing down of knowledge, will spend periods of internship in administrative and decision-making bodies as part of their studies. They will be given opportunities to assume responsible positions on the staffs of such bodies later in their career, as they emerge from periods of study, teaching and reflection to put theories and ideas to the test in the service of society.

## LIFESTYLES

Lifestyles in the Age of Human Ecology will be keyed to refining and enhancing the quality of lived experience rather than raising the material standard of living. Material standards and quality of life will be clearly distinguished, and it will be generally recognized that, beyond a certain point, further increases in the former lead to deterioration in the latter.

Material conveniences will not be shunned, but they will be used to serve the purposes of existence, and not to dominate them. Pride of possession will be associated not with energy and resource-hungry devices bedecked in chrome and bright colors, but with works of art and handicraft, with aesthetic surroundings, with implements that are simple and efficient, and with products that are particularly sophisticated in furthering a sense of oneness with nature and a sense of communion with fellow humans. These trends are foreshadowed today in the almost aesthetic appreciation of riding a finely made bike, in the enjoyment of sailing and surfing, hiking and wilderness trekking, and in jogging and running. Status will be associated with authenticity and simplicity of personal lifestyles, with the purity of experience conveyed by them, and not with ostentation in the exercise of personal wealth and power and with conspicuous consumption.

Everyday ethic will dictate frugality in the use of nonrenewable natural resources. Parsimony has long been valued in science and art; it will come to be valued also in lifestyles. People will prefer walking to riding, biking to motoring, convenient, comfortable and safe public transport in company of fellow passengers to the isolation of private cars and the frustration of traffic. Recreation will bring people closer to nature rather than further from it in noisy stadiums and amusement parks. Sports of skill and teamwork will be preferred to competitive contact sports, and participatory sports to spectator sports. Athletic events will regain something of their Greek origins in being displays of skill rather than contests of power. Competition will be among individual athletes and teams, rather than among representatives of rival promoters and firms, or rival cities and countries.

The nature of progress will be redefined. In today's world progress means to increase one's material standard of life, and the collective wealth of one's company or country. Social, intellectual, cultural and spiritual progress is assumed to follow in the wake of material progress. In the Age of Human Ecology the focus will shift to progress in the non-material spheres of life. And such progress will bring about notable enhancement in the *quality* of life. For some segments of the world population, material standards will increase dramatically. For others, material standards will decrease. These adjustments will be dictated not by abstract valuations of material standards themselves, but by emphasis on quality of life indicators, which in some cases will call for more spending on material goods, to assure the fulfilment of legitimate needs, and in others for less, in cutting waste and overconsumption. After its remarkable love affair with consumerism and technology, mankind will regain its perspective as not merely an economic, but also a social and a cultural species.

# INDEX

Abstracted systems 12
Adaptation 55–58
Aesthetics of music 122–137
Age of Human Ecology 248–256
   Citizenship 248–249
   Culture 253–255
   Economics 252–253
   Lifestyles 255–256
   Politics 249–251
Alexander, S. 39
*Allgemeine Systemlehre* 13
Analytical method 5
Anomalies in science 72f.
Ansermet, E. 123
Aristotle 123, 172
Ashby, W.R. 17, 42, 43, 99, 122

Bacon, F. 172
Behaviorism 163
Bergson, H. 39, 165
Bernard, C. 104
Bertalanffy, L.V. 4, 13, 17, 48–49, 76, 98, 99, 103, 122
Bigelow, J. 53
Biological systems 103–104
Biperspectivism 62–71
   basic premisses of 70–71
Boltzmann, 25
Boulding, K. 4, 17, 55, 100, 122
Brezhnev, L. 157
Bronowski, J. 26, 86, 87
Buckley, W. 155, 177, 178
Bunge, M. 109

Cadwallader, M. 155

Cameron, N. 166, 182
Carnot, S. 25
Carritt, E.F. 123
Cassirer, E. 123
Children 187–190
Clausius 25
Collingwood, R.G. 123
Common Regional Heritage 252–253
Communication among scientists 119–121
Communication in music 133–136
Compartmentalization of knowledge 214–215
Complexity 55–56
Conant, J.B. 6
Conceptual synthesis 139–143
   Functions of 141–142
Conceptual systems 12
Consciousness 68–70
*Cooperator* 158
Creativity in music 127–129
Croce, B. 123, 170
Cultural universals 57
Culture lag 191f.

Darwin, 25
Darwinian theory 83–84, 85
Design Science 179
Deutsch, K. 122
Development in science 81–95
Dewey, J. 39, 53
Dignity, def. 162
Disarmament 191f.
Dissipation function 42, 43
Dissipative structures 27
Diversity 44–45
Dualism 63f.

257

# Index

Easton, D. 155
Early warning system 219–234
   Conceptual foundations of 224–229
   Implementation at the U.N. 232–234
   Practical applications 229–232
ECDC/TCDC (Economic and Technical Cooperation among Developing Countries) 238
Ecology 76–78
Ecosystems 155
Education 213–218
Einstein, A. 6, 72, 75, 97
Emerson, A.E. 154
Empirical adequacy 73, 88f.
Energy 202–204
Evolution vi, 21 and *passim*
Experience 63
Expressivity of music 123f.

Fagen, R.E. 12
Falk, R. 156
'Feeling' 68
Feyerabend, P. 39, 74
Firth, R. 57
Forrester, J.W. 58, 156
Frankl, V. 15
Fuller, B. 178–179
Functionalism 32

Galileo, G. 6
General system model of science 85–95
General system theory vi, and *passim*
   definition 17–18
   factors blocking 8–17
   factors favoring 5–7
   fallacy of generality 16–17
   fallacy of generalization 15–16
   metatheory confusion 14–16
   practical applications 11
   principles of 17–23
   prospects of 3–5
   research approaches 23
   resource availability for 10
   semantic confusion 11–14
   specification (formal) 18–19
General theories 72–80
Generality 73, 88f.
Genetic fallacy 68
Global goals 197–212
Global negotiations 237–238
Global problems 199–205
Goals: Africa 208
       Australia 206
       Canada 205
       China 207
       Communist world 207
       India 209

International organizations 210–211
Japan 206
Latin America 207
Middle East 209
Southeast Asia 209–210
Transnational Corporations 210
United Nations 211
United States 205

Hall, A.D. 122
Handy, R. 183
Hanson, N.R. 3
Hardin, G. 7, 11, 198
Harris, E. 74
Hartmann, N. 46
Helmholtz, 25
Heraclitus v
Hidden strata of stability 86–87, 89–90
Hierarchization 33–35, 44–47
Hierarchy, def. 45
   internal/external 46
   macro/micro 117–118
Holton, G. 84
Homeostasis 104, 165
Human dignity 162–185
Human ecology, def. 248
Hunger 201–202

Ideals of science 40–88f.
Industrial revolution 191f.
Insecurity 194, 200–201
Intellectual inertia 8
Interdependence vi, 188f.
International economic system 204f., 236f.
*International Journal of General Systems* 11
Intervening variable 163
Invariance under transformation 125f.
Irreducibility 28–30, 41
Isomorphism 100f.

Kacser, C. 103
Katchalsky, A. 26, 30
Katz, S. 155–156
Kedrov, B. 81–82
Kepler, J. 6
Kluckhohn, C. 57, 183
Koestler, A. 107
Kohler, W. 182–183
Kuhn, Th. 39, 49, 73, 74, 81, 83

Lakatos, I. 74, 81
Langer, S. 123
Language 112f.
Leadership 213–218
Learning in music 129–132

# Index

Lévi-Strauss, C. 104–108
Linton, R. 57
Living systems 31

Mackay, D. 122
Man 40, 52, 63, 71
Mankind 149–160
Margenau, H. 6, 73, 74
Marx, K. 182
Marxist philosophy of science 81–82
Maslow, A. 54, 78
Maxwell, J.C. 8
Maxwell, R. viii
Matter 65
Meadows, D. 58, 156, 219
Meyer, L. 123
Miller, J.G. 4, 12, 55
Mind 64–71
Mind-body problem 62–71
Modern Age 188
Monod, J. 84
Morphogenesis 89
Morphostasis 89
Morgan, L. 39
Mumford, L. 171, 172, 174–175
Music 122–137
Muskie, E. 157
Mutation in science 82, 84

Nation-state 156
Nature 74
Need 108, 181, 183
    def. 165–166
Needs, national 224–226
Neolithic revolution 187, 191
Newton, Sir I. 6, 73
Northrop, F.S.C. 72, 74

Obsolete perceptions 191–196
Order 28, 40, 46–47
Ordered wholeness 41–42
Organization, def. 143
Organizational inertia 9–10
Organized complexity 99, 110
Outer limits 219

Panpsychism 64–65
Parmenides v
Parsons, T. 75, 155
Perry, R.B. 53
Pepper, S. 39, 53, 54
Phases of leadership education 216–218
Physics 63
Piaget, J. 52, 100, 101
Plato 123

Platt, J. 158–159
Popper, K. 74, 81, 82
Potential strata of stability 27, 34
Prigogine, I. 26
Process metaphysics 24
Progress 256
    in science 72–80
Purpose 149–160

Radcliffe-Brown, A.R. 106–108
Radnitzky, G. 75
Rapoport, A. 4
Rashkis, H.A. 12
RCDC (Regional Cooperation among Developing Countries) 243–247
    Need for 243–244
    Objectives 246–247
    Obstacles to 244–245
Reductionism 110
Regional communities 236–242
Regional/Interregional Strategy for Collective Self-reliance 240–242
Reich, W. 159
Relations, internal/external 144
Resources, national 226–227
Resources Needs Development Charts 227–229
Resources/needs ratio 229–230
Richardson, K. viii
Rosenblueth, A. 53
Russell, B. 55–56, 63, 114, 115

Sciences of complexity 4
Self-organization 32–33, 42–44
Self-stabilization 30–32, 42
Simon, H.A. 34
Sinnott, E. 104
Smith, A. 59
Social anthropology 97f.
Social Darwinism 109–110, 183, 193
Social influences on science 7
Social systems 30, 58, 177
Society for General Systems Research 4, 5, 119
Sociocultural systems 155f.
Solipsism 66–67
Spencer, H. 24, 25
Sports 255
State of the World's Future Report 233
Steady-states 30, 103
Strauss, R. 9
Structuralism 97–110
Structures 101f., 105
    Social 104–108
Systemic invariance 27–35, 40, 99f.
Systems, adaptive/manipulative 178
Systems Biology 98f., 103–104

# Index

Systems, categories of 20
Systems, def. vi, 12, 144
Systems evolution 26, 27, 33
Systems, intertype relations 21
Systems Philosophy 38–47, 48–50, 62f.
    Constructs of 41–47
Systems Science 48–50
Systems Technology 49

Taylor, A. 110, 156
Technology 162ff.
    def. 162
    inhumanity of 171 f.
    potentials of 167f.
Teilhard de Chardin, J. 64
Theory Selection 39, 82, 84–85, 88f.
Thermodynamics, Second Law of 25, 26, 76, 87–88
Thompson, W. 25
Tolman, E. 166
Törnebohm, H. 75
Toulmin, S. 83

UNESCO 233
Unification in science 76f.
Unified field theory 75
UNITAR 159, 233
United Nations 157, 219–220, 222–223, 232–234

U.N. Third Development Decade 236, 237
UNU 159, 233
U Thant 157

Value judgements 51
Value mistakes 59
Value theory 50–55
Values, manifest/normative 59
Volterra, G. 100

Waddington, C.H. 84, 90
Walter, W. 53
Weaver, W. 4, 17, 76
Weiss, P.A. 4, 12
Whitehead, A.N. 4, 39, 178
Whorf, B.L. 112f.
Whorfian relativity 112–121
Whorf-Sapir hypothesis 114
Whyte, L.L. 74–75, 109
Wiener, N. 53, 104, 172, 178
Wigner, E. 74
World order 144ff.
    def. vii
World picture 112f.
    fragmentation of 114–121
    scientific 114–119
World population imbalance 221